A JESUIT
TALE

A JESUIT
TALE

JOHN SHEKLETON

Rutledge Books, Inc.  Danbury, CT

ALL RIGHTS RESERVED
Rutledge Books, Inc.
107 Mill Plain Road, Danbury, CT 06811
1-800-278-8533
www.rutledgebooks.com

Manufactured in the United States of America

Cataloging in Publication Data
Shekleton, John

A Jesuit Tale

ISBN: 1-58244-103-0

1. Fiction.

Library of Congress Catalog Card Number: 00-107131

in memoriam

Pedro Arrupe, Jesuit General
Donald Fehrenbach, Jesuit angel

Thanks to readers and editors whose advice I valued and whose comments gave me hope, direction and helpful criticism: Francesca DiPiazza, William Glenn, Avis Jensen, Frederick Mertz, Kristine Oberg, Carol Olson, John Padberg, Jane Rafal, Michael Skelly.

Prologue

Two hands, both marked by the shallow spur of a short lifeline, quietly tacked a white envelope to the cool mahogany door of the Jesuit residence at Landívar University on the evening of the Feast of the Three Kings, 1991. The letter inside was one hand-written sentence:

> *The Union de Derechos Absolutos orders all Jesuits to leave Guatemala by October 12th or be dragged from their residences and executed, their blood let to flow in the streets.*

The next days and for months afterward the Jesuit communities in Guatemala met, prayed and discerned the will of God. They discerned the same will of God that the Jesuit General in Rome, a tiring anthropologist with hair as gray as Neanderthal ash, succinctly urged upon them: *Maneatis.* Stay. Stay all.

The gringo priest had been the strongest proponent of staying. After six years in Guatemala as economics professor at Landívar University, he had transformed from a foreign observer whose concern was muffled by polite, *yanquí* smiles into a full-throated critic of Guatemala's oligarchy and of that tight-linked circle's murder and intimidation of the Mayan peasantry, even as fewer were slain in 1990 and powerful forces advocated an amnesty packaged in silence.

Try as he might, the gringo priest could not achieve silence. Anger about the massacres and nighttime marauding welled up inside him. As preacher he no longer used amplifiers. The spirit of his youthful, sinewy protests was again commandant of his soul. Whether he stood in pulpit or on altar step, everyone heard his words and felt their sting. No heads bobbed in currents of dreams while he preached.

John Shekleton vii

He cried out the names of towns and provinces, and everyone knew the grim story. Santa Cruz. Huehuetenango. Rabinal. He cried out atrocities, and people covered their eyes. Tears spilled off his cheeks. At times he invoked the grand name of the defending archangel with such fury that all present thought Heaven would open and celestial brightness—hard, swift and pulsing light—would engulf the congregation with its cleansing surge.

The other Jesuits began to whisper that the gringo's righteous anger added inches to his height and bulk to his lean frame. They noted that after the threat an even hotter stream of prophetic condemnation spewed out of him, massive and mobile, a river of lava streaming out from a deep rift.

What fueled this molten flow? Decades-buried Vietnam War protests? Frustration with Central American social intransigence? A dangerous romance with whip-snapping Jesus in the Temple court?

His superiors wrote down all these appraisals and sent them to the provincial who sent them on to Rome.

But if they could have seen him at night. . . .

At night the gringo presented a surprising figure, on his knees and bent in a corner, crumpled and floor-facing, a poet's discarded first draft.

In those cloistered hours, in that square Guatemalan room, only one thought lived bold within him. The gringo priest knew, the knowledge overwhelming and body-twisting as a gift of the Holy Spirit, that he had made himself the prime candidate for the executioner's machete.

The Calling, 1967

CHAPTER ONE

Mark

It was the beginning of Mark's senior year at Georgetown University's School of Foreign Service. The pressure was on. What was his next move?

His father had been after Mark all summer to choose between law school or starting out in some entry-level position at the State Department.

"It'll take four months to call in enough favors to get you the right job at Foggy Bottom," Mr. Sappingstone said as he drove his middle son to the Minneapolis airport.

"I've got the picture. When I decide, you'll be the first to know."

Mark stared forward, grinding his teeth until he felt an incisor, loosened four years previously in a rumble of football glory when he slammed over the De La Salle defense for the game-winning six points, begin to wobble.

"I don't need to be the first, I just need to know in time," Mr. Sappingstone said as he drummed his fingernails on the steering wheel of his ink-black, sensible man's Impala.

Mark had heard the rhythm before, usually at the dinner table when one of the seven Sappingstone children was late, or at Mass when a padre spouted Vatican II dogma that his father would later deride as "rum-soaked speculation, porous as an old woman's Christmas treat."

Mark had learned to block out the finger tapping, and the hard man's fury behind it, by concentrating his thoughts until they were laser-thin and flowed at one level frequency.

"You understand the need for a quick decision?" Mr. Sappingstone asked, his head facing traffic.

"I get your time schedule," Mark said, glancing at his father. Mark modulated the frustration out of his voice and added a slight, wet vibration of apology, a trick of the vocal cords he'd perfected a year after puberty. Today at twenty he didn't want his father, the litigator whose phone number every criminal of note in the upper Midwest kept in a wallet or wall safe, to probe deep. Mark's struggle, his personal secret, still just a desire, almost a whim, was expanding fast in the cavity of his soul, ready to burst out. If only he could get to Georgetown. If only he could talk to Charley.

"You've been on me all summer about this," Mark said.

"I've been on you because you don't *seem* to understand the importance of this decision." Mark's father reached over and placed a hand on his son's left leg, squeezing lightly. "Timing is important." He clipped the words, the way he spoke with underlings.

Mark didn't respond. His worry, his fear, his almost rebellion, turned a layer of his body into liquid and steamed up his blue Hoya rugby jacket. Mark could smell the acid wetness of these emotions as they rolled over his collar up into his fine, bust-of-a-Roman-youth nostrils. He wrinkled his nose and looked away. Mark smelled this way whenever he talked alone to his father. During high school, he'd showered every night.

John Thomas Sappingstone, progenitor of five sons and two daughters, was sitting judge and sharp-tongued prosecutor in their well-run Kenwood brick mansion, whether the issue was a sibling's feud or politics and religion. Mark, the third son, bested verbally and bullied by his father's two darling elder boys, ever vigilant of an attack by one of the chosen princelings, had never acquired the skill to oppose the ruler himself.

Mark didn't lack the logic of argument. He lacked, surprisingly, the stamina, the stand-alone inner fighter.

And he loved his father, who had lost one eye and half a foot in the greatest battle of the Pacific, loved him in a way that kept Mark's mouth dry and empty in his father's presence. This man, his father, was hero. He had suffered for others. He was like Jesus. Commanding and worthy. Elite.

Since the days when his bristle-topped head only reached his father's knee, Mark had relished the stories of Marine triumphs on the atolls and coral islands of the Pacific. Brutal, heroic epics. Manly deeds. Told by a rough, proud man, a man whose one uncovered eye sometimes glistened at their telling.

On occasion, when he was alone and small as a puppy, Mark hid in his parents' closet and leafed through the black-paper albums. These sacred books overflowed with pictures and news clippings and map fragments. Sometimes he picked up the special relics and caressed them: the green helmet, the three shining medals of white and blue and gold. Then he, too, cried little drops that crinkled the yellowing papers.

As far as Mark could remember, those mothball-scented scenes of adoration were the only times he regularly shed tears in his childhood. It was once a sign of pride to have numbered and kept small that number the times when a woman's weakness overtook him. He hated tears. At St. Anne's grade school, when he was seven, he'd cried at the end of a story hour tale: a poor man's son dies and the father becomes a hobo.

Tad, his childhood nemesis, looked over as he cried and hissed the name "Sappy," a term the other boy's took up as they leaned forward in their pen-scarred desks, their small hands covering their mouths so that Sister Benedict, wimple-wrapped, shrunken, and largely deaf, wouldn't pick up the buzz. They kept mocking Mark as they walked through the hallway at the end of reading class and headed to the playground. "Sappy. Sappy. Sappy," they chanted in praise of Tad, the tallest in their class, chanting until Mark rushed up from behind and slammed his storybook into Tad Ewald's carrot-red head so hard that Tad wobbled on his tiny feet and crashed into a wall. All were silent and amazed.

Mark didn't confess that assault during his springtime first confession. Defense was not a sin, as his father had instructed him, correcting any errors of doctrine introduced by farm-bred nuns. But that St. Anne's scene had curled up inside Mark for a long sleep. It awoke when Tad Ewald's body was shredded by a land mine in Vietnam in 1966. After reading the one-inch obituary his mother had folded into her weekly letter, Mark went to Dahlgren Chapel, center of the campus mandala, as he sometimes dreamed, and confessed the years-ago assault, weeping, ironically, even as the phrase "Bless me, Father" spurted out.

Tad and Mark had been enemies into high school, savaging each other's lockers, flinging names as they passed in the hall, until the day that Tad dropped out, the day he was caught driving Mark's car, the day Mark's father offered Tad redemption if he joined the special forces.

On a cloudy April afternoon in New North, 207, the obit still in his hand, Mark had examined his soul with a distant, older eye, an eye curving freshly with Jesus words. He felt as if his venom, still strong, sour at the back of his mouth, had tripped the wire, splattering Tad along the Mekong. Hate could bleed out of a human being, steam into fog, take shape with the form of a night creature and finger destruction. Mark felt a patch of his soul dripping with that hate, that anger. The only way to dry it up, at least for a while, was to confess.

And this task of forgiveness, seeking it, giving it, both hard things to do, especially for Mark, the admission of faults to the Father, were manly tasks. Charley had made this point clear to him.

Being a priest, Mark had come to believe over the last year at Georgetown, was becoming a man. A man of God, yes. A man, without doubt.

Saying farewell at gate A5, Mark continued to skirt his father's coal-black eyes, staring unashamedly at the dark-haired stewardess rushing down the gangway with small, tight steps.

"Stare all you want at that cute ass, but give me a decision within a month," Mark's father said, boffing his son's marine-cut head.

"You bet," Mark said with a sharp nod.

Mark turned toward his father. One foot separated them. He shook the older man's hand, serving up his valedictorian, good-son smile, stifling the blood-gorged urge to blurt out his secret: He might sell his inheritance and go prodigal.

His second night back on campus Mark paced outside Healy, up and down in front of its gray mass, waiting for Charley Keegan. Mark was all nerves, from clipped toenails to stubbly scalp, a hemisphere with a rock spine of anxiety. The campus itself, in contrast, was quiet as the Visitation convent hidden away over the northern wall, softly contemplative. Only a few gawky, dark or olive-skinned boys in flared jeans, internationals who had arrived early for the semester, walked along the red-brick pathways. Mark's buddies, the American sports boys, were elsewhere. They'd taken their ruddy cheeks and rippled muscles off campus to indulge in all the illicit liquids.

Mark had told the rugby boys, as they battered him with adolescent jibes, surrounding him at the O Street gate with admiring jest—"Yuh got some piece hid'n 'way somewhere?"—that he was meeting with Father Keegan. The sound of the Jesuit's name, a deep-muscle drug, calmed the nervous herd of Vietnam War-fodder. Father Keegan and Mark were tight. It was a respectable relationship. A coveted one.

Mark had fancied Father Keegan as soon as the priest strode into his freshman religion elective, Christianity and Existentialism. Mark was enthralled the moment he heard the man's voice, a large voice, senatorial, worthy of the Jesuit's phrases that snapped up air or hollowed out souls.

Mark had expected to hate the over educated cleric, a man of awe whose employ of a short-stemmed, silver cigarette holder to smoke his perfectly rolled fags during evening strolls had made him a figure of legend on campus.

Mark had expected to hate the fancy pedagogue the way his father would have. "Whereas Thomas would say . . ." he could hear his father commenting in an imagined face-off against the dandified, Ignatian foe, his father's voice quiet as a wolf humming in its lamb's clothing, a stalker who has begun to circle his victim with lengthening strides.

Soon into the first lecture, Mark was sure Father Keegan would be tough meat for his sharp-toothed father, even poisonous meat, meat with its own bite.

"After an hour," whispered the knowing students, "when you're battered and brain-gore spatters the walls, Keegan wipes up a drop here or there with a tiny chamois of an answer, maybe a story, a quote, a joke, then scrawls the next reading on the blackboard. Kierkegaard. Hegel. Sartre. Camus. 'Read them at dawn. Read them at midnight,' he commands as he scans the class, locking onto every pair of eyes. 'You need imagination and curiosity, qualities sometimes available to you metaphysical neonates at the cusp hours. Do calculus and history in the daylight. Go now. *Ite. Labor omnia vincit.*'"

Mark came to admire everything about Father Keegan—form, face, idiosyncrasies. The professor priest was tall, his neck long as an aristocrat's. Short dark hair, edged with a hint of gray, wrapped around the crown of his forehead. Mark thought the neatness of Father Keegan's hair, the clean line, had its own sense of purpose, conforming eloquently to a higher purpose, which was evident in the perfection of the line. The newly middle-aged Jesuit was the last scion of a wealthy Washington family, lawyers all, corporate law and government, two of them ambassadors, one to France and one to Argentina. Father Keegan confessed once to Mark that his entry into the Jesuits had wounded his father so deeply that they never laughed together again.

Mark had stared back silently, stunned and hungry.

Mark's classes with Father Keegan were a continuous, soul-refining search for meaning, a ripping into the tight fabric of the day, of the personality. Father Keegan had announced in his greeting to the newly assembled freshmen on January 14, 1965, the words exploding from his lips as if he were a prophet unleashing his first revelation: *The old growth forests of patriotism, family, and immigrant piety have been felled by the wrong war, sprawling individualism and aggiornamiento. Ours is a time of challenge, of discovery, of reformation. If you're not ready for this reforestation, take a class on Thomas!*

Father Keegan's arguments captured and nourished the struggle within Mark's own spirit, a battle as visceral as the yeasty hormones that kept Mark and his taut-thighed rugby buddies jittery and wide-eyed most of the day. Mark needed to plant and nurture something of his own within himself. The air in Father Keegan's class was ripe with spores. They settled into Mark's soul and germinated.

It was Father Keegan's lecture on Dag Hammarsjkold that began their friendship. Mark had admired that mystic world diplomat ever since high school and went up to speak with Father Keegan after class, standing back until Jennifer, half Chinese and half black, voluptuous and bright, tall on her platform shoes, had moved on.

Mark told Father Keegan he'd "lapped up" every word the priest said about Hammarsjkold, especially that comment, half thrown away to the small clump of white pines outside the classroom's wide window, about the Norwegian's ability to weave together in his personal life "the raw complexities of a modern world with a life-sustaining, yes, life-sustaining, spiritual existence."

Mark had sat up straight as the priest's words bounced back from the glass. The words were revelation to him. That's what he wanted! A life of greatness, a life of worth, a life glowing from within.

"Lapped up?" Father Keegan had responded, smiling. He laughed. "Am I the she-wolf? Is the Potomac the Tiber? Are *you* about to found a new Rome?"

Through Mark's persistence and Father Keegan's admitted enjoyment in youthful searching, teacher and student became pals. They ate breakfast together most Fridays. They talked about the Vietnam war, about church reform, about racial justice, about premarital sex, about women's rights. Mark discussed the same topics with his rugby pals and reporter friends on *The Hoya*, but even he heard a different tone in his voice when speaking with Father Keegan. It was a tone that moved beyond debate to a warm concern.

"Summer was good to you. You look great," Charley said as Mark jogged up the short incline to the north of Healy.

"Thanks. Working at my dad's law firm was OK. It didn't interfere with my water skiing, and the chicks at the beach were especially fine!"

"Ah, the twin interests of the young male: recreation and procreation," Father Keegan said as he placed a fatherly hand on Mark's shoulder.

Charley was acting the pleased parent, not the quirky professor. It gave Mark heart. He'd played this scene in his mind over and over for the last two weeks. Still, it would be difficult to get the words out. They were words that shattered, even when spoken on a Catholic campus. Distancing words. But Charley should understand.

"You can tell me all about your summer," Charley said, "and I'll tell you about my studies in Milan. I'm sure stories of cold Lombard mornings spent paging through neoplatonic manuscripts will edify you. As you'll hear, the life of the scholar warrior makes Hercules's exploits seem but a chug-chug for *The Little Engine That Could*."

Charley winked and headed the two of them off to M street for an evening of talk over pizza. Pepperoni, sausage and onion. Large. One coke. One coffee. It was another routine of theirs. Charley would mince down two slices, leaving the crusts for the alley rats, then sit back and indulge himself in coffee and cigarettes as Mark finished off the evening's food. For those forays into the undergraduate world of The Campus Inn, Charley abandoned his silver cigarette holder and the slender rolls he packed with the finest shag from an ex-student's North Carolina tobacco plantation, contenting himself with his next favorite nicotine source, a pack of Camels snatched off the well-stocked Jesuit residence's supply shelves.

"You know me pretty well," Mark said after he devoured the last slice of the evening's pizza and wiped his mouth with the side of his broad hand. "You know I'm no saint, no sissy. Right?"

Charley lifted an eyebrow at the appearance of that playground word. "I know some things about you," he said with deliberation, shifting his frame about on the bench as if he were suddenly uncomfortable, suddenly aware he'd been sitting on a rip in the vinyl fabric. "No saint?"

Charley leaned forward. He placed his elbows on the table and rested his chin on his joined hands. Mark felt a new heat in the priest's eyes. "I'd say you're a good soul, Mark, full of care, wanting to do right," Charley said, employing his moderately Southern, confessor-parent accent, the sound Mark loved, a sound so different from the quick drill barking of his father. "So, why did you ask?"

"I guess I asked," Mark said, his own voice cracking in mid-reply, sharp as ice in a Mississippi river thaw, "cause there's been something . . ." He cleared his throat. "You'd call it an interior movement."

Mark smiled at Charley. He'd chosen one of the phrases the professor priest spoke only in private or at Mass. Those words, appropriated by Mark in silence, had swirled gently through his soul the last months, as refreshing as an eddy in a high-season stream. "Something's been stirring inside me—all summer—something pretty odd."

Mark looked down at his greasy hands. Slowly, finger by finger, he wiped them clean with the remains of the stained paper napkin. He needed to get the words out. "I'm wondering if I could have a vocation. To the Jesuits," he said, whispering the admission to the table. His summer-bronze face had paled. He held the crumpled napkin balled into his right hand. He pressed it in his fist, directing all his anxiety into that ball of grease and paper as he cautiously raised his eyes to look up at Charley.

In the interval Charley's eyes had gone blank, distant. "I see," Charley said.

Mark's priest-confidant looked at the cigarette he'd just lit and, with a steady deliberation, stubbed it out into the base of the crenellated ashtray. "Have you thought about this—*call*—for long?" Charley asked, leaning back and folding his arms.

Mark made nothing of Charley's new posture, the priest's arms twined like a defensive guard's. Mark relaxed. His question was out. Released. The burn had already lessened.

"I've been thinking about it off and on for years." Mark's smile was broad. This confession—it felt right. "But this summer—I've been thinking about it all summer. I've been reading a lot, too. In particular Dag Hammarsjkold." Mark pronounced the man's name with reverence. "He was at the center of the creation of a new political world. He was a spiritual man . . ."

"Yes, yes, Hammarsjkold's an admirable figure, a hero for many of us," Charley said, interrupting Mark. For a moment the priest stared toward the ceiling, blinking rapidly as if cleansing his eyes of a sudden deposit of soot. "But let me ask a few questions about you, some questions about this vocation issue. OK?"

"Sure. Ask away."

"They're standard questions, such as, do you pray often?"

Mark went cold as the question pushed in. He thought they'd be discussing the works of the Society: education, missions, the crafting of public opinion. "Often? I don't know, I went to Mass every Sunday this summer."

That was stupid! Then from deeper: "My prayer is a lot like thinking, I guess. Sometimes I think about the beginning, before man, before Earth." Mark raised his right hand to form a bowl, a shelter for some round, soft object. "You know—I think about this power that created everything, about the mystery of it all, of existence, of life."

"And about Jesus. What do you know about Jesus?" Charley's face had drained of emotion. He sat unmoving.

"I know he was a great teacher. He taught the law of love, and he was the Son of God."

Mark looked over to see if the thirtyish couple in suit and office dress, nestled on one side of a booth across the aisle, were listening in on them, listening in on his first attempt to fit that curved, fetal spirit into a Jesuit mold.

"And he died for us, so the Church teaches," Charley said. "What does *that* stunning assertion mean?"

"It means—it means things needed to be set straight. And Christ's dying did that, he made the ultimate sacrifice."

"But *why* the need for a sacrifice?"

"Because of sin?"

Charley sighed as if disappointed and closed his eyes for a moment.

Mark's mind went blank. "Because—because new life comes through pain," Mark blurted out. "It's the same as childbirth, I guess." This was so frustrating. Mark was a darling of revered professor Carroll Quigley, articulate about politics and history. But about Catholic doctrine, dogma—he'd done his best to forget its catechism truisms, the way he'd abandoned most of his father's advice.

Charley suppressed a grin and took a sip of coffee. He peered into the brewed liquid and began to speak as slowly and clearly as a bishop at confirmation right before the slap. "What would you say is the most important thing you know about Jesus?"

Mark hesitated, only because he felt sure about these words. "That Jesus loved people. That he wanted to set people free."

"Free," Charley said, mulling over the word as he examined the chipped coffee cup, his face registering an urge to clarify the proper use of that core term. He lifted up his pale blue eyes and stared at Mark. "And what would it mean, in your words, to follow Jesus?"

"To follow . . ." A flicker of anger. Why all these questions? Mark slowed down to concentrate. He rubbed his eye sockets with his knuckles.

"It would mean to live the way Jesus lived," Mark finally said, quietly, first looking over again at the couple across the aisle. "To care for the poor and the weak, to teach love and forgiveness. That's what following Jesus means, we've talked about that before."

"Yes, you've probably said that before. But why follow Jesus as a Jesuit?"

Mark shoved back from the table and held his hands up in an open-palm gesture of frustration. When Mark's words finally took on sound, they rang out, half argument, half despair: "I want to change the world. I want to change *me*."

Hard-edged silence.

"You know, Mark, you don't need to be a Jesuit to change the world—or to change yourself."

Mark froze. He fought off a desire to get up and leave. Instead, he planted both feet firmly on the restaurant's red-carpeted floor and tightened his calf muscles.

"I know I don't have to be a Jesuit to change the world," Mark said. "But there's something inside me—it's been there for . . . It's a vine—a grape vine that grows on a trellis. It wraps around and grips. It's this question . . . ," Mark thought he saw concern in Charley's face, or fear, the Jesuit's eyes darkened by some private knowledge, " . . . should I be a priest?"

Mark's question silenced the couple across the aisle as it traveled about through the smoke-stained air.

"I don't know why I have that question inside me."

Mark relaxed for a moment, an unexpected smoothness along the walls of his soul after this refinement. He closed his eyes. He remembered his childhood awe of young Father Duffy, their assistant pastor, a professional baseball player turned cleric. Even Mark's father had admired the man.

"I've never spoken to anyone about this feeling before." Mark touched his heart. "It didn't fit with what I was supposed to do, with what I told everyone I wanted to do. But the question's not going away. It hasn't gone away. It's up off the bench and won't sit back down. That's why I wanted to talk to you, that's all." Mark could feel the sweat under his armpits, the old youthful sulfate.

Charley nodded his head, his eyes remote and calm, as if he'd just settled an inner argument for the thousandth time. He reached over to touch Mark's hand, a rare gesture. "You know, I'm asking these questions to get a sense about that very question. I'll be better able to help you if I understand."

"But you know me, you know what I think." Mark was pleading. He sounded adolescent and hated it.

"I know what you've said in some pretty informal conversations," Charley said. "Becoming a Jesuit is making a formal, public declaration. It's different, believe me."

They both turned for a second as a group of high school students tromped into the restaurant and poured themselves into a corner booth with the bumpy grace of a Disney beast.

"Let me ask one more question," Charley said, turning back, his voice softer, plaintive.

Mark said nothing. He nodded.

"What about celibacy? Have you thought about that?"

Mark closed his eyes for a moment. He thought of Claire, the girl he'd dated all summer. They'd been up at Bemidji at her family's cabin for a weekend. He'd told Claire he wouldn't go all the way. He'd told himself: This is a test. Still, after seven minutes of kissing, pulling, rubbing, their hands and tongues exploring everywhere, rock-climbers desperate for a foothold, he'd climaxed all over the soft mound of her stomach, arcing his back and closing his eyes, lost in that personal moment of pleasure. He'd ached to be surrounded by her as he shot out. It was the only flaw in that Northwoods moment, aside from the hovering sense of fault. His fingers were moist with her wetness. He'd rubbed them into her white-blonde hair and inhaled fully that body-rich fume again and again, swelling with desire to swim up to the source of the scent, past every ledge and fleshy obstruction.

At the time, on that hot August night with the call of loons in the pine-clean air, Mark's restraint had felt an act close to celibacy, requiring a control from far inside. He was not yet ashamed as he rose from her bed a few minutes later. He thought he was a step, a little step, closer to celibacy.

"Celibacy won't be easy, but you do it," Mark said. He knew Charley had once been in love. Charley had told Mark all about her. Mark thought love, marry-me love, must make celibacy harder. "I think I can do it. If I have to do it, I can do it. I'll need support from my brother Jesuits."

"You'll need support from God," Charley said, a quick retort. "And do you really think the Catholic Church is the best place to work toward your goals?"

Mark's eyebrows shot up, his smooth forehead wrinkling. Was Charley trying to warn him? Did he think Mark flawed?

"We're still a huge, cold bureaucracy run by old men." Charley was speaking louder. His arms had come into play. He was animated again. "Yes, there are signs of hope, opened windows, if you will, propped open for now by a few soft miters. But we're far from a perfect organization, the Church or the Society of Jesus."

The last word, the savior's personal name, Jesus, spun through the air with the mass of a cannon ball, whistling past Mark's ears. Jesus.

But Mark said nothing. He was shutting down inside. He felt bruised and betrayed, impotent as round-eyed quarry in a Kafka tale.

Neither of them moved.

Charley lit another Camel, inhaled, exhaled. "I've had decades to dwell on these questions, the personal ones and the religious ones,"

Charley said, looking away for a moment. "Maybe I was unfair tonight."

Charley reached for his pack of cigarettes with its indifferent dromedary and the beast's frozen smile. He held the pack in his long, delicate hand, quashing it slightly. Mark watched the priest's movement, avoiding Charley's eyes. Mark felt a separation grow between them, a dirty little feeling of failure.

"So, enough of this interrogation," Charley said. "Do you want to know what I think we should do?"

Hesitantly, "I guess so."

"I think I should put you in contact with Father Guinan, the house *primarius*—the man who deals with young men who are interested in joining the Society. He can talk to you at length about your vocation, whatever it might be. Do you want that?"

Mark's eyes had glazed over with a film of fatigue. He was tired. His arms hurt as if he'd been wrestling beyond his weight class.

"That'd be fine," Mark said, chasing the words with a sigh. "I'll talk to Father Guinan."

Mark had expected a welcoming embrace, a coach's pat on the back. He'd struggled all summer with this impossible dream and had hoped for support from Charley. Now he felt, in every sensate fiber of his being, truly alone, a city man lost in the desert, his loafers filling with sand as the cool white moon, mistress of night dunes, processed across the arid sky.

Remarkably, he thought later when he walked into his dorm room, opening the door slowly as if he were entering a hidden chamber, that the emptiness—the dome of solitude in his soul, gift of that greasy conversation, excited him as he stood within it. He was on his own. He, himself. He had opened the right door. The invitation was his.

Tom

Tom's days at Marquette University were all activity. He was an honors student, dorm R.A., parish youth leader, choir soloist, friend to dozens, lover. At night, always past midnight, he'd light one of the multicolored candles his prayer group had made in the fall and sit in lotus position on the tatami mats that covered the tiled floor. At that hour he contemplated the great truths of the 1960s: freedom, justice, and love. He made this contemplation into a dialogue with the divine-one-made-man, the great liberator, Jesus.

Throughout his university years Tom had formed an ever clearer image of Jesus. He saw a young man, bearded, sandaled, and doe-eyed. The savior's eyes floated in the sweet milk of kindness. Jesus was the new man. Any person, black or white, ragged or rich, could walk up to Jesus and touch him, talk to him.

Since childhood, Tom Burns had wanted to be a priest, which he imagined as a type of reincarnation of the Master. Tom could picture himself as easily at the altar as on the pitcher's mound or working a policeman's beat—his other childhood dream professions. For the young Tom, each of those professions sewed together the same warm threads: the excitement of the crowd, calmness amid desperation, knowledge of the right, heroic sacrifice, a life that was seamless with one's personal desires, whole as the body-stained shroud of Turin.

Even though Tom had chosen to go to a Jesuit university, he didn't want to become a Jesuit.

Tom wished to serve God, but as a populist American, a union man working for a better life, celebrating today's joys. He would work at the bottom of the rung. He would serve only the poor and ill-gifted. And, above all, he would not be bound against his will. God desired freedom. God did not desire ancient rigors forged in the over four-hundred-year-old imagination of a crippled Spanish soldier.

An acerbic comment from a Jesuit professor early in his freshman year started Tom wondering whether the Society might, indeed, be for him. Tom had told Father Melchior, his American history professor, after a passionate lecture on Irish immigration, that he considered becoming a priest of the Winona diocese. Father Melchior squinted his thick-browed eyes and said, his comment tipped with lightning, "You'd rather nursemaid a few thousand farmers on the way to paradise than change the way the world works? I thought you wanted to chase the horizon with those eyes, like Lewis and Clark, not plod content as a sod buster who stares all day at his horse's tired rear."

Tom laughed in response, a broad laugh, pulling his head back. But inside he swooned under the heat of the priest's taunt. Tom's response wasn't anger. It was shock. Tom understood repentance and turning from

18 *A Jesuit Tale*

sin. He understood discipline and forgiveness. He understood kindness and humility. He could envision himself speaking of those things, in linoleum-floored coffee shops or in confessionals of hand-carved wood, pressing his man's broad hand over the troubled hands of another.

Tom reeled back at Father Melchior's words, burnt by a thought, a possibility, a revision. His "calling," that word downy with divine meddling, perhaps his calling was not to preserve the well-tilled prairie he knew from childhood, to tend it and nurture it in little ways, pruning a stalk or hoeing a row. Could his calling be to ignite the prairie?

The idea of a Jesuit vocation was still all imagery for Tom. As he neared graduation, he wanted to test the roots of those images, taste the dirt clinging to them for alkali or acidity, discover what would grow and what would perish. Tom was excited about his interview with Father Riordan, the vocation director of the Wisconsin Province.

Tom had forged a passing friendship with a number of Jesuits. He and these priest-professors would stop to talk on a sunny day if they met on Wisconsin Avenue, raising their voices above the hum of urban traffic, or would share a beer and fish-fry in a pub along the Milwaukee river on a windy Friday night. He was comfortable with these priests. They called him "Burnsy" or "The Red Man" because of his dark red hair. Sometimes they called him "The Willow" because he was tall and lithe and had a graceful approach to the hoop.

Tom had met Father Riordan during halftime at last week's Warrior's basketball game. The round, short priest had appeared from nowhere as Tom was talking to Xavier, a six-foot five-inch graduate student from Sri Lanka. The Jesuit stepped out from behind that stand of foreign legs as if he were a leprechaun springing up beside a yew tree. His fat, wet face beamed up at the two students. After some patter about the game, Father Riordan elbowed Tom to the side and wrinkled his elf-peg of a nose, telling Tom to give him a call if he ever wanted to talk about a vocation.

"It's my job, Tom. I'm vocation director, so I ask," Father Riordan said, stifling a rill of a laugh.

"I know," Tom said, concentrating on the small cleric, wondering if fate, or divine providence, or some priest-teacher with a vocation quota had arranged this meeting. Tom had only spoken to one Jesuit, his basketball pal Father Ralph, about seriously considering the Society. He'd wanted his admission to Father Ralph to sound distant, intellectual, a studied comment from a man viewing the prime shapes of museum art. Could Father Ralph have been the instigator of this visitation?

"Father Ralph warned me about you," Tom said, bending down and studying Father Riordan's eyes, looking for traces of sincerity around the light retinas. "He said you were a hard-driving capitalist at heart, someone who loves a takeover deal."

Father Riordan's laughter burst out in waves around them. Two coeds sat forward in their seats, shocked by the unexpected, high-pitched cackle, and turned to see the Roman-collared ball of a man bend over, as much as he could, holding his jiggling belly with two stubby hands. Even in the auditorium's diffuse light, his forty-year-old oval face glowed red.

"I'll admit to being straightforward and honest. And I'll admit to acquiring capital—spiritual capital," Father Riordan said, still laughing. "If that interests you, Tom, give me a call." Before he hustled back to his seat, Father Riordan shook Tom's hand one more time, pressing tightly, his mouth drawn, saying, "Seriously." Tom called up Father Riordan the next day. He'd tell the man his story and listen to the vocation director's response.

They met on Sunday night at the Wisconsin Avenue I-Hop, about ten-thirty, before the place got busy again. Both men slid into their own side of an orange booth and immediately ordered black coffee. Tom undid the white paper napkin and placed its thin protection on his left knee. With no other chatter, he began to tell his story, only the highlights, the details he thought expressed his character, the plot lines that might show a pattern, what might be tracks of the prowling hound of God.

Tom volunteered at the Gesu, as lector, usher, teaching CCD, singing. He walked with Father Groppi when that fiery man crossed, as they said in Milwaukee, from Africa to Poland. That fall he'd spent hours forming a political action group to support Eugene McCarthy and failed his first Calc II exam. His loves? Radical politics. Radical faith. And the dream, an icon in his brain with one figure, mainly face, flat and strong, of becoming a priest. "I thought of being a diocesan priest, but since I've been here at Marquette U, I think the Jesuits could be the place for me. I want to be a priest AND change society."

"Many a Jesuit's declared the same thing," Father Riordan said, joyfully, leaving Tom no chance to amplify. He put down his pancake-laden fork, puffed out both cheeks and wiggled on the orange plastic seat. "It's exactly the story I've heard from some of our best young men."

Father Riordan steadied his rolling frame. His eyes became intense. "I really think you should pursue this vocation."

"You're right," Tom said. Then he unleashed the words: "I want to join the Jesuits." Once the words were out, he sat perfectly still—listening inside.

He had enjoyed saying them. They resonated within, around the heart. And he relished the sound of that bold, pushy word at the end: "Jesuits."

"I want to follow Jesus," Tom said, adding what he knew was the necessary counterpart of his first declaration. Yet that second sentence felt submissive in comparison. Less dangerous.

Father Riordan beamed at both phrases. He scrunched deeper into his side of the booth and rubbed his back along the plastic seam as if he were a muddy cow happy at a tree. "We're the right place, Tom. We're his band of men," Father Riordan said with the same sharp zeal Tom had seen in the Marquette auditorium.

"And as for change, for changing society, I've seen so many changes . . . I couldn't . . ." Father Riordan pointed to himself, boastful, as if he were telling something amazing: "I, myself—I used to be a real misfit. Tripping on my cassock. And Latin. I couldn't tell a *veni* from a *vidi*." He laughed. Tom smiled politely.

"Of course, they never tried to teach me Greek. I was being prepared to be the water boy in the Jesuit minor leagues," Father Riordan laughed again, but had now begun to pull at his Roman collar. A darkness spread over his pink face, quick as spilled altar wine oozing across white linen. Father Riordan gulped. "Even in the minor leagues I was second rate—and late for everything. I had to take my philosophy orals twice." He paused and spit out a quick Latin phrase: *Potest mus occidere se.* "Do you know what that means?"

Tom was getting lost in the little priest's ramble. He didn't say anything but lifted his shoulders and contracted the muscles of his face into a wordless gesture that combined "No" and "So what?" and "What's with you?"

Father Riordan didn't seem to notice the meaning in Tom's body language. He kept on.

"*Potest mus occidere se?* Can a mouse commit suicide? It was my second try at orals. Pass or no priesthood."

Now Tom saw the hurt in the little priest's eyes. He paid more attention. "That phrase was a sop from a friend on the panel," Father Riordan said, angrily. "A life saver, except I didn't know what a goddamn *mus* was! Thank God one of the *auditores* was my spiritual director! He leaned back in his chair, as if he were stretching, out of boredom—the other two never saw him shake his head. 'No', I said, thankful, ashamed, not really certain. '*Non potest mus occidere se.*'"

Father Riordan stopped himself, looking down at his well-padded hands, a single tear about to slide down his right cheek. He reached up and quashed it with his index finger. "This is the right time to enter, Tom. This is the right time. No one asks a Jesuit anymore whether a *mouse* can kill itself." Father Riordan took a deep breath and looked again into Tom's eyes. A small fear quickly paled the heated shame on his forty-year-old skin. More words tumbled out. "You know, you can enter the novitiate without making a commitment. Think of it as taking a car for a drive. After two years, if the Society isn't the place for you, leave. Follow your vocation somewhere else. The Church is a big institution."

Tom nodded his head. He wasn't paying attention to Father Riordan. He was back reviewing his own words, checking their echo. "Jesuits." "Enter the Jesuits." He stretched out his legs and exhaled until his flat stomach pinched inward. What was he feeling? Elation? No. Something akin to love? Maybe. He couldn't quite pin it down, assign it to a phylum or genus. But the feeling was sweet.

Father Riordan, on the other hand, was sweating. He wiped his face with his napkin twice all the way around. He was fidgeting, nervous. He looked curiously to Tom. "There's just a few formalities. Some tests, IQ, MMPI. Formalities. You've got nothing to worry about," the priest said, waving one soft hand in reassurance. "Father Donnelly, dean of students, will meet with you, review your academic abilities, not more than an hour. Then you meet with some special men, a few of the provincial consultors."

Father Riordan stopped. Tom focused more clearly on the priest. He knew the priest had been talking about the next steps.

"And we want you to meet with our psychologist—only once," Father Riordan said. A second of silence. "This isn't therapy, we just want to make sure there's no—no unusual impediment to your entering."

"Impediment," Tom said, slowly forming the four syllables as he began to take in the word. "Impediment?" This word he didn't fancy. Was it a Jesuit word he hadn't heard before? Was he moving too fast?

"Dr. Grosch asks about things that don't pertain to you, I'm sure. She looks for a psychological problem, a maladjustment, a problem with sex . . ." A band of sweat suddenly broke out along Father Riordan's high forehead.

Tom looked down and stared at the mound of blueberries coagulating on his short stack of pancakes, trying to hide his reaction. This new word, "sex," had pushed the canonical word out of his consciousness. Tom was to meet Rose later that night.

"I don't think you'll find much abnormal about me," Tom said, looking back up, chuckling.

Tom had told himself he would deal with celibacy later, when he had received the grace for it, just like Augustine. He was fearless of that stark vow. When he vowed celibacy, he would jump out into it, bold as a skydiver.

That night he was still in the belly of the plane. Even with the sweaty priest across from him, Tom began to think of Rose's soft body sitting above him, her breasts dangling at that perfect angle from her trunk, the nipple of the right breast pointing away a minor degree, naughty as a playground pin-up. He was ready to leave.

Besides, Tom had to explain it all to Rose, tell her what he'd done, what he'd said: "enter the Jesuits." She could reflect back the reality of it.

Father Riordan, Tom now knew, could not help him probe the inner layers of his soul. Rose could help. She knew what he felt there. She could read it even in his face. She always could. "You've got a Norseman's face, long, squared at the jaw, fierce in battle but mischievous in the longboat." That proclamation was uttered on their second date, and they were both drunk, and she was "waxing" as she put it, and repeated the Norseman analogy, or parts of it, until Tom finally thrust his tongue down her throat.

Rose's words, even when zig-zaggy as night bugs in an alcoholic haze, made everything inside Tom clear. She was mother-confessor. He had learned to kneel before her. Tonight, before they made love, he would present his newly announced spiritual quest for her blessing.

"Meeting with Dr. Grosch is just a formality," Father Riordan said, breaking into Tom's reverie, his voice tense as a used-car salesman still pitching his best out in the lot. "You're level-headed, Tom, not emotional about your vocation. You're guided by spiritual logic. That's the way it's been for me."

Tom nodded his head and suppressed a yawn. Father Riordan signaled to the waitress, writing on the air with his small clod of a hand.

That evening Tom felt a good, strong rhythm beat inside him. Exploring this Jesuit option was the right thing to do. He started humming, running through a medley of Dylan tunes, ending with "It Ain't Me, Babe." His college buddies kidded him whenever he sang that song's cautionary lyrics. Sex undraped by holy commitment? Tom's sexual involvement with Rose was as well known as his leadership with the Gesu parish youth group.

Prayer and sex were becoming two strands of one braid for Tom. He and Rose always meditated together before performing the most sublime of carnal acts. Their transition from prayer to intercourse was gradual, a slow meandering, intricate as the many orations and gestures the priest performs before he stretches his body in adoration after having bent low for the words of consecration.

Of course, their sex rite was more personal and improvisational than the precisely scripted Latin rite. It usually started with Tom rubbing Rose's inner thigh and humming "Kumbaya" until he would exchange the sacred vessel of his hand for the sacred vessel of his tongue and begin to moisten her skin centimeter by centimeter. Rose would smile benignly throughout, breathing deeply, regularly, absorbed as a Buddhist nun in full discipline, finding the something that shimmered in the nothing, losing herself and becoming one with the act itself.

Rose wasn't in love with Tom, so she said the longer they were together, and he knew he wasn't in love with her, not "I want to marry you" kind of love. He was sure she had no great need for him, for him alone. Their commingling was useful, calming, tidy. Once he wrote the word "organic" in his Calc II notebook, then doodled it into a shrub, thinking of Rose as a bush, as tree of life. She was, in many ways, more metaphor than person. But such a metaphor! Casting such shade!

After completion, in each other's arms, they spoke mantras that said it all. "Feel the energy," Tom would murmur. "Feel the calmness," Rose would reply. Never, did they say, "I love you."

Love was, for Tom, not a state but an act, primarily a political act, an act of conscious, public attention. Sex, for him, was not such an act. It was something else. More like play, a pick-up game. Tom's primary vision of love, holy love and holiness, had not developed to include children and tender intimacies. His vision was epic, its action played out before institutional battlements and on a rough social plain.

Only one unpleasant thought rippled through Tom's brain that night as he rode up the elevator in McCormick Hall: Father Riordan's comment, almost unheard, rescued for some reason from the trash bin where most of the I-Hop conversation went, that Tom's decision to pursue a vocation was not emotional. There was truth in what Father Riordan said. Tom's vocation seemed inexorable to him, weighty as the earth itself.

So he did experience an emotion, he realized as he got off onto the drab green fourth floor. It was confidence.

The provincial headquarters of the Wisconsin Province of the Society of Jesus took up the entire second floor of a two-story brick office building, which also housed a small accounting firm. Half the offices overlooked the Menominee River Valley and its rusting industries. Tom had put off his interview with Dr. Grosch for three months, deeming it unnecessary in light of a call from God. Father Riordan had begun to leave worried messages. The province's vocation director finally snared Tom by setting up several appointments on one day.

The temperature on that day of psychological inquisition had neared eighty degrees by ten in the morning, warm for a spring day. The cracked sidewalk reflected the sun's heat back up at Tom as he sauntered on his way, thinking more about the upcoming Democratic convention in Chicago than the necessity of interviews. Despite a steady breeze, Tom's paisley shirt soon stuck to his back.

Once he reached the provincial offices, he stalled at the outside steps. He saw no cross. No statue. No sign of a religious institution. He could've been going for an interview to sell insurance. Something felt wrong.

Inside, after his eyes adjusted to a blinds-shut darkness, Tom found himself half a room away from a long metal desk where a middle-aged woman sat lost in her work, clacking away at her blue IBM Selectric. Helen, a south side secretary with six inches of graying blonde hair carefully teased up on her head, was typing a letter, her spine as straight as the back of a pew. She spun around to greet Tom at the same moment she pressed the return of the typewriter, twirling with polka-beat precision.

"May I help you?"

"I'm Tom Burns. I'm here to see Father Riordan—and a Dr. Grosch."

"Oh yes, I have it here," Helen said as she turned to flip through the appointment book. Despite the magnifying aid of her dark-rimmed glasses, she squinted at the schedule. "I think—I think you're to see Mrs. Grosch, oh, I mean, Dr. Grosch, first. She's the province psychologist. Does that sound right to you?"

"Sure, I'll see her first."

"She's in the third office on the right. Just go down this hall," Helen said as she gestured behind her, the fat under her arm jiggling for two seconds. "The doorplate reads: St. Ignatius Room. Knock before you enter," she sang.

Diminutive Dr. Grosch sat on the thin pad of a high-backed tan chair. Her elbows, pointing up, rested on its wide arms. The dusty blinds of the room's one window impeded a long view of the Bradley factory tower. She continued to read as Tom entered. Without word or a softening of her face she pointed for Tom to sit in the opposite chair.

She read through three folders as Tom sat still, his knees bent correctly, his hands gripping the chair. He fixed his narrowing eyes on her skinny wrists, both of which were encircled by clumps of bracelets. Five rings, two of them set with one-carat diamonds, shone on the fingers of her right hand. Her cheeks were brighter than any flower's blush. Tom was deciding to describe her as the gypsy woman to Rose: "Someone whose art was at least half deception," he would say. Good comment.

"You're Thomas Burns?" Dr. Grosch asked, closing the last tan folder. Her eyes moved over Tom, a herder's gaze examining a new beast at auction, roving along the thorax, the haunches and legs, stopping a moment, then back up to the head.

"Yes." The muscles around Tom's mouth tensed. He almost added, "I'm not a piece of meat." Rose liked him when he was combative, the contour of anger on his body, the narrowing of his mouth, which she would trace with the tip of her nose in an effort to calm him, his small, balled-up breaths which she would ingest with her open mouth.

Dr. Grosch looked down at a ruled sheet where she had made five or six notes. Looking up, she exhaled a bureaucrat's dry comment, "Everything looks in order, young man." Tapping the fingers of her left hand on the arm of the chair, she asked, "Is there anything you should tell me?"

"No. It's all there, I guess," Tom said, pointing to the files she held on her lap, unsmiling. This woman was impediment, a gritty mixture of gravel and lime set as a wall. "The results of my tests, my request to enter," he added. Had the Jesuits set her before him as a test?

"Yes, it's all here," Dr. Grosch said, gathering up the folders and dropping them onto the floor next to her beaded red purse, which shook as the folders plopped next to it. "Tell me, have you any concerns about entering the Jesuits?"

"No, none."

A brief silence.

"Your parents are unopposed?"

"I've talked to them about my vocation to the priesthood since I was in high school." He gave her a morsel. "But I only recently told them I was thinking of entering the Jesuits. They worry the Jesuits will send me far away, and they won't see me very often."

A thin smile, quick as a garter snake, slipped across Dr. Grosch's face.

"And for you—you have no concerns, no concern with celibacy?"

Tom shifted his butt, releasing the lock of his knees, stretching his long torso. "I wouldn't call it a concern. Celibacy will be a challenge." The top of his cheeks began to warm. "But it's just a single part of the challenge. There's no need to highlight it or to make celibacy the—the pivotal issue."

Tom could read no reaction on Dr. Grosch's face. Had she seen that one fear? His being too weak in the flesh. He hated that phrase, its scorn ancient as child labor. "I'm human!" he had complained to Father McNulty in his high school confessional as he confessed his daily, multiple masturbation.

Tom knew he could be celibate. "But at what price?" Rose once asked. "I'm not counting the price. Price is not the issue, calling is the issue. This is who I need to be," Tom had answered.

"You've no concern with people telling you what to do? People you don't enjoy or respect," Dr. Grosch asked nonchalantly as she adjusted two of the silver bracelets on her left arm.

"You're talking about obedience?" Tom's ears started to itch.

"That's what obedience comes down to: people telling YOU what to do."

"Jesuits tell me it's not that way, that there's this process called discernment." Tom heard the harshness in his tenor voice. He was losing control. "In discernment a person's own inner desires are weighed heavily. God works there."

Dr. Grosch was immobile at the mention of the deity. She's turned herself into a statue, Tom thought, by spending too many years studying dream fragments and staring at ink squish.

"Fine. You may go," Dr. Grosch said, lowering her eyelids halfway.

Tom remained seated. He gripped onto the arms of the chair. A thought boiled over. "You know, I'm confident about my vocation. I don't know why." For some steamed-up reason, he wanted this gypsy woman's reaction. Would his confidence last?

Dr. Grosch's shoulders relaxed. Her right eyelid lifted, generous and dramatic in its arc. "I'm asked to give my opinion to the provincial and to his consultors, not to you. Nevertheless," she said, her bracelets clanging as she shoved that useless word to the side, "I've dealt with many Jesuits— on entering—on leaving. They all seek confidence. Some find it."

David

David had never known a live Jesuit. He had read about the Society, its history of exploration: geographic, intellectual, spiritual. When he considered a life in the Church only two religious orders appealed to him, the Jesuits and the Carthusians. In David's mind they were the extremes, the best, one a phalanx of powerful men charging over the spiritual landscape with banners furled, one the single contemplative lost in the faint glory of a petal frozen in ice.

David had chosen to charge over the landscape with thundering hooves and sweating bodies. He already knew too well the soluble delights of frozen petals.

David wasn't interested in parish life, in council meetings, marriages, and well-run schools. He wasn't interested in world peace. He wasn't interested in teaching. He was interested in spirit and words, swelling words, the holiest words that rang loud in church towers or quiet at death-bed anointing.

David, the younger man, still in high school, took Father Saunders out to dinner. His chauffeur dropped them off at Mitterand's, the finest restaurant on Lake Minnetonka. The Jepsons were a prominent family in the moneyed circles of Minneapolis, one of the old grain milling families who kept a low profile in that egalitarian city. David, from age eleven, to the chagrin of his parents, had insisted on having a driver available when his parents were away, which was almost always.

After settling into a window-side candle-lit table with a prime view of the lake, Father Saunders, the trim rector of the novitiate, explained to David that Father Riordan had asked him to do the initial interview.

"It makes perfect sense," David said, turning away from the bright reflection his face made in the shiny pane. All was dark outside. "You're here, Father Riordan's in Milwaukee. Surely you know a great deal about examining candidates, being rector at St. Bonifacius."

Father Saunders picked up his heavy tumbler of Johnny Walker Red, swirled it and sipped. "Not only do I know a lot about today's candidates, but I was once a young man wanting to enter. Those were anxious days for me," Father Saunders said with a smile David took as reassuring. "I was convinced the Society would reject me."

"And why?" David asked, wondering why Father Saunders assumed he, too, was anxious. David thought himself a perfect candidate, accomplished, self-confident, a proven producer, and clearly not someone seeking to hide away from the world. If he wanted to hide, he could build his own Mad Ludwig's castle. He had nothing to gain by entering the Jesuits. Except the salvation, which he thought of as a calming, of his soul.

"I'm reserved, you see," Father Saunders said, still holding onto his chilled tumbler. "I don't mix well. I feared the Jesuits would have no place for a wilting violet."

"You seem adept to me, socially," David said as he signaled the waiter with a turn of his head.

"Well, thank you," Father Saunders said, lifting his drink and tilting its crystal weight toward David. "I've learned over the years. You can't live with hundreds of men and not learn to communicate—at least at a rudimentary level."

"Hundreds of men?" David's eyelids fluttered. He'd meant to sound shocked. Some other emotion rolled out. He relaxed in its wake.

"In the old days. These days it's dozens of men, but the same principle applies. Your fellow Jesuits help form you. Their ideas, their experiences—they become part of you, open you up. Your brother Jesuits become your support group. They become the people you rely on for advice, for friendship, maybe even for love."

The waiter arrived as the word *love* escaped from Father Saunders' fine, thin lips. David looked down into the menu and ordered both his meal and hors d'oeuvres for the two of them. He felt Father Saunders' eyes stare at him. He decided to be wary. He didn't want to seem too adult, too set in his ways. Rigidity, he knew from his mother's chastisements, was a flaw difficult to undo.

"This is an elegant restaurant. Do you eat here often?" Father Saunders asked after the waiter bowed slightly and left.

"Not that often. We've a very good cook at home, an old Croatian from Zagreb. And eating out takes so much time. I've a busy schedule."

"So I've noted from your application," Father Saunders said, sitting back, resting both elbows on the plush arms of the chair. "You're active at high school, editor of the newspaper, co-captain of the debating team, a leader in the Catholic prayer group. At St. Olaf's you're a cantor and regular choir member. Plus you're writing this series for the local diocesan paper: the *A Day in the Life Of* series."

Father Saunders' eyes shone. He seemed happily absorbed by the outline of David's life. "I've got to tell you, I've really enjoyed reading those. The people come alive. I was so impressed by the nun who runs that home for the mentally retarded. The normality of their lives—the little love interests, the hand squeezes, the written messages, the hugs in the hallway."

David's return smile was polite. He was confident in his writing skills. He didn't want adulation from Father Saunders, he wanted a mentor. This was not the man. With that realization, a tiny winter-cold drift of sadness piled up inside him.

"I'm glad you've enjoyed the pieces," David said. "I was hoping to write as a Jesuit, maybe work for *America*."

"Oh, surely. For a man with talents, the Jesuits is the place to be."

When David arrived home that night he took out his diary and wrote as he did every evening. First he marked down whether he'd seen his parents that day. Since the age of ten, David had been keeping a tally. Each year at Christmas he'd give his parents the results of his counting, offering one of those little barbs that his mother said kept them apart.

His parents were currently in Barbados, so he marked down a dash in the 'not seen' column. It was spring. He'd seen his parents for twenty days that year.

Before writing his impressions of Father Saunders, David flipped back to his entry of January 7. He had discovered a poem that day by Gerard Manley Hopkins, a Jesuit priest they were studying in advanced English. "Brothers." David's heart had slowed down as he read the poem. He quickly memorized it and copied a few of the most precious lines into his diary:

> How lovely the elder brother's
> Life all laced in the other's,
> Love-laced

David didn't know what brotherly love was. David was an only child. He had no experience of brotherly love, although he knew it must be a bond as twisted and necessary as the intestines. Such love must be intense, mind-opening as the quiet in a forest. David often wandered through their estate's acreage, communing with the white forest's intensity. He found there a wise quiet, a shimmering birchwood quiet whose personality he understood.

David was intelligent and busy, but he was lonely. He thought loneliness made the words and feeling of Hopkins's poem burn into him. He used the dead Jesuit's image to pray about his own goal: the lacing, the entwining. That's what his spirit wanted. In his mind he dreamed of lacing himself up with the world through the Jesuits, tying himself to the very root of existence.

The morning after his dinner with Father Saunders, David was excited to talk about his vocation with Gina, his best friend and high school chum.

They were to meet for breakfast at the Hennepin Avenue Embers. David arrived early to claim their favorite booth, which overlooked the constant urban flow of the poor, hip, and elderly.

Gina made a later entrance. Twice she flung back her shiny black hair as she walked through the Ember's doorway, as if sun-rays had been trapped inside and clamored in her ears for freedom. David watched with pleasure. Gina was trying out a new hair style, a bob with a permed bend at the base of her creamy white chin. She said it made her feel a vamp in control. He watched her stride slowly down the aisle, swiveling her hips with adolescent care. David also kept one eye on the new blonde waiter whose own concentration on Gina nearly led him into an eight foot high column as he hustled along bearing an order of pigs-in-a-blanket.

Gina stopped at their booth to smooth her satiny black miniskirt, the one David had warned would dry up her birth canal.

"Don't say a word," Gina said, mischief in her green eyes. Slowly she undid the ivory buttons of her lime sweater vest, caressing each one as if she were fingering some soft organ. "I needed to feel unencumbered today."

David knew she was trying to make the words steam up the air.

"Unencumbered would be no backpack," David said with what Gina called his lord-of-the-manor voice. He shifted over to make room for Gina. They preferred to sit on the same side of the booth. They would bend into each other, conspirators of taste and judgment.

David looked up into Gina's eyes and grinned. "Just assure me you're wearing panties."

Gina's eyes narrowed. "Don't be naughty, people won't like you." Then she slid into the booth with a sudden fierceness, nudging David's shoulder and pecking him on the cheek as if she were a starlet of the first order.

"I'll never be naughty again," David said, crossing his heart with two of the fingers of his right hand and warbling back his assertion with the creaking voice of a great dame.

David leaned away from Gina to get a good view of her. He wanted to see the fullness of her reaction. "I spoke with the local Jesuit rector last night, and I'm going to be a priest."

"Don't tease me with religious profundities at this hour of the morning,"

Gina said. She looked down to rearrange her sweater and only looked back up when the cute waiter arrived and stared down at her young breasts.

"Coffee?" asked the waiter.

"Two," David said, annoyed, needing Gina's attention. The waiter didn't take his eyes off Gina. "Black," David added.

"Coming right up," said the waiter, Todd R., as he pried himself away from their booth.

Gina looked over at David, batting her eyelashes. "He'd do," she said.

"For what?" David asked.

"For many things, I'm sure."

"Such as? Gardening? Hoeing? Cleaning out the stables?"

"He has qualities I appreciate. Poise, for example." Gina segregated her silverware to their proper stations on the place mat.

"Would he make a good priest?"

Gina wrinkled her nose and squinted her eyes.

Todd R. was back with the coffee. "Are you ready to order?" Again he looked only at Gina.

"I'll have an English muffin," Gina said, smiling back. "Dry."

"A short stack and a side of bacon," David said. He wanted to shoo Todd R. away. This Norse bred food-jockey with the blonde locks and tight-fitting painter's pants was mixing in the wrong vibes.

"You're being jealous," Gina said, gloating after Todd R. left.

"Jealous?"

"Yes. You're irritated with Todd R., the way he's ogling me."

"And the way you're ogling back."

"See! You're jealous." Gina's voice was happy. She rested her right hand on David's arm.

"Gina . . ." David said, exasperated. He turned away to look out the window at the number 6 bus as it stopped across the street. Gina was his best friend. They studied together, gossiped on the phone, went to movies, even went to parties together. Were they in love? David knew he had no desire to kiss her, to fondle her breasts or put his hands up her skirt. He told himself it was because of his vocation. He knew there was truth in that assertion, and deception, and even innocence, which he recognized in himself, but an innocence as lamentable as Adam and Eve's innocence on the wrong side of the gate, an innocence with a deep, confounding birthmark.

"I'm sorry," Gina said. She reached out and turned David's head back to look at her. "What about the priesthood?" she asked.

It seemed to David that a dark sorrow had shuttered Gina's eyes. He was used to sorrow, so he ignored it.

"It's not just about the priesthood. It's also about becoming a Jesuit, joining the community."

CHAPTER TWO

The Jesuits of the Wisconsin Province had recently abandoned their rambling house of formation in the village of St. Bonifacius in rural Minnesota. By the late 1960s the building itself was nearly empty, a useless leftover of pre-Vatican II religious exuberance with that era's platoons of novices and juniors. The new novitiate, housing less than two dozen novices, was in the city.

It was 1968, and renewal continued within the Church and within the Society. New symbols were being tested, symbols that the superiors and scholars of the renewal hoped would lead people to new understandings and new practices, symbols to plot out the religious equivalent of airports and highways on a Catholic terrain that undulated with too much medieval cobblestone and meandering pilgrim routes. The renewed Society of Jesus would be unpretentious, accessible and practical, the modern equivalents of poor, chaste, and obedient.

The novitiate in St. Paul was an exemplar of these virtues. It was nothing more than a pair of three-story white stucco apartment buildings, the two structures set at an angle so that a triangular, modest yard grew between them. The apartments within had been converted into communal spaces: a refectory, a recreation room, a library, the novice master's office, and bedrooms.

One apartment, on the second floor of the southern building, had become the chapel. A plain blonde altar stood near the far end of the white-walled former living room. A ring of wooden chairs along the outer walls surrounded the altar so that the room had that slightly nervous, expectant feeling of a doctor's waiting room. A handmade star quilt from South Dakota's Pine Ridge reservation hung on the inner wall, a burst of red and gold as backdrop to the priest during Mass. The adjacent kitchen and one of the bedrooms served as a split-up sacristy where objects of the sacred liturgy were stored: vestments, wine, hosts, candlesticks, and chalices. The other bedroom was kept for visitors, who slept feet from the real presence.

The apartment's dining room became an alcove for private meditation before the ornate bronze tabernacle which had been transported from its altar perch in the old novitiate at St. Bonifacius and now was set on a sturdy wooden stand. Behind the tabernacle hung a six-foot tall iron corpus. Workers had sundered the corpus from the cross of the old novitiate's main chapel in preparation for the sale of that consecrated building to an evangelical Bible college. The heavy figure of the dying Jesus, his head hung low, was now affixed to the inner wall of the apartment's dining room by four metal studs. It loomed over anyone who knelt before it, dense and as sharply outlined as the shadow of a dead, leafless tree on a blazing sunny day.

In all, the chapel was a peaceful place, suited to its task, functional and clean, smelling more of Windex than candle wax.

Tom was the first novice to arrive. He said a two minute good-bye to his teary-eyed parents at the door of the novitiate. They'd told him they wouldn't stay around. Leaving him at the novitiate was different from dropping him off at college; to stay would seem an intrusion, as if they were spectators at a honeymoon.

Father Saunders greeted the three of them at the breezeway between the two buildings. After Tom's parents had left, he told Tom to drop his single suitcase in the foyer of the south building. First they would tour the novitiate.

"It's all pretty simple, I guess," Father Saunders said as they stood in the basement hallway of the north building. "The only thing you really need to note is the bulletin board." Father Saunders pointed to two large corkboard panels already covered with paper. "Here's where assignments are posted: the house schedule, phone messages, the names of guests, special provincial news, a copy of the latest status—where members of the province have been newly assigned."

Tom had little to say as they walked through the quiet rooms. Everything looked perfect to him. The residence was plain and utilitarian. The furniture, couches and armchairs, narrow beds and several box-crate bed stands, was all vintage Goodwill or university student hand-me-down.

"Let's go to your room," Father Saunders said after stopping for a brief visit to the chapel, the pair of them standing silently in the middle of the dining-room-turned-house-of-God. "It's just downstairs."

Tom was to live in a basement apartment, the one across the hall from the novitiate's library with its extensive collection of books on spirituality, Jesuit history, and the Bible. He could smell the must of the old books as they walked past the open door. He paused to look in, half excited by new books, half put off by the somber face of so many old tomes.

There were three bedrooms in the garden apartment: two small bedrooms and an even smaller kitchen that would be used as a bedroom, even though an enameled iron sink still hung to the inner wall.

Tom had been assigned one of the rooms that looked out onto Finn Street, a little-traveled side street not far from the College of St. Thomas and the Mississippi River.

His eyes lit up as he walked in and examined the room, its bed "cool as a eunuch's" (Tom thinking of the phrase Rose had slung at him their last night together, chuckling, as he packed for a return to Mankato and she packed to head off to the New School and a career in sociology). On the wall opposite the bed stood a three-foot-wide writing desk, a straight-backed chair, and one tiny dresser. The room's walls were chalk white, and Tom shivered at their simplicity. A black crucifix with a greenish-bronze Jesus hung above his bed. One dented single-jointed gray lamp hugged a corner of the desk.

"As you can see, it's not luxurious." Father Saunders stood in the center of the little space and grinned. "But everything's been freshly painted."

"It'll be perfect," Tom answered, still studying his quarters. He walked past Father Saunders to look out the Finn Street window.

"I don't think you'll have to worry about street noise. It's a quiet neighborhood."

"That won't be a problem, Father. Not after Marquette U." Tom turned.

There were more voices at the novitiate door. Father Saunders left Tom to greet the new arrivals. "You'll meet your novice master, Father Gorman, later. He's chosen to spend the day in preparation for classes."

Alone in his new room Tom continued to breathe deeply, as if this space exuded that mystical perfume he'd read about with skepticism: the odor of sanctity. He turned slowly around. He looked fondly at each plaster corner and each flat wall. He felt a warmth in his heart, happiness akin to a child's yearning for homerun glory being fulfilled by the snap of wood. He thought of kneeling to pray a prayer of thanksgiving. This was the right choice. He took the tattered Chardin text he'd tucked into the back of his jeans after getting out of his parents' Plymouth and placed it on the desk, gently flattening out its fresh bend.

Within moments, the silence of Tom's reverie was broken by a loud, brassy conversation.

"Oh, it's downstairs, as in the catacombs. Come on angel, fly down," David was instructing Terry Midland.

"I'm not a cargo angel! Even with two wings I can barely lift this trunk," Terry said, his voice full of cartoonish exaggeration. "What's in it— gold bullion from some sunken Spanish galleon?"

"Nothing so precious," David said, regally, with the Queen of Hearts' trilled 'r'. The two seemed kindred spirits. "It contains a few stitches of clothing. Mainly black, of course, books, a typewriter." Then with his own voice. "Is a typewriter OK? Books?"

Tom stood under his bedroom's doorway, big-eyed as a Californian in an earthquake, and watched the two young men struggle at the door of the nearly empty, red-shag living room. The one who'd been called an angel was tall and slender with curly brown hair and a wide, mischievous grin. The other, as tall as the angel, was softer, his face more cherubic. He wore chinos and a blue blazer with a gold crest on its pocket. His blonde hair, neither short nor long—giving no indication of his political bent, was perfectly trimmed. Sweat, however, had begun to drip from his forehead.

"The Society will supply you with plenty of books," Terry said, now serious. "There'll be typewriters in the library. My advice, give the typewriter to Brother Minister right away. As a novice, you don't need a *personal* typewriter."

"Hello, can I help?" Tom said, stepping toward the pair.

"YES," David and Terry answered in exasperated unison.

"Which room are you in?" Tom asked, looking to both of them, wondering who was the novice.

"The ex-kitchen, I guess," David said, frowning. "Is it far? Can we drag this thing from here?"

"It's not far," Tom said, concluding with displeasure that the dressed-up one was his new roommate.

"I'm the new novice," David said, extending his hand, "David Jepson. This is Terry, our angel."

"Good to meet you both," Tom said as he shook David's hand and nodded to Terry, who was stuck in the hallway. "I'm Tom Burns," he said, wondering what an angel was and why he didn't know. Freezing his smile, Tom walked over to help with David's end of the aluminum trunk. "Let's get this thing moved." Tom suppressed a laugh as he calculated the odds of getting that shiny rectangle of possessions into the kitchen bedroom.

After the three of them wedged David's steamer trunk into its narrow quarters, Terry returned to the makeshift sewing room on the third floor of the north building where he was sewing curtains for the windows of the novitiate. Tom went back to his room to savor the meaning of what he had begun, to relish that growing sense of pride and purpose. He reverently picked up his suitcase and placed it on the bed, opened it and gazed at his belongings, now possessions of a sanctioned searcher, sacral in their own way.

After a few minutes of quiet, David showed up at Tom's door. Tom turned to face his guest, but didn't invite him in, annoyed that his special moment of privacy, of confirmatory grace, had again been broken.

"You only brought three pairs of pants?" David asked, lengthening his neck and staring into Tom's battered Samsonite.

"Sure, two jeans and a pair of black slacks," Tom said. He picked up the slacks and walked them to the closet of the inner wall. "We're supposed to dress for Mass, so that's why the slacks," Tom said, returning from the closet to his tiny cache of clothing. "Otherwise, why would I need more? T-shirts and jeans should be fine. That's what I wore at Marquette U."

"What if you're invited to a party or out to a play—or to the opera?"

One of David's hands kept moving as he spoke, in the swishy manner Tom called "jellied." Tom contorted his face into an unbelieving question mark as the rich man's word "opera" inflated within him. Rose had warned him about the meanness of this facial expression.

"I don't plan on going out a lot," Tom said, almost growling as he bent over to pick up a stack of black and white socks. He took a breath and thought of Rose and then of Jesus. "We'll be pretty busy. And anyway, where would we get the cash?"

David still wore his blazer. He was leaning against Tom's doorway with his arms folded. "Well, I don't know all the arrangements, yet, but I can tell you that most of the priests I've met have known how to have a good time."

"I'm sure they have." Tom picked up his dozen pair of fresh jockey shorts, clutching them tightly in his hands and headed toward the four-drawer dresser that stood against the exterior wall underneath the window. "But I'm not entering the Jesuits to have a good time," Tom said, his declaration made to the wall.

David was silent for a moment. With Tom at the far end of the room, he slowly entered Tom's sacred space, heading over to the desk. David picked up the paperback.

"Teilhard de Chardin," David said. *The Divine Milieu*. Looking at Tom, "You've taken the high dive into the spiritual sciences. Were you a theology major in college?"

"No, political science and history." Tom had turned around to look at David, but remained next to the window. He felt trapped, the first pinching of his own will. Should he endure this imposition quietly? In the dorm, he was known for his rude assessments. He was bad at small talk but good at pronouncements, Rose had told him often, urging him to listen to her.

"So, did somebody discover you, recruit you? Were you the favorite of some poli-sci Jesuit at Marquette?" David asked.

"A favorite? I don't know about that. I knew a few. I volunteered at the Gesu, tutoring, working at the soup line. I was friends with a couple of my professors who were Jesuits. No one *recruited* me. I've had this vocation for years. How about you? Were you recruited?"

"I hardly know any Jesuits. It was the mystique of the order, the variety of opportunities, the emphasis on excellence that appealed to me." David started to flip through the Chardin.

"I see." Tom wanted to ask David to leave. He told himself to keep his door shut in the future.

"I want to get involved in communications," David said. He set the paperback face-down on Tom's desk. "Go ahead, keep on unpacking," David said, gesturing at the suitcase.

David sat down on the edge of the bed, crossing his long legs as if he were relaxing and preparing for a stay. "I was editor of our school paper. I've done some writing for the diocesan paper, nothing extraordinary, just covering a few local personalities, interviews, day-in-the-life-of type of stuff. I want to be a journalist, to let the world know about the Church."

Tom remained at the far wall. He wondered why David needed to be a Jesuit to be a journalist and almost asked the question. Instead, Tom thought about the detachment he had read about. He was studying whether he believed that the things of this world were of no value in themselves. He was most unsure about whether his own thoughts and opinions, those intimate possessions, could ever be set aside. Dealing with David was becoming his first challenge within the Society. Was this irritating visitor a grace?

Before Tom could make any response, Mark arrived.

"That must be our third roommate," Tom said as he headed quickly to the door. "Let's say Hello."

As soon as Tom saw Mark's fit body and his dark hair, cut close as a jock's before the big game, Tom began to relax again. This was someone he easily understood.

"Hi, I'm Mark Sappingstone," the new man said, extending his hand first to Tom and then to David. "Could one of you give me a help with my trunk. I think I brought more stuff than I needed to."

"I'll help," David said, his voice upbeat. Tom looked at David, astonished at this quick offer of physical assistance.

Minutes later Mark and David had lugged this second trunk into the third bedroom. Tom joined them.

"Have a seat, guys," Mark said pointing to his bed.

David and Tom obeyed, quiet as serfs.

Mark turned to his trunk and opened the lid. "Let's see, black sweater, black pants, black socks. Did you pack the same?"

"Pretty much," Tom said. "Just as Father Saunders' letter instructed."

"Me, too. However, I only packed white underwear," David said. "I'm sure we'll find black underwear folded somewhere in our rooms."

Mark's laugh was instant and loud. He went over and patted David on the shoulder.

Tom, however, leaned further back on the bed, resting his body on his elbows and staring at David. He'd never heard of black underwear. Why was that funny?

"Black underwear, one of the secrets of the Society, I'm sure," Mark said, still catching his breath. "Have you two guys been here long?"

"Not long," Tom said. "Have you seen the house?" Tom wanted to get back to novitiate talk.

"Father Saunders showed me around. He told me to unpack, then head over to meet the other guys. Have both of you finished unpacking?"

"I'm pretty much done," Tom said.

David said nothing.

"If you don't mind," Mark said, "I'll put some of this stuff away and then we can all go over together."

"Sounds good to me," Tom said, his voice tightening. He was suddenly aware these two men were to be his companions for years to come, his brothers in Christ as the vocational literature explained. His first reaction was panic. He could feel his heart beat quicker. This was not greeting new dorm buddies. These men were going to be a part of his life, a part of him, like skin grafts on a burn patient, or the pin in his grandmother's hip.

"Did your parents drop you off?" Mark asked David, who'd been mostly silent since they met.

David shot up off the bed and stuffed his hands into the pockets of his pants. "No, they didn't drop me off." The words were sharp. "They're out of the country." Mark and Tom turned to stare at David.

"Where . . . where are they?" Mark asked.

"Marseilles." David's eyes were slits.

Silence.

"I see," Mark said. He turned back to his trunk, then cocked his head slightly and asked, looking back at David, "They're on vacation?"

"Sort of."

"Hmm. Are you from Minneapolis?" Mark asked as he sifted through the trunk's contents.

"Yes. Well, from a suburb."

Mark picked up four pairs of socks and leaned over to place them in the middle drawer of his chest, laying them out in perfect pairs. "Which suburb?"

"Orono. We have a place on Lake Minnetonka."

Mark turned to smile at David. "Sounds nice. I've spent some time on the lake. We have a little land there, too." Back digging in his trunk, "What's your last name, David?"

"Jepson."

Mark straightened up and turned around, staring at David. "As in Jepson Flour? As in major supporters of the Walker and the Minnesota Orchestra?"

David nodded.

Tom had been taking in this exchange in silence, first sensing in Mark the quality he wished he had more of, an easy appeal, then wondering why David's mood had turned somber. Now something else was happening, this talk of flour and arts.

"My father's firm has done work for your family," Mark said. "On occasion."

"I recognized your last name," David said, nodding toward the trunk. "The law firm of Sappingstone, Fox, and Barber. John Sappingstone's your father?"

"Sure is."

"You live in Kenwood? In the old Finch place? Nine bedrooms and the best ballroom in Minneapolis."

"That's the place."

Their conversation had quickly veered in a direction Tom had not anticipated. A bond was forming between David and Mark, or if not a bond, an understanding. And Tom, though present in the room, was not a part of the bond. These two men, novices now, came from families perched high on the social ladder. Tom Burns, son of a Mankato hardware store owner, was clearly hanging onto the bottom rung of their ladder. He was becoming uncomfortable and reached down to scratch the skin of his legs.

At that moment Father Saunders knocked at the apartment door and cried out, "Hello down here. Are you guys finished unpacking?"

"Almost," Mark said.

"Good." Father Saunders came over to Mark's room and gestured for the three of them to come out. "You can finish later. You have two options now. We've got two angels helping out with this year's class. They're scholastics who've been in vows for a couple of years. Your options are to go with Dan Dreasen, a fine athlete and a terrific little guitarist, to play basketball over at the St. Paul Sem gym or you can help Terry Midland, our craftsy angel, in his sewing project. Terry tells me you don't have to know how to sew. If you're not arthritic, he can use you."

John Shekleton 45

"I'll help with the sewing," David said, stepping forward, a happiness back on his face.

"I'm for basketball," Mark said, imitating a free throw with his muscled arms.

"Me, too," Tom added, jumping off the bed, ready to get out of his new home and into a world he understood, with the feel of a basketball in his hands, knowing its natural arc and the clean meaning of another man circling you with his arms, blocking your path.

At the end of that first evening the twelve first year novices, three fathers, one brother, and two angels all gathered in the novitiate's chapel, some sitting on chairs, others on the floor with their legs crossed. The candle next to the tabernacle shone through it rich red glass. Two white candles flickered on the altar. The lone street lamp on Finn Street struggled to project its brightness into the room. Father Gorman had ordered the chapel's windows open, letting in a soft hum from the outside, a mixture of insect song and the murmur of rustling leaves.

The community sat in silence for ten minutes, the young men shifting around, not yet at ease with quiet or communal meditation. Some orders imposed great stretches of silence on their novices. That was not the Jesuit way. The Jesuit vocation was to become an active participant in the struggles of the world. Still, at the heart of all religious orders, at the heart of every spiritual discipline, is silence, and even Jesuits must learn to extract its balm.

Finally Father Gorman, one-eighth black and new to the position of novice master, broke the sweaty anticipation that filled the chapel. He rose to stand behind the altar, bringing his hands together before him and rubbing them twice together. He was an imposing figure, a chiseled athlete with the prematurely wrinkled eyes of a confessor, footed as they were with deepening tracks of human pain and mirth.

"You're beginning—we're beginning—a great journey. It's a journey unlike the journeys of most of your peers. Perhaps you've been ridiculed for making it. It's an uncommon path we take—a structured, studied way. We're starting on an interior journey, a pilgrimage, a voyage into the soul. It will require sacrifice and discipline."

"Some of the practices you'll learn will seem odd at first. You won't understand their meaning or their potency. And journeying inside can frighten. But if you stick with our disciplines, you'll find great joy, wherever they lead you."

"Take the time during this next week to write down your feelings and your wishes, your thoughts and your conversations. Look at them for a while, but don't stare too intensely. Instead, ask the Lord to open your minds. Ask Him to help you see deeply into your hearts. And let us all pray for one another, that we all can see into the depths of our hearts—and see within that necessary organ of life the desire the Lord has placed."

Father Gorman then dismissed the community and reminded the novices to be in chapel at six-thirty for morning prayer.

CHAPTER THREE

"Semper Tres, Nunquam Duo"

"Always three, never two"

A maxim common in many religious orders. It is meant as a guideline, that three rather than two members of an order or congregation should work together, travel together, stroll together through a garden. This practice avoids the fostering of "particular friendships" in which two people might become exclusive in their friendship, or passionate in their affection.

The next morning David got up at five-thirty so he could be the first in the shower. Only three times before, on two debate trips and one retreat, had he shared a bathroom with other boys. He remembered how his "peers" had layered the bathroom floors with their towels, young stags shedding on any bush, he imagined. Each bachelor herd had surrounded the toilet with piss stains so intense that a hard yellow lacquer mounded up at the base.

David didn't want to be disturbed with carnal matters on his first full day in the novitiate. He dressed quickly, khakis and pink polo, and sat on his bed in the dank basement quiet. He opened his diary and began to dig through it, picking out phrases, examining the slag heap of adolescent observations for spiritual gems, remembering tubercular Thérèse and the impact of her bold young longings.

As David came to the previous evening's entry, he heard Mark's baritone offer a bright "Good morning!" to Tom, followed up by a plea to use the bathroom. "I drank way too much Miller last night!" Mark said. "We killed off two cases! You'd think we were the rugby team!"

Tom croaked back, his voice echoing within the green-tiled bathroom: "I don't shower in the morning, so when I'm drained, the bathroom's all yours."

David could hear the sound of a hot, fast stream pound into the bowl. He stared at the kitchen's cracked plaster walls.

Tom's "All yours"—what did that mean? Had the piss-pounder Tom forgotten about him?

David hadn't stayed with his roommates last night at *haustus*, their new word for party. He and novice Smith Edwards had slipped out down to the Mississippi and strolled along its manicured bluffs, once leaning on each other, shoulder to shoulder, two trees bent after a wind storm. David wanted to write something about that encounter, maybe in code, in indecipherable twenty-letter words. But now—was he off Tom's list of roommates? Already? Or was David expected to remain as crusty as Tom?

David took a deep breath and returned to his diary, shutting out the sound of his companions' noises. Too much was changing in his life to pay attention to porcelain sounds. Boys would be boys. He knew their style.

Last night's diary entry was the first in which David did not keep a record of whether he had seen his parents or not. His life had moved into a new stage, evolving, he hoped, as saltwater-goo had once evolved into colonies of anemones, lengthening and extending and learning to ingest the tidal brew.

David picked up his pen and added a few more lines.

> We have set out on a great journey, just as our novice master explained in chapel. We're on the spiritual grand tour. We're going to visit all the sites that are the font of our world: our personal world, our religious world, our material world. We're going to walk around them, sit in them, measure them, smell them. We'll be changed by the experience. We'll become older and wiser and holier. That's what I think is going to happen.
>
> Or does that description sound too silly for words?
>
> So, who do I like here? I like my roommate Mark. Suave. Handsome. Capable. So beautiful he could never be viciously funny. I like the angel Terry. He's unedited. I say evil things around him, just the way I did with Gina. We were good friends, Gina and I. This Tom, however. I think he'll be wild-eyed, a prophet. He just doesn't know it yet.

The three basement-dwelling novices left their rooms at six-twenty-five. David offered a "Good morning" to the other two, suppressing a movie-mimicking desire to add an *Oratre, Fratres,* and head bow. Tom returned the greeting, his voice still dry and cracking, his face blank. Mark, already chipper, grinned and patted David on the back, then bounded up the stairs to chapel.

David and Tom walked together into the Finn Street chapel, into a room already filled with silent male bodies, most in jeans, all on their knees with their frames angled in every direction—the way iron filings splay out when the compass is set too close to the pole. Father Gorman had taken up position in the middle of the room, proud, David thought, as a mother cat surrounded by her purring kittens. The novice master knelt facing the tabernacle straight on.

All these "children in the spiritual life," as David had written last night, remained silent for half an hour until their ecclesial guardian signaled the end of that first morning's communal meditation by intoning an Our Father and instructing the novices to head quietly to breakfast.

Before taking seats in the refectory, the novices checked out the house bulletin board for the order of the day—with special attention to kitchen duty. Last night the priests and brothers had served the meal and done cleanup, making jest of it because it was the last time they would perform kitchen duties, except for St. Stanislas Kostka day.

Early that morning Brother Minister, a lumberjack of a man, had tacked up the kitchen roster, which ruled one of the most important parts of novitiate life and whose adherence was monitored closely. Last night he had welcomed bribes from the novices, patting his flat belly and lamenting his sinful "concupiscence" for chocolate.

Smith Edwards came up to David after prayer as they crossed through the breezeway and whispered in David's ear that at *haustus* the rowdier novices had begun howling and repeating Brother Minister's "concupiscence," stretching out the "pis" into a hissy shower until Father Saunders came down and ordered them all to their rooms, offering Brother Minister a scowl and stern jaw. David smiled in reply, shaking his head as they crossed from southern building to northern. Life in the Society was not shaping up as David had expected.

Mark, David and Tom were assigned to lunch cleanup.

Father Gorman had ordered apartment groups to eat together for the first week so they could get to know one another right away. Obediently, though David feared reluctantly, the threesome sat together with the angel Dan Dreasen at the furthest of the seven tables lined up along a wall of dark-stained paneling in the basement dining room.

David's eyes had rolled up into his sockets when he first peered into the dismal space. With whorehouse-red carpet and red-and-white checkered tablecloths, the refectory looked more a Lake Street dive than a room for religious camaraderie. Yet unlike the Poodle Club and its walls of dart boards and pin-ups, several pictures of a shaggy-haired Jesus hung along the walls of the novitiate dining room.

That first morning David stopped before one of the prints, a Caucasian Jesus flashing an Australian rock-star's toothy smile. "Just the way I envision him, too," Tom said, walking past David to the table. David turned and smiled, thinking: *At least he said something to me.*

"So, how did you guys rest?" Dan Dreasen, vowed scholastic and angel, asked after a droopy-eyed Brother Minister offered a quick grace.

"Fine," the novices answered with one voice.

The three of them looked at each other and laughed.

Dan sat back in his chair, pretending that a wave of sound had crashed into him. "Great, you three are melding your personalities nicely. You'll all do well in the Society."

"Does life in the Jesuits result in some sort of Vulcan mind meld?" David asked with half-real fear as he looked up from his plate of watery scrambled eggs that thick-glassed novice Andy Kurtz had just planted before him.

"Just a joke," Dan said. He laughed his nice-guy laugh. Smith had told David last night that Dan was "adorable." David was speechless in reply, and Smith's face had gone blank. "If Gina had said that . . ." David had been thinking. It was the topic he wanted to scrawl on every page of his diary, except he feared that someone, maybe even after his death, just as with Thérèse, would pick up those blotchy thoughts and read them and know. And others knowing made it more real. Undeniable, which sounded the same as unforgivable.

They all began to eat.

"Was Father Gorman your novice master?" Mark asked Dan as he buttered his blackened toast.

David looked over at Mark, remembering how Mark had wondered aloud yesterday, in a quiet moment before Mass when the three of them were hanging out in the living room, what type of man this Gorman was. So Mark was doing research again this morning. Efficient and tenacious.

Yesterday he and Mark had admitted curiosity, maybe anxiety, about their novice master's personality, the head man who stayed in his room until the predinner liturgy. Tom, however, had declared indifference: "I don't care about our novice master. I almost feel ready for vows." When the others had stared back in silence, Tom had backed off: "I don't mean I'm really ready. I mean—I know what I want to do with my life. I just want to be sure I should do it as a Jesuit."

David turned to look at Dan, who was shaking his head in answer to Mark's question.

"Our novice master was Father Ted Lerach, a man from the old school, never comfortable with people our age," Dan said, looking nervously around after the words were out. "Father Gorman seems pretty with it. He's just finished his doctorate in physics. The rumor is the provincial had to force him to come here. The good thing is, he's not old enough to be really tainted by all the old stuff, the way Father Lerach was."

"What old stuff?" Tom asked. He had devoured his breakfast and signaled to novice Kurtz for more coffee.

"The old rules, the old rigidity, the old worldview. When we were novices we weren't allowed to smoke—that was too secular. Here," Dan said as he picked up and examined one of the black ashtrays, "every table has an ashtray. That's the way it is in the real world, isn't it?"

The threesome looked at each other and shrugged their shoulders, nodding assent.

"I remember one day out at St. Bonafacius, in the novitiate wing. I was in Chuck Freeman's room, another novice's—after the great silence. That was a violation, a big one! And we were smoking, which might have been worse. A friend of Chuck's, someone he met working at St. Philip's on the North Side, had smuggled in cigarettes the day before. We had just lit up when there was a knock at Chuck's door. We knew we were had. No one would knock except Lerach."

"I took one final drag and flicked the cigarette into the sink. Chuck opened the door and in walked Lerach, his hands stuffed inside the cincture of his cassock, balled up. His eyes were so big, you would've thought he'd found us naked. He asked what was going on. I shook my head and coughed—blasting a cloud of smoke into his face, finally saying, washing my hands like an obsessive: '*I'm so confused—I don't really know what's going on, Father Lerach.*'"

Laughter burst across the table. Others turned to look. David looked over at the professeds' table. He noted Father Gorman's pleased grin. Brother Minister, whose pasty face brightened a degree, quickly looked over at a sleepy-eyed Father Rector, who didn't seem to notice. Laughter must be OK in this novitiate, David assumed, at the right hours.

"You told him you were confused?" Mark said after he regained composure. "*Confused?*"

"It's my favorite word," Dan said, radiant. "Authority never knows what to do when you use it. Anyway, Lerach ordered me to my room. He took away my television privileges for the month."

"Television privileges?" David said, putting down his halffull cup of acidic coffee and moving it away from him, his lips pursed as if they had just sucked, blistered and dry, on a lemon wedge. "What are television privileges?"

"There was only one TV in the whole place. Hundreds of rooms and one television. It was in the fathers' rec. room. Novices could watch five shows a week, and the novice master chose the shows. If you were being punished, you couldn't even watch those five."

"No one's told us anything about that stuff," Tom said, nearly angry.

"That's because those days are over," Dan said with finality. "That's why we moved to the city. The Church is changing. It's getting closer to the people. Those old ways were holdovers from a different culture, a different time. The Society doesn't want to be separated from today's culture. In our glory days, Jesuits never were."

David listened carefully to Dan. He loved this part of the Jesuit story.

"We should be using the culture of the day to teach the Gospel," Dan continued. "We used to have our fingers in everything, painting, plays, ballet, astronomy, exploration. We need to make the Gospel real for today, that's our challenge. You guys are lucky. You won't have any of the old baggage to discard. You're—we're—the hope of the Society." Dan's face was glowing. Then a cloud. "There are lots of Jesuits who don't seem able to change. Wait until you meet them."

"That sounds ominous," David said.

"Some of these folks are scary. They're preoccupied with apparitional things, an unseen communist infiltration, or the secret message of Our Lady of Fatima. They think Vatican II was a heretical plot. Believe me, there's plenty of division in the Society."

"But what about—what about the vows. Isn't everyone vowed to work together?" Mark asked.

"We all take the same vows, but we all live them out differently," Dan said, his fervor softening.

At eight-thirty on a steamy Monday morning in August, the official spiritual instruction of the class of 1968, Wisconsin Province of the Society of Jesus, began. In the green-walled living room of the west apartment on the second floor of the north building were packed a blackboard, a teacher's table, and eighteen chairs in three orderly rows.

David was the first to arrive, taking up a chair in the back. Smith Edwards, the Nebraska farm boy with broad hands and high cheekbones, who had helped with the sewing yesterday afternoon despite his loss of one eye in a combining accident and had meandered with David along the Mississippi bluffs in the evening, was second to arrive and sat down in the chair next to David.

"How ya doin'?" Smith asked, slapping David on the knee. "I didn't see you hangin' around outside."

"I was in the library. I'm thinking of volunteering to be librarian and thought I'd get acquainted with the stacks."

They sat quietly, David checking Smith out. He was feeling the same tension he felt in Mark's presence. It was chemical, little bursts and interactions somewhere under the top layer of his skin. David became aware of his own breathing. Smith had long, thick legs and nearly half a foot of black hair, caught up that morning in a ponytail. The sun turned it as silky as one of Gina's stallion's freshly brushed coats. David wanted to reach over and caress it.

Yesterday afternoon David had watched Smith stitch curtains, examining his muscled arms and making jokes about rural life so Smith would laugh. Now David watched Smith open his notebook and write down the day's date at the top of the first page. David's eyes followed Smith's hand. Even Smith's daily handwriting was calligraphy, David thought: receptive, wide ovals that funneled ink into fat tails below the line.

The two sat in quiet.

Three more minutes and the classroom was full. The noise of novice chatter broke into David's thoughts. He was reflecting that there were no bells in this novitiate to remind the novices of their communal gatherings, yet everyone showed up on time. Maybe it was group think. He'd read about experiments with high school kids who had bonded together during the experiment and terrorized other classmates with the fierceness of SS guards. David wrote the initials SS at the top of his notebook page, then crossed them off and wrote the holier initials: SJ.

Father Gorman walked in. Everyone stopped talking in mid-sentence. The novice master offered no greeting to his class. He did smile, however, a broad and undirected smile meant for anyone. He communicates best with his body, David thought, the idea strange and exhilarating. He almost wrote it down in his notebook so he wouldn't forget to put it in his diary, maybe with Gina-style stars around it.

Father Gorman began his first instruction in the spiritual life by detailing an exercise: each apartment group was to pray together for half an hour every evening. Prayer was to begin at nine-thirty. At ten, the entire community would gather in chapel for fifteen minutes of silent meditation. After chapel came quiet time. Novices should be in their rooms. There was no more television or radio. Conversations were discouraged. If they occurred, they should be in private and about spiritual matters.

"It used to be called the Great Silence," Father Gorman instructed. "However, in the old days it seemed we were more concerned about the silence part than the great part. Use your time well. The hours after chapel are for spiritual growth and rest. I hope you'll all respect that. If you're having a problem with it, let me know."

Or someone will surely let *you* know, David thought. This closeness, especially with those who weren't servants, was getting under his skin.

"Each week one of you will lead your shared prayer. That individual will select Bible passages," Father Gorman said, pacing slowly in front of his wards, his eyes as concentrated as an animal of bulk, a grizzly, David thought, an animal whose strength affords it the freedom of distraction, the indulgence in mystic things. In the novitiate, David's thoughts were racing.

"Just as Ignatius did, so do we build our spiritual lives on the events of the Bible, especially the life of Jesus. Acquaint yourselves with these sacred stories so you can make of the words *a diver's platform* . . ." Father Gorman stopped and grinned, his face suddenly childlike. "We will be showing you how."

Fixing his eyes on each novice in turn, Father Gorman announced the first week's exercise, "Each of you is to lead an evening prayer this week. During your conference with me we'll discuss why you chose your Bible passage."

As soon as the three men got back to their apartment, Mark volunteered, almost demanding, to lead the first evening's prayer session. David and Tom looked at each other, exchanging looks of surprise at this glint of fervor.

"It's not a competition to be first," David said.

Mark's stubbly face blushed. "I didn't mean it that way. I didn't—I guess I'm just used to stepping up to things."

"I think we all are," David said, turning to Tom and asking, "Right?"

Tom shuffled back a pace, saying, "Yeah, I guess so."

"But I don't have any problem with you leading tonight's prayer," David said. He hoped he hadn't sounded harsh. When his emotions were strong, his tongue became serrated.

In silence each man went to his room, the task to outline the first chapter of his spiritual autobiography before lunch. The headings, indenting and pattern of enumeration were up to each novice. They would be as perfect as the novice's attention to the Spirit's working, Father Gorman had implied. In his afternoon session Father Gorman would begin his lectures on Ignatius, "whose acquisition of self-knowledge through broken bones, poverty, and submission," the novice master had announced, "still drew the curious and the called."

The three men gathered for prayer that evening at nine-thirty. The day's heat had neared ninety-five degrees, fueled by Mississippi Delta moisture. There was no air-conditioning anywhere in the novitiate, except in the fathers' quarters at the top of the north building. All the novice windows were open. By evening the living room had cooled only a couple of degrees. The white walls were clammy and seemed to David to bulge ominously into the room, pregnant with a menacing plaster and lathe child.

David had noticed his roommates pad around the apartment in T-shirts and shorts. Before going to prayer, he took off his knit polo, leaving only his soaked undershirt which clung uncomfortably to his body.

Mark and Tom were already seated on the red shag. A squat green candle burned before them. David eyed the sofa and armchair, which he had previously christened, for Smith Edwards's ears, as "hunchback chic." In truth, he'd rather sit on that dowdy maroon presence than hunker down onto the floor. He hesitated a moment at its edge, but clumsily lowered himself, his legs bent and facing backward. He knew he appeared like a girl concerned about her privateness. He had never sat on Jepson Minnesota mansion floors or on the parquet of their London and Paris homes. Mark and Tom, seated as upright as Zen masters, watched him with curiosity.

Mark's Jerusalem Bible was open before him. On his right lay a pocket flashlight. The living room lamps, two towering gold-speckled green ceramic pods with dirty shades, were turned off. Only the candle gave light.

Mark flicked on his flashlight and pointed its spotlight on a passage from the ending of the Gospel of Matthew, a scene where Jesus instructs the apostles to go and make disciples of all nations.

David shifted constantly during the reading. Down in that basement, in that darkness, he felt as if he were partaking in a secret rendezvous, in a cell meeting of a dangerous sect.

"Imagine the risen Savior asking this motley crew of simple men to go and change the world," Mark said after finishing the passage. He prayed with his eyes closed and his hands clasped together yet still moving, as if he were a pitcher coddling the winning ball, feeling its stitching and the imprints of the evening's battery. David's eyes were glued to the praying youth. Is this the way holiness looks, he wondered. Well-formed and well-mannered? Boyish and bright? Cooperative. Had David missed the real form of holiness all those years, thinking too much about tonsured heads and bleeding hands?

"It was a stirring moment," Mark said. "Jesus offered these men a great challenge, the beginning of a heroic adventure. We're experiencing the same challenge—and I pray we can be judged worthy to accept it."

With that introduction the young men settled into silence. The word "worthy" reddened David's ears. Minutes ticked away, slow and hushed as the hands on an old woman's mantle clock. But David's stomach churned its contents bitter. He was unworthy. It was a barbed, poisoned word. It had been used too often by his valium-chugging mother since she first declared him unworthy of her love three Christmas's ago. As if she could bestow love!

"You're fifteen and already an ogre, a little, tight-brained, heartless ogre!"

Unworthy. It was a stinger ripping into soft flesh. In the presence of these two—so sincere, uncluttered—in their presence his mother's accusation seemed truer.

David knew the strength of his desire to enter the Jesuits, his desire to scrabble across a hot desert landscape, past scorpions and demons, to claim the land of milk and honey for his own. But the question. Was he a chosen one or camp follower?

David had studied the vocabulary of vocation and its curt little words: call, soul, trust. He had constructed the perfect response to each of the Society's vocation questions, sometimes lavish in detail, sometimes simple as a line in the sand, which the moon-pull would erase with the next tide. "Do you have a girl friend?"

"Gina, a brunette." He was wise as the serpent.

But wasn't vocation, his part in it, supposed to be a response? To a gift, a god-gesture. He was so much the fabricator of his life.

David had begun to fear that his decision to enter the Society was a grave mistake, grave as an opening in the earth, grave as a weight that holds down lighter, younger truths. He shifted on the floor because his legs were going numb. He desperately wanted to think of another topic, to be somewhere else. The silence, which was so often his friend, began to grate on him, annoying as a surly clerk.

Finally Tom offered a brief prayer, "Lord, give me the strength and the determination of those early disciples."

Mark prayed again, as if in response. "Lord, let us use what you have given us to further the building of your kingdom."

Kingdom. Kingdom had been the word of the day. Father Gorman had told his novices that when other orders talked of their *labora*, they did not visualize the nearly political, mappable reality of which Jesuits dreamed, a landscape nourished by rivers of grace and linked by roadways of good works. Of course Mark would start using that word, kingdom, David mused, that remnant word from mythic time when justice grew up in the protecting shade of thick Arthurian towers. Mark had already talked to him for an hour about the potential of the United Nations to bring lion and lamb to the negotiating table. "Kingdom" would be Mark's word.

As the half hour ticked away, David kept quiet. This was his lowest moment so far in the novitiate. His body was aching. It was hard for him to concentrate on anything spiritual or calming. He felt a pressure to say something, to be more than the other body on the carpet, so he finally prayed, "Lord, let us be cunning in your service." After the words were out of his mouth, David gasped. What had he meant? Mark looked over at him, quizzical, batting his long brown eyelashes.

The prayer ended. The threesome leaned back on their elbows and relaxed together, remaining in the dim light of the candle.

"Well, two years of this," David said, breaking the quiet mood with a flipness that surprised him.

The other two turned to stare. A chill went up David's spine.

"What do you mean? Do you think this is stupid?" Tom asked, annoyed.

"No, not that. It's just—I don't know. It's not . . ." David dropped the sentence.

"Come on, tell us what you're thinking," Mark said.

"I was just thinking—this is not what I had expected," David said.

"What's not what you had expected?" Tom asked, cocking his head.

"Sitting on the floor in this room with you two. It's so unstructured, so undirected, as if we were on a high school retreat. I was expecting something more adult, more formal," David said, forcing the words out, fearing their hurt, unable to stop, the way he was with his mother. "I'm sorry I offend you, Tom." Those words were all apology, but he was irritated. He didn't tell the pair that he felt different from them, awkward in their presence, lesser, and that it was making him angry and sad, and that he knew he could be a prick.

"Now come on, you two," Mark said. "We're all new at this." He spoke to Tom. "And David does have a point. I expected something different, too. But maybe it's OK to learn to pray this way, maybe this is just the way prayer is."

"This *is* the way prayer is," Tom said. "It's simple. It's uncomplicated. A conversation inside you, maybe shared, always with God, who invented words, you know, and thought." Tom turned his gaze from one companion to the other. David saw an unexpected look of confusion in Tom's freckled face. "That's what prayer is for me."

The other two nodded their heads. Neither of them spoke.

Mark blew out the candle, leaving the three of them dark forms in the humid night, dolmens at the edge of the spiritual forest, huddled with inner desires.

The next night David led the prayer. He had decided to take a risk with his roommates. That entire day he had been wondering whether he should leave the novitiate. He had written about it in his diary, while the others were at *haustus* and Smith Edwards was learning to sew a chasuble.

> *The other novices are kind. Some of them are witty. But this sense of being unworthy. I know there's something wrong inside. I just don't know exactly what it is. It's complex, many tentacled. The thing has rooted itself in my soul. It's got a ganglion's grip. It's a deep-sea creature. It masks itself in jets of ink.*
>
> *I don't think this flaw of mine is the sort of flaw Jesus wants to build upon. But something inside me has relaxed here. And I want to stay.*
>
> *Can I share these comments with the other novices? What will they say? What, precisely, would I say? Everyone else seems so innocent, so on track, so right for this life. Maybe I'm best off on my own. As an anchorite—or God knows what.*

Again the threesome settled into a small triangle in the middle of the dimly lit living room. This time David lay his Bible down next to the candle, but left it unopened. He had memorized the passage. It was Isaiah 49: 15. *Does a woman forget her baby at the breast, or fail to cherish the son of her womb? Yet even if these forget, I will never forget you.*

David placed his hand on the black, pebbly surface of his Jerusalem Bible, solemn as a man swearing an oath, and recited the passage. He saw Tom and Mark glance at each other and exchange a quick smile when he spoke the word *breast*. He felt alone, but he had to go on. Maybe this would be his last prayer in this Jesuit house.

A pause and then David began to pray, his voice scratchy and barely audible: "Lord, help me to forgive, to thaw out. I know a woman can forget her baby at her breast. My mother did that. She bore me, cuddled me for a month, as if I were her Siamese Benji, then set me down and flew off to Nice to escape the cold." David reached up to dry the wetness that was gathering in the well of his right eye, amazed at its renewed presence after so many years. "Nanny kept me warm that winter. Thank you for sending me Marie. And please, Lord, never forget me. Never forget anyone."

David could feel his companions' shock, waves of upset conveyed in their rigid stares, in the muscle tightening that curved their backs until they were taut. David assumed Mark and Tom were flipping through memories of their own mothers, cells in a home movie with warm skin and love that breathed milky and close in. How could they understand? How could he express the emptiness?

Before David's words had disappeared into nothingness, Tom reached over and touched David's lightly fuzzed leg, saying, "I'm sorry."

David startled. Warm-wet flesh on skin. He locked onto Tom's face, whose hazel eyes reflected back the candle's steady light. David's mouth was open. Tom's hand was still there, now gripping slightly. David felt his legs relax. Calmness, swift as a narcotic delivered right into the heart, overcame him. He wanted more of—something.

"Thank you," David whispered. The phrase was fresh and light. "Thank you." It was hard to look away. This Tom. This Tom was good. Tom was good.

David bowed his head and prayed words he had never prayed before: "I believe in love." He looked back up at Tom, the novice with flickering eyes. Tom had removed his hand, but didn't look away. The tall novice with pretty red hair and faint, innocent freckles was smiling now, not judging, not pitying.

"I believe in God's love," David said, narrowing his faith. Then back at the flame: "I believe in a benign universe, despite the terrors we experience. If I didn't believe this, I wouldn't be here today."

For the first time in the novitiate David thought he might have a true vocation. It had to do with pain. It had to do with the healing touch of men.

CHAPTER FOUR

Unlike the rule in other orders, the vows of poverty, chastity, and obedience a Jesuit novice pledges two years after he enters the novitiate are permanent. Those vows are not renewed. There is no time limit set on them. They do not expire.

In the summer of 1970, Mark, Tom, and David, nearing the end of their second year, were preparing with every new day to recite the words of the over four-hundred-year-old Jesuit profession on Saturday, August 22. Each of them had told the others they were resolved to ask for vows, to continue on in the Society, to enter deeper into the holy of holies, to proceed forward into the next court of the Temple. Yet only one of them was gifted with certainty.

Before professing vows and becoming philosophers, they had to spend three more weeks as novices, two on vacation and one in vow retreat.

For vacation, *villa* in the American Jesuit vernacular, they would have fourteen days at the province's dying boarding school, Campion Preparatory School in Prairie du Chien, Wisconsin, a river town at the confluence of the Mississippi and Wisconsin rivers where the novices could walk under Joyce Kilmer's leafy alleys or boat up the two rivers to fish or lie naked on summertime sandbars.

After *villa*, the nine men remaining in the novice class would travel in the novitiate's two 1969 egg shell blue Ford station wagons to the Trappist monastery of New Melleray, a hundred-year-old religious venture set on the rise of a hill in the rolling cornfields outside Dubuque. In that monastery of gold Iowa limestone, its walls logical as Aquinas' thirteenth century, each novice would review his decision to blend his twentieth-century American soul with the *Societas Jesu*, a powerful religious troop born out of counterreformation spirituality. Each novice would reflect again on his request to speak the formulaic words of initiation and become a Jesuit on the soil of the new world in a time of social upheaval and religious dissent, in an era as chaotic as that of Ignatius, who had lived in an epoch of spiritual reform and world plunder.

The province had already decided which novices would receive vows. Invitations to the vow ceremony had been sent out; RSVP's received. New vow crosses were stacked in black, felt-lined boxes at the novitiate. The provincial had made arrangements for the housing of his province's freshly vowed scholastics in the philosophate, Fusz Memorial Hall at St. Louis University. Transcripts had been sent to the College of Philosophy and Arts. The bureaucracy of Jesuit formation had nearly finished strapping tight the reddish-brown accordion folders that held the life stories of this latest crop of Midwest American novices. The ecclesial bureaucrats awaited only the signed and witnessed copies of the novices' vows before tying tight the folders and hand delivering them in St. Louis to a new rector and his four consultors.

Still, as some feared and others hoped, the Spirit might stir a new wind in either novice or superior during vow retreat. The Spirit's agent, the angel of consolation, so often vested in unexpected garb, might offer new enticements, suggest a new path, garble a message once miraculously clear.

All summer Mark had dreamed of being near the river. He had spent three dusty months in South Dakota at Pine Ridge, one of the Lakota reservations where the province had schools. During his last sweltering weeks on the prairie, he had decorated his prayers with scenes of river life. He prayed about Jesus as the living water and envisioned himself sitting on a sandbar of the Wisconsin river, his legs dangling in the warm, lush, life-giving current. He had risen each morning and knelt on his room's narrow pine wood slats, vowing to rise early in Prairie du Chien so he could fish in the wistful haze of the Mississippi.

Every night during the last weeks on the reservation Mark fell asleep in his narrow bed dreaming of water skiing, his body thrilling at the luxury of speed and the sensuous massage of cool spray against hot skin. He went to sleep dreaming of water. Every night he jacked off just as he was about to plunge into unconsciousness, pumping himself with a sudden fury, his legs tight as if he were bracing himself on water skis, readying himself for a quick turn.

As he drifted into the depths of sleep, Mark noted the problem he was having with masturbation. It had been building for months, part frustration, part desire, part confusion about his vocation. Father Gorman was being rough with him, asking hard questions, challenging Mark's vocation.

As his eyes fell shut and thoughts of Gorman faded away, Mark gladly ignored this sin. His mind was unfocused, dissipating into a fog. *Later. I'll deal with this in my vow retreat. Later.*

Tom had been with Mark all that summer, teaching school while Mark worked during the day with reservation politicians and bureaucrats on housing issues. Every morning when they got up and met at breakfast, Tom told Mark how great it was to be there with the Lakota and with him. Mark had begun to joke with Tom over their breakfast of coffee and Wheaties, a little scripted exchange.

"So, don't you love it here?" Mark would ask as he poured a quarter cup of almost-sour milk onto his mound of cereal. That summer the residence's industrial size refrigerator was constantly on the copper-coiled edge of meltdown.

"Love it," Tom would answer, his angular grin making his face look more sincere than usual, which goaded Mark on.

"What do you love?" Mark would ask, silently grinding his teeth over his own interior flatness but keeping his lips upturned in a milk-soaked smile.

"I love the kids. I love the endlessness of this place," Tom would answer.

Since driving onto the reservation, Tom had taken to using "endless" as his adjective for perfection and joy. "Endless love." "Endless taste."

"Endless is right," Mark would respond, nodding to their unobstructed view of the prairie, mocking his friend's exuberance. Tom seemed unaware of the daily mock, taking Mark's comment as nothing but friendly jest.

After two weeks, Mark had become bored with the routine of reservation life. The boarding school kids were shy around him, ignoring him, calling him "Mister Sappingstone" instead of Tom or Brother. The Lakota knew the power of names.

With Tom, the endlessly serious one, the kids had become quick chums. One evening in a secret dormitory ritual, using a smuggled pipe and a hundred-year-old eagle feather, the band of thirty residential summer students, headed by senior Billy Two Bulls, bestowed on Tom a Lakota name, which he could use when he spoke in ceremony, a name which Tom had to swear never to reveal to Mark.

Mark couldn't understand why the reservation kids liked Tom and not him. It had been the opposite on every other occasion, in Omaha at Creighton Prep, in Milwaukee at Marquette High, in Minneapolis at St. Mary's clinic. Mark was the attractive one, the gregarious one, the self-assured one. He was a planet attracting lesser bodies into his orbit. Observatories aimed their most finely ground lenses at his rugged geography.

All that attention had made his spirit glow. He had admitted it often in conference with Father Gorman over the last year and a half, expecting his novice master to see this reflective brightness as confirmation of his vocation. People, influential people in the Society, principals, confessors, rectors, had told Father Gorman that Mark was gifted by the Spirit. Mark felt holy, in a way. Chosen. Anointed by attention. But on the reservation, the buffalo eyes of those prairie-dust children made him feel a new sensation, the frigidity of the universe with its cold maw open wide to gorge on light.

Mark thought there must be something wrong with his vocation. His spiritual director that summer, Father Hughes, reassured Mark that his vocation was fine. Mark tried to believe him.

"You've got to accept the fact that you won't be all things to all men," Father Hughes told Mark as they sat one Sunday evening on a hillock just north of Drexel Hall, the clay-brick Jesuit residence with its tin, shiny steeple. "You've also got to accept that as a Jesuit your life is not only yours. Sometimes the Society will ask you to do things that drain you of energy. That's when you need to turn to Him."

Mark stared off into the horizon, still pink at its core, remembering the Friday evening he had spent in the rec. room with Father Hughes and Tom during their first week on the reservation. Everyone else had gone to bed or to the kitchen for *haustus*. Mark had noticed a guitar propped up against one corner of the room. "Do you play?" he asked Father Hughes. The narrow-hipped priest smiled coyly, as if he were a fifteen-year-old at a powwow leading his first fancy dance, and crossed the room to pick up the guitar, dusting it off with his hands.

"I leave it in here," Father Hughes said as he walked back to the window, toward Mark and Tom. He held the guitar away from his body, treating it as if it were an object of danger, a rattler, or the sheer robe of a succubus whose mere touch could snare a guardian angel with narcotic restraints. "Sometimes I play late at night. Rarely, though. Only on nights as empty as tonight." Father Hughes paused, then mumbled: "When hardly no one's around."

The priest stood silent a moment, standing a few feet from Mark and Tom, who were splayed out in two deteriorating arm chairs, their eyes quiet as cat hair. Father Hughes examined the guitar, turning it around, testing the strings with his cigarette-orange right thumb, holding up the belly of the guitar to his ears. Finally, a twist of satisfaction jutted out in his lips.

Mark decided that Father Hughes had forgotten about him and Tom, that the leathery priest thought he was solitary in his cell and could perform in that semisacred square his own intimate orations.

Mark watched Father Hughes take up position on a bench next to the western window and place the guitar over one knee. The priest bent over the instrument, concentrated as a sorcerer on his spell, and began to tune the guitar. The G string. The E string. Sometimes he revved up a little tune only to let it sputter out into silence.

Mark and Tom said nothing. Mark began to wonder: "Is this me in twenty years? Alone and wasting my life in some termite-trap mausoleum? Playing one song every weekend?" He wrapped his arms around his chest and slid his hands into the armpits of his T-shirt. Mark's thoughts were far from Jesus. His thoughts were on his future. If he were assigned to live here, in this rattler-infested desolation, he'd turn into a ghost, all billowy, his flesh wilted into oxygen. He knew it as sure as he knew anything, as sure as he knew that Jesus thought him a worthy companion. But something about that future seemed inevitable. Mark had to turn away from it.

Thankfully, at that moment of turning away, Father Hughes came fully to life. The slender cowboy-cleric twisted slightly to face the moonlight head on and began to shake. Shake first at the neck, then shoulders and thorax. Then he began to strum. Hard, bold chords that mocked the size of his left hand. Mark and Tom both shifted in their chairs, sitting to attention. The chords rang so hard that Mark was sure the priest's consecration fingers would have bled if he hadn't been using a pick. But the music soon pushed out all other thoughts from Mark's brain. The guitar's belly, circumscribed with mother of pearl, sired wild, soulful blues. They crossed the room and swirled around Mark.

Mark saw Father Hughes transformed. The priest was now fierce, fine and fierce, tapping one booted foot and stiffly rocking his long torso, the four chambers of his heart pumping a wild sorrow. Ten minutes he played, sometimes singing, words of loneliness and abandonment and spent youth, Mark wondering if Father Hughes were composing the lyrics just before they flowed out. Each sung phrase pulsed under the man's sun-scorched skin and through the arteries that lined his long neck.

Then he stopped. Abruptly. The keening of the strings faded. Father Hughes, who had continued to play while staring at out at the moon's half face, turned back inward and shut his eyes as tight as any mummy's. He sat motionless, a monk bolted into his choir stall.

Mark looked over at Tom, hoping to get a reading. What did this performance mean? Tom didn't look back. He was staring at Father Hughes, his mouth wide open.

Neither Mark nor Tom moved. Mark wished David had been there. David would've said something, stepped in, maybe sung his own song, a show tune or narrow Maronite chant.

Finally Father Hughes opened his eyes and stared unfocused into the room. He took a deep breath, held it, exhaled, got up from the bench and walked across the room. He set the guitar back in its corner and uttered a simple, almost inaudible, goodnight to the novices.

That night Mark had decided on Father Hughes as spiritual director. Mark told Tom, who had chosen a red-headed nun as spiritual guide, that his choice of the blues priest was a risk, an abandonment of will. Novitiate words. In a starker voice: "I think Father Hughes sees some frightening truth—and knows how to stare it down."

"I'm definitely experiencing that energy drain," Mark said as he stretched out on the knoll, turning his tired face up toward Father Hughes, wondering again if this man of sorrows was a vision of his future, or a visionary for his future. The image perplexed him, constantly in his mind, but he could never bring it up with his director, ask him: "Tell me about yourself." Mark was afraid to hear the answer. Instead, he said, "I pray for help, for inspiration, but nothing changes."

Father Hughes broke off a sprig of sage from a young bush next to him and twisted it in his hands, lifted the tiny purple bud to his nose and inhaled as if it were opium, his nostrils flaring. Then, "Things change, Mark. Little changes. You may not notice, you may not be looking."

"Change?!? Nothing changes on this prairie!" Mark had wanted to respond. That's how he explained to Tom why he hated the place.

But Mark didn't blurt out the bully's response. More than his hatred of prairie life was his reaction to the appraisal: You may not be looking. Father Gorman had said the same thing, in his therapy-filled, meandering phraseology: "I'm concerned with you, Mark. I'm concerned that you're not really looking, looking inside, seeing what's there, examining your motivations."

None of those Pine Ridge thoughts occupied space in Mark's psyche as he woke up on the eighth day of sun and humidity in Prairie du Chien. He was once again in his glory. Sought after. Reaping the rewards of his nature. Today would be a special day. His older brother Rich and year younger sister Kate were bringing one of the family boats down the Mississippi from Lake Pepin. Mark had invited Tom, David, and two jock first-year novices to join them on the *Tina Louise*, a fifteen-foot Chris Craft christened for their pearl-loving, martini-mixing, chiffon-wearing mother, the woman who exhausted herself riding tight on her man.

All day the boat was in constant action, two skiers in tow. Everyone was drinking Leinie's, Rich's favorite, and within half an hour the chill between the religiously skeptical Sappingstones and the novices had turned into hot, shared irreverence about everything: parents, country, and Church. The planned two-hour stay stretched to four.

Mark was sitting in the back of the boat, gleaming, proud that his family and his Jesuit buddies were getting along so well. He even smiled as he watched his sister flirt with Tom. Kate let her dark hair drape over the squareness of Tom's left shoulder as he bent over and she pointed out two blue herons standing in a nearby marsh. Mark had never before noticed how attractive Tom was. His novice buddy was lean and muscular, but Mark had to see him in his swimming trunks to appreciate it. And now that he looked, he saw that Tom's teeth lined up perfectly. More a surprise:

When Tom smiled and ran his hand through the wet curls of his hair, Mark noticed a red softness fill out Kate's face.

"You two havin' a good time?" Mark asked after lurching forward onto the pilot's deck and putting his arms around both their shoulders.

"Great!" Tom said, raising his bottle.

"Yeah! I'm glad you convinced us to come down," Kate said, her good cheer as ample as her twenty-two-year-old breasts. She leaned over and pecked Mark on the cheek. He was pleased with her, with her looks, with her charm.

At the same time David came up from behind and announced that Mass was in an hour and that maybe they should head back to Campion.

Kate swirled around, glaring at David. "You don't have to go to Mass *every* day, do you? It's Saturday, for Chris' sake."

"No, not every day," David said, stepping back a foot. "But our novice master is here. And he watches. You know, he's just like a parent: Concern is his business."

"Well, it's not mine," Kate said, her voice sharp as her father's. She turned to look at Mark. Mark's face had drained. He agreed with Kate. Mass was an intrusion on their good time. None of the Jesuits he respected had ever been sticklers for religious formality. He was ready to stay as an act of protest, Jesus chasing the money changers from the temple. Jesus saving the wedding at Cana with miracle wine. But the mention of Father Gorman chilled his defiance. Their vows were only weeks away.

The day of his return to the novitiate from Pine Ridge, Mark heard Father Gorman's continuing doubts, his concern with letting Mark take vows. Father Gorman questioned Mark's ability to do whatever was asked of him—to accept a mission in the language of the Society, any mission. Father Gorman had been blunt. "Mark, do you really understand your own motivations? I hear your words, but I wonder if the words are truly are yours? Or enough yours. You've got to be straight on with yourself to deal straight with anything else."

Mark didn't want a new incident to cast another confusing cipher into his novice master's equation-loving mind. Mark hadn't even told Tom and David about Father Gorman's comment. To everyone in the novitiate he was the golden novice, the spokesman for his class, the sought-after dinner guest, the one interviewed for the provincial newsletter. And Mark knew the witness of his commitment was important to all the other novices. He knew they watched him. He wanted to measure up.

"David's right about Mass," Mark said, his voice now distant. Mark leaned over and tapped his brother Rich on the shoulder and told him to head into dock.

Kate stepped back from the three novices, turned sharply, and snaked over to sit on one of the boat's benches, crossing her legs and shaking her head. None of the threesome moved. They stood and looked straight ahead as the boat returned to the Campion dock and slowed down, letting the two first-year novices, who had been doing beer-swollen pranks on their skis, sink into the brown calm of the Mississippi River channel.

Only the first-year novices said much as they tied up at the dock, complaining about the end of their joyride.

"Do you two want to join us?" Mark finally asked Rich and Kate after they had cleared the day's debris out of the boat. The other novices were standing politely on the dock.

"No thanks," Rich said. "We've got to get home. We're late already."

"OK. Thanks for coming." There was defeat in Mark's voice. He shook Rich's hand and went over to kiss Kate on the cheek. She was still sitting on the bench, with her anger deepening in the shade of the trees.

"Will you say good-bye?" Mark asked as he bent over her.

"Good-bye," Kate said, turning her cheek away from Mark.

"Don't do this, Kate."

"Don't do what?" Her anger was clear, crisp.

"Don't be mad at me."

"I am mad at you. And I'm mad at Tom. And I'm mad at that—at that David!"

"It's not their fault," Mark said, sitting down beside her, putting his arm around her.

Kate threw off his arm and inched away. She turned to stare at Mark. Everyone was hushed. "Yes it is their fault! It's all your fault. This stuff is crazy!" One hand was flailing in the wind; the other held a green Leinenkugel bottle with a tight grip. "I can't believe you're doing it! What a waste! What a waste!" She turned her head completely away from Mark and looked up the tree-lined channel, slowly pronouncing her words into the wind, "You can go now."

Mark sighed and got up, pulling on the bottom of his swimsuit as he rose, moving his legs the way a high diver who's just bombed jitters at the edge of the pool. He shook his head at his brother Rich before he got out of the boat. Rich stared back, motionless.

"You, too?" Mark asked, balancing on the edge of the boat.

"I don't know," Rich said and revved the motor.

Mark leapt onto the dock, avoiding the eyes of his fellow novices. He stared only at the boat, at his siblings who were about to speed away. David came forward and put Mark's folded T-shirt on top of his hairless shoulder, saying nothing. The boat sped off, oblivious to the channel speed signs.

"We've got to go out tonight," Mark said to Tom and David as they walked back to the residence, several yards behind the first-year novices. "I need to be crazy."

Whenever things got too tight in the novitiate, too much a mind game, the three of them had gone on a bender. Maybe five times. Mark had learned the practice at Georgetown. At least the next day his head would be concentrated on something else, something it could overcome.

"Me, too," Tom said. "I'll drive," David added. Mark heard the concern in David's voice. Not just about road safety. Mark knew David saw into his soul. David had those confessor eyes. Mark avoided them when they were too intense.

About nine in the evening the threesome drove out to the Red Dragon, a boat warehouse turned bar. The renovation of three years earlier had left the building a smoke-infused metallic rectangle with two pool tables at one dingy end and a bivouac of booths and tables at the other. Strips of walnut laminate darkened the back wall. The other walls were plaster board painted a pale gray and hung with beer signs, deer head, and stuffed fish, shiny and bent in their last joy.

As they walked in the threesome found a half dozen middle-aged regulars already hunkered down in their spots, sipping tap beers and staring over their baskets of fries and well-done burgers. A couple of the evening's patrons were nodding to the juke box lyrics. The night was as hot and humid as the day, and the two wall air-conditioners at the ends of the bar did nothing to extract the bar's steamy moisture.

Mark pulled at his T-shirt as he strutted in. It had begun to cling to his body, showing off its contours, muscle-shapes enhanced by the last weeks' sessions in the Campion gym. Exercise, like drinking, was a way to clear his mind, to forget his troubles. He would think of the Apostles walking to the ends of the earth as he bench-pressed his two hundred pounds. Their bodies had been disciples as much as their souls. "Keep at it," he'd say to himself as he struggled to push up the bar. "Keep at it."

Inside the Red Dragon, Mark breathed a sigh of relief at its masking darkness. After Mass and before dinner, he and David and Tom had all downed two gin and tonics in half an hour. They had kept their distance from Father Gorman during preprandials in the rec. room, grateful he was spending time with the first-year novices. They went down late to dinner to make sure they could sit by themselves. At dinner they each had two glasses of wine. Mark had said nothing in the loud refectory. David and Tom had talked excitedly about the next year in St. Louis and the topics they'd be studying, Missouri Valley Thomism, Renaissance Popes, Descartes, Kant, and the modern Germanic density of Rahner. Every so often David would look over at Mark, tilting his head and smiling. Mark began to wonder how much David knew.

"Millers all around," Mark declared to the red-lipped brunette waitress as the three of them slid into a corner booth at the Red Dragon, David claiming the interior comfort.

The waitress stared at Mark a moment, finally saying, "OK, honey," with her made-up drawl. Then she added, as if a special idea had dawned on her, "My name's Mary Ann, but everyone calls me Misty," pointing to her name tag.

"OK, Misty, good to meet you." Mark smiled back, his Georgetown leer. He knew he was losing control. "We'll be here a while tonight."

"I hope so," she said, flipping her curls as she turned to leave.

Mark watched her walk away and thought she might be working her hip muscles just for him. Her black dress, obviously overwashed—its dun color visible even in the bar's yellowed light, barely reached her knees. The two ties of the white apron ended just below its faded hem. Mark was thinking how electric it would feel to stand behind her and undo that white knot.

"What's going on?" David asked Mark, reaching across the table to touch his arm.

"What do you mean?" Mark grinned wide. He was feeling good. The gin and wine had pretty much settled all the earlier disquiet of the day. Now he felt lust.

David rolled his eyes and turned to Tom. "Did you notice anything? Anything in that exchange between novice and waitress?"

Tom leaned back in the booth and stretched his arms along its red top, smiling broadly. "I noticed *something*."

"And how would you describe that something you noticed?" David asked.

"I would describe what I noticed as a sultry wet flirtation. A hot, summertime, Mississippi flirtation." Tom winked at Mark. "A temptation. A near occasion of sin, if not a sin itself."

Mark grinned back at his friends, proud that they had noticed Misty's attention. He was thinking that for two years he hadn't gotten this close to a woman. For two years he hadn't felt the urges in his groin the way he had this week on the river. He closed his eyes for a second and breathed in the smoky air of the bar, luxuriating in its complexity and impurity.

"Speaking of sins of the flesh, you seemed to appreciate my sister," Mark said to Tom. "And she seemed to appreciate you."

"Yeah, she's hot," Tom said just as Misty arrived with their beers.

"She's hot?" Misty asked. She looked first at Tom, then sideways at Mark.

"Yes she is," Mark said. He looked up at Misty, his mouth set firm, his head held bent and curious as a puppy's.

"Good," Misty said, straight on to Mark. Her tongue licked the top of her lips, which shone with what seemed a recent glossing.

"We were talking about Mark's sister," David said, almost laughing as he interrupted the tension between Mark and Misty.

"No, you weren't," Misty said. Her voice was as slow as the river. She concentrated her eyes fully on Mark, extending her hand. "You're Mark?"

"Yes." They shook.

"Nice to meet you, Mark," Misty said, slipping her cool fingers out through Mark's rough hold. With a wink, she turned and walked away.

Tom clasped both hands around his Miller, grabbing firmly onto the base of the cool bottle, looking intently down at them.

"We're giving this up, you know." Tom looked up to stare at Mark. "You are, aren't you?"

Mark gulped. "I want to be a Jesuit, if that's what you're asking."

"That's what I'm asking."

"That's what I want. You know that, don't you?"

They had all begun to slur. The sharp awareness, usually clear in their banter, that word play that had eventually etched friendship, had turned dewy, softened by the still-hot river basin summer air and by the evening's alcoholic indulgence, which the three near-Jesuits were pursuing as zealously as cloistered novices pursue cowled sanctity.

They rambled on. For three hours. They complained about the first-year novices, about their experiments during the novitiate, about Father Gorman. They listened to tunes on the juke box, getting up every ten minutes to plug that music box's navel with copper-centered quarters. David played The Carpenters' "Ticket to Ride" five times, and the last three times the threesome sang along. Other patrons applauded.

They ordered another dinner of fries and burgers, which Misty placed within the bottle Stonehenge their avid beer drinking had erected.

Mark flirted with Misty whenever she came over, although the bar had gotten packed, and she was busy.

Every so often the sharp question intruded into Mark's evening of abandonment, Tom's question: whether Mark wanted to be a Jesuit. Wasn't his vocation obvious enough? If it wasn't obvious, did it exist at all? Even drunk, that question was high-noon clear.

After midnight they got up from their booth and wandered over to the pool tables at the other end of the bar. They put down their quarters and played one game. It took forty-five minutes. Twice Tom dropped his cue.

A little after one in the morning, Misty came over to watch them play. She wasn't wearing her apron. Mark was chalking his cue for the shot.

"Nice stick," Misty said, her butt resting on the table where David was slouched in a chair.

"It's a cue," David announced from his seat behind her. Misty turned briefly to stare at David, snarling at his sarcasm.

"It's a *clue*," she said.

Misty got up and walked slowly, slower than a snail's thought, over to

Mark's side. She stood to his right and put her hand on the crack of his butt. "Will you drive me home?" she whispered into his ear.

"Sure," Mark said, shifting his legs as he started to harden in his khaki shorts.

"We'll all drive you home," David said, loud enough for half the bar to hear. "He's right," Tom added, dropping his cue on the pool table. "Le's go. I'm exhausted."

"Why do all *three* of you have to go?" Misty asked. She spoke only to Mark. She had wrapped her hand around Mark's waist and had begun to nibble on his ear.

Mark closed his eyes and started to hum, no song in particular.

"Cause we live t'gether," David shouted out, rising from his chair. "Le's go," he said, pulling the keys from his pocket.

"You may live together, but that don't mean you *sleep* together," Misty said into the hollow of Mark's ear.

"Wer're Jeshuits," Tom said, coming up on Mark's left side and pulling at Misty's right hand, which was now clasped tightly onto Mark's waist. She finally let go, but reached around in front of Mark with her left hand and cupped his crotch.

"We'll all drive t'gether," Mark said, suddenly stepping back, prying himself from both Tom and Misty. He felt a jolt of anger. He became clear for a moment.

Mark jogged around the pool table, little steps, and grabbed the keys from David. "I'm drivin'. I'm no more drungk than you two." Turning halfway to look at Tom and Misty, he said, "Come on!" Then he stumbled toward the door.

Mark wasn't sure what he wanted. He knew he was drunk. He knew he wanted to screw Misty. He knew he wanted his friends' respect. And he knew he wanted to be a Jesuit.

Mark got into the driver's seat of the Campion community's red Chevette, and Misty ran to make her way to the passenger's side. David and Tom settled into the back. David leaned forward and asked Misty where she lived.

"Drop them off first," Misty said, her body turned toward Mark with one leg angled up on the seat, the hem of her dress now near her crotch. "Then you can take me home."

Mark started the car and began driving back to Campion. Sometimes slow, sometimes fast. Ten minutes. He drove through two stop signs. David yelled at him each time: "It's a stop sign! Even the French understan' that!"

As they neared the campus, Tom asked, his voice jumbled as if he had just woken up, "Where're you goin'?"

"I'm droppin' you guys off," Mark said.

"Your're droppin' us off?"

"Yeah."

In another minute they were at the back door of the four-story Campion residence. David got out of the car and started walking away, his head drooping. He stumbled, almost falling, as he moved up the soft incline of the grass. Tom got out, too, but went over to Mark's door and opened it before Mark knew what was happening.

"Gedow'," Tom commanded, reaching in to pull at Mark's left arm, which still clung to the steering wheel. "I'll drive her home."

"No you won'," Mark said, trying to pry off Tom's grip. For a moment he thought of backing up and hitting Tom with the door. That image frightened him, and he started to sweat even more. He put the car in neutral. At the same time Misty leaned over and began to run her hand through his hair.

David was at the back stoop of the residence, trying to open the door.

"Gedow'," Tom kept saying, his voice rising. "Gedow'!"

David turned to shush him.

"I'm jus' takin' her home!" Mark yelled.

"No your're not, I'm takin' her home!"

"I'm jus' takin' her home!"

"Your're lyin'. Your're lyin', you fucker! Oudda the car!"

"Donyacallmeafucker," Mark said, clenching his teeth. Then he shoved Tom into the open door. Tom staggered back with the door, but didn't let go of Mark's arm. Mark scrambled out of the car and stood chest-to-chest with Tom.

"Le'go'a me!" Mark cried.

Tom let go of Mark, brought both arms up between them and shoved Mark with such fierceness that Mark fell back, ricocheting off the car and onto the gravel road, flat on his back. Mark hit the surface hard. He was stunned for a moment. His head started to hurt. He felt trickles of blood moisten the back of his scalp.

"Geddup," Tom said. His arms were tensed, their veins showing, his hands balled into fists.

Dazed, Mark got up and sat on the grass. The pain made him feel even drunker, less aware.

David had come down and was examining the back of Mark's head, careful as an ape preening her mate. David's hands felt cool to Mark.

He was about to say "Thank you" when he saw Tom get into the car, shut the door, and speed away. The dust stirred up by the spinning wheels stung Mark's eyes.

CHAPTER FIVE

It was high spring in St. Louis with a half dozen joyous dogwoods and rows of yellow-pelted forsythia softening the brown brick severity and rectitude of the Jesuit scholasticate, Fusz Memorial Hall.

Tom, dressed in tattered jeans and white T-shirt, sat in his rocking chair and prayed one April evening, reflecting on his new life in St. Louis, on his relationships, with Mark and David, with God-person Jesus. He was having difficulty remaining clear headed during his prayer. Not that he was unhappy. He felt "fuzzy" as he'd described it to his spiritual father, like after a good hit, like when you're with your friends and everything is fine.

One dark thought, however, intruded noisily, accompanied by a low hum.

The Prairie du Chien memory was working its way deeper into Tom's life. He'd become nervous around Mark. He mounded small talk between them, stupid comments, fluffy and pink as cotton candy. He didn't think less of Mark because of that drunken episode in Prairie du Chien, but did Mark know that? None of them spoke much about the incident anymore. Not even David. Tom wondered if they were all too frightened by it—by its barmaid-lust, weakness-in-the-flesh, can-I-be-a-celibate meaning.

The memory of Prairie du Chien and the questions it lifted up into psychic space still made Tom's heart beat fast and his skin turn wet and salty. It was one thing to talk about the vow of celibacy and its noble root. It was another to talk about actual sex. Elder Jesuits smiled benignly when the topic came up. The younger ones kept silent or joked. The threesome had become ribald in the novitiate, earning a rebuke from Father Gorman. Tom thought their novitiate jesting had been a way to support each other in the tense struggle with celibacy. In St. Louis, sadly, he thought, they avoided talk of sex completely, avoiding the mention of "the wound that never heals, yet remains free of infection," as Father Gorman had described the gift of celibacy.

Tom struggled with that image of wound, wounded healer, wounded celibate. A self-inflicted wound? Or were there other hands on the blade?

Tom, Mark and David had taken vows together on a hot Saturday in August, 1970. They were gemstones that day, carefully cut diamonds shining in the eyes of their families and the nearly fifty Jesuits who traveled to St. Paul for the ceremony. The frescoed faces of the evangelists and church fathers smiled upon them in the Chapel of St. Thomas College. Their commitment was public, declared before the provincial, Father Sheely, families and friends, and, as the vows stated, the entire court of Heaven. No private affair, this Jesuit profession.

Tom felt the same thrill that had shivered through him when protesting in front of the Federal Building in Milwaukee, part righteous confidence, part itchy anticipation of an incident, part desire for peace.

The next day they'd flown together to St. Louis where they were once again the new men with new superiors and new spiritual directors, lean flesh and ready spirits passed off by a hopeful provincial staff into the second stage of formation.

Late on their first night at Fusz Memorial, they all packed into Mark's third-floor dorm room with its one wall of gold and green horizontal stripes, a color choice made by the previous decorator that David immediately christened Missouri Minimalist Landscape.

Mark had walked up and down the dark halls of the unfamiliar building that evening, checking out its four hundred rooms, searching for his friends. Tom thought it odd of Mark to want to get together so quickly with his Wisconsin Province pals. He imagined Mark busy making new connections.

Back in Mark's room, Tom sat on the narrow, lumpy bed. David settled into a straight chair at the drawerless oak desk. Mark rested his butt in the deep window sill, his arms folded across his chest.

"I've got something to tell you guys." Mark wiggled on the sill. Tom saw a tear squall about to push through Mark's eyes. He'd never seen those eyes swell up with distress. "It's something I'd prefer you keep quiet, just among us."

Tom and David nodded their heads. "After that night at the Red Dragon . . . later I confessed to Father Gorman. During our vow retreat . . ."

The first tears showed up. "He told me he didn't want me to take vows with the rest of the class." The squall broke.

Tom stayed fixed in place, shock overwhelming the impulse to comfort. A minute passed.

Mark forced himself to speak again. Tom struggled to understand the words. "Father Gorman said that the Dragon lady incident was the deciding factor. He said I'd failed the experiment on the reservation. He said other novices thought me too—proud."

David rose to hug Mark, but Mark pushed him away. "I've got to finish this."

Tom's heart began to race. He was unsure what to do.

Mark gulped for air. He stopped crying. His voice was suddenly chilled, brittle. "The provincial consultors intervened with Father Gorman. They noted all the good things said about me at Creighton Prep the fall I worked there, things from the Jesuit community and the families of kids I worked with." Mark's face was drawn tight. "Father Sheely called Father Gorman and told him he was being severe and paternalistic, unbending. Father Gorman was so angry with me the day he told me that Father Sheely had overruled his decision—he threw me out of his office. We haven't spoken since."

Mark fell to his knees, crashing onto the cold linoleum floor. "I feel I'm a cheat," he cried out. "A cheat! Second rate!"

Almost every night now Tom remembered how Mark had cried and fallen to the floor that confessional evening. Tom thought often of those tears, of the force behind them, of the reservoir that fed them. Those tears had offered Mark no consolation. They must've been from the evil one, Tom had decided, temptations to despair and doubt, to proud isolation. Perhaps this pain meant Mark was being called to something greater, to something awesome, to a battle on a spiritual plain set aside for the chosen few.

Tom hoped that Mark would one day feel what he'd felt when professing his vows of poverty, chastity, and obedience. Tom had felt a brightness. He'd been living in the afterglow of that feeling for months. He prayed three hours each day, morning, afternoon, night. Every Eucharist was rich with joy and spiritual peace. His soul was nourished. Sometimes after Communion he thought he might be floating up to the ceiling of the

Fusz chapel. He'd force open his eyes to make sure he was still firmly planted on the kneeler.

Tom was praying late that Friday evening in April about Mark's pain. He was thanking God that things were getting better for Mark. Mark was nominated to join the board of directors of St. Louis University, a step signaling that the Society and its institutions wanted to be in tune with the youth culture. David had told Tom, "Mark's coming back. He's confident again." That was true. Mark was more outgoing, less forlorn in chapel.

Just as Tom was about to finish his prayer of thanksgiving and go to sleep, he heard a quick, hard rap at his door.

"What is it?" Tom asked, jumping out of his rocking chair and running to the door.

"Your friend David Jepson's downstairs at the front door. He called up on the outdoor phone," said Father Kozolski, the sleepy-eyed Missouri province priest who was superior of Tom's community. The single phone on the block-long fourth floor was in the hallway next to the superior's room. Father Kozolski hated answering it. "He wants you to come down to see him." As much irritation as intrigue sounded in the priest's voice. "He's not really locked out, he says. He only wants you to come down."

As he walked away, Father Kozolski added, not turning around, "He sounded scared."

Tom put on his sneakers and hurried out, leaving his room door open, as he usually did, heading down the battleship green hallway of the fourth floor community for the side stairs. There were no decorations anywhere, no pictures, tables, or potted plants. Tom had chosen to live in the small community that was dedicated to living out poverty as best it could and to being active in justice ministries. He and three companions tutored at a North Side center four nights a week.

Two sets of glass doors encased a short hallway, the entry foyer to Fusz Memorial.

The first thing Tom noticed as he headed toward that entryway was David at the outside door, standing between two tall men, one white, one black, bulky figures in dark clothing. A dozen paces from the door Tom saw a flash of light glint off what appeared to be a badge on the broad chest of the black man. The man had turned to look outside where the streetlights kept the dangerous St. Louis night at bay. Tom jogged forward to press the buzzer to unlock the front door.

The white officer shoved David as they marched through the first set of doors. Tom's brain started to fill with fear. He unlocked the inner doors and stepped back.

"What's wrong?!" Tom asked. He stared into David's face. It was pasty, as if he were nearing shock. David made no effort to talk.

The white police officer stepped forward. His face was as ashen as David's. "Are you a Jesuit, too?" He seemed to be studying Tom, assessing Tom's jeans and overlarge white T-shirt that billowed out over his hips. The officer didn't seem pleased with what he saw.

"Yes. Yes, I am." Tom looked briefly at the officer, then back to David, trying to fathom the blank sadness he found there. Tom scratched the top of his head.

"Good. Do you know this man?" The white officer grabbed David's arm and shoved him forward. The officer squeezed hard. David didn't flinch. He just stared into the hallway.

The shove, the officer's grip, the question made Tom angry. This was stupid!

Then Tom noticed that David's arms were pulled behind him, hand-cuffs on his wrists.

"David? Sure I know him," Tom said, stepping closer to David, almost reaching out to take hold of him. "Why do you ask?" Tom crossed his arms and turned fully toward the pumped-up white officer, only a foot from his face.

"We picked up your friend in Forest Park," the officer answered, glancing at his partner who remained a few feet behind, "down by the cannon."

"So? Is that an offense? Is there a curfew?" Tom shook his head and raised his shoulders.

The white officer smiled back, as if he hadn't noticed Tom's cockiness. "You don't know, do you?"

"Know what?"

"Well, that's good. My partner and I've decided to give your friend a break. He's shaken—for now. But you've got to keep him in control." The officer hitched the thumb of his right hand into his thick belt and leaned toward Tom. "Understand?"

"No, I don't understand. What's going on?" Tom's sharp tenor voice resounded in the hall. The black officer turned to look behind him.

"Your friend can explain it all," the white officer said as he gestured to his partner to take the cuffs off. "Next time may not be so pleasant—for your friend, for the Jesuits or for the university. I'm an alumni and this stuff *disgusts* me." The officer looked over at David, who was staring at the floor, his arms now hanging useless at his sides. Tom thought the officer was going to spit at David. "You've got to get control," the officer said, his eyes inches from David's.

After the policemen had left, David continued to gaze down at the polished green tiles. Tom wanted to reach over and lift up his chin, but hesitated.

"What's going on?" Tom placed an arm around David's shoulder. David turned inward toward Tom and began to sob, burying himself in Tom's embrace. Tom held him tightly. His mind raced with explanations. *Had there been an accident? Did David get lost? Did he hit someone, or break something?*

Five minutes later David began to cry more softly, to breathe more regularly. He separated from Tom, his focus still on the floor, saying, "Let's go to Mark's room, and I'll tell you both."

It was about one-thirty when they knocked on Mark's door. The third-floor community was the community for straight arrows, young men who studied hard, played sports, were involved in campus clubs, spent time with coeds—all for the greater glory of God, which seemed best incremented by attention to the sociable life.

"Don't knock too loud," David whispered. "I don't want anyone else to see us."

Tom rapped again, and tried the door, which was locked, asking, "Why do they lock their doors anyway?"

Tom had expected a typical Jepson response: *That's why God made doors*, or *Let he who is sinless be the first to get the skeleton key!* Instead David stood quietly next to him, rocking on both legs, nervous. Another rap and Tom heard a voice swearing beyond the metal frame and pine slab. The door opened. Mark stood before them, shielding his eyes from the bright hallway light, dressed only in his white jockey shorts.

"Whadda you guys want?" Mark asked. His voice was fogged in, his face a ship battened down and anchored in harbor. "It's late. I'm asleep."

"We need to come in," Tom said.

Mark seemed to be sleeping upright.

"We need to come in," Tom said again, quiet yet insistent. He looked back at David who was spectral in his silence. Tom touched Mark on the shoulder. "We need to come in," he said, whispering into Mark's ear.

"OK, come in. But leave the lights off," Mark said, stumbling back to his bed, rubbing both ears. "David, light the candles on the window sill. I'm getting back into bed. You guys sit wherever you want. Or stand. Kneel. I don't care."

David lit the three candles on the window sill and the two thin tapers on Mark's table. That fall the third-floor community had celebrated with a candle-making weekend, and Mark had won the prize for most productive.

Since their arrival, Mark had painted the walls of his room white. Other scholastics had spent the first months decorating. His decoration was to strip his room. He had no poster on any wall. Only his vow cross hung over the foot of his bed.

Tom thought the candles brightened and softened the tense asceticism of the room. He relaxed a moment.

Mark rested against the backboard of his bed with his head on his chest. Tom was at the end of the bed, leaning back, his head and shoulders resting on the wall. David stood in a corner near the window.

"You're as faint as a twice dead soul," Mark said, seeming to come out of his sleeper's trance, looking up and over at David, using the phrase David had used to describe their Plato professor.

David said nothing, looking directly at neither friend.

"Something's happened tonight," Tom said, turning to Mark. "I don't know what. David said he'd tell once we were all together."

A long pause. The windows were half open. A breeze from the north caressed the candles. They licked at the heavy air and its scent of aging grain from the Purina plant.

David still said nothing. Now Tom was getting angry. This mystery had gone on enough. He hated private theatrics.

"Why did those officers bring you home? What were you doing in Forest Park? And what's the thing about the cannon?" Tom asked.

"The cannon," Mark said, his voice brighter. "What about the cannon?"

"These two police officers said they picked up David in Forest Park near the cannon."

"David. Near that cannon?" Mark started to rub his eyes.

"Will someone tell me what all this means?" Tom asked, irritated, sitting up straight.

"The cannon," David said, each word clear and distinct, "is where gay men meet."

Silence. A gust of wind. The flames swooped low and out. Mark adjusted the sheets over his legs and crotch.

David moved out of the corner of the room, closer to the center. Tom stared at David who seemed larger, defiant now.

Tom had heard about homosexuals, but had never known one. He thought of them as bent over old men, red-eyed, alone. David hung with a campy crowd, other scholastics with pointed wit who dressed up, loved ritual, sang show tunes, sewed and cooked. Were they gay? Tom gulped as he swallowed the thought. He squinted, sizing up David, realizing he had to say something. How could he want to be a priest and not know what to say? How could he be a friend and not know what to say?

"I guess I'm not surprised," Mark said, breaking the silence. "And I don't—I don't . . ."

"You don't what?" David asked. He could have been a mother scolding her child. One hand was on his hip, the elbow thrust out.

"I was going to say I don't care, but that'd be untrue." Mark fingered the stubble of his chin. "I'm your friend," he added quickly, as if the first thought had escaped, released without permission. Mark stared into the room. He spoke slowly. "I'm still your friend, I just—it's so different. I don't understand it, being gay."

"It's not so different," David said. He moved another step into the room, his shadow growing on the white wall. "You're attracted to women, I'm attracted to men. So I like a sharp jawline and stubble, it's still about love."

"But what were you doing out there?" Tom asked, gesturing over his head, west toward the park.

David hesitated, stepped back. The gray of his eyes darkened and turned porous. He sighed. "Meeting other men like me."

"To—to have . . ." Tom was unable to finish the sentence.

"To have sex," David said. "Or to meet someone, to cuddle, to hold." David sounded uncertain, perhaps unwilling to say the truth.

None of the threesome looked at the other. Tom closed his eyes.

"I know it's a sin," David said. He tensed the muscles of his chest and spoke a bit louder. "I know it's against the vows."

Tom looked up at David, into his friend's still moist eyes. David's head hung low. He seemed less the glorious new creature rising from the sea. He was going back under.

"And I've only done it twice before," David said, slumping, apologetic. "Twice last week. I don't think I'll do it again. I don't know, I'm very confused by it all."

David pulled out Mark's desk chair and turned it around, sitting face-to-face with Mark and Tom. He shoved both hands through his thick blond curls. "Since I've been here at Fusz I've met others—you know, since Smith Edwards left—other gay Jesuits. Not that you two aren't great! But their presence, *our* presence—this is revelation for me. And I need to stand in that revelation's light, even if it's only a moonbeam and I'm leaning against an antique cannon barrel."

Tom nodded his head. He understood the pull of that temptation or so he thought. On many a day celibacy was a martyrdom for him, a spectacle of dismemberment, a coliseum battle with a heavily-armored desire that wouldn't be slain. He had prayed so hard about it his second year of novitiate that his soul was raw and he had wanted to scream. Some days he kept modesty of the eyes because he couldn't be sane otherwise. And then there was Misty in Prairie Du Chien. Neither of his friends had seen him lean over to kiss her that night in the car, before she got out. Thankfully she shook her head and said, scornfully, "Not you!"

Tom still felt the shame.

"Please don't tell anyone," David said, breaking into Tom's memory. "Please don't tell anyone else."

The desire for silence. In Mark's cloistered room Tom understood the desire. He had yet to confess. Not once in St. Louis.

Via Purgativa, 1979

CHAPTER SIX

David invited Tom up to his room at the top of the triple-decker at 80 Lexington Avenue in Cambridge, Massachusetts. With neither Queen Anne tracery nor Victorian towers, the house was one of the more utilitarian residences maintained by the Society to house those Jesuits who had finished their stint working in a Jesuit apostolate and who had been approved to study for the priesthood.

The threesome lived in the same community, about a mile from the now urban Weston Jesuit School of Theology, whose city campus was shared with the Episcopal Divinity School that sat, as it had for decades, in stone serenity on Brattle Street just off Harvard Square. It was the beginning of 1979, a year and a half before David, Tom, and Mark were to be ordained, eleven years after they had begun their new lives in the novitiate in St. Paul.

On that cold night late in January, the twelve members of the community had only been back for a week from their winter break. Classes had yet to start. Raphael, the bald scholastic from Boston's North End, who strutted through life with the pounding steps of a striped Swiss Guard, had thrown together a meal of spinach salad, rotini, sausage, and tomato sauce. The kitchen was a mess. A thick red goo spattered all its surfaces. The ingredients for the salad and the makings of its fresh dressing, vinegar, oil, garlic press, paring knife, cluttered up the kitchen table like the ruins of a child's toy city. Tom was on cleanup duty that evening. He shrugged his shoulders at David, telling him it would take a while to finish in the kitchen.

David waited nervously upstairs, pacing the ten tight feet that made up the length of his bedroom. Two cloth-draped lamps warmed up the creamy chill of its walls, filling the room with a faint, seductive luminescence. That year Mark often told David his room resembled a high class whorehouse. "You might know, Mr. Libidosaurus Rex with your big— *tail*," David would respond, snapping his fingers three times in the pause.

But David knew with absolute certainty that Mark was as chaste as a dead provincial. Both Tom and he knew this.

"Have a seat," David said, inhaling deeply, greeting Tom at the door. He pointed to the eighteenth century Philadelphia rocking chair from whose arms roared twin lion heads. David had purchased the ornately carved piece for three thousand dollars at a rummage sale for the local Armenian church, the only extravagance in his room. After eleven years in the Society, he had learned to mute his worldly object transgressions.

Tom walked over to the chair, wide-eyed as a high school student in the disciplinarian's office. He gave David a perplexed look as he crossed in front of him, a look that said: "What's up? What's wrong?"

David sat down at the edge of his bed, facing Tom, the palms of his hands on his knees.

"I've decided to leave the Society," David said. "I'm not going to finish this semester. Rome's approved my dispensation." David paused, letting his announcement register. Save the details for later, he had warned himself. Deal with the pain, the shock. "I'm going to leave in a couple of weeks. You're the first friend I'm telling."

Sadness fell onto Tom's face, flat as an old nun's veil. It seemed to dim everything within him. His lips formed a question, "Why?" but nothing came out. He tried again, barely making enough sound to be heard a foot away. "Why?"

"I can't remain a Jesuit and be a gay man—at least not on my terms." That was the corner stone. Lay it out.

"On your terms?" Tom asked, cocking his head. "I don't understand." Tom slumped into the chair's turned slats.

David's mouth and eyes drew together. What had he heard? Tom said he didn't understand. But his calling had changed, David thought. Wasn't it obvious?

Tom emitted a low moan. He rocked back in the chair, pulling at the too short sleeves of his Harvard sweatshirt. "You've been out of the closet since St. Louis. What's the problem. Is it celibacy?"

"No, it's not *celibacy*, per se. It's that being gay—and learning to accept that fact—learning that there are psychological and social realities—realities that . . ." David stopped, sheltering his head in his hands for a moment. "This is so awkward, I'm not saying it right." David's voice had trailed off into a whisper. He shook his head a couple of times.

"Maybe you're not ready for this decision," Tom said.

"I'm ready, believe me. It's becoming too hard to grow into a gay man and remain a Jesuit." That was it. He'd stopped growing. He'd stopped growing outward. He only grew inward, in a bad way.

"It may be hard," Tom said, sitting up a little, "but does that mean you have to leave?"

"Yes it does!" David's clarity was deep in his body. It burst out without notice.

David's choice was made. He wanted it to be logical, clear-minded, sanctified. Still, the anger was there, "You know the Society isn't very welcoming to gay people anymore. Is it? It's gotten worse since we entered. Remember the latest provincial mandate: Gay people can talk about their gayness, in private, with friends and confessors—otherwise, keep it to yourself. We can't even bring up the topic at the community's dinner table!"

Tom placed his right hand over his heart. "I'm sorry about what's happened in the Society," he said. "You know I don't agree with all that drudgery about gays. You know that."

"Yes I know that!" David could feel himself starting to lose control. He'd planned a quiet, sorrowful meeting. He took a deep breath. "And I appreciate your acceptance. But I can't go on monitoring what I say and wondering whether somebody is watching me, whether someone is noticing that I hang around gay men, read gay novels, go to Dignity—my God, imagine the corrosive influence of praying with gay men!"

David stopped a moment and looked over at his icon of St. George. The saint was seated on a black horse, and his lance had already pierced the dragon through its throat. The dying dragon's blood splashed backward as if blown by a great wind.

There was more than glory in the saint's eyes, David knew. There was anguish. The death of his enemy was changing the brave knight.

"I don't mean to yell, but I won't live a double life, not if I don't have to. We're not back in the '50s now, we're not in Nazi Germany or Stalinist Russia. We're in a free United States."

"But what about your vocation? What about your commitment, your vows? Is being gay more important than following your calling?"

David heard the pain of Tom's questions, vested up as that pain was in the robes of the consecrated life. He didn't want his friend to hurt for long. He wanted the wound to heal quickly. He smiled back.

David decided he needed to speak more calmly, avoid that staccato attack that so easily clipped over his tongue and through his lips. Nevertheless each word came out flat and forcefully, the way heat marches through a furnace door.

"I've never understood as clearly as I do now the liberating power of the message of Jesus. He's calling me to set out, to go forth. I'm knocking the dust off my sandals! I will not preach what I do not believe."

"But lots of us have reservations about—about specific teachings," Tom said, rocking forward and bringing his hands together, pleating them in a supplicant's gesture. "That doesn't cause anybody any—unsolvable problems. We accept it." Tom seemed to lose himself in that statement for a second, as if he had just passed through a dense cloud. "It's a condition of being a part of this organization, this Church. Doctrines change, understandings evolve. Your *calling* remains."

David had known his leaving would be hard for Tom, that their friendship was a part of their vocations. No words would make the uncoupling easy. He kept quiet.

"Anyway," Tom said, "our religious lives are about way more than a statement of laws, about way more than the predicates in some yellowed medieval tractate!"

"You're right," David said. He relaxed, calmness covering his face, cooling his voice. "Our lives are about more than laws. That's what Jesus came to teach."

They both stopped to listen as Raphael clomped down the hallway to his room. "The Muppets" must have ended. Watching it had become a community event.

"It's this simple, Tom: I need to find me." David finally used the phrase he had spoken so often with his confessor, in his diaries, on his knees. "I know that sounds stupid, selfish, pop-psychish. And I know I'm supposed to find myself by losing myself—but that approach hasn't worked!" David laughed. "I'm still out there, somewhere!" he said, gesturing wide as his grin.

The phone in Raphael's room rang. As police chaplain he had his own line.

"And I want to find me, believe it or not," David said, serious again. "But I can't go searching for David Jepson—the way I need to search—as a Jesuit. It would be wrong."

David paused. "And I have no doubt in my mind that Jesus, the greatest of all sleuths, wants me out their tracking down my soul."

Their eyes locked.

"I'm with you on that," Tom said, sad-faced. Then he reached over to coddle David's knee in his right hand. "But, what about us? What about our friendship?"

"That's not going away, pal. I'm going to torment you for the rest of your life."

Mark, too, had decided to leave the Society. He, too, had experienced an interior vision whose image-roots dug deep into his maleness, into the hairy mat of x and y chromosomes.

Mark delivered his message to Tom a week after David's revelation, a night when a record-breaking blizzard overwhelmed New England's modern efficiency, settling in as comfortably as a hen on her eggs, and shut down commerce, education, sports and the arts.

Tom sat on Mark's bed. Mark was all movement. He stretched his body, paced up and down his bedroom. He was excited. This announcement was gospel.

"You're the first to know," Mark said, his smile congratulatory. He was as lit up as a father gushing over his first son. "Well, the first after David. I told David two weeks ago after he told me about his decision."

Tom was speechless. His eyes, in contrast to Marks' prophetic gleam, were blank ovals, holding only the watchfulness of an orphaned child about to be left with immigrant strangers.

"Tom, say something." Mark stood still. He continued to smile.

"I just—I feel—"

"Go ahead, you can tell me." Mark scratched his temple. He'd been positive Tom would understand immediately.

"You're sure it's not just about sex?" Tom asked.

Mark frowned. Yes, sex was part of his dream. He had shared aloud about the "limitations of celibacy" on their last retreat. But did Tom think him obsessed with sex? Was that the result of Prairie du Chien? And sex, well, it wasn't always a sin. It could be the netting of love.

Mark leaned back, arms clamped to his hips, and stretched his muscled frame, a runner before the race. He'd been dreaming of red-haired Cynthia for weeks. She was the new M.Div. student who sat next to him in Synoptics and whispered a billow of commentary into his ear. He'd fantasized about asking out Q-Gospel Cynthia—as soon as he'd told everyone he was leaving. They'd end up in her place, an attic loft in their Greek professor's Brattle Street mansion.

Mark hoped Tom didn't notice his excitement. Mark may have had many flaws as a Jesuit, but he'd remained as celibate as an anchorite, self-controlled and stationed high above the ordinary folk, flawlessly unjoined.

A now pacing Mark stopped to look down at Tom. He needed to construct his dream so Tom could walk through it, so Tom would know that his dream had other round, equally alluring shapes. In his brain was a clear image of the green expanses of the Marquette High playing fields. That was a good place to go.

"When I was teaching at the High, I used to watch fathers pick up their boys after practice or after a game. Some of the fathers would wrap their arms around their sons and drag those lanky bodies home, protective and powerful and—intimate."

Mark closed his eyes for a moment and stood totally still. "I'm afraid I'll be missing out on the best thing in life," he said, opening his shining eyes, wet and busy as they were with a sea swell of life, "missing out on life itself, as if this vocation has fenced me off, separated me from the truest desire of my soul." He strung out the word *soul*, the word that now, for him, had more hip rhythm in it than spirit flutter. "That's why I need to leave. I'm afraid this vocation is a fantasy love—with the wrong kind of pain and the wrong kind of pleasure."

"Fantasy love? Wrong pain? Wrong pleasure?" Tom said, murmuring his words. "Are you sure you understand what you're saying?"

Mark nodded and placed his hands in his back pockets. His students at Marquette High had joked that when he took that stance, his mind was set. He couldn't be moved. They called it the "Butt Hands" pose.

Mark didn't want to argue with Tom. Perhaps he hadn't been clear.

Mark had discovered a vacancy within himself. David had it. Didn't Tom have it, too?

Mark had decided how to fill the vacancy. His plan had to do with family, with fathering. That's all he was saying. He needed to make love hot and physical, not mystic and universal like drizzle in the British isles. Surely that would make him happy. The thought of this new love, perhaps impure—scented as it was at that moment with Cynthia's breath, soared in him.

CHAPTER SEVEN

Tom had been a priest for one summer before entering his graduate program in economics at Harvard. His first priestly summer lasted only sixty-one days, from mid-June to mid-August. He spent that gleaming sacerdotal time in Minneapolis where he worked in an inner-city parish made vibrant with congregants who volunteered for ministries, sang with unprodded excitement during services and reached out to newcomers as if they were Jesus, tired and needy.

Tom spent his nights in a community of eight Jesuits. La Storta House was an aging granite mansion on the periphery of an urban American Indian community, mainly Lakota, many with connections to the reservations of South Dakota where the Society had worked since the days of roaming buffalo and where Tom had spent his regency.

The community's name referred to a vision of St. Ignatius where Father and Son had both spoken to him. Ignatius later described the vision at La Storta as an invitation, perhaps meant only for him, perhaps including his companions, to stand at the side of Jesus as servant, a perilous yet sweet spot.

That summer it seemed to Tom that he walked in a lighter atmosphere than the rest of humanity. His professors at Weston Jesuit School of Theology would've been dismayed by what sounded like the tocsin of clericalism and the murmur of ancient cant in Tom's comments. Despite what Tom had believed—that the priest was not instilled with a unique holiness because of the sacrament of ordination so that *alone* he could work the miracles of faith, Tom did feel different, changed, blessed in a way that modified his being.

"I can't explain it. Surely *you* understand," Tom said to his confessor in Minneapolis, his look half fright, half glee. "It's a—special feeling. Celebrating the Eucharist is so momentous. The approach to the altar, the raising of bread and cup, the pull of the chasuble flowing out around me, encircling, the simple and clean words of blessing, the exaltation and the hush in the souls of believers. It's—it's sensual! I *feel* as if I'm doing something pure, something holy. As if I'm touching something—I don't know," Tom said, shaking his head, "something beyond."

Tom stood up from his chair to roam about the large, nearly empty parlor at La Storta, startling his confessor. He rubbed his hands along his torso in an attempt to defuse the current of his emotion.

"I know it's not really me, or me alone—that it's the faith of the whole congregation at work." He began to paint his explanation with his hands. David would've been proud of him, of this forthright expression. David had become the apostle of personal truth toward the end of his stint in the Jesuits, just as Tom had become the apostle of world social renewal.

"And in confession—people approaching me as if I were a sage, revealing hidden things to me, waiting for my wisdom. And their clear relief when I've forgiven them. It's amazing stuff. I feel—I feel I'm more than a messenger, that I've got access to a powerful, transforming energy."

Even all the old temptations, that morning sexual habit, that tendency toward protective silence, that enjoyment of a weekend buzz with his smoking buddies, even those things fell away during that first summer of priesthood. That summer Tom had felt fresh as a snake wriggling free of its old skin—maybe to cross species, to grow hair, to give milk, to give birth from within.

In late August Tom settled into a slate-blue Cape Cod in Cambridge which housed a Jesuit community of graduate students, most of them in their final years of studies. The ten members of the community were rarely together, their schedules so diverse. Tom had known none of his new housemates before arriving. The ones he chanced upon those first weeks were more concentrated on their research than on helping the new community member adjust.

"Will you be home for dinner?" Tom asked Father Leonard, an ex-gymnast-medical doctor who was finishing his Ph.D. in moral theology, concentrating on the nuances surrounding the modern ability to change one's sex.

"I'm off to dinner with my advisor tonight. Sorry," Father Leonard said, tucking his battered satchel under his arm as he rushed out the door, a bagel in one hand.

Tom was generally left alone at the kitchen table with the untouched bulk of the *Boston Globe* and a well-thumbed *New York Times*. His primary outside contact was with the parish at St. Bridget's where he'd started working the week he arrived back in Cambridge. He said weekend Mass and heard confessions.

"They're a tough parish," Father Leonard had told Tom one morning, standing at the narrow wooden counter while smearing cream cheese on his bagel. "They're not going to be impressed by another tall white man who is well read and speaks with a quirky, Harvard-sounding intelligence. That definition, except for the gender and height part, would describe most of your parishioners. You'll get their adulation if you're brief and witty," Father Leonard said. He punctuated that comment with a thrust of a stubby butter knife. "They're a heady crowd, but they prefer their religion with an MTV beat. Welcome to America: Father, Son, and Holy Spirit. Love is all there is. All there is is love."

Before leaving Father Leonard stopped at the kitchen door and stared back at Tom, saying, "Concentrate on your studies. Don't take on every burden. Only Jesus saves."

Tom smiled back and nodded, muttering to himself, "I'm really not looking for salvation right now. A little companionship would do."

Tom was early for his class in advanced theories in microeconomics. He was the first student to arrive and had taken up an aisle seat near the front of the hall. It was a Monday morning at ten. He began to leaf through the primary text, already lost in discovering its structure, his mind focused. He didn't turn around when he heard the heavy metal door at the back swoosh open. He only half listened as the footsteps came down the aisle. When he heard them pause, he turned and looked up.

"Oh, hi," Tom said, rising from his seat. She was three feet away.

"Hello. My name is Guadalupe Escobar." Her speech was slow. Guadalupe didn't reach out a hand to Tom, but nodded her head politely. She held a leather briefcase in her right hand and kept her left hand on the black purse that hung from her shoulder. A tight, blue skirt wrapped around her waist, and the high collar of her plain white blouse stood partway up her neck.

Tom's smile flashed across his face, his "This is a Beautiful Woman" smile. Guadalupe's shiny hair was youthful, thick, and loosely braided. Useful, direct, he thought. Her skin shone. A little moistness, perhaps nervousness, perhaps the result of exertion, gathered on her cheeks. Her skin was reservation cream, the way a native family looks after generations of intermingling. Her eyelashes distracted him most, their dark length curving out and up, moving with easy grace as her eyelids made their cleansing cycle.

Guadalupe looked down for a moment. "May I join you?" she asked, gesturing to the seat next to Tom.

"Please, please." Tom pointed to the spot next to him, on his left. She squeezed between him and the row of seats in front. Tom looked down for a moment at his faded jeans and dirty white sneakers; he felt bumbling and stupid.

"You're taking this class?" Tom asked as the woman moved in front of him. He was actually appraising the fact that her head reached up to his neck, and that to hold her he would have to lean over and hunch his broad shoulders.

She smiled at him as she sat down. "I am." Pausing, "Are you?"

"Yes." He laughed. "I guess that was a stupid question." He grinned.

She shook her head, and Tom noticed the two curls of dark hair at the edges of her forehead. He wondered if she had added that detail in the morning. It made her look sophisticated. She was simple, solid, and sophisticated.

"You're from?" Tom asked, raising his red eyebrows.

"Nicaragua. Out in the provinces, not Managua. Do you know Nicaragua?" She lifted the ends of her lips with a hint of amusement.

Guadalupe stared at his eyebrows for several seconds. He hoped he didn't look freakish to her.

"No, I don't know Nicaragua," Tom said. "I was in Mexico one summer, but in the north. I don't know Central America at all." He smiled at her accent. It was playful and energetic.

"Few do," she answered. "Not since bananas were as precious as oil." She laughed lightly. It must have been a common, silly little joke to her.

On Friday that week Tom and Guadalupe went to lunch at a diner frequented by solitary students and their stacks of texts and notebooks, a dusty outpost just beyond campus on Massachusetts Avenue. "This place is OK with you?" Tom was worried that his choice was too common for Guadalupe. The more he knew her, the more he recognized the refinement, the exposure to the better things money and leisure offer. She would have been at home with David.

"It's exquisite, we can talk easily here," she answered, leading him to a table near the front window.

For a while the pair said nothing, looking up occasionally from the menu, looking out through the window at the world passing by, looking at each other.

"I checked on the map this week to see where Boaco is. Your ranch is just east of the city?" Tom asked.

"Fifty miles. It's really several ranches. When my—*bisabuelo*—great grandfather, no?, moved from Mexico, he bought the Finca Guerrero. Over the years we have purchased others, but Finca Guerrero is where the family lives. It is, in my mind, the most beautiful place. The hills are gentle. You can see great distances."

"Like South Dakota," Tom said.

"Perhaps, but more green, I think. Verdant. That's how the guidebooks describe our land."

The waiter came to take their order. Both ordered hamburgers, fries, and a Coke.

"You eat hamburgers in Nicaragua?"

"No, but I have acquired the taste since my year in Washington."

Tom nodded and smiled. "Was your family supportive of your working at the World Bank, if I may ask."

Guadalupe faced him squarely. She brought both hands forward and placed them, folded, on the edge of the table. "There are still many restrictions on what young women can do in our society. But in my family, we have always been workers. I worked every day on the ranches, alongside the *vaqueros*. Wealth has not made us—apart. This is important to our family. We do not wish to live our lives as did the *patrones* of the past. So, it was not so hard for my family to think that I might want to do something other than marry three years after stepping out of my *quinceañería* dress."

Guadalupe stopped speaking as a police car drove by, siren blaring. They both craned their necks to watch it speed down the busy street. Tom looked at the length of her neck and the tightness of her cheeks. She caught his look and smiled at him.

"That is not to say," she continued, stopping to sip from the cool glass of water, batting her eyelashes as she raised her head, "that I met no resistance. You see, we have no family in Washington. There was no one to—chaperone, no to—guide me. Would you say guide?"

"Guide, yes. Look out for."

"Look out for! That's the phrase. No one to look out for me." She smiled, placing her right hand palm down between her breasts. "Well, only me to look out for me. I knew I would be fine. My family feared, of course. We think of America as such a dangerous place."

The waiter brought their food, and both began to eat. Guadalupe looked up, saying, "Tell me, why are you studying economics. Is it your family's wish?"

Tom shifted in his chair, putting down the hamburger. He felt an uncommon moistness gather under his arms, soaking his light blue cotton shirt. He decided to get it out in one gust of honesty. "I'm a Jesuit. A priest. I plan on teaching—after. I've been sent here to study."

Only when he was done with his declaration, did Tom sense how the words had seared the air, metallic and blunt-nosed in their flight. He could see the tightness grip Guadalupe's face, her jawline pull in. Her eyes narrowed slightly. She smiled back, but without mirth, an iron smile.

"I suppose I should have told you earlier," he said. He could feel the sadness creep into his own face. His lips drooped. He exhaled. Tom now knew for sure that she was feeling what he had been feeling. The attraction. The tension. The excitement. The current moving up and down the blood skein. Tom knew he must have finished all that off with his admission. He was wet. The damp weight of his words silenced him.

Neither spoke. Neither ate. A fly buzzed by and settled on the rim of his glass of Coke.

"As you know," Tom said, deciding to fight the spiral of sadness with an uprush of words, "I have some experience in Mexico. One summer I made a pilgrimage in Mexico, during my first year in the novitiate." Guadalupe said nothing. She stopped eating.

"I can't remember the name of the town," he said. He looked straight into Guadalupe's eyes. He wasn't certain she was listening, her eyes turning opaque, but he kept on. "It was in the state of Jalisco. My companion, Ed, and I were resting on the steps of the church when a toothless woman wrapped in a black *rebozo* spied us. I thought she was going to shoo us away, as if a couple of young *gringos* were desecrating her holy place." He made a sweeping gesture with both hands, but Guadalupe remained rock-faced.

"Instead, she told us to follow her and brought us to her adobe house. There she sat us down at the small table in the main room and started putting together a feast: *tamales, pollo con mole, arroz.* It was great! When we asked her why, she said it was her duty to feed travelers, and that we appeared to her as angels. After we had eaten, she asked us to bless each of her three rooms and to light a candle at her altar to the Virgin of Guadalupe, which was set in a niche next to her cooking hearth. Can you imagine?"

"I can imagine," Guadalupe said, her hands now hidden in her laps.

Guadalupe and Tom began to eat lunch together two or three times a week. Tom would regularly invite Guadalupe home to his community the evenings he had cooking duty, and together they would make dinner. As the school year got more serious, at least half the members of his community ate dinner together every night. They joked about Guadalupe being the next female Jesuit, following in the rumored footsteps of a mantilla-draped Spanish princess. But when Guadalupe and Tom went upstairs to Tom's room to study, Tom saw his housemates exchange glances that were more worry than humor.

Tom knew what he was doing. He was walking a tightrope. He had exchanged the broad flatland of the vows for a thin line high up in the air. He had never walked there before, not with Rose, certainly not with Misty, the Rock-Smashing Siren of Prairie du Chien (RSSOPDC) as David began to call her during their last year of philosophy in St. Louis. This encounter was so totally different. It was driving him crazy.

At St. Bridget's a member of the congregation came up to talk with Tom about the way he held the host during the consecration, shaking it as if he were involved in an argument: "This is *my* body."

Tom had begun to discuss his *problem* with his confessor. Prayer had become worthless, a time of torment. He felt weak, confused and out of control, a fakir whose bed of nails pierced and drew blood. He rose from his knees wanting to howl, to take his vow cross and hurl it through the single-pane window. He only felt peace with her now. Her eyes were a haven. Her touch, renewing.

"I think about the times I am most happy," Tom told Guadalupe the night they first slept together, four months after they had met. "They've always been connected to religion, to the foundational principles: love, good works, prayer. I think that's because those are the basics, the root activities of human beings."

"And what is love like for you?" Guadalupe asked.

"Love is like a sunset over the South Dakota prairie, a sunset when the great grassland seems to ignite with a fierce red light."

"And does not love have to do with touch, with holding on to another being, with a feeling that rips across the body and through the heart?"

His eyes widened. Wordless, Tom answered Guadalupe by leaning over and kissing her, first lightly on the lips as he passed his right hand over her cheek, then forcing open her mouth with his, pressing his breath into hers.

"Yes, love can also mean touch," Tom finally exhaled.

Father Gendler, rector of all the Jesuits living in Cambridge, had known many young Jesuit grad students during his six years at the post. He knew they were the flowering of the Society, a Persian garden filled with the bright, aggressive, and accomplished. Many had demonstrated the potential to become intellectuals and leaders for the future of the Society. This planting of men he watered and pruned was a special growth. Their fiber and nutrients would become topsoil for the Society of Jesus in the decades to come.

And so Joseph Gendler was deeply happy when a young man came to him to discuss a problem with one of the vows. The rector knew this would give him a clearer idea of the direction of this young man's life. Everyone's life had a direction; everyone's life turned toward a special slant of the light.

Problems dealing with celibacy offered the most exhilarating opportunity for Joseph Gendler. He had come to believe absolutely that the desire to love another was the twin of the desire to sanctify.

Tom knocked softly on Father Gendler's door that March evening. Father Gendler, his marine good looks barely softened by the signature chocolate-brown corduroys and black turtleneck, met Tom at the door. They stood at the door a moment, Father Gendler smiling, Tom hesitant and wary. With little chitchat and a gentle pat on the shoulders, the rector directed Tom to the gray couch. Father Gendler took up his regular spot in a Shaker rocking chair on the other side of a knotted rug.

Tom looked around the room, avoiding the rector's eyes. The room was full of knickknacks, the one possession, other than clothes and a professor's books, which Jesuits could collect and transfer with them. Four icons of Mary, in cruciform pattern, were nailed to one wall. A jade Buddha sat on a half-table and attracted a pool of ambient light. Spaced along the bookshelves were a portrait of Ignatius, pictures of Father Gendler with various family members and notables of the Church. Every corner had something in it, giving the room a coziness, a feeling of good use, of senses alert to the sacred in all its manifestations. For a moment Tom relaxed.

Father Gendler sat still. Every few seconds Tom would look at him. He saw that the rector's eyes were active and his small mouth seemed on the verge of speech, as if the man were only waiting for a star to reach its zenith.

Finally, Tom looked straight on and held Father Gendler's gaze. He straightened himself up and pulled up his knees. He rubbed the stubble on his cheeks with the palms of his hands, brightening the ruddiness his face still kept from the evening's chilly walk.

"You look anxious," Father Gendler said. "I hope it's not because of me. I'm here to help, in any way I can. You can talk to me about anything." Father Gendler elongated the *anything*, as if he had looked up into a sky-domed atrium and sat gazing at cosmic mystery. "You realize that, don't you?"

"Yes, Joe, I do. I'm not nervous because of you. Because of what I have to talk about." Tom should have leapt right into it. Instead he paused, a horse refusing to take the jump. His calf muscles tightened. His lips clamped together.

"And what is it you want to talk about?" asked Father Gendler.

"My vocation."

Tom was almost crying. The blessed word was pierced. It seemed a dying creature, a doe limping at the edge of the road with an arrow in its breast.

Tom's eyes were wet, but he had screwed up the muscles of his face to stem the flow. He didn't want to cry. He didn't want this to be so painful.

"I see," Father Gendler said. "You can cry if you want to, Tom. These issues are never easy to discuss. And remember, you're not the first Jesuit to confront the issue. I'm here to help."

Tom sat back into the low couch and brought his hands up to his face, finally letting himself sob into their chamber, cradling his head in his palms. His chest ached as it heaved his emotion. He couldn't remember the last time he had cried with such fury. Nothing had so troubled his soul.

Eventually Tom told the story, only the details of transgression, assuming his anguish was evident in nervous hands and tear-washed eyes.

"And how often do you sleep with her?" asked Father Gendler.

"Several times a week. At her apartment, of course. I spend most of my weekends with her, rushing from her bed to say Mass at St. Bridget's."

Father Gendler didn't move. "I see. And have you spoken of this with your confessor?"

"Many times, yes. He suggested I speak to you. He thinks I need to— to do something about this."

"I'd agree we need to do something." Father Gendler's tone held no accusation. He was placid and thoughtful as if they were discussing a matter of taste, how much pepper to grind on a crisp salad. "And do you have any idea what to do?"

"Well, I could go away. Leave Massachusetts. Go to another community, maybe study in Europe." Tom was counting out his options on the fingers of his left hand.

"Or—I could stop seeing Guadalupe." Tom paused, staring directly at his superior. "Which is not likely."

Tom looked away, staring now at the indifference of the illuminated jade Buddha. "Or I could leave the Jesuits and the priesthood, which is what I want to talk about."

"Yes, those are all options." Father Gendler had been rocking softly, back and forth. Now he stopped the motion of the rocker, placing his feet firmly on the floor before him. "However, it appears you've come to a conclusion already. But this is not a light matter, nor is it a strictly *personal* one." A brief pause. Father Gendler seemed to be waiting for Tom to look back at him. "Before we go too far, I want to know if you're willing to hold off acting for a while?"

"What do you mean?" Tom's eyes were jimmied open with surprise.

Father Gendler cleared his throat. "I mean, your decision will change the course of your life, your life and Guadalupe's. I don't want you to make that decision tonight, or tomorrow night. There's so much to review, to discuss, don't you agree?"

"Yes, yes, I guess so," Tom said, nodding his head several times. "But I don't want to prolong the pain of living this—this lie. Besides, Guadalupe and I have discussed it at great length. I love Guadalupe, I want to live with her."

There was a sudden emotion in Tom's voice. He could feel the muscles of his arms contract, the way they did when he was up at bat, a combatant's grip, tight and concentrated.

"I hear you," Father Gendler said. He accompanied those three words with one hand held out, modeling the Pantocrator. "As your superior, the man who must make recommendations to your provincial and to Rome, I need to know you better, to know the details of this case. I need to understand these issues in light of your entire history. So, let's take this tack." Father Gendler's face softened. "We'll set up regular appointments, twice a week for a couple of months. That will give us both time to discuss the issues involved and pray about them."

Father Gendler paused, leaning forward slightly. "Are you with me on this?"

It was traditional Jesuit rhetoric, an approach to reality that Tom had lived by for many years. Prayer, discussion, the passing of time. Instruments of the spiritual life. Sitting on that couch he felt it was his duty to comply with this one last request from this one last superior. He knew it would all be over soon enough.

"Yes, I can buy that, I guess."

"Good. There's one further request," Father Gendler said. He rocked forward, stopping the arc of his chair at its furthest point. "I want you to stop sleeping with Guadalupe while you and I are discerning your future in the Society and as a priest." There was silence in the room. "Will you do that?"

The request shocked Tom. Hadn't he made his love for Guadalupe clear? He was getting angry. Was Father Gendler toying with him? Did Father Gendler think he shouldn't leave? Wasn't his physical enmeshing with Guadalupe sufficient evidence that the door out of the Society and priesthood should be opened wide. Instead, Father Gendler wanted to spend time lingering in the foyer.

"I'm not sure . . ." Tom began.

"That's why you need time," Father Gendler said, interrupting. "You're not sure." He pointed his right hand at Tom. "If there's one thing you should have learned in the Jesuits, it's how to arrive at a decision, a decision you're sure about. The history of the Society is a history of men who came to solid decisions about how to live their lives and so could concentrate on achieving their goals. That's what the Spiritual Exercises of St. Ignatius are about. That's why they're the cornerstone of our formation program." Father Gendler's voice had risen to fill the entire room. "They are the reason for our greatness. The same rigor should be applied to every important decision in a person's life. If you know where you're going, you'll get there."

Father Gendler leaned again into the room, clasping his hands together. "So, Tom, are you willing to give this decision the time, thought, and prayer it demands?"

Tom could feel his body force out the answer despite the resistance in his soul. "Yes, I guess I am." He was a boxer being struck from behind by a foe he had never seen. He stumbled, unclear about what had happened.

Father Gendler didn't smile back, but Tom thought he saw the relaxation of a victor. "I'm glad," Father Gendler said. "I think we'll both feel better about the outcome, whatever it is. And—you are going to stop sleeping with Guadalupe while we consider this matter?"

"Yes. I can do that—for a while." Tom's hands were cupped together, resting in his lap. The earlier redness of his face had all drained out. Something had been subdued.

"I'll have my secretary arrange our appointments with you tomorrow, based on your schedule. To begin with, I want you to tell me about why you entered the Jesuits, OK?"

"Yeah, fine. But, this isn't going to be easy for Guadalupe," Tom said, finally countering, recalling what the meeting was all about. "What am I supposed to tell her?" He raised one hand in question. "I've more or less made a commitment to her."

"I expect she understands the nature of your situation," Father Gendler said, rising from his chair. "You've already made a life commitment. You shouldn't break such a commitment without careful consideration. Would she want less from you?"

"No," Tom said, still seated. He looked up at his rector, not ready to end the conversation. "But it will seem a rejection."

"It will *feel* like a rejection, yes. That can't be helped."

"What about your promise to me? You said you would leave the Jesuits." There was no calmness in Guadalupe as she sat across from Tom that night at the chrome and Formica table in the kitchen of her rooming house. Her breasts rose and fell with her deep breaths. The stitched pattern of reindeer trooping across her white wool sweater knocked about with distress.

As the damp cold evening quickly edged its way into the harsh light of the room, they both clasped their arms across their chests, containing their emotions for a few moments.

"I said I would talk with Father Gendler about it," Tom said. "I didn't say it would be immediate—that I would leave the next day."

"And so, what do we do now? Tell me that." Guadalupe's face was stamped red as if she had just been slapped.

"I promised Father Gendler I would follow through on this, that I would spend time praying and reflecting."

"You've been doing that for months, Tom. What's going to be different?" Guadalupe held his gaze, her black eyes unmerciful.

"What's different is that now I'm making a formal request to be released from my vows and released from my priesthood." Tom was trying to be calm, pastoral, thinking of the other, but he choked on that final phrase. "It's not just you and me and my confessor now! This stuff is *hard.*"

"OK, you pray and reflect," Guadalupe said. Tom could see the rigidity of her muscles, someone pushing on an unseen stone. "You go through your Jesuit routines, you and your priests figuring out what you want. And what, *por favor, si no es tan incómodo explicármelo,* what do I do all of this time?"

"I—I'm not sure, Guadalupe." Tom reached his hands across the table, but Guadalupe leaned backward, sharply, as if she were a spring-loaded trap unsprung.

"I wait. That's it, no? I wait," Guadalupe said.

"We both wait." Tom could feel the weariness around his eyes. They ached. He continued to rest his arms on the table.

"What are *you* waiting for, Tom?"

"I'm waiting for clarity."

"I thought you had clarity. You acted that way, your body acted that way." Guadalupe's voice was loud enough for her roommates to hear. They had probably put down their books to listen.

Tom watched Guadalupe tighten her fists. He had never seen this before, in her, in a woman.

"I don't mean I lack clarity," Tom said. He was beginning to plead. "I have clarity, but I owe them this . . ."

"You owe them nothing, not any more. We had made a decision. A commitment. Don't you remember that night? The night you said you couldn't live *without* me?" Her eyes spit fire.

"I do, Guadalupe, I do." Tom exhaled. "But I'm a *priest*, remember, this isn't a meaningless thing to me." Tom clasped his hands to his chest. "I've told you how hard this is, this leaving."

"I never said this leaving of yours was meaningless. I love you because of your meanings, your ideals, but I hate this—this indecision, this childishness, this weakness, this . . ." Now Guadalupe was pounding her firsts on the table.

"Please, Guadalulpe, don't . . ."

"Don't what? Don't be angry? Why not? I am furious, I gave myself to you. In my country, that is not a minor thing. Do you understand? I gave myself to you, I entrusted *me* to *you*."

He was at fault. Her words stung. He wanted to console her, wrap her in his arms. "And I gave myself to you, I gave myself back to you," Tom said. He hated the anger and despair in Guadalupe's voice and eyes. He hated the resonance of those emotions inside himself. He pushed back his chair, got up and began to walk around the table toward his livid companion.

"And now—I'm so angry!" Guadalupe was screaming. She shot up from her seat, shaking her head in disbelief. "You've cheated me. You're no man! I should have known better. No wonder you became a priest, you're a coward. *Cobarde!* Leave!" she cried as she muscled Tom away. "Leave now!"

Tom heard the sound of her roommates' chairs scrape the floor above.

That conversation took place a week before Señor Héctor Alvaro Escobar y López was gunned down by a band of *contra* rebels who claimed to be wrestling control from the Sandinistas, a party to which Señor Escobar had never belonged. A stunned, tearful, defiant Guadalupe left the United States within days of the news of her father's death.

"I'm so screwed up," Tom confessed to Father Gendler the day Guadalupe left, his eyes swollen from hours of crying, his skin as pale as crypt marble. "I don't know what to do. I don't want to lose her, I don't."

"It's good you feel that way, Tom. If you weren't torn apart by your feelings, then you wouldn't have been in love. Then you would have been using that young woman, using her in a very harmful way."

"You agree I was in love with her?"

"I have no doubt of it."

"Then you think I should go after her?"

"Of that I'm not sure," Father Gendler said, his words clean of emotion.

Tom set his head with a new defiance. "But I was in love with her, I am in love with her."

"Love is never bad, Tom. We all love other people. Love is never bad." Father Gendler was rocking gently in his chair, smiling as if he were feasting on the most succulent meal. "But because you love Guadalupe doesn't mean you should leave the Jesuits or abandon your priesthood. That I don't believe."

"Why not?" Tom's jaw was tight.

"Because life's not that simple," Father Gendler said, solemn and slow, careful as an officiant intoning the prayer. "Because God has a wish for each of us. We cannot factor out His desire."

Tom chose not to leave the Jesuits or to pursue Guadalupe after she returned to Nicaragua. She had written, telling him that if he truly loved her, he would come to be with her. He never went. "Perhaps," he wondered for the first week, "if she hadn't gone so far away . . ."

He trembled at the gel that quickly surrounded those words.

Guadalupe's absence, he would later reflect, gave him distance, objectivity. Her absence did not make his heart grow fonder; it made his heart grow more complex.

Her absence created a time for reflection, a listening to other spirits. And Father Gendler's insistent questions made Tom reexamine everything. He weighed his desire to be with Guadalupe against that other long cultivated desire of his soul. He chose to stay with his original dream.

"I don't understanding everything about God's will. I know it's about more than my personal fulfillment. I know that when I work with people as a priest, when people expose their wounds or the blossomings of their souls, that's the time I most feel His energy and His desire," Tom admitted to Father Gendler after twelve weeks of discernment. Tom hadn't touched himself since she'd left. He assumed that was all over. He began to sleep less, to push himself in every way possible, to run ten miles a day, to be more humble at the altar. He vowed to finish his doctorate in only four years.

When Tom next heard about Guadalupe from friends in Nicaragua, she was fighting somewhere in La Mosquitía, near the Atlantic coast. She had become a Sandinista. His Jesuit friends in Nicaragua said she had acquired a pulsating distaste for all things North American. She returned every one of Tom's letters unopened.

CHAPTER EIGHT

David moved immediately from his cramped Jesuit room in Cambridge to Manhattan's Upper West Side. He packed himself and his scratched and scuffed aluminum novitiate trunk and his pair of new two-tone Louis Vuitton suitcases into a pied-à-terre he had inherited: twenty cove-ceilinged rooms and a rooftop garden outlined by five stately cedars, with a grove of three orange trees hugging the garden's interior, a well-coddled orchard that bloomed every spring high above Central Park West.

He had a living from his grandmother's estate. More than a living, really, that term appropriate for the minor benefice of a minor son. David had inherited an immense wealth. He was independent of means.

As a Jesuit the easy access to cash had been a constant challenge to him, a Gordian knot he never severed, leaving the Asia of total dependence on God vastly unclaimed. Even as he was vowing poverty during his nearly two-minute profession on that sultry 1970 afternoon in St. Paul, he had kept a credit card bending in his wallet, its account funded in the name of his childhood teddy bear, Mr. Biggins, an often-patched brown creature who managed to stow away in every trunk David pasted with transport labels, some to St. Louis, one special label for his London regency year writing and researching at Farm Street, bastion of high-collared British Jesuitry. This *ursa minor* credit card, as he had first described it to Gina in the Lake Street Embers, batting his eyelashes with the precision of an overbred English gentleman—much to her disdain, had seemed an eccentric yet proudly adult act when he set up the account at eighteen, halfway through his senior year of high school. He had been inspired by an Evelyn Waugh character, a dandy with a taste for booze and dusky men.

At the time, alone at the Jepson estate with only a Croatian cook and a lanky, farm-bred bachelor groundskeeper for conversation—which arrangement left so much adult advice hidden in odd vocal shadings and shifting posture, David didn't realize the depth of the Waughian pool of inspiration from which he had drunk. When he moved to Manhattan, he nearly drowned in it.

So much changed when David left the Jesuits. He burst out of the confines of the religious life with its sure goals and regularity, with its well-maintained pathways and routines of grace. His life changed in big ways and in small.

David no longer examined the eyes of others for the trace elements of Christ. His regard was for the individual's luster, for the fragments of personality that floated as motes in the vitreous humor. For the reflection of himself in the stillness of that thin, aqueous world.

Community was now the friendships he made. He stopped timing the minutes it took him to finish the Sunday *New York Times* Crossword Puzzle. He was no longer in competition with fellow Jesuits who would demand his puzzle time at Sunday's preprandials. He would construct his own traditions, around brunch and the opera, gyms and bars, online bulletin boards, and the occasional exploration of pathways in a little replica of a glacial moraine in Central Park. He was the new dog in the neighborhood, sniffing out the smell of every queer-odorous venue, the scent of its creatures. The externals changed. David packed his books of Latin and Greek into a sturdy Green Giant Whole Kernel Sweet Corn box he had picked up at the Cambridge Stop & Shop and stuffed that box into an unused closet in the seventh guest bedroom, leaving its contents unmarked. With a regimen of jogging and a diet inspired by the training grounds of Sparta, he lost fifteen pounds. He was trim, toned, appealing.

David's personality underwent a similar redefinition. He met people with a steady handshake and a well-practiced, deep voice that announced only the necessities of name, origin, and pastimes.

David abandoned the role of dandy as best he could. His new model was Mark, whose masculine butt-slapping ways David had often mocked, much to Tom's delight. David had claimed, in jest, in those early basement days, after his first conversion of heart and trust-in-God decision to remain the Jesuitical course, that his vocation was to make Mark humble.

"Hey, Mark," adolescent David would goad, puffing out his chest and grunting his words on those occasions that young man Mark seemed most aggressive and content, "Didja butt heads wid anybody today?" In response Mark would narrow his wide, round eyes, saying, "Yeah—and they're lying out in the gutter, freak." Then they would run at each other, both glancing off the other's chest, Tom watching on the sidelines. All three would burst into laugher, a sign of good cheer and male bonding in the house of the Lord.

From the real Mark, the man who permitted himself to be mocked, the man whose face was so honest, David had learned a new poise centered not in the electrical dazzle of wit but in the heat and purpose of gut.

David spent his first summer out of the Society practicing this poise on Fire Island where he met Randy Jones-Smith, another recently-out gay man born to money and endowed with fashionable, Italianate good looks. They had spied each other at a tea dance on a crowded, weathered deck that jutted out over the water of the small Pines Inlet, Cyndi Lauper vibrating the air. David fixated on Randy's square jaw and the dark shadow of a beard and his V-shaped gymnast's form. Randy told David later that evening that his height and bright blonde hair and ready laughter had caught his eye.

The two young men met near midnight on the broad Atlantic beach, both strolling off the nine-course meals they had consumed with their share mates, both indulging in a few solitary moments of reflection. David's contemplative side had been trained by the Jesuits, hopeful he would be one of theirs, Randy's by his avid research into the history of Egypt, with hours deciphering hieroglyphs from the Old Kingdom and studying the ancient rituals of animal mummification, losing himself in research into mysteries less personal or horrifying than those occasioned by being the gay son in a hotly religious Methodist family.

The two of them passed each other on the strand as they were walking alone barefoot through the surf. Their white linen pants and white silk shirts were so brightened, so intensified by the cloudless moon they could have been angelic Dominions or Principalities of a lesser rank on coveted shore patrol. They passed each other and nodded. Ten paces further they both turned to look back, smiled, paused, and returned.

"Hi. My name is David Jepson," David said, his anticipation working him the way hearth flames do a fresh birch log. He reminded himself: aim for cordiality, not wit.

"I'm Randy Jones-Smith," Randy said stretching out his hand and holding onto David's, lean flesh firming up on lean flesh. More than a few seconds. "Are you out contemplating the wonders of the universe—or giving in to a more feral impulse?"

They both let go.

"Feral?" David's grin was wide as a regent's about to pounce on his favorite student with a hot new phrase. "Nice vocabulary. Do I look as if I'm prowling? Or predatory? Or about to build a nest?"

David placed his freed hand on his hip, taking up the pose he had used at Marquette High for delivering his best hoop skirt, high camp commentary, displaying the body signal that called for his chosen coterie, "whities" in the Marquette vernacular, to gather round. This Randy, he knew, relaxing into the sand, could enjoy the less virile David.

"No, no. I wasn't thinking of some low-slung, big-toothed quadruped—or a brood hen. I was thinking . . ."

Randy's face turned serious. "I was thinking of peace. You look peaceful. Pleasing. The moonlight bending . . ." Randy said, gesturing with his chin from the moon to David. " . . . all white. And in this moonlight, you, your face, are inviting."

Quiet.

Randy's words were a sea wave. It lifted David up.

David's hands dropped to his sides. His eyes moved back and forth from the moon-washed highlights in Randy's curly black hair back to the soft obsidian at the center of this new man's eyes.

"That's a good word: inviting," David finally said.

They headed down to Cherry Grove, passing several miles beyond the village.

"So tell me again why you left the Jesuits, in order to have sex?" Randy asked for the third time as they began their return.

"Are you writing for *People* magazine? If so, I'm no cover story. I mainly kept my vow."

"Mainly?"

"Well, here and there," David said, looking at the waves and wrapping his arms across his chest. "Actually, I had my first sexual experience with another novice, a young farm boy, big hands, big eyes, big all over. We got carried away for a couple of months. But he left the Jesuits soon after we broke up. He's a costumer for the Guthrie now."

Tentatively, his desire fragile, David wrapped his arms around Randy's waist. "I was afraid back then. I didn't have the courage to confess that entanglement, so I just stuffed the whole issue of sexuality deeper into my psychic vault and became what I became—a Jesuit, a little repressed, a little manic, a little acerbic."

"But that was years ago. You haven't had sex since then?" Randy turned the two of them face to face. They stopped walking.

"I fooled around a little during college—anonymous stuff. After that, nothing until I left."

"I don't get it."

David sighed. This Jesuit tale so often got in the way. People fixated on it.

Randy began to play with David's hair. David gently shook his head, pre-occupied for a moment by old thoughts. Was this truly a generation that didn't understand sex, just as the century's best had preached, a generation too satisfied with simple dichotomies, with a binary worldview even when it came to the firestorm of love and lust?

"Celibacy was a vow. I did my best to keep it." He smiled. Could he make this vow thing clear without sounding stupid? Randy's face was so close to his now. "It helped define me, give me form. And besides, I think—no, I thought, I'm still not sure about this—that sex should be accompanied by love. That it would be good only with love."

"Your sex with the farm boy wasn't good?" Randy asked, a small worry dashing past his eyes.

"The sex was great, the feelings afterward weren't."

"And how do you feel about sex without love now?"

David knew they were getting close to the desired end. He became more confident. "I'm doing research into that phenomenon," David said. Moonlight caught the whisper of a smile on his face. "The final paper isn't ready yet. Right now I'm still leaning toward sex with love." Then he kissed Randy, softly, then wild.

AIDS ended David's research. His friends began to die. He started spending several nights a week at hospitals or hospices or at the bedsides of weakened acquaintances. He stopped having sex altogether. He feared for his prostate. Each morning he examined all the dangerous pockets of skin for lumps or lesions. He stopped dancing. He nearly stopped laughing. That was a slow decline. One evening he went through his wardrobe and discarded every item that wasn't black or white. It was as if he wanted to return to the Society, return to the vows, to the surety they had provided, to their purity.

In 1984 Randy lie dying at Mt. Sinai. His brain, that jeweled lockbox, though rusty, could still open and display its sheltered treasures, although David noticed the inner gems were finally losing their brilliance. The rest of Randy's body, the mechanical parts, to David's increasing despair, were becoming utterly useless, their hinges and gears sticky and slimed.

The two of them had attempted lover-type love in 1979, but found that friendship-type love suited them better. The Greeks, David thought, subtle in so many ways, would have created unhyphenated names for these interactions. In the eyes of the queer and gifted Manhattanites who knew them well, David and Randy were the ideal pair: witty, attractive, wealthy and deeply supportive of each other.

"David, please don't stay here after I die," Randy said, the purple splotches of his face moving as a descant to his words. "Leave Manhattan. Go elsewhere. I don't want my spirit to see you wandering these streets of possibility without me. Besides, you need to do something. I wish I'd done more these past years."

"You've done plenty. We've been constantly busy."

"With what?" Randy asked, starting to slur. "Travel and parties, reading and rearranging furniture, falling fast in love and falling slow out. Is that a life?" Randy closed his eyes.

"Yes, that's a life," David said, reaching over to massage Randy's shoulder, his own sadness deepened by the factory-man's clock-out admission. But his job at this bed, with his precious friend, was to soothe and inspire. Saints had done less. "That was *our* life. And don't forget your studies, people respected your opinions. Your two monographs on those discoveries in Sudan were well received. And the past year, before you got sick, we've been doing our own social work, attending to our friends, escorting their families through the final days. It's as if I were back in the novitiate on long experiment. Except I truly loved these departing queers."

"You never loved the sheep in your novitiate flock?" Randy asked, opening his eyes and batting his eyelashes. David laughed, despite Randy's death-yellow glow. What pleasure that Randy could fix his wit on anything, even on David's erstwhile membership in that solemn religious company. Randy had confessed to David early on in their relationship that he had once dreamt of becoming a monk.

"Novitiate love was different. Duty love. First base love, not home run." David looked down at his large hands, which appeared clumsy and bizarre. "I was really playing hide and seek, child's play, searching for me—and not very effectively. Back then I didn't have good clues."

"And have you found you?"

David watched Randy struggle to raise his right arm, perhaps to touch him. Then Randy gave up and let his arm fall limp at his side. A glaze started to form over his eyes.

"I have found me," David said, beginning to worry. He'd seen the look before. "I've found big, architectural chunks of me with you. A hearth . . ." David pressed his palm onto Randy's forehead, fervent as a priest giving a blessing, his mouth breathing the sacramental words into Randy's left ear. "And a load-bearing wall." He brushed Randy's oily air. David's eyes brightened. "And a breakfast nook full of laughter and gossip—and this baroque cornice of naughty putti."

Randy laughed a sharp laugh, lurching back into life, then convulsed, three jolts jerking through his body. He began to fight for breath, fight to keep oxygen in his lungs. His thin arms shook at his side. Just as swiftly he quieted down, an empty rattling diminishing in his chest. David kissed his forehead, then softly murmured as he frantically rang for the nurse, "Go laughing into Heaven, honey. You go laughing!"

After Randy died, David returned to Minneapolis. Randy was the glory of his days in New York. Not a lover. Not a minor friend. More a brother, a twin brother, who knew the rhythm of his heart. And with his dying, a segment of David shut down. His joy ended with the sealing of the casket. Something was over. David's attachment to life had lasted throughout the last six months of Randy's existence, the months of the long, painful dissolution, the loss of normalcy, the loss of control, the loss of keen eyesight and finally, death. But as long as Randy was there, even only a suffering spirit in a tortured body, no matter how forlorn a body, David kept going. Once Randy's body was buried in a well-mown field outside of Canton, Ohio, David's interest in life dropped beyond zero.

Mark and finally-pregnant Ann went up from Washington for the memorial service. They couldn't believe the transformation in David, so they called Tom, who had to stay in Boston for his doctoral orals. "He'll listen to you," Mark said. "With me, we either laugh or spar."

Tom called David, and the two of them talked for three hours. It was Tom who suggested David return to Minneapolis for a while, to get away from New York, the city that had become plague-central.

"You used to love Minneapolis, the lakes, the parks, the easy access to beauty, the sanity. Why don't you go back there?"

"Who's there for me? My parents are dead, thank God. Oops, I shouldn't say that. But I'm sure they're not listening, even now, probably too busy dining on something deep-fried. And you and Mark aren't there. I don't know anyone in Minneapolis anymore. I've been away too long."

"You don't have to stay. It can be a retreat, you can get up early and walk through the morning mists. You used to do that a lot during novitiate! You'd goad the rest of us to put on our sweatshirts and head down to the river bluffs. Remember?"

"Yes, I remember. It was my attempt to be spiritual. Father Gorman suggested it. He thought religion was too intellectual for me. Unfortunately, even nature made me hear Wordsworth or Keats rather than Jesus' mordant lines."

"So bring poetry—Oh, I hope that doesn't sound callous!"

"It doesn't. You don't do callous well." David's face lit up for a moment as he enjoyed this rare attempt at Burns irreverence.

"I hear you want to get missioned to Guatemala?" David asked, finally moving the conversation away from the still-yelping pain of loss, watching his right hand play with the twisted cord of the phone, wondering if the twists helped propel sound on its transcontinental luge-run. "Why go there?"

"I want to go where the need is really great. I can do a lot in Guatemala."

"But aren't you afraid?"

"Afraid? No, not really. In Guatemala, it's mainly the Maya they're after, not like in El Salvador."

Not long after his conversation with Tom, David returned to Minneapolis. He closed up his penthouse, leaving his furniture covered with percale sheets, his statues quiet on their shelves or in their niches, his paintings and photographs unviewed on the walls, except for the three O'Keefe Abuque vistas and two late-Monet collages of daisies and stars which he locked away in his vault. His 4,523 books sat collecting dust in their bookcases and stackings, and the contents of his two walk-in closets remained hanging their perfect distances from each other.

In Minneapolis he rented a furnished efficiency on the ninth floor of a '60s building sided on its front with a pale-brown brick. The main room, the only room other than the bathroom, contained the efficiency's prize feature—a single-paned picture window set low in the north wall. It looked out on Loring Park, Minneapolis's downtown island of green hills, old oaks and elms, which was no Central Park, lacking both size and monumental charms. Floating in that island were two small ponds, tennis courts, basketball courts, and five unpretentious plots of annuals. Most importantly, it was near enough to a string of lakes that were the walkways of Minneapolitans.

His first month home David walked one of the lakes every morning. Lake of the Isles. It took him nearly three hours. He rose at dawn. On the way back he stopped at Gelpe's, bought danishes and the *New York Times*, and spent the rest of the morning reading about the city he had loved. He put on some pounds and passed his first days "on retreat" reading Michener and watching TV, becoming a fan of Oprah. "I'd invite her for preprands," he'd mutter to himself, half-smiling, sitting down with an early afternoon Johnny Walker Red, a cheap gouda and a packet of saltines as Oprah's theme song disturbed the dead quiet of his hermitage.

At Christmas Mark came home to visit his family, much to David's surprise. Charley, Mark's son, named after a fatherly priest Mark told everyone who probed, and not his pharisaical father, was a preemie with a heart problem and only recently out of the hospital. Ann had stayed back in Washington with their child "swaddled in wires," as she'd written in her Christmas card. Mark explained his presence in Minneapolis on the phone to David, who didn't hide his shock that Mark could be in Frozenopolis at this very moment of his child's weakness. "Senator Brandon wants me to go on a junket to Beijing. I'm only passing through. It's my job."

The friends met for coffee Saturday night. David insisted they stay at his place, telling Mark it was too cold to venture out in the arctic wonderland of twenty-degree-below-zero windchill. "I'm sure a herd of mammoths is on its way, skipping and whistling Dixie through their hairy trunks."

They passed the first half hour in near silence.

"You don't have to stay," David said. "I know you've got a lot on your mind."

Mark checked his watch. He leaned forward, holding his hands together as if he were a gentle ten-year-old caging a butterfly. David wondered how he had learned that pose. It was fatherly, reverent. Straight men could be tongue-tied about feelings, David was thinking; he so agreed with Oprah's guests. Straight men were on empty when the topic was relationships. But their bodies, somehow, with this angle and that flex, they could learn to speak with their bodies.

"David, tell me what's going on with you," Mark said, softly, unctuously.

Not the question David expected. He stared into the middle of the room, avoiding direct eye contact, rocking back and forth in the creaky chair he had picked up at the Franklin Avenue Goodwill.

But it was the right question. The problem, David's problem with the question, was with the timing. Was it time for the answer? He could've said that he was an oyster with a lodged intruder. That maybe a pearl would form inside, only much later. He could've said that.

"Going on? Nothing. Nothing's going on," David said, reaching to pick up his cup of coffee, then changing his mind, deciding to say something, to slice off a little bit of what was inside him. "I'm a routine, a domestic animal. I wake, I walk, I chew, I read, I recycle food. That's it."

"That's it? Is that enough? Have you made any friends since you've been back?"

"I don't want any *new* friends," David answered, thinking: You and your new politico friends, you and your expanding influence. "I don't want any more attachments. You know what I've been through—well, I'm not going through it anymore." David raised his right hand as if to say: Enough on this topic! Then he smiled and looked down at the tan carpet, a path wending through the tired fibers from the doorway to the window, and laughed, mockingly. "Oh, such tragedy! Cue violins. Bring out the smelling salts. Wheel out Liberace!"

Then more somber, stopping even the slow movement of the rocker. "I know I sound as morose as a Russian princess, but I *am* an exile. I don't belong here, and I don't want to belong here. My real life is elsewhere." David stared out the large square of glass into the black winter air. "Unfortunately, elsewhere is no more. That's the plight of the White Russian: the lands, houses, jewels—everything's gone. No chance for redress. You just live with it, bear it. And that's what I'm doing, I'm bearing it."

Mark shifted his head to angle a look of criticism.

"Come on," Mark said as he clasped his hands tighter together. "I know it's been rough since Randy died, but you're no dispossessed Romanov. Your life is full of possibilities, you still have your talents and your friends. You're still—*you're* still alive."

That last remark: Mark sounded tentative, as if he were trying out an argument for later use. David listened more carefully.

"You can make something with your life," Mark said, scowling now. He began to move his hand around the room, pointing out objects. "Look at this place: a cheap rocking chair, a fake-bronze lamp, a tacky metal bookstand with a few torn paperbacks. I can even see a layer of dust in this dimmest of all possible light." David looked at each object as Mark pointed at them. How odd of Mark to pay attention to these details, he thought. Something's happening in Mark. Ann, a Chicago debutante, kneeling Catholic with a Mother Teresa heart, had often joked that Mark never knew whether he was sitting on leather or on cloth, that the Jesuits had made him truly indifferent to the things of this world, or at least furnishings.

"I mean," Mark continued, "you used to be so caught up in things, in everything around you."

David looked again out the window. A patch of moonlight had settled over the white stucco of the Dutch-inspired park concessionary, whose bathrooms were often trafficked by suburban men cruising late in the night. He looked back at Mark, thinking: he's cruising around me, hoping for something to happen, to unzip something.

"I've changed," David said. "I stood up one morning in New York and felt as if the world could barely support me. I breathed and there was no oxygen. I'm a zombie, Mark, a zombie. I don't even rant anymore about all the wrong people dying. I used to be good at that. It always infuriated Randy—he was so kind. But I felt good afterward, after a good rave. Not anymore."

David almost got up out his chair, suddenly feeling as if he were sitting in filth. But he wouldn't admit the feeling to Mark. "I'm sorry my state disturbs you."

"I'm sorry it doesn't disturb you," Mark said, the delivery sharp. He tugged at the collar of his black wool sweater.

"That's not fair!"

"Fair? Who's talking fair? I'm talking life," Mark said. "Life isn't fair, it's unjust. This world's disordered! Remember? Father Gorman's lecture on the Christian *weltanschauung*? Second or third week. I even remember that weird word. We were to be signs of a different world, a haven—not like this, this—crazy, stupid place!"

Mark's theological imagery and the fire of his delivery shocked David. He hadn't heard words as bold as these from his friend since they'd left the Society. As a scholastic he had loved to listen to Mark go on about morality and society. Mark's muscles would mass into firm shapes, and his eyes would shine. He became an Athenian soldier readying for battle. David would imagine him naked and oiled, virginal. He chose to think of Mark as virginal.

David had a finely chiseled image of the nude Mark, having gone with him often to the St. Paul Seminary gym during novitiate. Not that David had ever stared fully at his companion in that long communal shower or at their lockers as they dried off. He had been too afraid of being caught, the rapt peasant, envious, desirous in the presence of a lord, too afraid of the feeling whose name he batted away. But the discoursing Mark, his skin wet with truth, David would look at full view. It was at those moments, when Mark was heated from inside, that David was most aware of how much he loved Mark, more so than when he thought of him in those sinful, sticky moments at night in his narrow beds. Of course, he had never told Mark he loved him, loved him in that way. Now David felt beyond love.

Mark looked again at his watch. The surge of energy had drained out of his face. "My flight's early tomorrow, I should be going."

At the elevator they offered each other a brief, brotherly hug, only their arms touching, their chests, holding their beating hearts, inches apart.

Back in his room, David shut off both lights and padded quietly over to the window, furtive in his movement, as if he were sneaking up on someone.

He stood and watched Mark get into his car and drive off. He remained at the window for a while, rocking slowly back and forth, his hands clasped behind him. After several minutes of this mindless *davening*, he turned and went about the apartment lighting the odd collection of candles he kept scattered throughout, placing one pair of tall white tapers on the window ledge. He pulled up a chair, sat and stared out over the landscape.

The cold of the night swept past the window pane, singing the tune of a wet, southern wind. It was beginning to snow. That whirring melody and the icy fingers of the wind that bore it reached inside the apartment, forcing David to move his chair back a bit. He went to get a heavier sweater and returned, this time studying the fossil formations of frost at the edges of the glass.

He shifted his gaze from the intricate etchings on the window pane back to the frozen park below.

David noticed a lone figure enter the park from near the brilliantly lit ivory-colored mass of the Basilica of St. Mary. The figure paused to scan the whitened slopes of the park, pulling his stocking cap over his ears, and started to walk down the path toward the small arched bridge that spanned the channel between the two ponds.

The man's movement, the man's aloneness, triggered the memory. The awful, worst memory—the memory he had never shared. The memory of Jeffrey Addickson, the sophomore who came to speak with David during his final year of regency at Marquette High before he went off to Farm Street. The memory of his betrayal. David Judas Jepson. One of the reasons, clammy in his heart, he had left the Jesuits.

"You can't know you're gay at this age, Jeffrey," David had pronounced.

It was late at night in a tiny room in the Marquette High counseling center, after Jeffrey's basketball practice. The boy's mother would pick him up in an hour. Jeffrey had been so nervous setting up the appointment, looking down at the floor, scuffing the floor with his feet, smiling too broadly.

David could see the life drain out of Jeffrey after his official comment had dropped hard on the room's dark green linoleum.

David was afraid to tell the boy it was OK to be gay. "I can't say that. I'm not permitted," he repeated in his mind. He was afraid to stand up against the Church. He was afraid, a fear as vertical as mortal sin, which sits on the precipice of nothingness. He was bold in everything else. Relentless. Not about this, however—not then, not yet.

A week after he began his theology studies at Weston he heard the news. A Marquette High senior was found hanging from the lowest limb of a hundred-year-old oak tree on the Lake Michigan bluffs. The lad had impaled his letter jacket on the sword of a winged victory, which stood her ground beneath the tree.

Above Loring Park, David began to tremble. He held himself and started to cry. He thought of Jeffrey, seeing again the rejection that had slashed the boy's downy face. "I'm sorry! I'm sorry!" David wailed. "I'm sorry!" He cried the words so loud he thought the man in the park would look up and stare back. He held himself tighter and sobbed uncontrollably. "I'm so sorry!"

He felt as if he cried for an hour.

Finally the tears abated, and he saw a new image in the evening's reflective white. An image of Randy on the beach, dressed with the breeze itself. Bright in the moonlight. Two old words, pre-Jesuit words, the poet's words, sifted out over David's lips: love laced. Love laced.

He fixed his puffy eyes on the man still standing on the bridge in the park. David's mind was focusing tight again, summing things up, as if he were a grocer alone at his counter: "All Jeffrey wanted was love. All Randy wanted was love."

CHAPTER NINE

Mind is the pulse of time; body is the sweat of energy; energy is the dance of existence. We swirl outwards; we swirl inwards. We are the dancers.

Heretical comments made by Father Hugo Beltrán y Lanzarote, S.J., when brought before the Sacred Congregation for the Faith in 1950. When confronted with the doctrinal errors contained in the words, Father Beltrán recanted, apologizing, saying he did not know what the words meant. He had uttered them as if possessed.

In the late spring of 1985 the threesome spent a long weekend in New York. Gotham was the favorite choice for their semiannual reunions. Just the three of them together. They invited no spouses or lovers or other Jesuit friends to these gatherings.

David had kept his co-op in Manhattan. He paid all expenses.

Randy had been dead for nearly seven months, and David had published his first edition of *The Loring Intelligencer*. One spring day in Minneapolis, walking home after his lake-side meanderings, David had been struck with inspiration. A tornado of words had taken him up and turned him around. Titles from long ago spun about him, lifting their knees high and dancing. *A Separate Peace. The Scarlet Letter. Magister Ludi. The Grapes of Wrath. Zorba The Greek.* These stories had given his youth life, fed it with the proteins of existence: mystery and joy, tragedy and courage—and triumph. He saw the book covers as he rounded past the elegant facade of The Loring Office Building: paperbacks, torn, worn, read.

What could he do? A magazine. He'd been reading Michener and picture-laden pulp for months. He could start a magazine. A quarterly—no overwhelming exertion. It would be local. It would be queer. It would be sharply written and dicey. It would whip when necessary, allude and primp with style. He began to laugh.

David was on his way back to the land of the living.

Tom was preparing for the next big step. He'd accepted the position at Rafael Landívar University and was preparing himself for his new life in Guatemala. He was more quiet. Reserved. Concentrated.

Mark's face, on the other hand, in the middle of the decade he had once envisioned himself stole-bearing and counseling those about to marry, stirring congregants with words of justice and peace, was being drawn flat, dermal cell by dermal cell, with worry and other inner abrasions he no longer bothered to name.

Half his days Mark sat slouched in a chair with his legs apart, sitting on the sidelines of medicine, half he basked proud-chested in political glory. He'd been promoted to chief of staff for Senator Brandon and spent evenings strategizing and conferencing. His only child, Charley, however, had been in and out of hospitals all his short life. He was one of those institutions' special creatures, his body a sacrament of biologic inquiry. Charley was six months old. His diagnosis: unknown. With operations, with luck, with some experimental medicines . . .maybe he'd live. A normal life for his son? Not as Mark had imagined it. But he loved that boy so. How could his love have created . . .?

When the doctors first whispered their concern, during the third month of pregnancy, Mark had thought of abortion. He'd never mentioned the idea, the grim possibility, to Ann. He'd thought of it often, though, as often as she'd fall to her knees in prayer, "Bernadette in damp muck" he'd think to himself, biting as his father.

Maybe that was the beginning of his problems, when his father started to sprout inside him, rhizomed and suddenly everywhere like fiddle-head fern in the back of the garden.

All three men knew that this reunion would be the last of their regular meetings, that the shape of each one's existence was shifting rapidly, that their friendship was becoming a thing comprised more of memory than real presence.

Their first morning together the threesome taxied down from David's co-op to Soho for breakfast, finally stopping to check out a little place on Mercer. It was a delicatessen with three small tables on the sidewalk. The tables huddled beneath a maroon canopy whose lettering read: Serenity's Kitchen. "That's where I need to eat," Mark said, signaling to his friends, he hoped, subtly for he still felt the pride of chosenness, that not all was right in his life, that he hated being the martyr-father of a sickly infant.

They decided to stay because the young waitress from Wisconsin, who quickly announced she'd come to Manhattan to scale the walls of the fashion industry with her preternatural ability to use any household item as an accessory, chatted freely with them, in an unhurried way. A string of up-bent spoons, all different sizes, evidence of her skill, were strung together along a slinky that circled her waist.

David asked, "Can you play tunes with that belt?"

"You just listen!" the waitress said as she danced around a table.

The threesome nodded and smiled, pursing their lips. Serenity's was the place.

"So, Kristie, how's the career going?" Mark asked as they sat down. He'd bent his head at a twenty-degree angle to stare at Kristina's name tag, which she had pinned askew on the side of one of her cloth-stretching breasts. Her skin was milk white, Wisconsin pure.

"It's hard," Kristina said, pouting her plump lips. "I don't make much headway, but I'll stick with it." Her head swayed nonchalantly in the wind. She's so at ease, Mark thought. Untroubled by her troubles.

"I come from white trash, you should know," Kristina said, almost giggling. "Trailer park folks." Kristina rested her right hand on the small fold of her tight hip. "But I've always made good—so far. I got A's in school despite working most nights at the Country Kitchen." She looked down into Mark's eyes. Intent. "I know how to survive."

"Watch it, lover boy," David said after Kristina jingle-jangled back inside with their order of fresh fruit and omelets. "I thought she was starting to evaluate you for more than tip-making material. She might be wanting to fetch you home to mama and chain you naked to the Harley."

"Oh, get off it, David, I was just being friendly. I'm married: Look." Mark raised his left hand over the table and turned it around with the graceful sweep of a model. "My ring is big and bold and clear for everyone to see." Mark smiled as brightly as he could, straining so no one would see the pain. He and Ann hadn't had sex since the last time the ambulance came to take Charley to the hospital—over three months. Neither of them talked about it. Mark assumed Ann needed all her energy to help Charley. She'd already quit teaching calculus, resigning from Georgetown Prep. For him, it was different. It was the first time in their marriage that he'd wanted to have sex with someone else, anyone else. At night, before going up to the bed of worry, he'd pick up the yellow pages and finger the listings of escort services, slowly, the way a good priest reads his office. He'd dream of dark-haired women with lips pulpy as Kristie's and with long, opening legs. Quietly, quickly, he'd jack off in the downstairs bathroom, then scrub his hands with soap so Ann wouldn't catch the scent.

"Your pearly teeth and broad shoulders are also pretty obvious, Mr. Dad." David smiled his comically wide, bearish grin.

Mark had savored that Jepson smile, but scowled this morning. He was becoming a scowler, more sour with each angry grin.

Mark had awakened that morning in one of David's canopy-covered Edwardian bowers trying to remember why he'd fallen in love with Ann rather than with the three other women he'd bedded after leaving the Jesuits. She was the best athlete; she could beat him at tennis, herself a near-member of the 1976 Olympic team. Her father owned a block of Chicago's gold coast, with a Mies van der Rohe in his portfolio. Her mother's family ruled Springfield and had connections throughout the Democratic world. Those attributes had all counted in Ann's favor. And she was beautiful, blonde, lithe, a bosom made for his face, but, still—there were so many other beauties.

About Ann herself, the thing that shocked him, enticed him, the thing open in her that made him tremble. Her Catholicism? Was that possible? Was that the draw? That *reverence*, one of the kinder religious words, when she closed her eyes at Communion?

Their Sunday brunch dates began with Mass in Georgetown at Holy Trinity. She'd listen to him afterward, his comments on the homily, on liturgy, on the Church. He enjoyed her listening. The enjoyment, supple in his gut, like tight abs after a workout, had surprised him. He'd left the Church, in his mind, before dating Ann. Catholicism, mystery-laden and sin-obsessed, had become irrelevant to his life—to his career. His Jesuit existence was only a source of stories, useful stories, yes. He knew that being a Jesuit gave him shape and character. He could see it in the eyes of those he told. It was as good as being a marine. With Ann—with her faith—maybe—he woke up and anticipated her listening on those Sunday mornings, her attention when he talked of justice and the shaping movement of interior spirits.

Having a son should've made religion ever more meaningful, giving him the opportunity to transfer the best stories about the family and its history of eccentrics and heroes. Mark would hand on God to his son, God the blessing-filled, still busy ancestor.

Instead, with Charley's birth and its aftermath, that desert-dwelling father-deity became for Mark a stone-faced idol who lays back and devours beating hearts, a God who rises only to lead into temptation.

Ann insisted Mark keep going to Sunday Mass. She went daily. "We've got to pray for Charley."

Mark went with her—a good pet. But he seethed inside, composed dirty limericks during the homily, "there once was a prick in the pulpit," and undressed the attractive women.

At home, with Charley in his bedroom, they'd torment each other with an energy as fierce and wobbly as that of the rock of ages when it had blasted into the thickening atmosphere above pangeia.

Mark would manage to blame God, who sat in his mind, bent over in the shape of his own father at the end of their Kenwood table, narrow-eyed and in command.

Ann would rebuke. "Don't blaspheme! He's our only hope!"

"You won't let me touch you!" He had learned where to prod, where to dig. He'd unleash it all. Sundays were the worst.

"I don't want you to touch me, you Pharisee! You care only about your career! What did they do to make you this way, those black-robed friends of yours!?!"

For the first month Mark had honestly thought Charley's health might have been a punishment for his abandoned vow, the sin of the father oozing out, sharp as stomach bile, into the flesh of the son. That month he goaded Ann into such torrents of rage that her face would turn lupine, not hairy but big-jawed with bulging veins.

Yes, hadn't Ann changed, too? Hadn't birthing this sickly child warped her? She complained. A lot. Mainly about Mark, it seemed, especially about his new job with the sexually avid Senator Brandon. The Senator had once cornered her at a party, when she was first pregnant, and rubbed his knee up her thigh. She stood still for a second, then called over to Mark, "Over here, honey!" Later Mark told her to avoid the senator. He was angry, yes, but what could he do? Senator Brandon was his best hope for success. Ann stared at him in disbelief.

But neither of them talked of separating. Of ending the torment. Mark thought, "Maybe when Charley's dead. He can't live too long." Maybe it was just a question of time.

"Now you two behave," Tom said, shaking his finger in mock rebuke of his friends. "It's only breakfast. We'll have plenty of time to discuss the things of this world, such as bodies and their natural uses."

"Bless you, Father." David brought his hands together in the form of a prayer.

"Bless *you*, my son," Tom said as he began to delve into the freshly arrived bowl of fruit.

"Now wait just a little minute, Father Tom," David said with a false look of shock. "We're only discussing the obvious: an attractive man talking to a luscious young woman. You can't tell me you're totally at ease ignoring the lusty pleasures of this earth."

"David!" Mark said as he stretched out his hand to grab David's right arm and squeeze tightly. Mark feared that Tom still hurt from losing Guadalupe, that Tom was clinging even tighter to the rule of the Society than he had in the past—in response to that loss, throwing away a promising academic career to teach in the dusty torpor of Guatemala. Mark had talked to David about it before he came up from Washington.

"I bet he still loves her," Mark had said.

"Maybe," David answered, "but he's really a loner, don't you think? Don't you think his current vows will last him?"

"I don't know."

Mark had spent many hours in the last months thinking about Tom's affair with Guadalupe. It had found a place in his dreams. It was the only time he ever imagined another man having sex. He saw Tom's lanky body, still the adolescent body he'd seen so often in the '70s, hairless except for a patch of red in his crotch, bend over the woman's brown skin. Mark imagined Tom's affair to be a blossoming of real love, something beyond sex and comfort. Romantic love. It was without plan. It had happened, a lovely, beautiful spiral within the universe. Mark was glad for Tom. He thought of Tom's affair and wondered whether it had, in some way, saved Tom, at least for a while—that it had refreshed Tom, relaxed him before the next sprint.

Kristie was back filling their coffee cups. She smiled at Mark and winked, a glint of mischief in her eye, then left the three men to their talk.

"Ease was never the point, as you know," Tom said, throwing out his chest and straightening his spine, "whether it was about pride or lust." His words droned with a cool, logical monotone, the sound he always produced when imitating their novice master. *"Lust will sap you, blunt your ability to penetrate God's message."*

"Yes, of course, one of the gems of our novitiate." David cackled, nearly snorting coffee out his nose. "Father Gorman managed to use the word 'penetrate' in every truism he uttered. Penetrate truth. Penetrate pain. Penetrate love. What could that have meant!?"

David's eyes darted over to Mark, who sat back watching the other two. "Is this conversation bothering you?" David asked.

Mark said nothing. His eyes were following two sapling-thin women who walked past their table into the delicatessen. "I'm—not bothered. Perplexed, though. Why are we talking about sex?"

"We've always talked about sex," David said. "Right?" he asked turning to Tom.

Tom set down his coffee cup. "It took us a while to get to sex. I think we started out talking about other desires."

"What other desires?" David asked.

Tom cleared his throat. "Self-sacrifice. The search for meaning. The kingdom."

"Oh, yeah." David shifted in his chair, adjusting the fabric of his shorts over his muscled, light-haired legs. "But don't you think it would've been good if we'd gotten to sex earlier than we did?"

"I got there pretty early," Mark said, leaning forward and putting both elbows on the table. "Celibacy was a big issue with me, I discussed it often with Father Gorman. It's one of the reasons he didn't want me to take vows.   He saw how weak I was in that area."

"You were *weak*?" David put both his hands palms down on the table, as if he might push himself away from it. "I—I—I don't know what to say. What do you mean, *weak*? You were human!"

"I mean," Mark answered, his gaze toward the center of the table, "that I was in constant temptation, I was constantly randy."

"But you didn't screw anybody," Tom said, quietly from the side. "I'm the one who was weak."

"I don't mean weak as in actually screwing someone." Mark turned to look at Tom. "I mean, this is the way I see it now, I was weak because I took in something, and I let it torment me."

Mark sat back in his chair and laid his hands in his lap. There was a tear at the edge of his eyes. "It was a hardness. A ball of—something plastic and—I don't know . . ." He breathed deeply, closing his eyes. "As you can see, I still don't understand what happened between Father Gorman and me. He said I was 'ineloquent' about my soul. That I wasn't struggling with celibacy, I was struggling with love. Why'd he say that?"

For the last six months Mark had wondered if the Jesuits had made him cold, the way Ann accused, if those years of self-critical introspection among like-minded men had denatured him in some way. Some men might be best off without that drilling analysis and its drift toward parade-ground conformity.

Kristie brought their omelets, asking if everything was all right. "Fine," David answered.

None of them began to eat. Tom and David stared at Mark. "Go ahead, eat," Mark said. "I'm just telling you that I don't understand those feelings, the ones I had in the novitiate. That's all."

David picked up his fork and worked off an edge of his omelet. The others did the same. "Do you still have those feelings," David asked, "whatever they are?"

"I'm maybe too rigid," Mark said. "At the office I have this reputation for being a hard-ass about the way things are done, which is good," he added, gesturing a downbeat with his fork. "I'm the chief of staff for a very important American senator. It's a big responsibility."

Mark didn't want to talk about his problems with Ann, not in a direct manner. He wasn't sure what to say about them. But he had already played a card from the deck.

"I understand about discipline," David said as he wiped his mouth. "I keep on my staff about the details, too. Check the facts, check the spelling, check the punctuation, check the ad placement." He took a sip of the fresh orange juice and puckered his lips. "But I don't feel uptight about sex."

Mark and Tom stopped chewing.

"I don't feel uptight about *sex*." Mark said, his response sharp. He put down his fork and shifted to face David.

Tom cleared his throat, getting both friends' attention. "I don't know exactly what you feel, Mark, but for me, sex—sexual desire and loneliness—or, is it isolation—damn, why are they so entwined!"

Tom took a deep breath and looked away.

"I thought everything was going to be beautiful with Guadalupe."

All three froze. Only the gentler Sunday sounds, muffled conversations, people walking by carrying newspapers and coffee, hung over the table.

"But I know today that everything wouldn't have been beautiful with Guadalupe. I know that my vocation is a rock inside me. A stone, a slab of granite. Anything not built on it wouldn't last, satisfy or last. How could I have made a life with Guadalupe and remained a Jesuit?"

"So, you still think about Guadalupe?" Mark asked, transgressing his vow to avoid the forbidden topic.

"I think about her a lot," Tom said, sadness in each word. "But it's this way: Happiness is a percentage. My Jesuit life is not a hundred percent of happiness or fulfillment. I'm pretty sure living with Guadalupe wouldn't have been either. Right now, being a Jesuit priest is a good—say—sixty-five to seventy percent. That's pretty remarkable."

"What's this percentage stuff?" David asked, loud and annoyed. "Is love an algorithm, a mathematics problem?"

"You were the first among us to quantify love, Mr. Jepson," Tom said with no think time. "Your last year in the Society you kept on telling me that gay people had taught the world at least one thing: that you can make a life with just a *little* love."

"Well, I . . ." David stalled, " . . . I didn't mean the goal was to *minimize* love, the way you minimize expenses."

Quiet.

"So, Tom, if you could be a married priest, would you do that?" Mark asked.

"I don't know." Tom stopped a moment. "Remember how we talked about celibacy in the novitiate—as focusing, single minded, single hearted? Rodriguez faithful and insignificant at the door, filled with one task, his task. Those thoughts—images of our souls alone with God—binding, struggling, forging a union, a particle exchange between two souls . . ."

"But you can have a particle exchange with someone else *and* with God," David said, jumping in again. "That's the physics of the Trinity, if I may assert."

"I know," Tom said, sitting up straight, exhaling deeply. "All I'm saying is—this idea of being married and a priest—it's something I don't know about."

Tom smiled at his friends as if to say, I'm sorry. "I think being a married priest would be confusing for me—so probably confusing for her. And

I couldn't be a *Jesuit* and be married. You have to leave the Jesuits to marry."

No one spoke. Mark replayed the phrase in his mind: leave the Jesuits to marry. The phrase, which he had not thought of for so many years, made him shudder, deep in his organs, and caused him to slide back inside.

CHAPTER TEN

Justice is a lily of eternal beauty and sweet fragrance that grows in a vast, gaseous swamp. Dare we drain the swamp?

— Excerpt from a letter Father Beltrán wrote
after his first year in Japan, June 1937.

Two months after his arrival in Guatemala, Tom went one evening to dine at the city home of the Vargas family. Their son Sergio was a student of his. Sergio was bright and curious and proud to have this distinguished Jesuit pay him attention.

After dinner and two bottles of Chateau Blanc de Baune, Señor Vargas began to relate tales of his latest business ventures. Señor Vargas sat in a chair of plush velvet and puffed on the deep richness of his Gran Corona Montesino, which he would frequently take out of his mouth and admire with the same appreciation a breeder might show when examining a prize bull. He had not bothered to offer Tom a cigar, keeping the Abatenza humidor shut beside his chair.

Four years previously Señor Vargas had joined in a partnership with a couple of *compadres* to raise cattle for export to the United States and its insatiable fast food industry. He wanted to give Tom an example of how Guatemala was a part of the new global economy.

"I am treasurer, Padre," Señor Vargas said after blowing a cloud of white Dominican smoke into the placid air of the living room. He had unloosed the already tight notching of his belt and had settled into his chair, content, contemplative. "Señor Martínez runs the operations. Señor Echeverría has the right connections," he added with a knowing wink.

"We needed land," Señor Vargas said. His voice had suddenly expanded to fill the entire room, bouncing off the black marble floor. Señor Vargas began to paint circles in the air with the red embers of his cigar. "We found some government land near Tiquisate—land that was owned by no one. There was no finca there, only some Indian squatters. It would make perfect pasture land. You can grow corn anywhere. The Maya know how to do it. They did not need *that* land."

Señor Vargas stopped to examine the tip of his cigar and frowned at its faint glow. He reached over to the table next to him and picked up his gold lighter, rubbing the soft wings of the lighter's embossed eagle. In a few seconds he had puffed life back into the roll of dead leaves and continued his story. "These Indians wander down from the highlands, you see, little bands of them following in single file the way they would up a mountain pass, looking for more land to plant their hectares of corn and beans." Señor Vargas wove his left hand in the air as he described the line of Indians walking from the highlands. His gesture reminded Tom of a serpent all aglow, vamping in the ether.

"They complain that too much of the highlands have been turned into coffee plantations. Nonsense!"

The boom of Señor Vargas's judgment startled Tom, nearly ejecting him from his tight little room of private terror. Tom was wondering what words he could speak to his host. His host had turned into a caricature. In the coolness of the evening, Tom began to sweat. Señor Vargas was so natural, so arrogant in his explanations. The man was happy to be one of that group of landowners who attacked and cleared Indian settlements. Tom had expected such a person to give off a sharp, acrid smell. During dinner Tom had found Señor Vargas genial, forceful, proud. Their conversation had been about religion. Señor Vargas was for reform, the vernacular Mass, a de-emphasis of mysticism and murky ritual, more right living. "The Ten Commandments are an owner's manual," he had exclaimed.

"There is plenty of food and land in Guatemala," Señor Vargas continued, standing to stretch his lumpy frame. He walked over to look at a weathered map of Guatemala which hung along the inner wall of the living room. On both sides of the map were photos of his family: Señor Vargas, his wife Renata and their three children in Miami, all windblown and bright teeth; a photo of the extended family in the grand courtyard of a *finquero*'s home with a ring of servants standing in the shadows. Turning to look at Tom, Señor Vargas pointed to various areas of the country. Esquintla. Santa Rosa. Jutiapla. Chiquimula. Zacapa. Alta Verapaz. He announced the population density of each province. "Anyway, Padre," he said, indicating a little village on the coastal plain with his burning pointer, "this land near Tiquisate was ideal for grazing cattle. Señor Echeverría got us the right to lease the land for one hundred years. Señor Martínez hired the—workers—and rented the caterpillars so we could level the makeshift village and raze those small fields. Of course, it was all legal."

Señor Vargas returned to his chair and settled back into its softness, humming as he again relaxed. It sounded to Tom like a strand from "Granada". The *finquero's* eyelids drooped. "They offered no resistance. Left to themselves, these Indians are passive, fatalistic. If men as bold as me and my friends were not here, this country would be going nowhere. We would still be in the Dark Ages. Surely you, Padre, as an economist, understand that."

Tom sat quiet, his mouth open as his brain raced through phrases and scenarios. He sat mute at one end of the couch with the observant Sergio at the other. Señora Vargas had just dismissed the maids, *las muchachas*, and returned to sit, a proper *dueña* in an ebony and leather chair near the main door. Everyone's eyes were trained on Tom.

Within him burned a low anger that was charring a path through his consciousness and along the sinews of his muscles. Yet he held his tongue. What words could he say? He wanted to scream: "You bastard! You coward! You greedy sonofabitch!" But that string of words was too bright. He was a Jesuit, a sophisticate. Keep the end in mind. Wasn't his mission to ingratiate himself into the power structure of the country in order to fashion the greater good? The early Jesuits had brought astronomical toys to China to win over the emperor and his phalanx of mandarins. Tom had brought economics to Guatemala. Surely the power structure would listen to his discussion of viable economic development. He wanted their attention. Hadn't he discussed this plan with his superiors, pleading that he could make a positive contribution to Guatemala, convincing them that he should be given permission to teach at Landívar University?

"What happened to the Indians?" Tom asked blandly, his hazel eyes Nordic steel, his lips tight and drained of blood. He hadn't felt such anger since the Vietnam War, since his raving about Johnson and Nixon, since the nights of protest, the marching, the placards, the shouts of disgust and "Shame, Shame, Shame!"

Señor Vargas squinted at Tom. Tom knew at that moment that Señor Vargas had heard the disapproval in his question. He saw Señor Vargas twitch from the minor sting.

"They were sent to the Petén," Señor Vargas said. His mouth tapped out his response, clear as Morse code. "There they can reclaim the jungle. I am sure they are content." The *finquero's* face was grainy and emotionless, his jaw set with the lines of a Maya stella.

"But the Petén is a miserable, awful place," Tom said. His horror had burst out. "How would they survive?"

"Indians are happy if they can grow corn," Señor Vargas said, the shadow of a benign smile passing over his face.

"Corn and land is all they need. You are new here, Father. You will learn, if you have an open mind."

The evening quickly ended. Señor Vargas's farewell was brief and formal. Tom's stomach churned unmercifully during the ride home. He paced the red tiles of his small bedroom the entire night, comparing his quiet acquiescence to Peter's denial the night of Jesus' abduction.

"I betrayed them. Out of fear, out of discomfort, I betrayed them!" He raised his hands palm up, then formed them into fists with the swift movement of a man grabbing onto a rope. "I betrayed you, Jesus. I am worthless! Spineless! I shouldn't be here!" Then he beat his chest.

The blood-tinted clouds that would cast their troubling darkness over Tom had begun to crystallize and billow above Central America in the 1960s, raining down death, terror, and political turmoil for decades.

Several years after Tom's dinner with the Vargas family, a thunderhead of frightening dimension and intent blossomed and rumbled over the narrow, rugged lands between the earth's great basins of water. At one in the morning on November 16, 1989, the professor Jesuits of the University of Central America in neighboring El Salvador, whose teaching of liberation theology had finally tripped the death wire in the minds of their enemies, were all hustled out of their residence, forced to lie face down on the damp grass of the *jardín*, and shot. The executioners had been thorough, completing their work by killing the community's cook and her daughter and an elderly Salvadoran Jesuit of little concern to them.

The Jesuit communities of the region were on the phone that entire evening, rising in stupor to ascertain facts about the deaths, to check if other communities had been attacked, to contact the remote brothers and alert them of danger. Prayers rose immediately, quiet prayers of disbelief, loud prayers of denunciation, tearful prayers for friends. Eyes surveyed the entire landscape, peering out windows and doors, memorizing the profiles of trees. Ears listened to every noise with the concentration of a small, hairy mammal in the Jurassic jungle. Souls struggled with the meaning of sudden, brutal death, of a loaded gun pointed to the back of the head, cringing at the ring of the shot and the thud of metal crashing past bone into the soft brilliance of brain tissue.

Tom was numb for the rest of that evening, neither praying or speaking. He sat on the sole wooden chair in his room, senseless and unaware of discomfort. He felt his beard turn gray. The next day he had a phone call from David.

"You're coming home, aren't you?" David asked, the first words out of his mouth.

"No," Tom said after a second's hesitation. He had considered the option. Already Sergio Vargas had begun to scoff at him. He'd seen hatred in Sergio's eyes and the disdain of a self-satisfied young man, a warrior of his caste.

"Why not?" David's question burst across the line. "How am I supposed to relax knowing that some band of—*banditos* are roaming around knocking off Jesuits? I don't have that tranquil a personality, you may recall."

Tom started to laugh. Brief, relaxing. His sense of isolation dissipated. He stretched his back for the first time, working out the knots from his evening's stiff meditations.

"I'm going to wait and see," Tom said.

"Waiting is all right if you're pregnant! Wait nine months, have a baby. Waiting is not all right if the *locos* of the world are training the sights of their CIA-supplied weaponry on you. This requires action!"

Mark called an hour later. "What's the situation in Guatemala?"

"It's different, yet it's the same. There haven't been any threats. The government is posturing about civil unrest and vigilantism, declaring they won't have it in their orderly country. Anyway, none of the great Jesuit orators or liberationists are here in Guatemala. They were in El Salvador." Tom's voice was limp. He knew, as he spoke those words, that a hole now existed. The front line of the war against injustice had been battered. Others needed to take up the empty positions.

"So, you're just going to keep a low profile, huh?" Mark asked.

Tom said nothing. Mark asked again, "Isn't that right?"

Tom exhaled, pulling up his soul into his mouth, "I can't be silent."

Once Tom began writing and speaking on land reform and community-oriented development theories, working with the radical economists at the public University of San Carlos, the intellectual greenhouse of Guatemalan revolution, the invitations to the homes of his students dried up. Once he began to preach about a justice that questioned the great disparity of wealth in Guatemala, he became one of the lightning rods of the left. His words buzzed with a power that could illuminate and ignite.

"And when we speak His name we hear ringing in the air the word 'Justice.' Justice is my rod! Justice is my strength! Justice will roll down from the mountains like a great and terrifying flood, cleansing all before it."

Tom echoed the words of prophets. The words filled him the way ocean air fills the masts of great ships. He struggled to keep his course as the wind pushed him forward. He stood tall and imagined he preached before a throng of believers, as had Martin Luther King Jr. in Washington. In contrast, in reality, his congregations were often small and wary. Some people would leave as he began to speak, fearful of where it might lead, perhaps embarrassed for the awkward gringo who seemed overcome by another spirit.

"Are we not shimmering images of our Almighty Father? Are we not His servants? Has He not made this truth clear enough to us?"

Tom had learned to use his height. He could stand and be seen everywhere in all the churches that invited him. He would walk into the congregation, the sacred robes billowing as he strode out.

"Who is sick? Attend him."

He would look into the eyes of individuals, the eyes of the weathered peasant woman in the black *rebozo*, the eyes of the wealthy matron in her fine, yellow silk. Sometimes into the steely eyes of single men sitting in the back pew.

"Who is hungry? Feed him. Who is captive? Release him. Who is without? Give to him."

Tom would open his raised hands and clasp them shut: "How pale our need to possess!"

He would stretch out his arms and gather them to him: "How pale our righteous theories of accumulation!"

He would open his arms to the heavens: "How pale our proud lifestyles in comparison with the crimson brilliance of these commandments of justice and freedom!"

When the threat was delivered to the Jesuit community of Guatemala in 1991, Tom was still struggling to make sense of the red robes of martyrdom. Over the last years he'd seen them handed out like dime store costumes at Halloween, dressing up a parade of blood-drenched ghouls. Again people questioned whether he should stay.

"Tom, do you realize what staying means?" asked Jim Meeker, a Jesuit friend of his working in Nicaragua who phoned every month. "It means you may be killed. Are you ready for that?"

"How do you get ready for that?" Tom asked with a querulous brevity. He'd asked himself the same question many times. In response, he readily conjured up pain and the petty details of death.

First he recalled Raúl Ixchan, a 20 year old *ladino*. Raúl had helped teach catechism at the school near the *Finca Gutierrez*, the biggest cattle farm in the province. Unfortunately Raúl had heard too much about the dignity of the poor from people such as Tom and had taught as much to the children of the *finca's* laborers. He had organized a group of laborers to demand better treatment from the *patrón*, more rest during the day, fresh water in the fields, the right to gather firewood for free—and for the *patrón* to leave their women alone.

They found Raúl one Monday morning lying in a ditch at the entrance to the *finca*. His throat had been cut through—before they chopped off Raúl's hands and feet, Tom hoped. There had been no warning for Raúl. Rather, his corpse was the warning for others. One word was carved on his naked torso: *Cuidado. Careful.*

"You must see it all around you in Guatemala," Jim said, "just as we've seen the face of death in the *contra* war. You know the way death looks. You've seen the disfigurement and the marks of torture, the mouths frozen in the form of their final scream. You know death means the end. Those bodies never rise again, those friends never speak again, those souls are gone from you. I'm not really sure that it's much of a contribution—being killed, that is."

"I don't think fleeing is much of a contribution," Tom answered, his words flashing his anger. He'd become frustrated by the culture of self-destruction that perpetuated itself in Guatemala. He held onto the black phone receiver with a grip meant to crush. "That's why I'm staying. It's my vows, my commitment to preaching this truth about justice. I will not break that commitment." Tom spat out the word that both ravaged and exhilarated his soul: commitment. "But I'm afraid, Jim, I will not deny that. I'm afraid. Sometimes it boils my blood." Pausing, "But I see no alternative to staying."

Tom's superior suggested he consider obeying the UDA command to leave the country.

"Tomás, I really think you should leave Guatemala, at least for some time, until things settle down here, until there is a peace," said the soft-spoken university rector Father Alfonso Espinoza as the two strolled through the ramped gallery of the university's art department, admiring the glazed figures of tropical birds and jumping, nearly dancing deer found on the pots and vases of the most recent class.

"Things are still bad here," Father Espinoza said as he reached up to touch Tom's arm. "People have lost respect, simple human respect. Old customs, old boundaries, old restraints are gone. You should go."

"I cannot leave," Tom said, stopping to look at the slight old man. He raised both hands the way David would when he got beyond frustration. "What would that say to the students? What would they learn from that act? That Christians need to watch out only for themselves?"

"No, Tomás, that is not what they would learn." Father Espinoza shook a patrician finger at Tom. "They would learn that even Jesuits make sensible decisions, decisions based on the greater good. It is a simple calculation. You can live to do good."

"It is a wrong calculus!" Tom planted his feet on the floor, grounding himself. "Every week we read of more dead. The death toll is unending. Should we Jesuits be exempted? Not if we want to be a part of the equation. This blood bath is caused by a—," Tom stretched out his right hand the way someone would grab hold of a moth that fluttered by, "—a cabal straining to maintain an unjust system that allows the few to tyrannize the many. I can't remain quiet about this!" He pointed the finger of his still-clasped hand at the center of his chest. "I know what it does to people I care about, the people of the slums, the people of the *fincas*. If I were to remain quiet, I could no longer look into their eyes."

"You are not a citizen. You can be forced to leave," Father Espinoza said as he turned to move on, his authority quiet but clear.

"Then I'll become a citizen!" Tom answered. His right hand continued to crush its contents. It held no moth, no word, no idea. It held anger. It was the anger of a man battered by a storm, by an act of God. It was an anger at existence, a subterranean anger laid out along fault lines, an anger strong enough to scatter continents. It was an anger beyond the details of personality, not faceless exactly but composed with the details of too many faces, the ruthlessness of too many contemptuous acts.

Father Espinoza sighed and shook his head, looking down at the shiny terrazzo floor. His eyelids seemed to droop with weariness. His soft, white hair lay dull and formless across his fine forehead. "You must realize, Tomás, that you are seen as the worst of us. Your constant writing on land redistribution—your phrase 'amnesty not amnesia'—you don't let up . . ." He looked up over his glasses to stare into Tom's eyes. "You have become the clearest target. By teaching here, people say you are polluting the children of Guatemala's ruling class. And they will not stand for it."

One morning after the threat, the students discovered a crude sketch on the front wall of Building L. It was a stick figure. The head had been severed and was rolling off into the air. Atop this dislocated skull shot a blaze of red. Some thought it was the result of a scalping. That's what the newspapers said. But the members of the University community knew better. It was the hair of *el rojo alto*, the tall redhead.

Tom had an hour free between his morning classes and regularly spent it walking the edge of the campus, checking over his shoulders several times to be sure that no one was following him as he made his way. He needed to pray rather than shuffle a few more papers and charts past his critical eyes or spend a few more minutes with some importunate student.

During that hour, Tom would finally end up alone at his favorite spot, out past the playing fields, at a stand of three wind-shaped fig trees. His morning break was sacred time for Tom. It was his hour to walk. It was also his time for *examen*, the twice daily duty of every Jesuit to measure his progress on the road to perfection. A time to grapple with the spirits of the day. A time to remember his goal.

As he stood thinking and praying, Tom marveled at the pleasure of the wind on a warm day and the strong, semisweet scent of the eucalyptus trees, which wafted in the breeze, and the rugged beauty of the rain-etched ravines, *barrancas*, which added texture to the campus lushness that surrounded him. A storm had swept over the scene an hour earlier, freshening the color and intensifying the full-headed, dirt-rich smells. It was one of the two rainy months in *Guate*, as the locals referred to their capital city. He looked out toward the Río Contreras and imagined it swollen with new water, carving its bed deeper into the soil. But soon the *verano* would begin, the warmest and driest months in the western highlands of Guatemala, the time the rest of the northern hemisphere termed fall and winter.

Sometimes, when Tom's thoughts would drift from the rigors of the examination of conscience, which was more and more frequent during this period of torment, he would look out over the vista of the countryside to the south of Guatemala City and think of Jesus tempted on the cliff. What would Tom give to possess all this? Tom pictured in his mind the great beauty of that complex country, that vortex of history where two ancient strands of humanity had met and swirled about and still continued to dance that circular masquerade of conflicting cultures.

He saw in his mind the black sandy beaches of the Pacific coast with its flights of pelicans patrolling their warm and languid paradise, and the slow, determined movement of the indigenous peoples of the highlands, wrapped in the distinctive *traje* of their villages, rising early in the morning to work their own cornfields before heading off to work in the fields of the *patrones*, often times greeting the fog as it huddled about in predawn pools among the pine trees of the mountains and over the terraced, angled fields. He saw, too, the luxurious carpets of coffee beans laid out after the harvest, their mass dazzling in the sunlight. And lastly he saw the rows of low, wooden platforms covered with flickering candles and strewn with multicolored rose petals in the murky and incense-drenched darkness of the Church of SantoTomás in Chichicastenango, enacting a haunting scene of piety long gone from the sacred places of the cosmopolitan West.

This question posed by Satan to the Son of God was also an old question for Tom, one with an equally worn answer. A minute after he had contemplated his response, he would smile with the bliss of a poet taken up in the ecstasy of a moment's awareness. For Tom it was a moment that visited with the regularity of a trusted friend. It arrived, acknowledged him, then left. And afterward Tom would look down at his scuffed black shoes and walk on.

Every day Tom answered the same question the devil had posed to Jesus himself, every day answering it with the same answer. He would give up nothing to possess this world. *Vade retro Satanas.* Get thee behind me, Satan. Tom's desire was for something much grander, yet something more elusive. Something more akin to love.

Tom was thinking of love as the path he trod descended into a eucalyptus grove, a mottled haven. He was thinking of Guadalupe. Giving up his relationship with Guadalupe was a sacrifice he had made for his vocation, which had become a holy grail into which he poured himself. Yet Tom could luxuriate in the memory of what he'd given up.

Tom's decision to remain a Jesuit was, for him, a mark of hope, a hope in the power of God to transform pain into ecstasy, human despair into human bliss. Until the threat and his choice to remain in Guatemala, Tom's sacrifice of a life with Guadalupe had been the hardest decision he'd ever made. Rather than a turning away from love, he'd seen it as an opening to love.

In some manner, Tom's experience with Guadalupe got entangled into his very love for Jesus, amplifying his ability to care as Jesus did for all humanity. Somehow his rededication to his Jesuit vocation and his priesthood did not diminish his love for Guadalupe, so much so that Guadalupe often found her way into his prayer. Indeed, her young, alluring face was still on his mind when his eyes first noticed the new shapes amid the shadows, the shapes of three men standing straight among the dappled trees. Then he noticed their masked faces—and then their guns.

Tertianship, 1991

CHAPTER ELEVEN

We are like spiders. Yet unlike them, we are both the spinners and that which is spun. Pay attention, my brothers, to the substances you choose for your web."

Notes from the last retreat Father Hugo Beltrán y Lanzarote ever directed, this one to the tertian class of 1951 on Good Friday at the Jesuit community in Varanasi, India, the site of his exile from Rome. These notes were sent to the General in Rome by one of the tertians accompanied by a letter containing other unusual and idiosyncratic comments made by the long-haired Spaniard.

The news flew north minutes after Father Espinoza opened the ransom note. He had awakened from a brief siesta after a midday dinner of chorizo and beans and arrived at his office before his secretary and her spinster's afternoon cheer. The note lay flat on the floor, slipped halfway under the office's oak double door. His heart began to race as he carefully stepped over the folded sheet and turned to pick it up. No one stuffed messages for the rector of Landívar University under a door. It was un-Guatemalan, furtive, informal.

The rector's elegant and assured hands trembled as he felt the notepaper, its texture coarse, thick as parchment. The palsy in his hands intensified as he unfolded the note and read the words. Their meaning was unshaded, a blue cloudless sky: the UDA demanded two million dollars within two weeks, or Father Burns was a cadaver.

Mark first heard the news from his friend Gloria Eberhardt, director of the Washington Office on Central America, a human right's advocacy organization on Capitol Hill whose Central American network stretched wider and deeper into the landscape of that bloodied isthmus than the U.S. government's web of agents and electronic devices.

It was nearly five o'clock in Washington on a golden Friday afternoon in September. Mark was alone in Senator Brandon's office, probably a solo figure in the entire Dirksen Senate Office Building. He'd unbuttoned the collar of his well-starched white shirt and loosened the perfect knot of his favorite maroon tie, the one crested with Harvard Law. He sat with both feet digging into the navy blue, inch-thick carpet, his elbows resting on his teacher's desk, an oddment he had procured in a Hagerstown antique store. The weathered desk reminded him of his regency days and his last year at Marquette High as director of students, a position that had marked him for quick elevation within the institutions of the Society. "I'd be a university president by now," he'd been thinking of recent, "if I'd stayed in the Society." He was no longer satisfied with his job as Senator Brandon's marine sergeant, barking orders and taking beachheads.

That Friday Mark was checking his list of weekend tasks one more time, blocking out the policy issues and snippets of conversation that usually kept his mind busy with policy analyses and vote scenarios.

The list was short. Two items: mow lawn; lunch with Peter McLaughlin, Hennepin County commissioner. Too few distractions, he thought. Too much time with family. An acrid sweat moved up his body and gathered under his arms.

"I can't put it off," he mumbled. Over the last several weeks he'd been studying it as intensely as he'd studied the development, or near development, of the cardiac system after they'd received the first of Charley's diagnoses, or "conjurings" as he'd come to call them. At least all that doctor gibberish had been new to him then: gap junctions, connexion diversity, antipeptide antibodies. Most of it turned out to be bullshit. "Pure science." Useless as a Disney tale.

But Charley was still alive, physically limited but alive.

Anyway, it wasn't really about Charley, was it? Anymore. Charley's death wasn't going to be the answer, it didn't seem. The answer was about her. It was about him. That's what he was studying. And now . . . God, he'd made the one mistake he said he'd never make. He'd become what he said he'd never become.

The phone rang. Mark reached for it, but paused as he touched the receiver. He could off-load this call to the answering service, couldn't he? He thought of his father who worked every day of his seventy-nine years, busy from dawn to dusk on those 28,885 spinnings in the void. Folks in Minneapolis said his dad had worked himself to death. Mark knew differently. His father had worked for the exhilaration of it. Mark did, too. Except the exhilaration, and the solace it gave him, the protection, yeah— maybe it was an opiate, was getting thin, its chemical wizardry sputtering to an end.

He picked up the black phone. Her emotion made him rise to attention. Its beat, in her voice, half anger, half fear, stopped his heart. What was this call about?

"Mark, remember that friend of yours, the one in Guatemala."

"Tom Burns? Sure."

It was about Tom. Not the other thing.

"Something's happened. A kidnapping—today—this morning."

Gloria launched into the facts. Mark reached for a scratch pad to write them down. He wrote down her words into bulleted items, talking points.

She didn't have much, an outline: a ransom note, probably the UDA, a few hours ago, the Guatemalan government was already on the airwaves, denying any involvement, decrying the act.

Mark was concentrating on Gloria's message now. He shoved the other thing inward, back up as far as it would go.

But it wouldn't disappear, he knew. How could it? It kept staring at him, even when he began to cry. So unexpected.

"Mark, are you OK? Mark? Mark!"

He had no words. He'd stopped listening.

"I'm sorry, I'm sorry," Gloria said. "I can't talk now, I'm late for that dinner at the Honduran Embassy. Senator Gunderson'll be there. I've gotta go, I'm sorry!"

Gloria hung up.

Mark let the receiver drop onto the desk. He slumped back into his chair and sobbed, sobbed as stomach-hard as after Charley's first operation, the first despair. Nurses had huddled around him then. "We're not sure he'll make it." The beautiful man in sorrow.

Time passed.

Then he began to speak, to say words: "Not Tom. Not Tom. Not Tom." He closed his eyes tight, closed his hands into fists. The tears had stopped. He tensed every muscle, held his body until he was a balloon near bursting. At least he could feel himself that way—alive in the office.

He started to see images. Their first day. The three of them. August, a morning, bright and hot. The basement, musty, half-light filtering in through its windows, "mystical and kind," David had described it their last day in the novitiate. David was right.

Tom at his desk. That square writing surface was his choir stall, his connection point, his trysting place. Mark would come home from handball at the Saint Paul Sem gym. Tom would be at his desk, Chardin or Merton open in front of him, a candle lit, a highlighter in one hand. Sometimes Tom wouldn't look up, wouldn't know that Mark had poked his head in. He'd be lost to his thoughts. Were they just thoughts?

They'd had such good times there, the three of them. Laughing. Praying. Talking. Mark smiled and leaned back, relaxed a little, opened his fists, took a deep breath. He was happy to be back there.

Manualia days were the best, with David playing his Streisand tapes and dusting as if he were La Babs herself, lip syncing, dancing, *Make Your Own Kind of Music, My Man*—with Tom bent over in laughter, stomping his feet, joy spurting out of him.

He was a good man, Tom. Their first semester he'd taken the eleven-to-seven shift at Regina Coeli nursing home. Mark always heard him go out.

The late shift. How'd Tom do it? Why'd he do it?

Then no more images. Surprised, Mark opened his eyes wider and took another deep breath. He coughed for a minute and wiped at his mouth.

He had to do something. He'd confirm Gloria's story. Call Coleman Schaeffer, State Department, Central American desk. He reached for his Rolodex.

"You've heard?" Coleman asked, always unflappable, but a little annoyed.

"I've got contacts." Mark could envision Coleman shuttering his eyes. "So what are we doing?"

"The Embassy's contacted President Kepler García. He assured them that the Guatemalan state security forces were looking into the matter with the greatest vigor."

"Vigor, huh."

"That's their word."

"What are the news agencies doing?"

"We've got a news conference in twenty minutes. This could be big." A pause. "Why are you calling?"

"We were Jesuits together, before I left," Mark said.

"Oh. Yeah, I remember hearing that you were once a priest or something like that."

"Not a priest, a Jesuit, they're not necessarily the same." Mark always felt compelled to explain that distinction. He hadn't made it all the way. "Anyway, Tom Burns is a friend of mine. So—please keep me informed on any developments. In fact, if I can help in any way, call on me."

Mark looked out his office window over toward the capitol. The sky around it was darkening into an imperial purple. "I know you aren't over-ly fond of Senator Brandon's views—on the contras or aid to El Salvador or the School of the Americas—but this is something different. It won't look good for the U.S. government. And all I want to say is that we—we want Tom Burns safely out of their hands. We have to free him first, then discuss the implications."

Mark clenched his teeth. His stomach, acid flashing up in warning, had already registered just how far out of bounds he'd gone. Mark reached for the TUMS bottle he kept next to the phone. But surely Senator Brandon could be persuaded to see the situation Mark's way, to understand his concern, his sense of priorities, Mark thought as he popped two tablets into his mouth.

"I understand what you're saying, Mark." Coleman sounded cautious. Mark hoped his statement hadn't gone too far. He'd learned to win his political fights with many small moves. "And I appreciate your offer to help. Believe me, we aren't going to be soft on these good-ol'-boys who think they can pick up any innocent American citizen and hold him for ransom. And don't jump to any conclusions about who they are. We don't have any solid information as of yet, it could be either side."

"Gloria said it was the UDA, and that's what the note said. You don't think it's them?"

"All I'm saying is that we don't know for sure who did it," Coleman said. His assertion sounded neutral enough. "When we know for sure, we'll make a statement on it."

"And what about the ransom? Will we talk?" Mark knew the official position: No dealing with hostage takers. It was the administration's unques-tioned policy. Still Mark asked, hoping for some different interpretation in Tom's case. Maybe because Tom was a priest. Maybe because covert admin-istration money had probably purchased the kidnappers' getaway car.

"You know the administration, they're hard line when it comes to nego-tiating with kidnappers. We don't pay ransoms. That doesn't mean we won't try to get this friend of yours released. Believe me. Now I've got to run."

For a few moments Mark sat unmoving. The static of the phone line filled his ear, but he didn't notice it. Slowly he lowered the receiver onto its nest, his hand resting on the phone piece as if a net, a pall, had been draped over him.

Mark sat in his cramped office, the door shut, his eyes studying the small black-and-white photo of three college-age men. The three men stood outside a wind-washed clapboard church in South Dakota. There were no trees. The landscape was bleached of color except for the lavender-topped ridges in the distance. The threesome, however, hugged each other and smiled at the camera as if they were spending time at a tropical resort surrounded by sandy beaches and a turquoise sea. Next to this picture stood a photo of Ann and Charley, a speedy snapshot taken after a day sailing on the Chesapeake Bay. They were flushed and happy, the adults crouching over their young son, Mark's right hand resting on Ann's shoulder and his left hand on Charley's. It had been one of their good days. Charley had been healthy all that summer.

Every day that past summer Mark would look at those pictures, holding them in his hands as if they were sacred objects. The photos had power. They opened portals into life, but Mark never stared too long.

He had to tell David about Tom. He reached him with his first call at David's home in Minneapolis. He skipped all the formalities.

"Have you heard?" Mark's voice was weak.

"Well—Hi, Mark. Heard what? I guess not."

"Tom's been kidnapped. Today. It'll be on the news soon."

"What?! Kidnapped? By whom? Does—the threat—is it them?"

"I think so. The UDA claimed responsibility. But there's hope, they're demanding a ransom."

"Oh, good, bags of silver."

"Blood money." Mark got up to pace about the room.

"We tried to get him to take a sabbatical, but he wouldn't budge."

"He didn't want to die, did he?" Mark asked. The question had burst into his brain. He waited for a response. "To be a martyr?"

"No, he didn't want to die," David said, "and at least it's people after him."

"What's that mean?"

"His killers have faces."

"Faces?"

"They're not viruses. People with faces hate him. It's better that way, less stupid."

"Oh, Jesus, David." Mark pulled at his collar. He didn't want to argue.

David talked too much about that disease. "Tom's been kidnapped, they've asked for a ransom."

"So they want a bag of money. Will they let him go or return him in the bag?"

Mark considered the image. He thought of the bodies he'd seen in hospitals, the flat forms on gurneys with linen draped over them.

"Is there anything you can do?" David asked, his voice even, "we can do?"

"I'm getting all the information I can. I'll ask Senator Brandon to make a few phone calls. And—I was hoping you might help out, too."

"How?"

"Dial up your old cronies on the Jesuit news network, find out how the Society is planning to respond, whether they would consider paying the ransom."

"Is that possible? The Society isn't that well off, despite rumors they own ten square blocks of downtown Buenos Aires. Wouldn't it set a bad precedent?"

"Would they rather have Tom martyred? After the murders in El Salvador? I thought even the conservatives found that grizzly."

"You can't be sure about Rome. There's probably some rotund cardinal doing a pirouette right now."

"That's the Vatican, but what about the Jesuit curia? And the current General, what's his name—Karl von Ehre. He's an anthropologist? I don't know anything about those guys anymore." A sadness filtered through Mark's words. "What are they like? Will they deal with the UDA?"

"You and I are both pretty ill-informed on that topic. I haven't been hanging around the novitiate hoping for scraps of news about the sacred band."

"I can't believe this happened to Tom," Mark said.

"I can. He was charged."

"What?"

"Charged, as if he were a battery. He owned topics. The poor and their plight were his."

"Well, maybe."

"I'm not saying he was a saint."

"None of us were saints."

"Except maybe Tom, he was the closest. He certainly sinned like a saint." David chuckled.

"Sinned like a saint?" Mark stood still, held his breath.

"I mean—his sins were uncluttered. Brief. Focused. Easy to forgive."

"He broke his vows by sleeping with Guadalupe. He slept with her for months!"

"It was love," David said, dragging out the word. "He was lonely, he fell in love. Love."

Mark was tugging on his ear. "I'm not sure I understand what you're saying—about saintly sin."

"That's OK," David said, laughing. "I'm not sure I understand, either. But I know there was something unsullied about Tom. He never smiled unless he was happy."

"You're talking as if he were dead."

Mark could hear David gasp.

"You're right," David said, "I'm talking as if he were dead. Do we all talk that way about each other?"

CHAPTER TWELVE

"It has all been reduced to images. A lifetime of experience is now a quilt of images. It lays upon me, and I upon it."

— Words of Hugo Beltrán y Lanzarote, S.J.,
recorded on his deathbed in Varanasi, India,
by Joseph Sriram Kumar, S.J., his last confessor.

David said goodbye to Mark and set immediately to his detective work, sitting at his cherry wood Ming scholar's desk with its Taoist meditative stone at his right. He concentrated on making a list of names, numbers, and questions, talking aloud about how best to approach each acquaintance, straining to block out images of that possible end scene. A scene so different from Randy's long death procession and final gasp.

But David had seen pictures. He had seen them at a church service during the Sandinista revolution, when he was a theologian struggling with the "C" vow, when his mind bent over with a desire to break, no, not break—to blast away that sanity-depriving vow.

The service, no wild, revolutionary gathering, was a somber Quaker-sponsored event in a neo-Gothic Episcopal church. David had hoped for something stormy, a fist-clenching service with red bandannas dripping with frustrations and angry screams. He had hoped to mingle his own spiritual turmoil with that political wail and let it explode through the saint-packed rows of stained-glass windows. Instead he sat amid tapers and quiet grief.

In the Church of St. James, ranks of elegant candles bathed the photos of the dead with their forgiving light. The pictures, reproductions as large as a fifth-grader in pumps, showed men laid out on roadways or in fields, stiff as wooden carvings, young men whose bodies were beginning to bloat, filling out their death clothes with a pitiable ripeness. Except for the contortions of rigor mortis, a distant viewer might have thought the men were sleeping.

When the image came into focus David shot out of his comfortable Minneapolis chair, frightened, trembling, as if a ghost's teasing finger had crossed along his shoulder and ruffled the short hair of his nape. He'd seen a corpse, yellowing and naked, abandoned.

The face, his glimpse of it, quick because he had looked away, the face was empty of life. So empty. Flesh without breath.

David had known the face, recognized it in an instant.

He had loved the face.

David swallowed a sob and closed his trembling mouth around it. He struggled to keep it from bursting out. He pounded his chest. He began to scream, and screamed until his throat was sore, screamed the chant they should've sung at that anti-Somoza prayer gathering: "You bastards! You bastards! You evil damn bastards!"

David was not ready to mourn for Tom, not that friend, not the friend from before the time of liberation, the sweet friend who knew how to ask for forgiveness.

David wanted his own bruises and beat the air with his fists. He began to kick. With the fury of a night-dwelling shadow boxer, with an anger his karate instructor had attempted to soothe out of him, he kicked his way twice around the desk.

Calming slowly, David wiped the sweat from his forehead and sat down again to flip through the old booklet he'd fetched from a dusty pile on a bottom shelf in his home office. It was a *Catalogus*, the official directory of his former province. The sentences, all Latin, were nothing but cryptic abbreviations: *Dir. exerc. spir. pro Prov., Orat pro Soc.* David was getting angry again. Tom might be dead! What kind of people had time to fiddle with antique, useless forms? Where was justice? Where were the demands of *this* age? He almost tore the book in half.

David turned to the back of the *Catalogus* to the section titled *In Provincia Marylandiae.* It listed all of the Wisconsin Province Jesuits living in Maryland. He would start by calling people he knew in Washington, D.C. "Jimmy, have you heard about Tom?"

"You know already? It's spreading like wildfire here in D.C. There's a prayer service at Georgetown, Dahlgren Chapel, tonight. The provincial will be there, maybe even Bishop Stanton, probably to note down the names of all attendees and send them to some Opus Dei watchdog. But how'd you hear?"

"I'm a free man in Minneapolis, not a prisoner in some Chinese bamboo cell. Besides, I still have friends with connections." David's eyes were rolling with impatience. "Anyway, what's the official line? Will anyone in the Society or the American hierarchy take any action, other than offering a few carefully worded prayers?"

"You've given up on prayer?"

David's eyebrows knit together. James L. Rafferty had entered the Jesuits as a young man with the stated purpose of becoming president of Georgetown University. He was now dean of students. Paunchy, balding, and squat, Father Rafferty could make nearly anyone his friend by dint of his good cheer and an often cheeky humor. But public piety had never been his style.

"Let's not get into that," David said. "You know what I mean. Is someone going to make contact with Tom's kidnappers? Could they pay the ransom?"

"I doubt the Society of Jesus will cough up any money. Wisconsin Province has no official relationship with the Central American province. Tom was there because he found work he wanted to do. I just can't envision Wisprov getting too involved, they wouldn't know what to do."

"As for Rome," Jimmy continued, "the current General is disinclined to touch anything that has the slightest scent of revolution attached to it." Jimmy warbled the word revolution.

"Remember how John Paul lectured Fernando Cardenal's brother Ernesto when they met on a Managua tarmac in 1983?" Jimmy asked. "Cardenal, dressed in his embroidered blouse, knelt to kiss the Pope's hand. John Paul took back his hand and waved his finger at Cardenal, telling him to regularize himself, which meant, we all guessed, putting a cassock back on and getting behind an altar. That's set the tone . . ."

"But what about Tom!" David said, breaking into Jimmy's monologue. "Tom's no revolutionary."

No response.

"He doesn't carry a gun and ambush people," David said.

"There are rumors," Jimmy whispered.

"Rumors?"

"Clearly he sympathized with the rebels. They say he had contact with them. Whether he helped in any way, nobody knows."

"Innuendo! I've never heard any of this, Tom never said anything."

"True, the rumors are recent, but they're still there. And he'd become the wrong kind of thinker. He published a good dozen articles on Liberation Theology."

David was straining to understand Jimmy's words. He was starting to lose patience. He began to grind his molars. How important could this stuff be?

"Tom's ideas were even cited in a *L'Osservatore Romano* article identifying the extremes of Liberation Theology. And even worse, a year ago he gave a seminar in Mexico City in which, responding to a question, he openly expressed doubts about the Vatican's stance on women's ordination. It was at a Maryknoll Conference on Liberation Theology . . ."

"Fine, so he's not a poster boy for Polish Catholicism! He's a priest, a good priest and a good Jesuit!" David wanted to slam the phone down. "Are you saying the General won't do anything?"

Jimmy sighed. He became matter of fact. "He'll do something. He'll probably negotiate. We bureaucrats always negotiate. But he won't act until he gets the facts."

"And how long will that take?"

"Not long. I'm sure the process has already started."

By ten that night David's hope of quickly penetrating the mind of the Society was as dim as a Minnesota winter's night sky. None of his friends had access to the inner circles of Rome, but they all said the same thing would happen. The General would send a delegate, probably one of the regional assistants, calm, sensible men.

Late in the evening David called Mark to see what developments there were in secular Washington. The news was mixed. Mark had been able to contact Senator Brandon, who was livid about the incident. There would be speeches in the Senate on Monday and perhaps a special investigation. Those who had long fought against the free flow of arms to the military regimes of Central America hoped to make this a major episode. It had the drama, the smell of innocence abused that made Americans snort with outrage.

Unfortunately, Mark explained, few of the politicos mobilizing these efforts had yet to commit themselves, unswervingly, to freeing Tom.

"He's become fodder for the policy makers," Mark said. "That's what happens. You get caught up in global intrigue, then the policies become more important than you. In one sense, Tom's already played his role."

"So no one really cares about Tom?" David's heart sank low, as deep as when he first realized there'd be no cure for AIDS, no cure in time to save Randy. He wanted to lie flat out on the floor.

Mark said nothing.

"If he's still alive," David said, "we've got to save him." David didn't know what that meant. Was it mere bravado? Could the two of them figure something out? He could always pay the ransom. It was little more than a trifle.

"It's not that people don't care," Mark said. David heard a lecturer's voice, a voice steady in its explanations, a voice so different from the afternoon voice.

"There are things at stake here," Mark continued. "There's a movement toward reconciliation between the warring factions in Guatemala. Tom's kidnapping could be a test of the resolve of the guerrillas to end this war. No one wants to upset that momentum."

"So Tom might be sacrificed because of some greater good? Is that what you're telling me?"

"I hate it, too, but—Tom's situation has implications for US–Guatemala relations, for stability in Central America." David could hear Mark's deep breath, his gasping for air as if he were struggling against a compressing wave. "This kidnapping isn't just about Tom. That's the world we live in."

"That's the world YOU live in."

"And what does that mean?"

"I mean . . . where's the justice in this? Where's the outrage? Tell me how our government can look the other way!"

"It's not looking the other way. The government's looking. It's just not going to look so hard that it causes worse things to happen. But there'll be complaints. And Tom's situation will impact our foreign policy, that's for sure."

"That's not what I want!" David yelled. "I want Tom free! Someone's got to get him out of there, isn't that clear?"

"It's clear to me, but I don't know how. I don't know how. Do you know how? Really?"

Mark and David soon hung up, promising to speak in the morning.

David tried to sleep that night but rose every half hour. About two-thirty he finally gave in and dug through a basement closet for a shoebox stuffed with old Jesuit photos, little colored squares that only memory made vital. At dawn, David began to read his Jesuit diaries.

The fresh scent of a pine forest sifted in with the cold, slightly moist air. The atmosphere started to revive him.

Tom remained in the fetal position his captors had forced him into for easy transport. His eyes were useless because of the oil-stained bandanna pulled tightly over them. He had been warned not to take it off. He meant to obey.

Tom figured it was evening. Even the bandanna-imposed darkness had deepened by several degrees. He strained to factor time into what had happened to him. He calculated that his captors had lugged him out of their vehicle into some structure about an hour ago. He had expected something to happen right away, but nothing did. They left him alone. But how long since his kidnapping that morning? It'd been half a day of driving and stopping, driving and stopping along Guatemala's rough roadways. Maybe he'd been a captive for ten hours total. That sounded right.

Tom surmised he was somewhere in the highlands. Would he be able to sleep if the night got too cold? He was starting to tire again. His mind floundered. He tried to stay concentrated on the sounds around him, alert to the footsteps outside the hut, footsteps that could come too near too quickly. Yes, it must be a *choza*, he thought. A peasant hut. Maybe on a plantation. There was a smell of smoke oozing from the packed-dirt floor. There was a smell of smoke everywhere, the scent of some distant disaster.

CHAPTER THIRTEEN

Christ's suffering on the cross was not a simple, cleansing sacrifice, a servant's scrubbing of accumulated stains. It was an invitation, transformed from a passing moment in single-star time into a sustaining event in cosmic time by his pain and by his doubt, by his love and by his submission. By being who he was.

Christ's crucifixion was an anointing of this absurdity we call history. Even deity, caught up in history, does not destroy it. Deity transforms it.

So what was the moment of Christ's death? A trumpet call. An invitation for us to step forward into the shadows, beyond knowledge and judgment, beyond law and fulfillment, beyond time and matter, walking toward the eternal word, whose utterance is life itself.

Christ's death was the rending of the temple veil, a momentary glimpse at the ways of divinity, a passageway to freedom, an opening, an escape, an enlightenment, a place to start. Let us start.

The most scandalous sentiments found in the famous sermon delivered by Hugo Beltrán y Lanzarote, S.J., on the Feast of Corpus Christi at the Church of St. Ignatius in Rome, 1950.

Father Eger hurried from his small, cluttered room on the third floor of the Renaissance palace that several centuries previously had been converted into the Jesuit residence of the Collegio Bellarmino, across the Tiber to the General's residence, a sturdy, large villa nestled in the shadow of the Vatican. Father Eger was lucky. A 64 bus was rolling to a halt where the via del Corso emptied out alongside the Gesu. He jogged to catch it, hesitating only briefly before wedging himself into its standing mass. The 64 was a notorious transport, full of pickpockets and packed so tightly that the faithful regularly traipsed from the bus's steps to the Gesu confessionals to shrive themselves of their lusty encounters with the bodies of fellow passengers. Father Eger, statuesque in his simple Jesuit soutane and with a mild annoyance radiating in his light-blue eyes, was left alone that ride. He arrived at the Jesuit Curia ten minutes after his summons.

Brother porter, Frater Damiano, greeted the aging archivist in his toothless Neapolitan drawl and mumbled for Father Eger to go immediately to the General's office. There, behind a long and incongruously narrow walnut desk, sat the gray-headed German who was current General of the Society of Jesus.

Father Eger noted how tired the General seemed that morning, his shoulders bent down, his complexion as yellow as the volumes of paper *bullae* collected over several centuries and stacked on the shelves behind him. The hulk of Father General's cassock-covered body blended into the aged woodwork, a cheap oak that looked as if it had been roughly hewn when Ignatius still limped the earth.

Everyone, from Methodist news correspondents to the whores of Largo Argentina, knew that this General had been fighting a battle against the conservative forces now ruling the Vatican, a battle to keep the Society free from papal—or more precisely curial—intervention, perhaps to keep the Society alive, to keep its spirit alive. This morning Father General's bruin's body slumped over its paperwork with the exhaustion of a circus animal tired of drummy dance steps and the constriction of night time chains.

"*Buon giorno, Giuseppe*," General von Ehre said, slowly, hefting his 230 pounds of bread and pasta weight, both hands firmly gripping the chair's wide arms as he rose to greet his old chum. "Thank you for coming so quickly," he said, nodding curtly, switching to English as he plumped back into the chair, coughing his morning, ten-cigarettes-a-day cough.

Father Eger hardly noticed the switch to English. That island language, brewed from the mutterings of marauding Europeans, was their common tongue. Father Eger spoke perfect German, of course. Yet as a seventy-seven year old Hungarian, Father Eger's throat flinched from a metallic bitterness when speaking the tongue of the Central European tribe which had meddled so long, and so often, and with so much letting of blood, in Hungarian affairs—and in his own life. And Father General von Ehre, his old friend, ever the analyst of social patterns, had learned as a young man that fighting certain culture wars was useless. Long ago, after months of making do with the stilted Latin of Jesuit seminaries, they both agreed to use English for conversation. It was a polite language, well-known to both of them, the tool of quaint, mercantile foreigners, useful for conveying simple thoughts.

They had first met at Berchmannskolleg in Pullach, Bavaria, a recently-established and soon esteemed school of philosophical training, attended mainly by Jesuit scholastics. Eger, a Hungarian from a foreign province, was the prize student of the Berchmannskolleg class of 1937. He had quickly learned Scotus by heart and quoted from the *Opus Oxoniense* extensively, irritatingly to the Thomists of the faculty. Von Ehre, observant of the Hungarian, of his sureness, his deep feelings, his ability to annoy the *magistri* with his questions, maneuvered to become Eger's friend. They both loved taking hikes in the mountains and discussing, in that limpid silence, the current arc of the Hegelian swing as their hiking staffs made sharp holes in the alpine skree and their questions made openings in the elasticity of heart.

The war and dramatically different regency assignments split the two scholastics and interrupted a dialogue that was drawing them daily into spiritual intimacy.

Von Ehre spent the war in Africa, teaching at the Jesuit college in

Leopoldville alongside the Belgian Jesuits, persistently making forays into the vast rain forest to amplify his studies of tribal initiation rites, finally publishing a volume on the use of abstinence in these rites, a necessary symbol of control, he argued, much to the joy of the Congregation of the Faith, whose Jesuit members took note of him and mentioned his wisdom to others.

Eger had been less fortunate and much less favored during the mid-century years of world conflict.

The German superiors at Berchmannskolleg had convinced his Hungarian superiors that Eger might acquire a greater social discipline by spending a few years in Prussia.

The Canisius-Kolleg *gymnasium* in Berlin was twelve years old. The Society was rebuilding its presence in Germany since their expulsion in the 1870s. Eger would be a valuable addition to the faculty. The *gymnasium* needed a mathematician. Eger knew Leibnitz and Pascal. The Prussians promised to pay a hefty fee for his services, and the Hungarians acquiesced.

Although deeply read in German literature, Eger stood out as different, quirky, both at the Kolleg and within the community. His spiritual father shook his head, wondering why his reticent spiritual child was impervious to the small gestures of Prussian contempt he recounted in their sessions. He wondered whether Eger's indifference to these acts was a gift from God or an internal dullness. The Berchmannskolleg superiors had warned that Eger could be a trouble maker. Yet his Berlin confessor was finding, poking weekly, no burning embers. Eger's soul was not pig-iron in the cauldron, suspected the confessor. He was already a narrow rod of steel, fighting off bending force-waves.

When the Nazis shut down Canisius-Kolleg in 1940, Eger's local superiors decided to keep him in Germany. Returning him to Hungary seemed too perilous. Some bureaucrat would surely ask the wrong question, and Eger, honest when addressed directly, would speak his mind. He could get them all in trouble, unproductive trouble.

So Eger's name, along with the names of the three hundred and eighty German Jesuits remaining in the Reich, was inscribed in the Gestapo's Jesuit registry, a method for keeping track of that dangerous papal force, which action proved mostly unnecessary.

Eger spent his time in war-proud Berlin tending to the poor and continuing to meet with a few former students, the other odd ones, who had managed to find positions in Berlin, mostly in the large bureaucracy the Nazis created to govern their conquered lands. Without discussing it with his Prussian superiors, Eger had decided the Fuhrer's *krieg* was unjust. A number of his former students, after several years, came to the same conclusion. Ever inventive, he helped the young men resist, suggesting how they might delay supplies to the front, place an order for the wrong caliber of munition, misplace confidential files of enemies of the state.

But one of Eger's superiors, the one who argued loudest for keeping him confined in Berlin, was increasingly suspicious, fearful. Late in '43, as the war seemed endless and political madness intensified, Father Minister, snooping in Eger's room, discovered a fragment of the Kreisau constitution, a blueprint for a post-Hitler Germany. "You have this from Father Delp, no? How?" The man was shaking. The capillaries of his face had flooded with blood. "How could you bring this into our house?"

Eger said nothing. He was already an ascetic of silence.

"You know Count von Moltke has been imprisoned?" Father Minister could barely get the words out. He spoke as if his world were ending, as if the henchman were behind him, ready to lift him up at the shoulders and hoist him onto the hook.

Eger didn't respond.

"Have you forgotten your German!?!" Father Minister screamed. "Answer me!"

Eger shook his head.

The soft-bellied Prussian crumpled the dangerous papers in both hands and hurried to the kitchen to burn them. He froze for a moment at Eger's door, staring back at the tall scholastic, and ordered Eger to do penance with the discipline every night until Epiphany, "twice on Christmas Eve."

In May of '44 Eger was arrested and charged with spreading "defeatism," the common charge leveled against certain ministers and priests and unreformed intellectuals. Who had turned him in? One of his small flock? Another Jesuit? He never found out. Nor did he pursue the question, even after the war.

Yet that act of betrayal horrified the young scholastic, more than its ramifications, and unsettled him for decades.

Eger spent the final year of the war locked in a prison in Berlin, a small neighborhood jail near the SS office on Prinz-Albrecht Street. His superiors were never informed why he was kept there. Eger quickly turned into an object of ridicule for the prison guards. Not only was he Hungarian, beak-nosed and gawky, but on occasion he spoke with the slightest stutter.

When the Russians took the prison they assumed at first that he was an ordinary criminal, maybe a homosexual for he was not a communist and was refined in his speech. They kept him locked up, starving him along with the others.

When his new jailers found out he was a religious, the commander ordered him executed on the spot. Captain Groshenko was doing his own cleansing of the country, purging those individuals who would become obstacles to the new workers' state which all the Russian leaders were envisioning.

Only the insistent pleas of one of the Russian prison guards, himself the son of an Orthodox priest, saved Eger. Rifles had been shouldered. Eger was near the wall. The scene was totally informal, people wandering in and out of the area as if they were on the set of a play during a break in practice. There had been no trial. Groshenko had been reviewing cases. "Kill this one. Kill the priests."

Eger understood the words. Common Slavic words, part of the argot of Eastern Europe. The command itself was unemotional, straightforward. The memory of those words, uttered with the casualness of an order placed at a counter: "two coffees, please," the memory of the stillness of his heart as he stood next to the cracked ochre wall—the short guard with the distant eyes of the steppes and a broken-bulb nose calmly leading him to a spot in the middle of the wall and turning him around, delicately, to face the five-member troop, of the indifference of time, of the worn red tiles in the courtyard the captain had used for both his courtroom and his execution ground, looking at those tiles, wondering why those sturdy squares should figure into his last thoughts, of the worldliness of those thoughts, so taken up as he was in the external details, of the Russian guard's gentle pleading—all those memories zigzagged through Eger's being for years afterward, wakening him at night, piercing into his meditations.

Since Berchmannskolleg, Joszef and Karl had not seen each other until they met in their first class on Sacramental Theology at the Gregorian in Rome. Their teacher was an antique Castilian, Hugo Beltrán y Lanzarote, who had just returned from Japan where he spent his days at the Jesuit community in Nagatsuka, a suburb of Hiroshima. Tired and dazed from the atomic destruction of that city, Father Beltrán had become lost in an overwhelming lethargy, hobbling through the community's small garden, as was his wont, no longer stopping to smell a chrysanthemum bloom or feel the cool texture of a bamboo leaf, dazed—as if the bomb had exploded inside him, leveling the structures of everyday life. His superiors sent him to Rome, hoping travel back to Europe would rekindle some of his earlier enthusiasm for life. Father Beltrán could not return to his native Spain and its spirit-swept plateau. Quail-hunting Franco still maintained Father Beltrán's aristocratic name on a list of the truly hated, for Father Beltrán, once a polite teacher of seminarians at Comillas in Madrid had read *Rerum Novarum* too intensely and enmeshed himself with the miners' union up in Asturias, one of the first centers attacked by the fascist generals in 1936. As soon as its initial skirmishes devolved into a vicious civil war, Father Beltrán's provincial, Father Rivera, decided this aging worker priest, this murmurer of modern thought, this thorn in his side, needed to leave the country.

Father Rivera wanted him out of Spain for many reasons: Father Beltrán was working for the wrong side, he was an embarrassment to his class, he brought infamy to the Society. And the Republicans had already begun to round up and shoot priests. The lines in this war were clearly drawn.

Father Rivera scribbled an angry note and dispatched it late in September 1936. The note ordered Father Beltrán to return to provincial headquarters in Madrid and prepare for mission to mosquito-infested Honduras.

Father Beltrán never received the note. He and several older UGT labor leaders had made it to bayside Bilbao, driving with couriers when in the country, sneaking at night through towns and cities. They crossed in a fishing boat to Bayonne, stayed two nights in the newly established UGT safe house and dispersed. Father Beltrán headed to Rome, as Basque Ignatius once had, to the city of holiness.

The Roman superiors, years into their own fascist melodrama, didn't know what to do with the rebellious Castilian, didn't want him disturbing the social equilibrium of the eternal city. They wouldn't send him back to war-torn Iberia, but they couldn't let him take root in Italian political soil. He'd have to spend his days in the country, at the Villa Mandragone in Frascati, perhaps hearing confessions and visiting the deathbed sick, but constantly monitored.

Father Beltrán was forty-eight hours away from a train ride to his pastoral jail when the recently elevated Cardinal Deacon and one-time Jesuit visitor to Spain, Paolo Boello, intervened. Cardinal Boello had heard the case of the fascist-fleeing Spaniard from a former organizer of Italian labor as they stood piously in the shade of Bernini's piazza columns. The cardinal himself, ever since his elevation above the simple ranks of ordinary priests to the ruling body of the church, an extraordinary and unusual honor for a Jesuit, was suffering from a turbulent rumbling in his stomach regarding all fascist regimes. He knew the old Spaniard would rot in Frascati. He knew that type of Jesuit. He knew that agitating son of Ignatius deserved better. So Cardinal Deacon Boello used his influence, a visit, a letter, a dinner, a conversation with the Japanese ambassador, to have the Castilian sent off to Japan, to follow in the footsteps of Xavier, walking a path far from the Roman *regnum*.

There, near the southern end of the island of Honshu, in an imperium as daunting as any Felipe's, Father Beltrán holed away for a decade, writing his letters, which rarely were delivered, and agitating his new friends with his increasingly strange and mystical ideas.

When Father Beltrán returned to Rome, the Gregorian needed a teacher. Father Feuerbach had caught pneumonia a week before classes were to begin. The rector of the Gregorian assumed Father Beltrán would be a harmless substitute. Unfortunately, he turned out to be a radical of the worst sort, a warm and endearing old man.

The three years from 1947 to 1950 were bad ones for the rector. There seemed to be nothing he could do to keep the old Castilian from braying his odd theories about religion and spirituality. The last straw was Father Beltrán's sermon on the feast of Corpus Christi, the "Buddha Jesus" sermon as it came to be known. Within a week Father Beltrán was sent packing for the Orient, this time to India. The Americans, now overlords in

Japan, wouldn't let him return. They were nervous about Europeans and couldn't distinguish a Spanish fascist from a Spanish republican.

During their theology years, the two prematurely aged scholastics, Karl von Ehre and Joszef Eger, argued loud and long about what the old Castilian was teaching.

"We do not need to listen to the wisdom of the East, Joszef. Our tradition is full of wisdom. It is a clean and clear statement of laws. Why should we let people encrusted with errant ideas muddle it up?" Karl asked his question on a sunny day in May as the two strolled up and down the elegant oval of the Piazza Navonna, their cassocks picking up the warm breezes.

"If God is speaking in His many tongues, who are we to correct Him?"

"Who are we? Who are we? Joszef, it is all so facile for you. You're content to make an intellectual whim into a diamond and set it on a ring of gold. Don't you see the implications of these teachings, of where they will lead us?"

Eger's burly friend was pleading, with an Italian intensity, all arms and head movements.

"Where did that Swastika come from?" von Ehre asked. "From Hindustan. What does that mean? You understand, no? Some people, crazy people, take ideas from here or there and stitch them together into theories that, draped over the populace, drag us into terror. Terror, Joszef! We don't need new ideas, we need to understand and live the old ones, certainly in the realm of morals."

Eger smiled a sad, gentle grin and touched von Ehre's shoulder.

"You can take even one verse from the Bible and ruin a life," Eger said, soft as a mother offering a minor rebuke. "Take several, take this phrase and that one, this truth and that truth. *Et voilà*, a regime of hate and oppression. You see that, don't you? You smell the danger in our own sacred book?"

"I smell danger and I smell the way around it. We rely on the magisterium to divine what is true and what is false," von Ehre said, stopping their stroll to emphasize his point. His broad hands shook with a renewed energy. It seemed the most important concept, this apostolic authority, buoyant as a plank of wood sheared from the hull of a sinking ship. Karl seemed to be hanging onto it tightly.

"And Holy Mother Church, on whom the magisterium was bestowed, relies on us," Eger said, stepping back a step, "on our searchings, on the movements within our souls." He was looking straight into Karl's beer-brown eyes. He wondered why Karl seemed so afraid.

"Holy Mother Church relies on the Pope," von Ehre declared. "*Super hanc petram aedificabo ecclesiam meam.*"

"On the rock, not of the rock. We are more than the rock. We are a people, a people on the move, the rock, if you will, in motion."

Lecture after lecture, the old Castilian's theories drew in Eger, enticing him with their oddly heroic view of the universe and its innate nobility. These whimsical ideas, concoctions part Castilian mysticism and Eastern wisdom, steadily offered up by Father Beltrán as he paced back and forth on a creaky dais hidden from the bright Roman sun, ultimately led Eger into a study of Eastern religions.

Father Eger spent his working years teaching and studying in India and Japan. He never achieved the academic glory his early superiors had anticipated. Nine years ago he returned to Rome to work in the Vatican library, curating oriental texts that had found their way into that Western archive over the many centuries.

In contrast, von Ehre's path was an autobahn leading swiftly to administrative positions within the Society. First he was president of the Jesuit high school in Beirut, then at the Jesuit college in Baghdad. In Baghdad he was responsible for the painful closing of all Jesuit institutions in Iraq, the inevitable fallout of the demise of the Hashemites and the expulsion of Jesuits. After Iraq, Father von Ehre was brought to Rome to work in the Jesuit curia.

When Father von Ehre was elected General, nine years previously, everyone acknowledged he was the compromise candidate. The majority saw him as a man who would lead neither to the right nor to the left, not too much Trent nor too much Rahner nor Cardenal nor de Mello. And he was a man who knew how to run an institution, even, some whispered, if he were called upon the shut it down in an orderly fashion.

As if rethinking his approach, Father von Ehre got up from his chair and walked around his desk to join Father Eger in one of the four large high-backed chairs and its snug red velvet covering. "Can I offer you a coffee or anything to eat?"

"Nothing, thank you, I ate early." Father Eger was relaxed now that he was with his old friend. He folded his hands in his lap.

"I am sorry to disturb your morning, Joszef; however, we received news overnight about the abduction of a young American Jesuit from the grounds of Rafael Landívar University in Guatemala. There is a ransom for his release—two million American dollars."

Father Eger sat upright in his chair. "Who did it? What do we know? Is the American OK?" Father Eger was shocked. Every kidnapping story affected him the same way, as if he had entered a freezer and thoughtlessly, tidily closed the self-locking door. He recalled the moment of his own arrest, in the long residence hallway, whose terrazzo floor, grey and green, had been freshly scrubbed. He recalled the tinny emptiness he discovered in his soul as two Gestapo walked him down the five steps of the dour Canisius residence on Lietzensee. He was still in cassock. He'd been reading John of the Cross. That dark book he placed face down on the entryway table, as if to protect it.

"The *Union de Derechos Absolutos* are claiming responsibility," Father von Ehre said, disturbing Father Eger's memory. "They are the same group who threatened us if we did not leave Guatemala."

"So they finally acted. But why the ransom?" Father Eger asked, reaching his right hand up to stroke his goatee. "Why not kill him? Isn't blood what they want? What they promised? A flow of blood?"

"Perhaps in that hemisphere money is more important than blood." Father von Ehre tried to smile. "Or maybe it is publicity they want, the new coin of the realm."

"Will you pay the ransom?" Father Eger knew what the response would be. He still had a habit of asking the wrong questions.

"No," Father von Ehre answered, nearly bellowing. "We cannot begin to pay ransoms for captured Jesuits. I would soon be papering this office with ransom notes," von Ehre said looking around. "But I don't want to abandon this young man. His name is Thomas Burns. He comes from the Wisconsin Province, in the central part of the United States. He has been in Guatemala six years."

"So you will negotiate?" Father Eger was keeping his questions short, employing a habit of intellect he'd perfected in the East. He was gathering the important facts, his tone cool as a close-lipped journalist's.

"I may negotiate. First I need to know more. I need to know more about this young man, I need to know more about this situation in Guatemala." Father Eger heard the frustration in von Ehre's voice. The large Bavarian leaned toward him. "What I really need is to send someone there on whom I can rely, someone who knows how to discover the truth."

"A suggestion? Send Bellini."

"I am not looking for a suggestion, Joszef, I am looking for a volunteer."

"A volunteer? Certainly you are not . . ." Father Eger's eyes bulged, sparrow eyes of fear and amazement. The General would consider giving him this assignment!?! He was a scholar and an archivist, thoughtful, slow, unsure, no diplomat or negotiator. After the war, his life had become ever more solitary, his time spent reading and reflecting. Only Father von Ehre's command had dragged back to the West.

"Yes, Joszef, I am asking you to volunteer." Father von Ehre, in contrast, was calm and steady. Clearly he had made up his mind.

"And why me?"

"Because I am looking for the unexpected. We must discover a way to deal with the captors. You are a man who is always examining new ways."

"Oh, please, Karl, what kind of a reason is that? What do you mean . . ."

"I trust you. Times are difficult. This situation will attract attention. People will ask: what was at the heart of this young man's message? The Society is going to be scrutinized again, I assure you." Father von Ehre's voice was all warmth and smoothness now, but Father Eger knew he could turn hard and cold in a minute. "I need someone I can trust, someone who will help me get the Society through this."

"You know I want to help, but I have no experience in anything like this. What would I do?" Eger gripped the arms of the chair. He wanted to leap up and run out of the room. He had no energy for political intrigue. He avoided television news programs, magazines, movies, fiction, even the factional discussions within the Society and the Church. He only wanted to grapple with one issue, one discipline.

"First you must go to Guatemala," Father von Ehre said, a steeliness entering into his instructions. "I have arranged tickets for this afternoon's flight to Miami. You'll be in Guatemala the next day. And you will take this mobile phone," Father von Ehre said, leaning forward to pick up a small black case from the top of his desk and handing it to Father Eger. "The number you are to dial is in the phone case. You will call me every morning at 7 your time."

"I . . ."

"You must hurry now," Father von Ehre said as he stood up. "There is not so much time to pack and to get to the airport. Here is a briefing document," Father von Ehre said as he handed Father Eger a thin manila folder. "I will hear from you tomorrow." The General's face was blank. It had resumed its bureaucratic blandness.

Father Eger stood up, slowly, shaking his head. He clenched the phone.

"Stop by my secretary's desk for the tickets," Father von Ehre said as he walked around to the other side of the desk and sat down. He started to pick up a document from one of the stacks on his desk. He stopped and looked up. "Good luck, Joszef."

Father Eger stared down at his old friend. He had learned over his many years of obedience to superiors that he should take the mission as a request from Jesus and act with the fervor that the situation required. Inside he wondered, doubted, whether this mission could really be a request from Jesus. Why would Jesus do this to him?

Both men nodded, as if on cue, and Father Eger left.

Father Eger's return home was less frantic. He walked the last half mile, taking slow steps so not to absorb much of the morning's sweltering heat. It was an unusually hot and unpleasant fall, although the heat did relieve the pain he felt in his aging joints. As he sauntered through the now crowded Piazza della Rotonda on his way back to the Via del Seminario and his diminutive rectangle of a room in the Collegio Bellarmino, Father Eger looked up for the thousandth time at the wonderful circular majesty of the Pantheon. It was then that the thought struck him. "He has a plan," he muttered in Hungarian. "That old German has a plan! And he needs an unnoticed servant to pull it off. I am that servant. Surely he will give me further instructions when I call him."

In other parts of Rome there had also been meetings. The round and red faced cardinals of the Curia had been talking about the Vatican's role in this "Guatemala affair." None of them wanted another Nicaragua in which the Church that had finally fought against the dictator Somoza had become the enemy of the Sandinista state. With the election of the Chamorro woman in Managua, at least the Church could begin to reassert its privileges and teach more clearly. Nor did they want an El Salvador where factions within the Church were tearing it apart, one group aligned with the poor, the other with the ruling class.

In Central America everything was so dramatic. Such situations were too dangerous for the Church. She was already under assault in Central America, under assault by the angry message of justice preached by the left wing and by the loudly proclaimed testimonials of personal salvation and wealth of the exploding evangelical movement. Both these creeds were unraveling the cultural fabric of Central America, a fabric in which the Church had been so dominant, had so much power, had everyone's attention. Now, fewer and fewer people seemed to listen to her.

The cardinals feared not only that this activist justice message might place the Church in a weaker position, but that another more profound message of truth, a message wrapped up in the symbols of their daily rituals, was being laid aside. And as princes of a two-thousand-year-old realm, these old men knew that once these profound messages, and the bonding force of daily consecration, were laid aside, whole societies would crumble.

CHAPTER FOURTEEN

Soul of Christ, Sanctify me. Body of Christ, Save me. Blood of Christ, Inebriate me.

Pleas from the *Aspirationes Sancti Ignatii*, a prayer beloved by Ignatius Loyola, founder of the Jesuits, and traditionally published at the beginning of all copies of *The Spiritual Exercises*, his method for achieving spiritual confidence.

By the time the man left the hut to stretch his muscles in the morning air, dawn had sauntered out over the expanse of the abandoned *finca* in the remote highland valley, casting its golden light and chasing away the worst of the evening chill.

The man is a *ladino*, although the *indígena* blood is nearly bred out of him. Still, that branch of his ancestry is noticeable in the curvature of his eyes and the ruddy hue of his skin, perhaps in the short but muscular build of his body evident through the fatigues he rearranges several times.

Tom could not see the man's face or clarify his shape. The blindfold, held in place by a nylon stocking pulled over his head, kept Tom from clearly distinguishing any form. He could barely sense that the man was three feet away.

Tom lay crouched in the middle of the room, his chin resting on his knees, his hands and legs still bound by a rough cord. All Tom felt with surety was his isolation and the continuing ache of his muscles and the panicky fear that jumped him every time footsteps came near.

Now someone was in the room with him! The thought struck deep into his gut, nearly emptying it.

"Call me Marcos. I'm in charge of you, gringo pig!"

Marcos stepped a foot closer and leaned over to spit at Tom, striking him on the forehead with a wad of mucus.

Tom lifted his bound hands to wipe away the spittle, awkwardly rubbing at it, fearing, suddenly, halfway into the act, that this cleansing might incite Marcos to hit him.

"Go ahead, speak my name!"

Tom heard the captor's boots circle nearer, small, precise movements.

"Speak my name!"

The accent is good, Tom thought. He's studied in the States.

"Marcos." Tom croaked the word. His mouth was parched.

"Tell me what you want, gringo."

What I want? Doesn't he know?

"Water, please."

The boots stopped.

"Why not piss? Would not piss do?"

Tom stared toward the voice. It was over his left shoulder. Should he respond? Say "OK"? What would that mean? Too submissive? Yes! A ripple of anger worked through him.

But Tom had heard of people stranded on mastless boats who drank their urine to stay alive. Bread and water. The body's needs. If not bread, at least water.

He was so thirsty.

"Too disgusting for your excellency?" Marcos asked as he stomped out, slamming shut the rough plank door.

Was this a new game? Tom wondered. What were its rules? He had to learn them quickly.

A few minutes. Marcos was back in the room.

Despite the blindfold's barrier, Tom sensed Marcos bend down. To set something on the floor? There was a scratching sound.

"I hate tending to the useless, so do not annoy me!"

There was arrogance in his captor's voice. But the man had said "useless," not "condemned." Marcos moved toward him. Tom's body jolted at the sound of sharp steel slipping out of its sheath. He could hear Marcos's breathing. The man hovered near him. Tom moved his hands to cover his face.

"Lay on your back."

Slowly, gracelessly, Tom complied, stretching his tight muscles. He was too concentrated on fear to moan.

"Hold up your hands and make the arms stiff."

Tom couldn't figure it out. What was going on?

"Hold the hands apart!"

"Into your hands . . ." Tom breathed in his mind. He grit his teeth. His body went rigid.

"Do not move!"

A sharp, swift movement cleaved the air.

Tom's arms flew apart. His body shook with fright. With his freed hands he patted his arms to see if they were bleeding.

Marcos had cut only the rope.

"When I am here, keep the blindfold on. If you take it off or steal a look at me, I will poke out your eyes with the tip of my machete, a quick prick and one slow turn. Understood?!"

"Yes," Tom said. His voice was weak.

"Do not forget: If you see my face, you will never see another thing."

At the door, Marcos turned around. "There's water in a cup on the floor. Your last water of the day." Marcos latched the door as he left, locking the chain that wed door and frame.

Tom was afraid to move. Was the man really gone?

He waited. When he felt alone, sure the man wasn't hiding somewhere, crouched in darkness, Tom ripped at the nylon stocking and the bandanna. He clawed at them.

Finally they were off.

He blinked and blinked. His eyes were dry and scratchy.

A little daylight brightened the *choza* darkness. Still, it was hard to focus. Tom made out the form of the cup. He scrambled on his knees to the center of the room and picked up the tarnished cup in both hands, gulping down its contents.

His throat softened a bit. He closed his eyes with relief. Then he looked back into the cup, into its dented, scratched bottom. The water was all gone. He licked the cup, tasting the cool tin. He was still thirsty.

Tom needed to piss. Muscles inside him were relaxing, nerve endings hooking back up. He looked at the cup and smiled, thinking he might yet have to mix a cocktail of urine. He crawled to a corner of the room away from the door, unzipped his pants and pissed at the bottom of the wall. Most of the stream splashed onto the ground outside. The urine stung. It was dense and yellow. He sucked in a foot of air with the sharp pain.

Tom crawled away from the wall, back to the bandanna.

His feet were still bound. He leaned forward to untie the knots. His hands were useless. He was a Raggedy Ann doll.

He kept trying. Slowly the clumsiness shook out.

After he'd unbound his feet, he massaged the long muscles of his legs. Then it was time to stand. He struggled, wobbly as a newborn calf.

He shuffled around the room and stretched his aching body as he moved.

What should he do? Escape? How?

What would they do if they caught him?

The most obvious question, however, strutted before him, back and forth. Why had they not killed him? Did they have a special plan for him? Some special death?

The fear intensified. He began to relive the kidnapping: the first rush of terror as he realized he was surrounded by angry men, their faces covered with ski masks. He remembered the roughness of their hands, the anger and excitement in their voices. "*No grites! Pónte las manos en los bolsillos!*" One of the henchmen, the tall one, taller than Tom, hit him on the crest of his back, emphasizing the command: "*Marche tranquilo.*" Tom had stumbled, nearly losing his balance.

His heart started to race.

He had to stop those thoughts! Fear gave the enemy power. It was a blade in their hands.

An anger came back into his heart, a defiance, a pride.

He would not be the first Jesuit martyr of this new world.

Others had walked the path before.

For a moment, peace sifted into his soul. It smelled of dried leaves in autumn, something ancient and honorable in the decay, something ordained beyond time.

A phrase: the way. The path. *I am the Way.*

Tom smiled. He didn't want to die a broken man. If he was going to die, he wanted to die free. Free from hatred. That was the way to die! With dignity at the moment of passing, to feel the balm of that sacred egress as his naked soul drifted through panels of stainless silk.

Tom needed to pray.

He settled down, cross-legged, his back upright against the wall that faced the lone door. He blinked his eyes to clear them. They scratched less. He focused more easily.

Many times he'd found himself sitting before a closed door. At the beginning of every retreat. Alone in a simple room with nothing to do but turn toward God, hoping to open himself with the same sun-hope as pink-white sweet pea blossoms on a curving green strand in morning's calm light.

But the first days of retreat silence were always the worst, an unsalved itch. Time plodded on, constant as an old horse at the mill, heavy-eyed, flyswatting.

Since his second Jesuit retreat at Campion, in an era of Jim Fixx and the runner's high, Tom had begun his retreats with long runs, fifteen, twenty miles, striding until he felt the God-pulse in his muscles. Then he could pray. Later he'd learned to knit, producing at least one lumpy retreat sweater each year. David had five, Mark three. Charley, two. Anything to get him to the prayer spot. To hold him there.

In the *choza*, sitting, his hands idle, newly awake, Tom felt desperate in a way he'd never felt before. Part of him, he knew, was afraid to pray, to contemplate the God he'd come to know in Guatemala, the smithy God, sinewy and busy at the forge.

In Guatemala, Tom's prayer life was half torment. In Guatemala, silence rested above a deep, sustained roar. Yes, he saw injustice at its most brilliant, but he also saw—experienced—his own flaws raw as blade wounds. He'd always known there were gaps in his nature, missing or fragile links in the chain, fractures that required the blacksmith's mending. Since the threat, the gaps had made him shake with panic, sometimes shivering at the altar, wishing he could turn his face away from the congregation, to stare alone at white linen, gold chalice, grainy wheat and his own light-skinned, hairless, nervous priest hands.

Tom resolved not to begin with the gaps, with loneliness, doubt, anger, lust, fear. He scratched his back against the rough *choza* wall. He needed to bask in glory, soaking warm rays, recharging like a fat iguana on a flat Pacific rock.

He would begin with Ignatius's Exercises. Tom needed to fix his mind on some bright, distant point and move toward it. But which exercise? Which contemplation?

No answer. His mind blank. Empty of image or thought or prayer scene.

Damn! The only clear things were the details, the *choza*'s irregular walls, the coolness of the floor that was starting to freeze his butt, the tangy smell of dirt mixed with the acrid leftovers of a fire, the dullness of the metal chain that kept the door bound to its frame, those five planks of pine and their nine knots.

Nothing else, no spiritual image.

But the Exercises were all about image, the language of the soul.

Panic ripped into Tom again. He needed to get control. The veins in his right temple began to throb.

Desperation in his eyes. "How do they begin? The Exercises?" A sweat rose on his forehead.

"Weeks! They're broken into weeks!" He almost shouted. Four weeks. "Spiritual growth nurtured in a temporal illusion." David had said that; he was always manufacturing phrases.

And the first week?

"About sin," he muttered. "Thoughts, Words, and Deeds." Tom repeated the phrase twice, silently in his head. Silence was required by the exercitant.

Tom was back as a novice, week one of retreat. Despite his resolve, he would begin again with an examination of the gaps. God preferred to walk in through the gaps.

He'd been at the novitiate for five months. It was time for the long retreat, thirty days of internal dialogue, prayer, fasting, reading, and silence. Night silence. Morning silence. All day silence. "Peace be with you" at Mass, then silence. No singing. Reading at table.

And the every-other-day meeting with Father Gorman and their dissecting of his contemplations, an analysis as intricate as any Freudian dream study, following the method cave-dwelling Ignatius had begun to develop as he prayed throughout the night in his rock home above the flowing Cardoner.

Day one. St. Paul, Minnesota. So far away. He was remembering.

Only ten remained in their novitiate class. They'd all gathered in the chapel early in the morning. It was January in Minnesota. He remembered running across the icy walk from building to building. He remembered shivering at the door to the chapel, not quite ready to enter. He listened at the door and heard nothing. Was he the first one? The night before the novices had been warned that as of midnight, they had entered into silence. Was everyone else inside? He entered.

Nine pairs of eyes landed on Tom, some greeting him with smiles and some shifting quickly away, as if recognition might be a trespass of the required isolation. David and Mark were already there. David winked at him. Mark had his head in his hands. Tom found a seat near the altar and closed his eyes. Something had changed in that novitiate group. The energy was there, but it was being restrained. Some special event was about to happen.

Then Father Gorman emerged from the sanctuary, dressed in his clerical collar and well-creased black slacks. A fine gray cardigan sat unbuttoned across his chest, curving over muscles sculpted by nature and years of sport. In his right hand, large as a pig farmer's, he held his Jerusalem Bible, its black jacket supple and its title gold-embossed and shimmering on cover and spine.

Father Gorman walked to the altar, his gait more coach then presbyter, and faced his small group of charges just as he would if Mass were about to begin. He set the Bible down onto the altar and opened it up. It was a sensual indulgence. He flipped through several pages until his right index finger rested on the verse from Jeremiah:

> "Heal me, Yahweh, and I shall be really healed, save me and I shall
> be saved, for you alone are my hope."

And then it began. The drilling down into Tom's soul and the soul of his fellow novices, the beginning of the great list of faults, the preparation for the general confession, a confession that spanned a lifetime. The time to examine sources and patterns. Of good. Of evil.

And why had he been so drawn into this mystery of faith, into this religious vocation? The question seemed so important now, there in the hut. The answer might give him control.

From earliest childhood he'd wanted to help out. In the kitchen preparing meals with his mother who sometimes looked at him strangely, with worry, as he offered to cut carrots or peal potatoes. In the hardware store with his father where he swept the oak floors in the evening or counted boxes of nails. In the domain of the octogenarian Jewish neighbor lady where he mowed and shoveled and managed light switches on shabbos.

He saw it clearly then, in the novitiate. He saw it clearly now. The urge to help and the urge toward sanctity had become intertwined in his youth, intertwined such that his young mind knew that the deepest movement within him was a movement toward holiness, toward God. He had told Father Gorman that as a boy two streams of thought had occupied his mind: baseball and Roman Catholicism. He had collected icons of those two enthusiasms, accumulating both playing cards for the entire Yankees team of 1958, the year he fell passionately in love with them because of their World Series triumph over the Milwaukee Braves, and statuettes of every one of the North American Jesuit martyrs, plus a special, tattered holy card of Blessed Kateri Tekakwitha, a sacred object that had once belonged to an old Mdwaketon Lakota who came into his father's hardware store in Mankato and told stories full of criminals and oak-grove hauntings from before the pioneer days.

Tom remembered his family dinner table. His father would get Tom talking by asking one of two questions: Who were the best players in baseball? and What was the history of Catholic missionaries in America? After that, Tom's toneless young male voice would drone on without stop, explaining every detail of the topic as he played with his meat loaf and drying macaroni. He could still hear his own voice:

"The early Jesuits in North America were not killed just because the Indians disliked Christianity. Oh, no. It had a lot to do with politics. For example, the Iroquois killed Father de Brebeuf because in 1699 the governor of Massachusetts offered them money or whatever they wanted, guns or beads, if they would bring him any Jesuits they found, dead or alive, that was because the English and French were at war over North America and, of course, the Jesuits had been sponsored by the French . . ."

Tom knew his enthusiasm for Catholic facts drove his sisters wild. They avoided him in school. They kicked him under the table. But their sisterly assaults didn't deter him.

Martyrs had been central to Tom's early religious life. He'd examined the lives of those chosen ones, straining to imagine their torment and their determination. The memory of that enthusiasm for gore almost made him laugh in the confined air of the *choza*. Tom recalled the words of Sister Mary Michael: "The road to sanctity is no smooth interstate. It's a dark and thistled undergrowth that stretches all the way to the pinnacle of Mount Zion!"

The young Tom had wanted to travel that heroic road. He wanted to battle its monsters. As a child he had sought out every challenge available to him. He pushed himself into mathematics, played football despite his slight build, worked with slower students even though he was so quick to lose his temper.

As a novice, Tom had seen the roots of his vocation with clarity and freshness. He also began to understand the diseases that would attack those roots. He'd been struggling with the diseases for years. They were no odd mix: arrogance, self-reliance, anger, and other desires deep in the flesh.

Tom remembered the discomfort he'd felt standing outside Father Gorman's office before his general confession. He'd begun to dislike Father Gorman and distrusted the man's ability to help him grow. He hated Father Gorman's confidence, the same vice Tom knew was his own virtue.

That first general confession was etched clearly into his mind.

Father Gorman had been hard on him, hard on Tom's surety, hard on Tom's easy dismissal of sexual sins.

Father Gorman was already seated, waiting for Tom. They exchanged no pleasantries. Tom sat in the opposite chair and began his story, starting at the beginning, with childhood. But he had not been a bad child. Perhaps he had badgered his parents and sisters. So what?

"Would you say you were a hippie?" Father Gorman asked. Tom was now confessing sins from his college years. Father Gorman was yawning. It was three in the afternoon and getting dark in winterbound Minnesota.

The question had annoyed Tom.

"You could call me a hippie. I had long hair and wore embroidered clothes. I smoked a lot, but I only did acid once." Tom had never done acid. He wanted to rile his confessor. Father Gorman's back stiffened. "Some people think hippies are angry, confused. I wasn't angry or confused, I was having fun. I believe in what our generation is all about, about freedom and harmony."

"And you had sex?"

Since their first course on the vows, Tom thought his novice master spoke as if sex were the primary sin, the curse of Eden itself.

"Yes, I had sex," Tom said. He knew his tone was dismissive, even as his heart was changing. He was having new thoughts. Tom had begun to wonder if he'd been wrong about sex. His novitiate reading on celibacy had convinced him there were nuances, a spiritual side. Celibacy wasn't necessarily a vacuous discipline. It could be an earthen levee that rerouted the river's flow. The flow was still there.

"Mainly with Rose," Tom confessed. "We dated seriously our junior and senior year. But I wasn't in love with her, and she wasn't in love with me. We were both convenient for each other. We were friends."

"Hmmm." Father Gorman's face was tight and empty, a confessor stunned and unsure how to respond. He rubbed his face. "Friends?"

"I've been very active—sexually, but not since I entered the novitiate."

"You've only been here five months," Father Gorman said. He shook his head back and forth.

Tom had left Father Gorman's office absolved, but less sure of his vocation, of the rightness of his response. Why had he thought he had a vocation? Were his dreams all celluloid? Their thin story made believable only with lighting and make-up and masterful language?

His consolation came later.

The next week of the Exercises, during his meditations on the three classes of men, Tom had a recurring vision of himself as an old man, one who'd spent years working with the poorest. The old man had lost his body's elegant form and now stooped in constant examination of the ground. Only wisps of gray hair covered his pate. Deep furrows of wrinkles had been ploughed up and down his face. He sat on the steps of an aging, one-steepled church. Little children played on the street before him. Hopscotch. Hoops. Some on bikes. Some wrestling. Cars went by, radios blaring. One girl rested her head on his knee. He touched her head and silently blessed her.

The cawing of a highland crow broke Tom's reverie. He snapped his head toward the sound and sighed.

Would he ever be that old man? This was not the time to die! There was more to do! And he had not yet reached that moment of perfect detachment. He wasn't ready to die.

For a few moments, Tom felt empty, hollow. He had not prayed well. Then that one, powerful living memory came back.

Even captive in the desolate *choza*, surrounded by fear and in search of God's purest love, the memory had found him. It was painted with her face, scented with the smell of her cheeks on a cool evening.

The story of Mary Magdalene. Jesus saving the despised.

In Tom's mind the Magdalene was the woman Jesus snatched from the hatred of those who would stone her. With his Jesuit's training in meditation, beginning with the composition of place, he arranged the scene. He placed the sun high in the sky. The crowd had gathered on a dusty road at the outskirts of a town, several dozen mud-brick buildings. Her hair was long, black, a waterfall of curls carousing to the small of her back. She was sweating. Her dress was torn. It was really a nightgown with no sleeves. It barely covered her knees. It was white and soft and clung to every curve of her body. And in the contemplation in the hut he, Tom, Jesus, reached out and ran his hand through her hair. Guadalupe turned to look at him, first full of anxiety. Their eyes steadied on each other. "Forgive me," Jesus, Tom, prayed into her soul.

CHAPTER FIFTEEN

"De e hos H m nos"

H man Ri h s

The few faded letters still visible from a long political statement scrawled in red paint on the concrete highway wall that helped define the limits of Colonia Samaria, the impoverished barrio at the northern edge of Guatemala City.

Father Eger's flight landed in Guatemala City at 1:30 in the afternoon, just as the city settled down for siesta. He shuffled into the airport's grand hall feeling tired and dazed, a disoriented relic in the spacious but deteriorating shell of Aurora International. He stopped near the middle of the hall to scan the crowd for the promised driver. Father General had arranged for him to stay at La Merced, the main Jesuit parish located in the heart of the old city, now referred to as "Zone 1" by his Miami-purchased guidebook, a stiff phrase, he found, soul-less and mechanically precise. Would that be his experience of the New World?

Father Eger knew the driver could easily identify him. He'd arrived in a shiny black suit with a stiff, oversized Roman collar declaring his station in life.

He stood patiently and waited with his single carry-on secured between his feet.

Suddenly an old Indian appeared before him. "Padre Eger?" the Indian asked, bowing his head and clutching a brown fedora in both hands. "I have been sent by Padre Garza at the Church of La Merced. I am to drive you there. May I carry your suitcase?"

The Indian spoke a clean, correct English. Father Eger assumed he'd practiced it with many a visitor.

Smiling, he hoped—he was so tired, he examined the old Maya. The hair of this native of the New World was thick and silver, but his cheeks were shallow. A man with inner burdens, or bad digestion.

"Thank you. Please, and your name?" asked Father Eger, moving beyond his first assessment.

"Joaquín, Padre, Joaquín Chiyá," the Indian answered, courteous to the stranger but now busy as he put his hat back on and picked up Father Eger's single bag. With a smile and a shoulder gesture that invited Father Eger to follow, Joaquín spun around and began to make his way through the crowd that had gathered to greet the fifth plane from Miami. Father

Eger noted how much younger Joaquín seemed in movement, zigzagging ahead through the airport throng, leading him to a stairwell.

"A Mayan name, is it, Chiyá?" Father Eger almost yelled his question as he hurried after Joaquín.

"Yes, Padre, Tzutuhil," Joaquín said turning back only slightly. He seemed intent on his mission. "We live in the region south of Lake Atitlán," he said, nodding his head with geographic detail. "Have you heard of the lake?"

"Oh, yes, Joaquín, it is deep, no?"

"Yes, Padre, very deep." Joaquín's shoulders drooped.

Father Eger wondered if he'd said something stupid. Did he seem another ignorant tourist? *The lake is deep.* That was an idiot's comment. The Lake has meaning. People live there, different peoples. Joaquín had called himself Tzutuhil. Who were the others around the lake? Father Eger's mind flashed with the history of the Balkans and of India, lands tattered with diversity. That must be Guatemala, he realized. He braced himself. Another land packed with long memories and souls addicted to melodrama? He felt an ache, a longing for his archives. He clutched his veined hands.

As they exited into the bright sunlight, Joaquín continued his quick pace, telling Father Eger that he had spent his adult life working at La Merced. "A Baroque jewel of the city. Now, sadly, a scratched diadem. The last earthquake." Joaquín shook his head.

Father Eger marveled at Joaquín's use of the word diadem. Such a word of luxury from this man in worn tan pants and flat rough sandals. Father Eger noticed that Joaquín's right toe seemed irritated by an ingrown toenail. The man favored his right foot. Father Eger recalled that in India he, too, had worn sandals and the soles of his feet had callused.

After the two settled into the Jesuit community's aging green Impala, both men turned quiet. Joaquín assumed a new persona, distant as a kitchen servant. Father Eger said nothing to correct that relationship. He was intent on observing the city and countryside. He'd never been to Central America and was ready to number its features and compare them to the sub-continent of Asia, which he knew so well. He'd expected green hills and fresh air. Instead their car emptied into a cloud of fumes and a disorganized flow of traffic that never diminished as they wound deeper into the metropolis, a plain and unspectacular expanse of single-story buildings. Battered signs hung out over narrow sidewalks. It was another cityscape covered with dirt and the choking exhaust of aged buses and thirty-year-old flatbed trucks.

There were fewer poor folk huddled on the streets than Father Eger had expected. Guatemala City was no Bombay or Calcutta. Still, occasionally he caught glimpses of shanty towns climbing up and down steep gullies. And he noticed plenty of unwashed beggars resting on their haunches. They reminded him of the vast expanses of poverty he'd once adjusted to during his mission in Asia. It was the same old international tableau: the hunched-down suffering of the poor.

The Jesuit residence at La Merced was a mid-1800s structure built in the colonial style, as if its designers were expecting *caballeros españoles* to dismount and swagger into its interior comfort. At the residence's heart was a courtyard with fountain and pool surrounded by a green patch of lawn. Clusters of rose bushes and pairs of palms stood at the stone meeting places of the walls. Well-bred blossoms of pink and red roses opened up in the sunlight. A brick path wound around the courtyard's edges. A covered walkway, supported by seven stone columns, jutted out on the side of the quadrangle that now glowed in the sun. The street wall, its inner face shadowed, was topped with wire and jagged glass.

Father Eger sat down on a bench of pink granite near the fountain. With him he had a sandwich of ham and tomato, a glass of red wine and the single, compact orange, all of which the housekeeper had prepared for him in accordance with his wish for a pilgrim's meal.

Father Eger sat alone contemplating the quiet and beauty of the scene, peacefully eating the sandwich and then meticulously pealing the orange. Even as he thanked the Lord for this moment's sanity, he felt the guilt of his own pleasure. It was, again, an old friend renewing his acquaintance. How had he come to be graced with these luxuries of food and shelter and long life?

As he paused to breathe in the soft smells of the garden, Father Eger noticed the face of a tiny apron-clad girl staring at him from the doorway that led into the kitchen. Her dark hair wrapped around and under her oval face. He looked over at her and waved, presenting what he hoped was a welcoming smile. Her eyes grew large, and she bolted from the doorway into the security of the kitchen. Father Eger shrugged his shoulders, hoping this brief drama did not foreshadow a mission plagued with unwilling witnesses, or worse, truths he could not fathom.

He quickly finished off the juicy meat of the orange, thinking to himself how small but sweet it was. Then he went up to his second floor room to catch up on lost sleep.

At 4:30 in the afternoon, there was a rap at Father Eger's door. He was startled from his rest, confused about where he was, and rose halfway up from his narrow bed blurting out "*Avanti*," as if he were back in Rome.

The door opened.

"Father Eger, I am Father Antonio Garza, rector of La Merced," announced the equally aged Jesuit, his wrinkled face marked by a half-dozen splotches, a common gift of the Central American sun. This short priest's eyes were large ovals behind thick lenses.

Father Eger stared back, his mind still waking, but also dragging up the new data. He'd learned a few important things about Father Garza. Despite his evident age, Father Garza remained in charge of this important church after thirty years of leadership, an oddity within the Society but very normal within the rigid social norms of traditional Guatemalan society.

"I have disturbed your rest. I am a foolish man, please, forgive me," said the rector of La Merced, barely shuffling away.

"Oh no, Father Garza, there is no problem. I was about to get up." Father Eger rose from the bed and stood pressing the wrinkles of his clothing with his long hands. "It is late, no?"

Father Eger noticed the clean darkness of Father Garza's simple black cassock, the habit which the majority of the Society had abandoned in favor of clerics or civilian clothes.

"It is 4:30, Father. Only 4:30."

"But time to get back to work," said Father Eger, smiling as he had learned to smile in Berlin with men he distrusted.

"Yes, time to get to back to work," said Father Garza.

Father Eger heard dismay in the rector's voice. Surely it was the topic of time. In India it had been the same. And in Rome. He scratched his head.

"May I speak with you awhile? This afternoon?" asked Father Eger.

He was still groggy, but needed to get moving, to make connections, to discover the undiscovered.

"About the kidnapping?"

"Yes, about the kidnapping."

"Let us talk in the recreation room," said Father Garza. "It is just off the courtyard, you will find it easily." Then Father Garza leaned forward and spoke in low tones. "I will be there alone. We can talk openly, as no one else is home. Until then."

With that the old Guatemalan bowed from the waist, almost a third-degree bow, and closed the door.

He seems pleased, thought Father Eger. For the moment he approves of me.

Father Eger went over to the room's narrow writing desk and opened up his notepad. Leaning over the paper he wrote down a phrase on the first line of the first page: *history of conquest*. And then on the second line: *faithful steward*. The first things that came to his mind. It was a trick of Father Beltrán. An attempt to catch the movement of the Spirit, which can leave subtle tracks in mind-sand.

After changing clothes and rinsing his face with water from the ceramic bowl he'd found on a stand in the darkest corner of the bedroom, Father Eger went to the kitchen to speak for a moment with Joaquín. Then he crossed out into the courtyard and over to the recreation room.

At first glance the recreation room seemed to be the high-ceilinged, somber twin of the dining room. If the dining room smelled of cleanliness, the recreation room smelled of old books, leather, and the occasional fine cigar. The wall facing the courtyard was volcanic stone and glass; a pealing, dingy plaster covered the inner walls. Standing at the doorway, Father Eger noticed a strong flow of natural light, which entered from the court-yard at the top of the six-foot-high windows. He stopped for a moment to watch particles of dust float about in that light's amber, slanted current.

Then he looked back in.

Father Eger counted five scratched leather armchairs and two leather couches, whose sheen had been worn by years of clerical relaxation. A row of bookcases, a vast network of wooden slats stained a chocolate brown, blotted out the northern wall. The shelves nearly reached the ceiling.

As he was about to examine a row of titles, Father Eger heard the muzzled summons of a small cough. From the corner of his right eye he identified the frame of Father Garza, sunken, so it seemed, into a chair, one of two set back into the innermost corner of the room. The old Guatemalan had been watching him with what Father Eger now thought of as the calculating gaze of a mountain gnome. And was there a look of disdain on Father Garza's narrow face? Because he had changed into khakis and a pink rumpled sport shirt? Such garb must not seem appropriate for a Roman visitor. Sartorial pique would fit Father Garza's profile.

"You look more relaxed, Father," said the rector, continuing to stare at Father Eger over clasped hands. "Your journey was long, no?"

"Yes, long and sweaty."

Father Eger would take his time. Let the Guatemalan think him unsuited for the task of Roman delegate. It was easier to hide secret activities when considered a dolt, a lesson he'd learned in Berlin. Yes, that wartime ruse had worked—mostly. "Supposedly he was brilliant at Berchmannskolleg, but in our Berlin community he's a simpleton!" That was on his first Prussian *informationes*.

He froze with the memory. He mustn't let those thoughts back in!

Father General should've sent someone else!

Abruptly he turned from Father Garza's stare and took a deep breath. Stood quiet a minute. Another deep breath, and the memory stopped. But he felt moisture under his arms and in the small of his back.

He moved closer to the bookshelves and started to read titles. The first shelf he examined contained volumes of scholastic and moral theology. Above it were other resources: dictionaries, atlases, small histories, and, of course, Virgil, Homer and Cervantes. Half the titles were Latin, the others divided among the great European languages. Is this a house of classicists? Father Eger wondered.

On a lower shelf were two stacks of newspapers and magazines, leaning as precariously as medieval Italian towers. Father Eger picked through one of the stacks, careful to keep it upright. *Der Spiegel. L'Express. Time. El País.* All printed within the last two years. From the world over. Residue of guests who had passed through, Father Eger surmised. He imagined Father Garza thumbing through their worldly print, finding stories that disturbed him about decadence in other countries, tidbits the Guatemalan would use in sermons or in conversations with parishioners or family members.

Or in more sinister conversations.

Father General's briefing document contained five pages on Father Garza. The family Garza was a family of note, a family one could read about in histories, first as conquerors and landowners, then in the last several hundred years as politicians. And as politicians, they ranked among the least farsighted or humane. Their roots went back to Antigua, the now-abandoned Spanish capital, where the family still maintained a colonial residence, one of the most remarkable restoration projects of that city.

The Garza family currently numbered nearly one hundred members, half of them *finqueros* and half of them professionals. There was a small, though most of them would say insignificant, split between the two halves of the family over the future of the country. Both halves understood the need for change. Both halves understood the need for gradual change. One half spoke constantly about the word "gradual." The other half, even some who had been stopped by guerrillas on roadways and forced to pay "war taxes," spoke about the word "change." Father Garza was on the right wing of the *gradualistas*.

"Do you desire something to drink?" asked Father Garza. He sounded annoyed. "A Coca-Cola? Water? Juice?"

"Water would be splendid," said Father Eger, turning around and smiling. He needed the old Guatemalan to trust him—at least for a while. Father Eger had assumed from the General's briefing notes that this small priest either knew or could find out every relevant fact.

Father Garza reached over and rang a plain iron hand bell that had been hidden among several stacks of books and papers on a table next to his chair. Father Eger was amazed. It had been many years since he'd visited a Jesuit house where servants answered every whim.

"*Dos vasos de agua, María*," commanded Father Garza to the young girl who had been so shy in her observation of Father Eger in the garden. She nodded her head with a child's exaggerated bob and disappeared as quietly as she had appeared.

"She seems a pleasant girl," said Father Eger.

"She is. Sadly, she is the granddaughter of our cook. The mother died in childbirth. Now they both live here."

"And what of the father?"

Father Garza shook his head. "A bad thing," he answered. "A bad thing. Luís. I knew him since he was a baby. So sad." He waived both hands in the air as if he were a man shooing away a deformed, big-eyed fly, then gestured to Father Eger to sit on the nearby couch.

As soon as Father Eger settled onto the cool leather, María arrived with a tray and two glasses of water, each with a single ice cube floating at the top. Both men thanked her. Father Eger paused briefly, wondering how unkind it might be to ask about the quality of water here in the capital. Instead, he had no chance to ask, for Father Garza was anxious to do some investigating.

"So, Father, it is a sad event which brings you here. I hope, however, you do not think all Guatemalans are madmen and criminals. These things happen everywhere. Whole countries are under Communist rule, no?" Father Garza squinted as he peered at the Roman visitor.

Father Eger wondered if the Guatemalan gnome had forgotten about the precipitous fall of Communism in Eastern Europe. It was well documented in all those magazines. He nodded back and smiled.

"Still, it is a stain on our national honor, this I can declare." Father Garza took a sip from his glass slowly, with great contentment, as if he had delivered himself of a well-crafted argument.

"And what does Father General von Ehre think he might do about this tragedy?" Father Garza asked, looking over the top of his black-rimmed glasses.

To the point, thought Father Eger.

"Father General has sent me to investigate," Father Eger responded, then sipped from his glass. He thought of the mountain streams near Kezhthely, which had cooled his childhood's heat. He closed his eyes a moment. "I am to advise Father General as to his options."

"So, what are your plans?" Father Garza leaned slightly forward.

Father Eger would tell him the obvious.

"First, to talk to the various officials, to governmental authorities, church authorities, Father Espinoza at Landívar, and of course, to the American embassy."

"Ah yes, the Americans. They will pay particularly close attention." Father Garza put a finger alongside his nose. Was that his family's way of indicating a secret? "There are even some of their news reporters here."

"Yes, that is their way. But, perhaps you, too, could be of help to me." Father Eger smiled.

"And how?" Father Garza was unable to disguise his glee.

"Well, you could tell me about Father Burns or about the UDA. Do you know anything about either?"

"About—Father Burns, I know nearly nothing." Father Garza had hesitated to pronounce the name of the kidnapped priest. A thin sweat appeared above his brow, then evaporated in the dark coolness. "We rarely met. The university community is very—apart, no? Is that not the word? Yes, they are apart from the other Jesuit communities here. Maybe they see more of the community at the Colegio San Ignacio, the high school, as they say in English. But most of the university community is apart. A number of them are foreigners, you know."

"But did you know Father Burns?" Father Eger decided to probe a little. Father General's briefing document was vague on this point.

"Yes, I knew him. A nice looking man. Introspective. I heard his confession once or twice, when he first arrived here. He made special trips to see me. I do not know why."

Father Eger noted this fact: Father Garza knew the young priest's soul. That could work either way. Father Garza could admire Father Burns or detest him, detest him but never show it.

"He was involved in social justice works, I understand. Do you know about that?"

"We are all involved in the work for justice, Father."

"Yes, yes. But Father Burns did work at a particularly poor area of the city. I think that place was named . . ." Father Eger put a finger to his lips.

"Samaria," said Father Garza.

"So you know it?"

"I know it, we all know it. It is too bad all those country people have come here to the capital." Father Garza sat back in his chair, melding into it. "There is no work for them here. Better that they go back to the country, don't you think?"

"But these people have come for a reason. I can only suppose that all is not right in the countryside."

"All is not right in many parts of our land," Father Garza sighed. "All is not right in many parts of our world, even within our Church."

"Well then," Father Eger, said, trying not to snap out the words, "one of the things not right in your country is this UDA. Surely you can tell me about that organization."

"The UDA," began Father Garza, holding his head in his hand, as if he were remembering something from long ago. "The UDA is similar to a *cofradía*. Do you know that word, Father? It is a fraternity—or a brotherhood. A guild in English, I believe. Such an odd word. Anyway, we are a country of *cofradías*. In the villages, the *indígenas*, what the Americans call Indians, organize themselves into *cofradías*. Yes, there are civil authorities and ecclesiastical authorities. But then there are the *cofradías*. They have existed since the conquest, before it." Father Garza was looking straight at Father Eger, smiling, as if he were a sweet old man instructing his grandchildren. "Their role is primarily spiritual, to care for the statues, to make processions. The men of the *cofradía* also exercise power or influence in the running of their communities. During certain centuries of our history, they were the only power."

Father Garza paused, his eyes narrowing, seeming to estimate whether Father Eger was listening closely. "It is that way for the UDA. They are a type of *cofradía*. Their concern, however, is not just statues or saints." The old man's face darkened. He sat up straight. "Despite what you read, the UDA's concern is with the moral fabric of this country. That threat," Father Garza waved his hand dismissively, "that threat tacked to the university door was propaganda, a message. Their concern is that the socialist and atheistic habits of other countries not take root here in Guatemala!"

"Are you defending them, Father Garza?"

"I understand them, Father."

"And do you understand Father Burns's and the Society's commitment to the poor?" The question had slipped out of Father Eger's mouth. He blinked his eyes.

"I understand much about the poor, Father. I understand much about the forces striving to control the Society. About Father Burns and priests of his stripe, I understand little."

Father Eger was on the verge of losing his temper. It came on suddenly. It must've been the trip and his lack of sleep.

"And what do *you* do to walk with the poor and humble, Father Garza? Our General Congregations have asked that of all of us. Surely in this country, there are many opportunities?"

"I am only too pleased that the fathers of the General Congregations found it in their wisdom to make official what I learned in my youth as the corporal works of mercy, dear Father Eger." Father Garza settled back, even deeper into his chair. "I am an old man and can do little today to help the poor other than to look out for those special ones God has entrusted to me, such as our cook and her granddaughter. I hope you will report this to Rome and give me a good evaluation."

A masking smile froze on the faces of both men.

"I am not here to judge you, Father Garza. Your life and its conformance to the canons of the Society are not my concern. I am here to deal with terrorists."

Father Eger felt his back stiffen. He pulled in his stomach. "I apologize if I have offended you. It is only that you have seemed—reluctant to acknowledge that a grave evil has been perpetrated against one of our brothers. A brother Jesuit has been kidnapped, perhaps killed. I am saddened that you do not seem more—offended."

"I am offended by many things," Father Garza wagged a finger in rebuke. "I am offended by priests who take up guns and join revolutionaries who hide in jungles and ravage defenseless villages. These priests, at least one a member of our own order, another American, from the same province, do these scandalous acts in the name of revolution, declaring that they are overturning the satanic world of capitalism!"

Father Garza's face morphed into a gargoyle's disdain, surprising Father Eger with its contorted hatred. "I am no fool that I do not see how some are given much in this world and some are given little. But I am not so bold as to proclaim that the Lord God would have it otherwise. It appears to me that the Lord God fashioned heaven for the next world and gave us this world for testing and purification!" Father Eger saw the tight fists and white knuckles of Father Garza's hands. He hoped the old man would not do damage to himself. "The world has always been that way. I know that in my very stomach, Father Eger. I know testing, and I know purification. But heaven, that is a vision of something to come. *Adveniat regnum tuum.* May thy kingdom come. I pray that phrase daily, as do you. Daily and often."

Father Garza's speech slowed. "But I know that the kingdom will not be wrought by man. The kingdom will be of God's making, not ours. It will be when He comes again," Father Garza said as he pointed back to a copy of a Zurbarán crucifixion that hung over his chair.

The association infuriated Father Eger. His next question leapt from his mouth. "Then why, Father Garza, are you a Jesuit? Are we not a company of men dedicated to working for the *coming* of the kingdom with all due speed? Is that not at the essence of our mission?"

Silence.

"Surely you are no dupe, Father Eger." Fr Garza was grinning. "Please, do not be simple-minded with me. I, too, work for the kingdom of our Lord. But I acknowledge the limits of what can be constructed in this world."

This new tone annoyed Father Eger more than the words. He raised his voice. His accent became stronger. It was then that the Germans had most mocked him. "Then what would you have us all do, Father Garza, in *this* world?"

"Pray, Father. Pray," replied Father Garza, calmly.

"Indeed," Father Eger said. He flashed back to the sharp grimace his Nazi warden would display whenever he came upon Joszef in prayer. "*Wirklich*," the commandant would mutter, the word awkwardly stiffened by the speaker's attempt at thin-lipped wit. "Really."

Father Eger calmed himself, took another deep breath. "However, in the matter of this kidnapping, I must do more than pray. I must get a message to the UDA. Do you know how I might do that?" Father Eger remembered the last paragraph in the briefing on Father Garza. The rector's ties with the UDA were well known. Still, the briefing concluded that the Guatemalan was a harmless curmudgeon. Father Eger was starting to fear the opposite.

"I do know how to contact them. The UDA has sent another letter to Father Espinoza at Landívar. It arrived today. In it they state that I am to deliver messages to the officials of the Society and to take their messages back to the UDA. They have provided me a contact and location."

Father Garza's face went blank. "I see the curiosity in your eyes. More than curiosity, certainly." He paused a moment. "And, no, I do not belong to the UDA. I belong to no *cofradía*. I belong to the Society of Jesus. So, do you have a message?"

Father Eger stopped to consider what he'd heard. The shape of it was unexpected. For the first time in decades he looked on the face of political evil as it sat content in its chair. Today, however, it was darker and sun-ripened. "I will deliver you a message for the UDA, tomorrow."

Father Eger's eyes narrowed to cellblock keyholes. In Guatemala on this new continent, he was still full of old-man sadness, and now a new anger and other tense concerns.

CHAPTER SIXTEEN

Old warriors learn by contemplating of old wounds.

Nations, unlike warriors, never learn by contemplating old wounds. Nations need new wounds. Contemplating new wounds they sometimes abandon the idiocies hummed into them with milk-drenched tales of glory.

— The message Father Beltrán sent out on Christmas 1946.

Heat and humidity draped over the body of Managua. Only random breezes, teasing relief, blew off storm-sky-blue Lake Xolotlán.

Jim Meeker was at his desk in the Nicaraguan Treasury, daubing his forehead to keep little bombs of sweat from dropping onto his work and dissolving its labored columns of figures. A Jesuit from the Wisconsin Province, he continued to work in the Treasury Department of the Nicaraguan government despite the Sandinista's fall from power in the 1990 election and despite growing ecclesial pressure for him and other priestly laggards to abandon public office.

Twelve years had passed since the Sandinista revolution and Jim Meeker's excited entry into Nicaraguan governmental service. In those glorious days of Central American peasant rebellion, priesthood and leadership in the secular realm were not seen as a matter/anti-matter reality, even by Americans with their creed of separation between the two societal estates, even by a college-educated public who had read of the cruelty of Richelieu and the poisonous intrigue of the Borgias. Many in the land of the free thought it laudable for a priest to callus his hands transforming a government from within. More than laudable, hopeful, exhilarating. Only the most conservative American clerics and laity had questioned Jim Meeker's choice to serve in the Sandinista bureaucracy.

Much had changed over the last years in Nicaragua, in the halls of the Papal Court, and in the religion-rife politics of the northern giant.

And in Nicaragua, by 1991 the hopeful poor had seen the vagaries of shirtless poverty, hemispheric pariahship and poor management grind the revolution's dreams into trash heaps of frustration, misery, and despair.

Guadalupe showed up in Jim's office near the end of the official work day, hours before the good sun would be content to end its toil. She found the graying ex-jock puzzling over sheaves of ruled paper that spread out on his desk.

Guadalupe stood at the doorway, looking at the shape of this priest-bureaucrat, bent, as he was, over his caretaker's work. She remembered a visiting Jesuit telling her years ago that in America Father Meeker's name smelled of adventure, pungent as jungle fumes. She covered her mouth, stifling a laugh as she watched the sweating accountant rise from his chair.

"Welcome, Guadalupe, another hot one," Jim said as he circled the desk to greet her with two quick smooches. He gestured for her to sit in one of the trio of high-backed chairs, relics from a Somoza family dining room, that faced his desk. Their origin was a fact he had long ago stopped explaining to indifferent visitors. "The Somozas? Who?" History was fast approaching and blotting out the memory of past tyrants as it spewed out new names.

Guadalupe smiled and sat, preparing her first words, when her eyes picked up Jim's double take. She was sure it was her looks. Her cheeks, she knew, had lost their color. Her housekeeper Fernanda had complained to her in the morning as she left. "You look pale, *querida*, ill."

"Yes, Jim, if only we had tourists here to soak in the heat."

Guadalupe smiled—her gracious trade-conference smile, perfect teeth and hidden disdain. She and Jim had argued often about creating a tourist industry in Nicaragua. He was for it, she against. The idea of turning her heroic country into a vacation spot for the gawking gringo turned her stomach. It would be a mockery, a cynical exposition of the bones of dead heroes. And of the dead, there were many.

"It would be good for the country, Lupe," Jim said, shaking his head and sighing. "But let's not argue about it now. You want to talk about something else."

Guadalupe smiled back, a vague, diffuse pleasantry, momentary as a butterfly's peck.

As the celibate sat back down, his eyes wandered over her form. This was the look she had expected! Her cheeks may be sallow, but she was still beautiful. She knew why men admired her. She saw the wet satisfaction in their eyes.

Of course, many admired her for her political and economic savvy. And some still feared her because of what she had been.

Over the last years people had begun to comment about how well preserved she was, her face and body still lustrous after fighting a civil war and suffering political defeat. Was it because she had never given birth? Or that she lived erect as a nun? Or was it because she had frozen herself in an ancient tragedy, she who had been cheated by love and toyed with by fate? Once her story had inspired songs. She blushed to remember the lyrics young men had sung around campfires. She felt a warmth return to her cheeks.

For five years now Guadalupe had been living alone. When she had returned to Nicaragua after the death of her father, she joined the Sandinistas.

In the Sandinista army she met Colonel António Virgílio Zurbarán Roldos. He was a dashing young man, filling out the standard-issue army uniform with the form of a Greek warrior, an Achaean with the arms to throw his opponent in seconds and the legs to launch himself with shield in hand high into the air. As for revealing his inner form, Colonel Zurbarán offered a constant barrage of anger against the Somozas and all Western institutions. He was a defender of true human civilization against the capitalist barbarians. It was precisely this emotion, acrid with its whiff of explosives and revenge, for which Guadalupe had begun to hunger on her return home, sniffing around with the frenzy of a starving dog, checking every corner and cranny for a morsel of food or the smell of a marauder. With Colonel Zurbarán, she had bared her teeth and lapped up her fill.

Colonel Zurbarán had been the perfect mate for Guadalupe's mood, the perfect anti-dote to the reflective gringo she had left. Guadalupe had arrived back on the soil of her native land with an anger that lashed out at insult and kindness with the same stinging tongue. Within two days she had gone from the ornate iron door of the family's mausoleum to revolutionary Managua to demand of her distant cousin, Sergio Valenciaga, a place in the Sandinista defense against the contras. Sergio was as amazed as the rest of the family. The Escobar clan had always remained aloof from politics and everything fervent, even religion. But Guadalupe could not be stopped.

"You are a woman of the upper classes. What do you know about the jungle or about struggles or about suffering? If you want to serve Nicaragua, you can work for the government in other ways . . ."

"I am strong. I am capable. I do not care whether I have been bred to silk or to cotton. I *can* fight. I *will* fight. I will not allow these cowards and thieves to terrorize my country!" She had lost ten pounds and her face, as she rose to demand her right to battle fatigues, appeared chiseled as a stella-warrior's.

"Of course, of course, we are all angry," said Sergio, patting the air with his hands in an attempt to calm her. "It is a spiteful United States that sends out drunken pirates to attack us. But we should not allow their actions to dictate ours, we must reflect . . ."

"I am tired of reflecting!" Guadalupe slapped her hands on Sergio's desk and rose to lean over it into his face. "And I am tired of men who cannot make a decision even when their hearts scream at them! Let me sign up, Sergio, let me sign up today!"

Guadalupe's death-lust anger finally bled out of her. She had been wounded in a fight near the Rio Bambana, outside of Rosita, in the eastern reaches of Nicaragua. It was a marshy wetlands, half forest, half swamp. Her platoon had been sent to search for a handful of civilians taken prisoner by the Miskitos, the *indígenas* who made up the majority of the contra forces. She and her troop were crossing a small stretch of land.

When she had first glimpsed the light that reflected off the tall grasses, she figured it would be easier terrain to walk across, easier than continuing to trudge through the forest. She should have known better.

The first two rifle pops came so far apart, she was unsure it was an ambush. The second one wounded Guadalupe. She screamed in pain but managed to order her troop to get down and return fire. Perhaps because of her pain or because of her rage, her spirit focused. She caught sight of a figure squatting next to a tree trunk. The edge of his shoulder was out of place for the geometry of jungle trees. She hunched up on a paddock of grass, gritting into silence the searing pain of the wound above her heart. She aimed, narrowing her eyes, and pulled the rifle's trigger with an unhurried determination. It required as much energy as turning a key in a lock. Within an instant Guadalupe saw a portion of the young man's skull separate and fly away from his head. It was the last thing she remembered before falling into a coma.

Everyone remarked that Guadalupe was different after that battle. She returned to the mountain town of Boaco for treatment, and then to her family's main *finca* to convalesce. She should have recovered quickly, her wound being clean and her body young.

Colonel Zurbarán was on a mission in China for two years. He sent long diatribes to her every week, letters pounding with his love for her and his love for revolution.

A young doctor, Edgar, would visit her daily, taking her pulse, examining her eyes, placing his stethoscope on her chest, chirping little sounds. She smelled his desire, but his white teeth and dark brown eyes meant nothing to her. She thought neither of Edgar nor of Colonel Zurbarán. A black robe of memory draped over her spirit. She could not find within her the will to discard it.

After six months her mother told Guadalupe she needed to do something, to be about something. Her mother hoped Guadalupe would settle down and produce children, even if it meant travel to China. Obedient in this one desire, Guadalupe turned her mind into a brood farm, her chicks hatching as deformed memories of that last day in the jungle.

Guadalupe had never seen the young shooter after his death. She had been unable to transform him into the known enemy, to stand over him in disgust, to spit into his vacant face, to decry his ancestry and kick his ribs. Such was the fury she had felt in battle. But this particular fury, this child of a young man's disdain, this hate-child of the forest encounter, she never birthed. Instead, it grew up inside her, nourishing itself on her spirit so that she went numb.

Her mother cried over her morning and night. Guadalupe's quiet was limitless. Light bounced back from her eyes.

One morning in the town of Boaco, as she sat listless in the family's jeep, she spied a young man leaning against the bright blue wall of a wooden store. The brim of his cowboy hat hid his face. She could see only the contours of his lean body. She felt the useless torpor of midday, a heat scented with desire and long caresses. Even from that distance, magical as a momentary gift of communion, she felt the blood flow through the young man's limbs, up his legs and into his groin. In her mind she toyed with the rope that held his baggy white pants around his waist, her hands nervous, her heart pumping wildly. What would she find there if she pulled it? She thought of her young Miskito, now decaying at the stump of a mahogany tree. She thought of the red-headed gringo who had once suckled at her breast. The spirits of both men arose inside her and smiled, boyish and unsure, desiring.

That night she stood on the veranda and watched the moon paint the leaves of the *cedros espinos* silver and black. The hill-shaped wind sang into her soul, a mournful song of love lost, of youth wasted, of early death. That night she didn't sleep. She wrapped herself in a white shawl and entered into the moonlight, where she encountered herself lying in a jungle bower, lying silent in a coma. She kissed herself on the lips. She reached down a hand and helped herself up.

With dawn, the grim emptiness had begun to leave her face.

At breakfast she announced she would go to Managua. Her family startled at the table, turning to eye one another, happy yet frightened, as if a foreign spirit had come to live among them.

"Have you heard anything about Tom?" Guadalupe asked, posing her question to Jim Meeker with the directness she had acquired from her time in the land of the gringo.

"Not much. We call every day. The Jesuit community in Guatemala doesn't know anything, there's been no communication." Jim picked up a ballpoint pen and began to twirl it in his fingers. "Father General's sent a delegate. He was to arrive today or tomorrow. What this guy'll do, nobody knows. He's an unknown, not one of the regular Jesuit overseers, the General's Assistants. All I can find out is that he's Hungarian—and an archivist. Not the sort of guy who's going to move mountains."

"Rome doesn't want to move mountains," Guadalupe said. "They approve of current terrain. Their maps still work, at least for them, even with the unmarked ravines. The shepherds avoid those dangerous lands and let the sheep explore."

"Maybe so," Jim said. "Maybe so." He set the pen down and folded his arms across his chest. "Anyway, nobody I know is clued into anything that's going on in Rome—whether the Vatican is involved or why the General sent this man."

"This Pope has no love for radical priests, true?" Guadalupe knew full well how much the Pope had despised the clerics who took part in the Sandinista government and how constantly the local hierarchy, glowing with Vatican approval and Opus Dei fervency, had fought to topple that anti-clerical regime.

"But Tom wasn't a radical in any sense that should annoy the Pope or conservative Vatican forces. I mean to say, Tom wasn't political."

"He worked for the poor, didn't he?" She tilted her head sideways, mockingly, as if she were talking to a monkey. "Blessed are the poor, no? You touch the poor, you touch politics. Everyone knows that!"

Jim winced. "I mean—Tom wasn't organizing a political movement—or fomenting a particular party's plan."

"You're sure?"

"I'm sure. Tom was clean when it came to politics."

"Then why did the UDA choose him?"

"Well, because of his teachings and his preaching." Jim scratched his small earlobe. "And maybe because he's an American. His kidnapping is noticed."

"So he was teaching against the government?" Guadalupe crossed her legs. Her pants had retained the crease Fernanda had ironed into them that morning. She admired the crease.

"He didn't teach against the government in a *direct* manner, only in the sense that he talked about how economies affect the poor, perpetuate poverty . . ."

"That's why they took him." Guadalupe interrupted, annoyed to be discussing the obvious. "He shone a light on their bank accounts, pointing out how they grew fatter the more others labored and suffered!"

They both paused a moment, nodding their heads in agreement. Outside they heard the noise of workers and students heading home, calling their farewells to friends.

It was time to get to her point.

"And what can be done?" Guadalupe asked. She settled back into the uncomfortable chair, despising the Somoza taste for ostentation.

"Well, I see three options," Jim said. He ticked them off on his right hand. "One, the ransom gets paid somehow and Tom is released. Two, there is a negotiated release in which the UDA get something they want other than money, what that might be I don't know. Or three, they kill Tom."

Guadalupe reached up to twirl a strand of hair. His words had not shocked. "I see it the same way." Her eyes blurred. She continued to twirl her hair.

Jim stared silently at her contemplation, at the strands of black hair and her fingers, fidgety with thought.

A moment later Guadalupe got up and turned to leave. She had only one final request. "Please, find out everything you can—through government channels or your priest network. Keep me informed. I need more facts. But don't involve *me* in your questionings, OK? Don't use my name."

Jim nodded.

"I'll visit again tomorrow night to hear what you have learned."

The evening sun's gift was a warm bronze that covered the walls of the battered buildings of Managua. Soon Guadalupe was surrounded by couples strolling up and down the streets. The light had drawn them out. Packs of children ran through the adults, bouncing balls, calling each other names, tagging friends with glee. Tiny dust devils and antiphonal shouting matches rose from the empty blocks of the city where bands of children and adults played *béisbol* or *fútbol*. It was one of those perfect nights, one of those nights decorated with moments of beauty, sudden perceptions of the loveliness of a spouse or of the goodness of one's life.

Guadalupe barely noticed any of this magic, so intent was her concentration.

Guadalupe had been living contentedly the last several years, a regulated life with more silence than friends, more reading than theater. No more Colonel Zurbarán. He was divorced five years ago. They were childless. Separating was easy. Anyway, he'd bedded most of Hunan. He was a swollen Yellow River, and she was no longer tempest. They were wrong for each other.

Guadalupe's mother was dead thirteen months, a great sadness and a great release. Señora Talavera Espinoza had been the lone figure who reminded Guadalupe how dust-free her life was, how unmarried she was, how alone she was. No one brought up these facts to Guadalupe now, no friend, no family member.

The kidnapping, however, was a wild blow. Guadalupe had gasped and cried out, high pitched and loud on a street corner, after Jim Meeker caught up with her and told her the news. All the swear words of the Revolution poured out of her.

This Jesuit tragedy, this threat to Tom—the real person, not the man of her dreams—this Guatemalan escapade was a hot sun that evaporated what had become the most important support column of Guadalupe's life, a rigid column of memory and feelings. So much was bound up in that column: words of love, phrases of delight, the shape of a body, anger and pain. She had imprisoned them all inside the column. Now the column had transformed, taken on life, grown heart and hands, feet and face. It had moved out into the light.

It wasn't that she loved Tom anymore and that her love was threatened, although she did love him, she thought, in some manner. A sinew of pain lay buried in the muscle mass of her heart, a sinew of rejection, of loss. Was it the pain a mother felt when her child died before her? These last days the sinew would contract at any hour, day or night, clouding knowledge with pain.

She had learned so much that winter in Massachusetts. She had learned that Tom had another love in his life. She had tried to woo him away from that lover. She'd nearly succeeded. But how could she, a mere woman, compete with baroque dreams, with a spirit thirsting for noble deeds, with eyes that strained to look through matter into the kind heart of energy? She was but a smudge of matter, the soft mounding of a few trace metals and the fluidity of water. She was a spirit of the land, rooted, distinctive in her smell, impure—a strange sister to the cosmic spirit Tom worshiped, draped as that spirit was in a glowing mantle of galaxies.

Guadalupe stopped at a street corner. Her eyes blurred. She clutched her throat. She remembered the intense dryness of that valley of disappointment. She had fallen into the valley from a green, flowering cliff. Tom had told her he was a priest.

She had asked the question. "Why are you studying economics?" They were at lunch. It was a dirty little student place off Harvard Square, full of the smell of animal grease and the scratchy chatter of a cheap radio.

"I'm a Jesuit, a priest. I plan on teaching—after. I've been sent here to study." The words had slapped her. She lost her balance. She fell. He kept on talking. Her soul was empty and airless, but he didn't seem to notice. Occasionally she laughed. She said: "I see." "Ah, yes." Hadn't he read her eyes? Why did he keep on talking? Wasn't he the one with priest-eyes that could see through veils?

Guadalupe could not remember anything else Tom said that day. However, she remembered how his dimples transformed his cheeks as he smiled, as if his personality lived there, in those little hollows, as if it danced there. She remembered the color of his eyebrows, a light red, perhaps tinted with blond unlike the nearly rust red hair on his head. Several times she quashed an urge to reach over and touch his eyebrows or to put her hand through the tight waves of his hair. She observed his hands opening and closing and the light red fuzz that marched down to them along his well-shaped arms.

That night Guadalupe had cried so loudly that she knew her housemates would ask her about it in the morning. She also knew she could not speak of it in the morning. Nor could she think of a way to speak to Tom about her feelings. It would shame her and her family to discuss those feelings.

For an entire month Guadalupe and Tom arranged to spend parts of each day together, meeting for coffee or a lunch of gringo tomato soup spiced with Tabasco sauce. They spoke little of their personal lives. They discussed classwork or the politics of the day. Guadalupe assumed that Tom had withdrawn into that personal cloister in which priests maintained themselves, a sanctuary of ritual purity which she should not seek to penetrate.

Eight weeks after they met, the rites of the Church opened up a dangerous door. It was the last day of what had been a luscious, warm and long fall. Guadalupe found herself moping about Cambridge, still struggling with her attraction to the wrong man, wondering if there might be any possibilities in the relationship, fearful of how alien all of this was to her, how little experience she had in relationships, how simple she had supposed her romantic life would be. As she rounded Arrow Street in front of St. Bridget's, she decided to go into the church to pray.

Guadalupe had intended to light a candle to the Virgin and pray for guidance from this other woman who'd been bound up in the ways of men, struggling to be holy. As she walked up the left aisle toward the Mary altar, she noticed four or five people gathered near the cabinet of the confessional. Then the idea dawned on her. She might get relief speaking to an unknown priest about her feelings. Even a lecture would be an improvement, something concrete. She could touch it, feel its texture, poke it with her hand.

"I do not know the words in English, Father," she spoke as the priest nodded to her through the confessional grille. The dim light of the confessional and the thin white covering over the grille hid the features of his face. She could not determine his age. "And I come to speak more of a question than of a sin, at least I do not think it is a sin."

There was a pause. She could see that the priest had leaned his head toward her. He propped up his head with one hand as if he were straining to hear, or as if the teeth in his jaw had stunned him with pain. She was afraid he had totally misunderstood her. So, as anyone unsure of the language, she began again. "Father, I speak Spanish. I do not know the ritual words in English . . ."

The priest interrupted her, saying, "Guadalupe, I don't think we should do this."

She held her breath.

"Tom, is that you?" she said, finally exhaling. Did he know what she wanted to confess?

"Yes, it's me." His whispered response had barely escaped from his throat.

They remained quiet for several minutes. Footfalls echoed on the marble floor outside the confessional. She was waiting for him to say something wise, something spiritual.

"Maybe we should talk—about us," Guadalupe said, breaking the silence. "Maybe this is God telling us to talk."

"Oh, Guadalupe, I don't know. Maybe it is, but not here in the confessional. I can't speak to you here, I can't hear your confession. Please, wait outside. I'll be done soon. We can talk then."

"What will be different outside?" She was unwilling to lose the moment of truth.

Another pause.

"I'll be able to see you," Tom said.

"And seeing makes a difference?"

"Seeing makes a difference. Seeing you—seeing you, I—I can't deny my feelings."

"And what are your feelings?" she asked, her heart warming to the day's atmosphere.

"I—I feel—I'm attracted to you—in a romantic way." She could see him rub his face. She heard him inhale deeply. He made a hand gesture, an awkward, searching movement. "And I dream of you—all the time."

There was agony in his words. "My prayer life is a mess! I have no concentration, no peace. I've begun to think of you whenever I'm alone, and I . . ."

"Finish up here, Tom," Guadalupe said, ending her confession. "I will wait outside."

Guadalupe had seen her future. It appeared as quickly as a Caribbean hurricane roaring across coastal silt and tangled mangrove thickets. She knew she and Tom would be lovers, that their love would twist them, that they would experience a passion neither had yet known, eye-popping as a trip into space.

Guadalupe arrived at the green door of her Managua apartment, just off Bolívar, a street with a clipped view of Xolotlán, and sat to rest on the stoop, fiddling with the iron key, nodding mindlessly to passing neighbors. All day she'd reviewed facts and sorted through memories. It was time for resolution. She was forcing herself to a decision.

Finally, she stood up and unlocked the door, pushing open the worn wood with a convert's certainty. Guadalupe had decided to do something to help Tom. She would extend a hand to the man who had hurt her, who had infected her with a stony hatred when most she had needed potions of love. She would take up arms one more time.

CHAPTER SEVENTEEN

Human happiness is a game. The playing field is a wide cylinder that wobbles precariously on the fulcrum of fate. Inside we struggle to stand, our arms outstretched and pushing against the walls, our feet dancing for stability. At one end of the cylinder is hope. At the other end is submission. No one wins at happiness unless he struggles with all his might to hang on to the side of hope until, exhausted, all that remains is to fall out of the cylinder through submission. Where are you, old friend, in the game?

Excerpt from a letter of Father Beltrán to his friend and correspondent Pierre Teilhard de Chardin, S.J., written after Father Beltrán's exile to India.

On Saturday David told Mark he'd fly to Washington next Thursday. David and Mark decided they needed to be together to support one another in this crisis, to be near each other to concoct the perfect plan. Mark complained, ever so quietly, that Ann didn't *really* understand what he was going through.

"Come on Mark, what do you mean?" David asked.

When David and Ann had first met they quickly formed a relationship that verged on the sororal with giggles and block-long fashion critiques. Ann had even confided in David about Mark's habit of collecting his toenail clippings in a mayonnaise jar. "He still does that?!?" David had exclaimed. "It made my skin roll up under my eyelids!"

"She doesn't know how this experience is unfolding my guts," Mark said on Saturday.

"Why not? Hasn't she known loss? Or the fear of it?"

David's days were filled with memories more vibrant and unpredictable than life, memories that crowded at the head of the table.

He was concentrated on that one event, whether talking on the phone, watching TV, reading up on Guatemala, or telling his friends endless stories about his times in the Jesuits and especially about Tom and Mark.

But nothing good seemed to be happening in Tom's case. The United States had sent no special envoy.

David yelled at Mark during their daily conversations, "So those jerks you work with won't help! Where are the repercussions? What's going on? I thought you and your politico pal had some power!"

"I do, David. So does Senator Brandon. But things have changed in the past years. There may actually be a chance to bring *peace* to Guatemala. Nobody wants to stir up passions right now."

"Oh, so kidnapping's no longer a crime? Does this administration sanction crime?"

"That's not it, David. It's complicated."

"Oh, yeah." David was wringing the cord of his phone with the fury of a farm boy ringing the neck of the dinner chicken. "So, because in a week they may want to sit down with these UDA thugs, the American government needs to keep its mouth shut about the terror their *allies* inflict. Hell, we probably trained that pleasant little posse at our best finishing camp, the School of the Americas. I see nothing complicated here. We sell out our principles! We sell out Tom!"

Mark's sigh flooded back across the cables of David's newest T-1 phone line.

"I'm sorry," David said. "I know you're trying. It's as if . . . it's as if Tom will be the last soldier killed in the war. The last person to die of AIDS. . . ."

David jumped off the Evian wagon and drank pots of Costa Rican coffee. He stayed up late listening to the half dozen records of religious music he kept packed away in the back of a basement storage closet along with the glory albums of the '70s, Streisand, Taylor, and Barry White. The religious records had been stamped when he was studying philosophy in St. Louis. He'd written the jacket notes for a couple of them. Twice he stayed up until dawn playing the same record over and over during those boundary hours. It was the one record, *Trust in Love*, on which he could listen to the lilt of Tom's young voice: Tom, the best soloist of the Fusz choir.

David's Minneapolis friends began to fear. His actions, many infused with a disturbing Catholic scent, spooked them. Few of them knew Tom. None of them understood David's reaction.

Since leaving the Jesuits David no longer went to Mass or prayed or gave any thought to the ways of his religious past, which he saw as a sad child's delicate yet deranged nest of dreams.

His current vocation was the nurturing of the magazine and AIDS activism, hopeless as that task seemed.

After Tom's kidnapping, David attended Mass four days in a row, refusing breakfast meetings with his best friend Samuel.

A comely young priest with close-cropped black hair and Castro-clone moustache celebrated those Masses. The priest spoke, unfortunately, with the flatness of a well-ironed soul, made more painful to hear by the degree of his physical beauty. David closed his eyes and ears, however, and brought back memories of other liturgies, '70s liturgies bursting with the goodness of life and of celebration rediscovered.

"OK, David, what gives?" Samuel demanded on the phone Tuesday night.

"What do you mean?"

"I mean—I know this is a stressful time for you. It's obvious. And I've been happy to listen to all your old stories, but what's going on with this religious schtick? You told me you don't believe in any of that stuff, not anymore."

"I don't, in one way. Maybe I do, in another."

"Oh God-the-unnameable, what's that supposed to mean?"

"That means—that means . . ." David wasn't sure what to say. "OK, the images, the rituals—taken in the right light, mind you, they have power. You know, Samuel, it's the same with your first gay pride march, your first loud, public, brave statement, your entering into the crowd to change history. You touched something special that day."

"That's politics, David. That's elation. That's personal freedom and self-discovery. I don't get how it's the same as—the same as kneeling before a wafer—or toast or whatever!"

"It's not toast. We don't burn our sacrifices."

"You know what I mean."

"I know what you mean. And I know these rituals seem bizarre to you, nothing but boys in brocade, but for me—they're putting me in touch with a big spirit, and its good mystery, and with an old truth, a really old, aunty-of-all-aunties truth."

"Don't get me wrong, I'm all for what you just said. But I don't under-stand. Forgive me for repeating myself: You don't *believe*."

"I don't have to believe. It's not up to me. Something *inside* me is believing."

David pressed his left hand onto his stomach. "Maybe it's only a cul-ture ghost."

David was standing in the master bedroom of his Mount Curve man-sion in front of a great, bronze-encased mirror, a prized relic from the hey-day of the French Revolution. He eyed himself skeptically. "Or is it just something private, just my own synapses, their pathways misfiring under too much stress?" His voice trailed off into a whisper. "In any case, there *is* something inside me—and, well, it's *awake*."

Wednesday morning, after an evening-long session with his memories, David stopped in at dawn to light a candle at the smooth and shiny alcove of adoration at St. Olaf's in downtown Minneapolis where the light of a hundred brightly colored votive candle holders reflected off the mottled brown marble. He watched a pair of stubby candles flicker and die. He felt their end. The final swoop. He thought he tasted the grit of those two little black death-clouds on the tip of his tongue.

At one point that morning David saw Randy's last-day face stare back at him through the swirl of marble. David gasped, shook his head, and cried out, "No!" His shock seemed to wake up the church itself, the pews straightening their bent backs, the marble walls pulling in their stomachs, the tabernacle inhaling another gust of human distress in through the keyhole. David wrote in his diary after returning from Mass:

> *I see Tom in a hut. I see him bruised. I reach out my hand to touch*
> *him, but nothing happens. My hand disappears. I hear his voice*
> *singing: "Make me a channel of your peace." He looks up, the way*
> *he would after Communion. Hundreds of times I watched him*
> *return to his pew and kneel to pray. I loved to watch him. He*
> *winked back at me and smiled, all teeth and dimples. I loved him.*
> *He loved me. "Channel of your peace." Did that phrase betray*
> *him? We relished those words. We heard guitars and angelic har-*
> *monies. How could those words lead to this?*
>
> *Beware the words.*

Ever since the thing happened, not Tom's kidnapping but the *thing*, Mark had become quiet, withdrawn into inner chambers. The kidnapping nearly sealed him in.

Even without the distraction of Tom's kidnapping, Mark couldn't figure it out. He hadn't meant for *the thing* to happen. That was an act of God, if any act were. Hah! He didn't believe that! But Tom's kidnapping—were they connected? They were. Somehow they were. He was sure. Surer and surer.

Mark began to carry a yellow notepad wherever he went and wrote down his thoughts, or the curt phrases that wafted in and out of his consciousness, repetitive and explorative as infant speech: break through, break down, break up.

"Twelve years," Mark muttered to himself as he walked near the Jefferson Memorial, his head low. It was a forlorn, set-aside place. "Twelve years ago I had the crisis—and the breakthrough. Twelve years. But the problem's still there, only now I'm dragging others down with me." He clenched his fists and softly beat his thighs.

"What are you writing?" Ann asked Tuesday night after Mark had come home late.

He had greeted his family haltingly, brushing Ann's cheek with his lips, a hand shuffling Charley's golden hair. He said he was tired and walked through the pair to his study.

Mark was sitting at his desk. He covered his words and turned to look at Ann. "Notes. Notes for a speech. I'm working on a speech for Senator Brandon."

"You don't write speeches. Jill Henry does that. She's good, too. You're too wordy."

"She can't do this one, so I'm getting a chance."

"A chance? Fine," Ann said, walking away shaking her head.

Mark wrote the word "rent." Then he wrote: "in the fabric." Then he wrote: "of existence" and began to cry softly. That night he slept in the study.

Ann didn't knock on the door to say good night or urge him to come to bed. Her silence was just what he'd hoped for. It gave him more time.

"Ann, over here!" David yelled above the crowd at National Airport. "This place is as dumpy as ever," he said as he enfolded her with a hug after gesturing widely to the space around him. "Where's Charley?"

"He's in school. He's getting old, you know. He's almost seven!"

Ann adjusted the lay of the garnet necklace that curved over the ecru smoothness of her blouse. The rest of her outfit was less formal, stone washed jeans and low green suede heels. David had loved the way fabric fit her. Ann was a woman made for clothes. Her skin radiated next to soft colors.

"I can't believe it—Charley's almost seven!" David said with a goofy brightness. Ann blanched.

David remembered Mark telling him for the first two years of Charley's life, when they had talked every month, that his son may not live to be five. Was that gruesome anticipation the specter that shifted across Ann's face? A worry that terrified her even with the mention of Charley's name?

"Children age so rapidly, not like we adults!" David exclaimed. Holding Ann at arm's length, with the joy of a proud father, David said, "My God, Ann, you could be a cheerleader! And that necklace is to die for."

David remembered that Ann wrote about going back to teaching in her last Christmas card and how that thought chilled her because for the last six years she'd dedicated herself to her son's health with the solemnity of a cloister nun at her devotions. He had wondered if she thought that comment were funny. He still wasn't sure.

"Mark couldn't meet us either? The Sappingstone men are about their great deeds?"

"Work, you know," Ann said, looking away. "Personal crises just don't match up to national ones." Her voice caught on the word "national" as if it were indigestible and sour.

On the drive to the Sappingstone's home in Arlington, it came out, a dirty secret, as if she'd said "the child's a bastard," that David was to return to the city in the evening for a dinner meeting with Mark.

"He wants you to meet with Gloria."

Ann gripped tightly onto the steering wheel.

"She's the director of the Washington Office on Central America, a human rights lobbying organization. Supposedly Gloria has contacts. She seems to know *everybody* and *everything* in the world of Latin politics. And she's radical nobility. Her parents were jailed in South Africa."

"Great!" David said, his tone too rosy for the message. He replayed Mark's comment about Ann's not understanding. Something was eating at her. It couldn't be Tom's plight.

David thought he knew. He'd seen this sort of face before, bruised, as it were, on the inside with an ache deep in the bone. Many of his friends had separated after years yoked in love. The last years were the worst. No one wanted to appear the shrew as he hacked at the binding.

"But—don't you want to come with us?"

"I have to stay with Charley. Besides, I wasn't invited."

David looked over and saw tears. He hadn't suspected. He assumed Mark had formed a strong bond. They'd been married nine years. But then, Mark had been a Jesuit for eleven years and left. And what about himself? Death had ended David's greatest love. Would his love of Randy have lasted beyond a decade?

"I'll invite you," David said, refraining from reaching over to touch Ann, who looked a Greek widow intent on her loom as she negotiated Virginia's weaving traffic.

But Ann glanced over briefly. She held out her right hand with the palm facing toward David and shook her head. A desperation settled into the car.

When they got in the house, Ann told David to put his suitcase and carry-on in the upstairs guest bedroom and began explaining the new gray carpeting with black and red borders, and the 1940s floral print wallpaper, her voice mindless as a docent's on her last day.

David dropped his bags in the entryway and grabbed Ann by the hand. "OK, let's get it out," he said as he led her to the small sun room off the living room.

She followed, obedient as a schoolgirl.

Too obedient, David thought as he pulled her on. She was tennis nobility, a sought-after trainer, a math whiz who calculated the number of hours between any two dates, a charmer with beauty, a miracle woman who kept a sickly child alive. This mood, this mousy, lowest order of nun, mother-superior-is-God submission disturbed David. How had it come to inhabit Ann?

She sat on the white rattan love seat, a palm frond caressing her hair. She began to sob. She bent over at first, cupping her head in her hands. David sat down next to her. He reached over to rub her back.

"I'm embarrassed to talk about it!" Ann said through her tears, wringing her hands as if she were forming a small, oblong pebble of clay. She took out a tissue from her pants pocket and blew her nose.

"Ever since Charley was born, we've had our troubles. I'm sure you know. I'm sure he's told you. But recently—recently he's disappeared!"

"Mark's always been secretive, a little boy with a forbidden treasure. I used to find it cute. Now it's—whatever's in his treasure trove is all he thinks about." Ann looked up at the ceiling for a moment, then out into the room. There was something worse, an older tale.

Ann took a deep breath, more tears marshaling behind her retina, but staying in formation. She looked at the polished oak floor. "My father had an affair once. He told my mother after it was over, but she never let him forget it. They were almost sixty then. They lived together another twenty years. I still hear her screaming at him whenever he came home late. Half an hour late, and she'd be Doberman furious."

Ann crumpled the tissue in her hands. "I can hear the hurt in her voice, as if she were a wounded dog unleashed and charging. I see her in my mind. Her eyes are red. Red! Do you know what that's like?"

David didn't move. For much of his life, until his novitiate years, his sole image of his own mother was as a demon. A subtle demon. In silk and pearls, martini glass and Mondrian face, swathed in azure, maybe, beguiling and bewildering, but never red. Barking, yes, but not red.

"And it's only her face I see, mostly her eyes," Ann said. She looked straight into David's eyes. "Mark's the same as my father. He'd never leave me, not since Charley." Ann started to run her hands through her hair, undoing the morning's waves.

"I keep wondering if things would be different if Charley's heart were OK." Ann paused, folded her hands again into her lap and looked down at them. "We do what we can. It's in God's hands, I guess."

David circled Ann with his arm. They remained quiet a few minutes. He'd totally forgotten about Tom until she'd mentioned "God's hands." He was suddenly exhausted. Too many tragedies.

Ann disengaged. "Something's happened. Recently. I smell it. There's a rat decomposing in the wall. I know Mark's going to tell me something, and I know how it'll be. He'll be the prosecutor in a court of law. He's going to tell me about the rat, and then it's judgment time. That's the way he is. Facts, judgment, sentencing. No chattering in the jury box." She looked at David, bold and accusing.

"I'll talk to Mark—about the rat, if you want," David said, his offer barely audible. He had no idea what he could say, but he was feeling a responsibility for Mark, as if he were an older brother.

"OK," Ann said, a flat hardness whitening her face. "Maybe you know some words I don't know. Maybe there's something Jesuitical you can say."

Ann drove David into Georgetown at four in the afternoon. She had to pick up Charley at his school, an expensive private institution with two fully equipped medical rooms and an ER-certified staff. "I'll just wander around until dinner," David said. "I'm sorry I can't see Charley yet. Say hi to him for me." He was relieved to be on his own.

David was to meet Mark and Gloria at Campo Bello. He had expected they would meet in some quiet hideaway. Instead, Campo Bello was a busy new pasta restaurant on M street with tables and booths set under a canopy of ficus trees and where the patrons ambled through that potted forest schmoozy as senators in their chamber.

After half a minute peering through the leafy camouflage, David spied Mark nestled into one side of a booth halfway down the outer wall of the main room. A woman sat close next to him.

Mark saw David and half rose, waving David inward.

David smiled, waving back at Mark, noting the modest space that separated Mark and the woman. It was almost as if Mark were protecting her. David's heart slowed to a dreary beat. He had a vision of Mark touching the woman, Gloria, disrobing her with a fevered hand.

David told himself to keep smiling and step forward.

He was relieved by Gloria's appearance. She was the anti-Ann. Streaks of gray wound in and out, unevenly, through her black hair. Her long face puffed out in two cheeky bulges. She wore a pea green dress and a flat brown scarf which spread out too extensively at her neck. Tapering gold earrings, in the form of a warlike pre-Colombian deity, dangled from her ears. But Gloria did have a bright smile, and a fervency radiated from her, even before she spoke, a regal certitude, as if she were the Virgin balanced on her half-moon and rising over the world.

"David, this is Gloria," Mark said as the two new friends shook hands across the table. "She has an idea for us to consider."

"Good," David said, settling into his side of the booth, reminding himself they were meeting to discuss Tom. "We need ideas."

"I think you need a plan with several options," Gloria said without further introductions.

"You have such a plan?" David asked.

He really wasn't ready to think about the kidnapping. For the last two hours he'd wandered through Georgetown reviewing everything he knew about Mark: his zeal, his sincerity. He remembered their novice master didn't want Mark to take vows. What had Father Gorman seen? David had long ago dismissed that man's insights. Perhaps the dismissal was a mistake. And what had Father Gorman thought of him, the loud queer one? That he had a bushel of talent. And bushels of talent were given out for a reason. That's what his novice master had pronounced to him month after month, urging more light, kinder light.

"I have the outline of a plan," Gloria said.

"OK, let's hear it," David said as the waiter appeared, asking David for a drink order. "Glenlivet, a double, straight up."

"Well, it involves travel. And money," Gloria said, examining David's face for a reaction. David was used to that look. The non-rich had no understanding of wealth.

"I assumed we'd get to the money part," David said, "but I don't know what you mean by travel."

"These are the facts." Gloria leaned into the table and spoke quietly, as if they were dissidents in the back-room narrowness of Communist Eastern Europe. "The UDA will not negotiate, they don't need to. They act with impunity. So, you guys need to meet their demands, to put up the two million in ransom." She paused, her eyes searching for a reaction.

David smiled back. So far no surprise. Where was his drink?

Gloria continued. "Our sources at the State Department say the Jesuits don't have the money and aren't willing to get into the ransom game. Certainly the United States can't get involved in making money offers. Besides, the government isn't party to the conflict."

The waiter returned with David's drink and hurried off before David could order food.

"So," Gloria said, leaning in a little further, staring into David's eyes, "we need to convince the Jesuits to agree to take your two million, or at least to use it in their negotiations." Gloria turned to look at Mark. "That needs to be negotiated with the Jesuits." Back to David, "which brings us to travel."

David gulped down half the Glenlivet and stared back at this new female.

Gloria settled five inches into the depth of the booth to deliver her next bits of news.

"It appears that a Father Eger, some obscure priest from Rome, has been sent by the Jesuit General to handle the situation. Our sources tell us he's done little since arriving, except hide from the press, which is becoming increasingly disinterested—as nothing is happening."

"You two need to go to Guatemala and convince this priest to do a deal with the UDA. If the Jesuits won't bite, then we need to get the American ambassador involved. The ambassador might know someone else, maybe a local Church official, who'd be willing to negotiate with the UDA. However, this ambassador's not apt to be an ally. He's been there too long, seen too much, been too quiet. Final option, you two do the negotiating yourselves. Much more risky," Gloria said, settling totally into the booth's floral smoothness.

"Do you even think the UDA will hold to a deal, any deal?" David asked. He finished the Glenlivet.

David wanted another scotch, and he didn't want to go to Guatemala, and he didn't want to have Gloria laying out their strategy. In his mind, she was already the enemy. He reminded himself to control his tongue.

"Will they let Tom go if we lay out the gold?" David asked, batting out the words with a rapper's rhythm.

"We think they'll insist on dealing with the Jesuits," Mark said, joining the conversation again, sounding dazed.

David stared at Mark. Why was this the first time he'd heard about Gloria's plot? Mark evidently knew all about it. The two of them had been yakking on the phone for days. Was this how Mark worked in Washington, always behind the scenes? No wonder Ann couldn't get anywhere with him.

"The UDA want to make a point," Mark said in the absence of any Jepson comment. He looked briefly over at Gloria, the skin around his eyes crinkling as if they'd argued about the topic. "If they also get money, all the better for them."

"And their point is?" David asked, his eyes still on Mark.

"That the Church must stay out of politics," Mark said, emotionless, "even in its commentaries."

"And will they let Tom go?" David asked his question again. He suddenly realized he was angry. He was angry at Mark. He was angry at the don't-I-look-innocent US government. He was angry at St. Gloria of the

Secrecy of Mary. But especially angry at Mark. His anger was steaming up. Six days of daily discussions, and Mark hadn't mentioned a thing about a rescue junket! Nothing about a marriage in chaos! David had shared every detail of Randy's dying, even the joke that killed him off.

"We think they'll let him go," Mark said, looking again at Gloria.

Didn't he hear my anger, David wondered? What's he all about? Does he want to screw her here? This must be the other woman. What about Tom?!

"They'll let him go if the State Department continues to put pressure on the Guatemalan government," Mark said, droning now, looking back at David. "The Guatemalan government can put pressure on the UDA. Besides, the UDA have already told the world what they're about. They want to frighten Church folk who keep talking about social justice. They don't need to kill Tom. Everyone already knows they kill. And they've already killed foreigners," Mark said, "a couple of Belgian missionaries, several Spaniards, two nuns from Italy. Tom would be an American victim, which is more significant in terms of hemispheric power politics." He paused.

For a moment David saw a pain in Mark's eyes. Was the pain about Tom or about his marriage? Or maybe you can't separate pains. Maybe all pain has one mother, and her children are close copies of each other.

"Their real goal is to send a message, and we think they've sent it already. Now they might be happy to pick up some cash."

"But nothing's certain," David said calmly. He wanted to leave.

"No, nothing's certain," Gloria said.

David watched this new Washington woman fold her odd little smile over the rim of her martini glass.

"And remember this," Gloria said, putting down the long-stemmed glass, "what's the life of one gringo priest to these thugs? They've killed hundreds of thousands, by massacre or night raid."

The group froze. David's heart sank deeper. Now Gloria was making a rescue sound impossible. What was her point? And what did Mark see in her?

"So, from what you're saying, this mission of ours could be dangerous?" David asked, "If they want to kill gringos, why stop at Tom?"

David leaned out of the booth and tst'd the waiter, whose tight butt he'd glimpsed poking out behind a date palm. He desperately needed another Glenlivet. And every appetizer they served in Campo Bello, which he had decided to christen the Last Stop in the Tunnel to Hades.

"It could be dangerous for the two of you, yes. In Guatemala, many people have guns—and itchy fingers," Gloria said.

She reached over to hold David's hand. He was surprised. Her hand felt boneless as a rubber toy. "But you won't be their target. You don't live there and preach about land redistribution, preach about social evils, preach about the great encyclicals that call for justice. You don't threaten them."

"Still, we'll be on the wrong side," David said as he removed his hand from Gloria's and waved again at the waiter.

"Yes, wrong side," she said, nodding.

"Well, we have time to consider this." David looked over to Mark whose eyes were staring off into the distance. "Right, Mark?"

"Time? Not much," Mark said. "There isn't much time. And to make the plan work, we've got to meet people. We've got to make contacts. To negotiate. We're leaving tomorrow." Mark pulled two tickets out of his blue suit jacket. "If you're agreed to go."

"Tomorrow? It's got to be tomorrow?!" David was shocked. He couldn't even concentrate on the waiter, who'd finally shown up. David raised a hand, asking him to wait.

"Critical," Mark said.

"You've told Ann?" David reached out and grabbed the waiter's arm just as he'd started to move away.

"No. I'll tell her in the morning," Mark said, looking down and slowly twisting his wedding ring.

"That's not fair," David said.

"It can't be helped."

David and Mark drove home that night in an alcoholic silence. Halfway through his third scotch David agreed to participate in the rescue plan, to leave on a flight in the morning for Guatemala City.

Ann was furious the next morning, adamant that Mark should not go to Guatemala, yelling at him in the kitchen in her tomato red bathrobe. Mark was half-dressed, his T-shirt resting outside his khaki pants. He stood at the counter gulping down a bowl of cereal. David had just walked in and remained in the doorway.

"You can't leave! You can't take the risk! You've got a small child, you have your responsibility to us. I can't believe you'd even consider doing this. Those people are killers down there. I refuse to let you go!"

Mark kept on eating. His face was full red. Veins bulged on the muscles of his neck. All the blood had massed in the top layer of skin. After shoveling in another mouthful of Cheerios he cranked out, "I can't let David go alone."

"Why not? David can take care of himself. He can hire a bodyguard! A battalion of bodyguards!"

"Ann, dear, be reasonable," Mark said, sounding the scolding father, superior in every aspect. "I can't ask David to do this by himself. That's unfair . . ."

David stepped forward, ready to jump in, to say something, but Ann gestured him to silence. She screamed into Mark's face, "This is not about David. This is about you! This is about our family!"

Mark slammed the half-finished bowl of cereal onto the countertop, saying, "I'm going to do my duty. I'm sorry you don't see it that way." He hustled past David, ordering him to meet at the car in ten minutes.

David edged into the kitchen. This scene was unexpected. He'd thought Ann's anger was hidden from Mark, subterranean.

Charley looked up at his mother and started to cry. A pile of Cheerios fell out of his right hand as Ann picked him up and held him to her. David thought Charley small for a seven year old. He couldn't be sure. He didn't know enough about children.

"I haven't talked to him yet," David said. "I'll talk to him during the trip."

Ann didn't look back at David. She'd gone over to the French doors and stared out into the dark yard, stared at the even darker shape of three evergreens.

Her voice distant, as if she were speaking in a trance, Ann said, "My mother gave me advice on my wedding day. 'Men get so they can't sort things out, that's when they make their worst mistakes.' She said that standing over me as she fitted my veil."

"Well, I'm sorting things out," Ann said, her face still gazing through the window, her hot will reflecting back into the room. "I won't be here when you two get back. Tell that to Mark on your jungle adventure!"

The only eyes in the entire Sappingstone household into which David could really look were Charley's, who was staring over his mother's shoulder. And Charley's eyes were swollen, inhabited by a puffy uncertainty and night-wall fear David suddenly recognized from his own past.

CHAPTER EIGHTEEN

Traffic and a dense fog added minutes and tension to Mark and David's pre-dawn trip to the airport. On their way Mark called his assistant, Janet, ringing her at home with his cell phone. He ordered her to handle the special investigation that Senator Brandon planned on launching into the "Jesuit abduction," as the senator termed Tom's kidnapping. They argued. David, straining slightly, heard Janet say, "It's unfair. I don't follow Latin American policy." Mark barked back, spitting out "nothing's fair," and hung up. He swerved a foot onto the black shoulder of the road as he put the phone in his coat pocket; his silver Mercedes's headlights brightened up a patch of dark pine forest.

"You'd better lighten up," David said as he stared at his friend, his legs tense, using both hands to steady himself on the dashboard. "This is dangerous stuff we're getting into, no trip to villa. We need to be level-headed."

Mark focused forward, silent, his hands gripping the steering wheel the way a top-notch wrestler settles onto his opponent. He signaled a lane change and sped up. David thought he heard a low snarl.

"I know this could be dangerous," Mark said. "I also know I need to do this, so get off my case."

The air hummed into David's lungs. He closed his eyes and concentrated on his own need for peace, preparing himself, perhaps too late, for what was fast becoming the most perilous journey of his life.

At Dulles, David stopped to call James Rafferty at Georgetown. They'd kept in contact about Tom's kidnapping, promising to share information.

"You could've used my cell phone," Mark said, looking at his watch as David made his way back to the gateway just before the annoyed crew insisted on closing the doors.

"I know," David said, as nicely as he could. He glared at Mark in the harsh light of the gangway. That hallway's false luminescence made Mark look wasted, a prisoner recently released from solitary. For a moment David toyed with the idea of handing over his checkbook to his fire-spewing friend and returning to the safety of Minneapolis.

"Are you sure you should tell anybody what we're doing?" Mark asked directly into David's ear as they hurried down the gangway.

David squinted until his eyes were medieval helmet slits and forced himself to count the windows of the gangway as they began to jog forward.

"Did you tell Rafferty about the money?" Mark asked at the plane's door.

"He asked," David said as they entered the cabin, hissing the answer. He smiled to the stewardess, knowing as he smiled that he looked the dismissive lord. "I didn't mention money, precisely," David said, turning back at Mark. "I was evasive."

"Damn it, David! Rafferty's probably figured it out! He's probably calling his provincial—or Rome—right now."

Everyone in first class looked up to follow their conversation, a luminous curiosity in the other passengers' eyes.

"Is that bad?" David asked. He was trying to whisper, to curtain off their conversation in a small space. "We want to make a deal, don't we? Maybe he'll grease the skids."

"Grease the skids?" Mark shook his head as he adjusted the belt in his aisle seat. "You're in over your head. Just follow my lead, will you?"

Settled into their seats, the pair's silence turned into a foot of ice thick enough to walk on. At first the flight attendant did her best to be cheerful with them, but all she got were gruff replies. "Coffee. Black. I'm fine, thanks." So she left them alone, turning away whenever she passed near.

David asked for three Tylenol and, as soon as they were in air, closed his eyes as tight as submarine hatches. His head pounded through a sea of questions, whose swift currents split the atoms of peace. He'd hoped to help Mark free Tom, which he imagined meant working the halls of Washington, maybe making a few phone calls to influential senators who might envision hefty campaign contributions for a little pressure on the State Department.

Only one thing was clear. David couldn't let his friendship with Tom dissolve in this meaningless way, by machete or bullet strike. If everything else failed, David would pay the ransom, open the Saracen's dungeon tower with Jepson gold. In his dreams the past week David saw Tom's captors as turbaned marauders from the fifteenth century, vile and small, ruthless men who had slit the throat of Byzantium. Gloria's story of the previous evening, footnoted with the details of mayhem, had made his dreams desperately real.

And now this man next to him, one of his dearest friends, an anchor into something sacred, into the best parts of David's personality, the parts that had once led to conversion of heart, the inner melting and reforging of personality, was cranky to the point of being irrational. Mark could snap in the wind, the way a haughty sapling with too many tight-angled, leaf-covered limbs is undone by an August storm.

With his eyes closed David could smell all too well. Testosterone wafted off Mark, pungent as the stink off a corralled bull. Did it make sense to continue with Mark? To continue on down this crusader's trail? Mark could act on hotheaded impulse, get them into real trouble, get them all killed.

David reached into his pocket for the small case of sleeping pills he'd almost forgotten to pack in Minneapolis. He took two tablets and was asleep in twenty minutes.

Mark had to pinch David's wrists to wake him in Guatemala.

"You're lucky I always travel with my passport, the way I did as a Jesuit, always ready for the unexpected mission," David said as they stood in line to exit the plane, acting out the jaunty and upbeat companion. He raised an eyebrow and smiled, his old signal for, "Can we start over?" The rest had done him good.

"I know you well," Mark said, jaunty in reply, as if they were old friends renewing their acquaintance. "You always insisted on carrying that thing with you, hoping for adventure."

Mark turned his head to examine the crowd, back and forth as if he expected some danger to be waiting for them with sign in hand, saying quietly to David, "The situation was deteriorating. We knew we had to do something. We couldn't work things from Washington."

"We?"

"Gloria and me." Mark's face turned blank, his cheeks gray. "She's OK. Her heart's in the right place."

Unblinking, seeing Mark now caught in a narrow cell, David said, "You know we need to talk. I mean *talk*."

"I know," Mark said as the exit line began to move, looking back again over the crowd. "I need to talk."

Three hours after the two friends departed from Washington, the first phone calls reached both Rome and Guatemala City relaying to their contacts the news that two ex-Jesuits, one of them immensely wealthy, a possible source of ransom money, had departed from Dulles Airport for Guatemala City.

David and Mark packed themselves into a dusty, mint-green Volkswagen cab and headed for the hotel Camino Montserrat in Zone 10. David insisted on paying the thousand-dollar-a-night for a suite in the best hotel in the capital. He told Mark it would give them credence—and reduce their stress, asserting quietly that a friend he'd called the night before, back at Mark's home, waking the friend from a deep sleep, had told David that the hotel was well guarded.

Their cab ride was silent.

David only began to relax as they checked into the hotel, a large, modern complex of nearly five hundred rooms that surrounded swimming pools, restaurants, galleries and shops. Their suite, rimmed with deep-carved furniture, led onto a balcony, which overlooked a courtyard tiled in white and blue, the tiles shimmering in the afternoon sun.

"I need a change of clothes, fresh air, and a drink," David called out as he flung his suitcase onto the bed in the master bedroom. "But not in that order. First I'm ordering the Glenlivet," he said as he picked up the black receiver of his princess phone.

"Shouldn't we start making phone calls?" Mark asked, gently, standing in David's doorway. His hands were deep in his side pockets. He was already less the Nazi camp guard.

David put down the receiver after a to-the-point rudimentary English conversation, shaking his head. "The Glenlivet is on its way. And no, it's too early here for work. The man on the other end was sleepy. Everyone's at siesta, at least all the good guys. And I need a drink. Traveling with you is like being flayed alive. I need to re-stitch myself."

"I'm sorry to drag you into that. It's such an awful time for this. . . ."

Mark gulped. He closed his eyes. It seemed Mark's beard had grown an eighth of an inch since dawn.

"We'll talk," David said, hurrying past his shadowed friend to get the door. "Room service is quick—they must know their guests and stash the scotch up here," David said as he opened the door to a young *ladino* uniformed in tight black pants and a red jacket. "*Aquí*," David said, pointing out a side table with black and gold inlay. "*Gracias*," David added as he let the youth out, handing him a fistful of *quetzales*, watching the dark-eyed waiter leave, appraising what was clearly a build as sturdy as a Mayan pyramid.

"You know some Spanish, don't you?" Mark asked, moving into the room, forcing David from his reverie. "You studied in Spain."

David nodded and turned to open the fresh quart.

"In Madrid for a month," David answered, raising the opened bottle to his nostrils and inhaling. "Then two months at Loyola in the Basque lands. Beautiful place. Quaint. Quiet as cork. No surprise Ignatius fled home to drink in the world."

Silent, the two of them dealt with the work at hand, listening to the sound of ice cubes stacking in glasses, watching the dark liquid spill over the cubes, the tang of its aged aroma sifting through the air around them.

Mark picked up his glass and stared into its contents. "Yeah, Ignatius left his homeland looking for glory, only he probably wouldn't have seen much of the world if he hadn't been hit by a cannonball." He downed the scotch with one gulp and poured himself another. "Not exactly a travel adventurer's fantasy."

"True," David said, his eyes wide in disbelief at Mark's alcoholic bravado. Last night. Today. As novices they'd drunk together when depressed. That hadn't been their primary emotion. "Not all travel is a pleasure trip to Xanadu." David took a sip and closed his eyes for a second.

They went out to the balcony and settled into its two wicker chairs, quiet for a couple of minutes.

"At least you've traveled and seen some of the world," Mark said.

"What does that mean? You're no beggar. You've got a full life."

Mark's features rapidly darkened. He blinked his eyes and bit his lower lip.

"It's OK," David said. He reached over to pat Mark's knee. It was starting to feel the same as their first night in Fusz, the night Mark's knees dusted the spinach-green floor and his tears pocked the layer of St. Louis philosophate grime like raindrops on sand. Hadn't Mark gotten beyond that, that whatever?

"Are you still my friend?" Mark asked.

"What a question, of course I'm your friend. I'll always be your friend." David squeezed Mark's knee. "Friendship is binding." Didn't straight men understand this? "More binding than any of those vows we made."

"And broke," Mark added, the words sharp again.

"OK, we've broken vows," David said.

In the afternoon's heat and softened by chemicals, David started to feel dreamy. He was thinking about Mark's sadness, about his friend's second set of deteriorating vows, about their common history of exclaustration.

"But the Society didn't reproach us," David said. "We were honest to our own callings."

"Were we honest? Honest honest?"

"I don't get you."

"I mean," Mark said, his voice damp, "I feel—I question—I can barely say this . . ." Mark set down his drink. He rubbed the hair on his right arm as if something sticky were affixed there.

"Go ahead, take your time." David sat still.

"Perhaps I cheated on my dream, the one big dream I had."

"Go on."

"When we were Jesuits, we fought for the kingdom." Mark's face flushed with the word. "We could smell the kingdom's air, even during the worst days, sitting through those lectures in scholastic philosophy in airless DuBourg Hall, drenched in summer sweat, listening to all that inanity about *substance* and *accidents*."

Mark spoke as if transported, or as if he were trying hard to be in a different place. "We always had the one thing, that guide, that pillar in the center of the canvas that allowed perspective. We always had our mission, and our special place in that mission. What do we have now?"

"What do *we* have? What do *you* have?"

"What do *I* have?" Mark leaned back and looked up into the sky. "Of course I have Ann and Charley. But they're not . . ." He sighed. He looked at David, ". . . my soul is empty."

Mark folded his hands in his lap and rested his chin on his chest.

Soul. The word glinted in David's mind. He hadn't talked about soul in years.

"So, are you—religious? Fervent? Is that what's getting at you?" David thought of his own recent contemplations, a gene-strand of young man memories and now desperate hope and continuing death-haunt. Had Mark been struggling with something similar, only for a longer time, struggling with the ladder-climbing angel that he, too, had trussed up and ignored for years?

"No, I'm not religious," Mark said, sad and on edge. He raised up his head. "Not the way I was—the way we were. But I have this longing inside me." Mark touched his chest near where his heart beat, off center. "It's a longing that I've had since childhood. To make things right for others. To be selfless. To be saintly, whatever that is. All my Jesuit life I prayed about that!" Opening his eyes, "Maybe that's what's slowly choking me, choking off my spirit, making me want evil things. I'm about the wrong things."

A single cloud drifted by, too insignificant to give shade to the silent men.

"Wrong things?" David finally said. "Well, we're about the right things today." Then he got up and announced his need for a nap.

CHAPTER NINETEEN

I ally myself with the trees and with the wisdom they set upon the air. Eradicate mankind, ignorant shredding of the earth's mantle, and wise green will cover the land, bringing water to deserts, healing city wounds—with roots undoing sidewalk scars, branches burrowing into the shame of walls. Song birds will sing. The trees will offer living creatures an abundance of fruit so succulent, one bite will suffice for a year. Yes, the Creator's will is for life, even mankind's life. Especially mankind's life. He cannot retract His Word. It is.

From the final Roman sermon of Father Hugo Beltrán y Lanzarote, S.J., delivered to five European scholastics, two from Holland, two from Spain, one from Hungary, in a dank chapel of the Collegio Bellarmino, 1950, as inscribed in the diary of Joszef Eger, S.J., who served the Mass.

Mark stumbled out of bed after a three-hour nap, his temperate brain shrouded in a tropical blue haze. He edged his way down the hallway to the bathroom, guided by his two hands as they fingered the smooth, plastered walls. Shuffling, he crossed the bathroom's white marble toward the shower, still keeping his sleep-caked eyes shuttered until he could open them under a hot spray.

For fifteen minutes Mark lathered and cleansed his body, rubbing all the parts, the firm ones, the malleable ones, scrubbing with the energy of a farm boy who longs to eradicate the clinging stink of animal waste and sweat. Mark had awakened from a dream memory of his last Saturday night alone with Ann and Charley. They'd played Uno. Ann assured him how Charley loved the game, that their son squealed with delight whenever he played the right card.

It was all in his son's eyes. His own burden of guilt. Big brown eyes that studied each card before a move, that looked up into the father's eyes, sentinels of the overlord, with the caution of a small child new to the neighborhood.

It was the distance that frightened Mark, the untrodden moonscape between himself and his son, which made him keep his eyes shut until warm water coaxed them open. In that Central American dreamland, Mark's spirit-self had ended up wandering alone in the middle of the South Dakota sagebrush prairie, walking its veined, rippling skin, listening for something carried on the air. A westerly dream-wind blew into his face and caked him with grit.

Awakening in Guatemala, Mark held his head, "Bust of a Grecian Warrior" Ann had termed it early in their love, into the shower's hot stream and prayed for cleanliness, for a clean start, for catharsis, Attic purification. He loved her adoration, but he hated her death fears, and their vapor, their lung-clogging vapor. He'd been raised to be without fear. He did not know how to make love and fear live together. Neither did she.

John Shekleton 277

Back in his room Mark dressed, breathless as an automaton. Inside, though, was exertion, the pushing aside of difficult thoughts. He focused on one task, one task alone, the next act in Tom's drama.

Mark spoke no words to the small memory of his son as he pulled on his underpants, T-shirt and khaki shorts. Nor did he speak words to that other one, still no longer than a shrimp swimming in the other woman, in the new Olympian votary who was considering her options.

Mark started to formulate his conversation with George Saxon, the security officer at the American embassy whom Coleman Schaeffer at the State Department said might help.

Coleman warned Mark not to expect much from George. "The man is harmless," Coleman said. "It's doubtful he'll help much, maybe some advice, some piece of information. He keeps to himself."

The phone conversation started poorly.

"Why didn't you tell me you were coming? Why didn't you have Coleman contact me? This is most irregular." George was grumbling as if he were a bachelor wakened from his nap by the cackling of street children. "Besides, I don't know much, I manage security here. You Hill types should be dealing with the political liaison."

"Coleman told me to look you up," Mark said. "I'm a friend of Tom Burns. I'm only here as a friend. Senator Brandon doesn't even know I'm down here."

That thought gored Tom. How would he ever explain this trip to the rigorous Senator Brandon? How could he explain that he was living on impulse to a man who planned out every conversation, even the lines he'd use on the summer intern, always a fresh maiden from Minnesota's farmland?

"This visit isn't official?" Mark could hear George reassessing the political implications.

"I just want to talk with you, George. OK?"

"I don't know. I'll have to check it out with the ambassador."

Mark covered the receiver with the palm of his hand and groaned. Everyone in Washington knew that the current ambassador was a genteel southerner more comfortable negotiating trade agreements atop a Tennessee walker than dealing with the political mess in Guatemala.

"What's wrong?" David whispered.

Mark rolled his eyes, whispering back, "Bureaucrats!"

"Come on, George," Mark said. "I'm not here on official business. There's no need to get the ambassador involved. Besides, I actually have some information."

"Information?" George paused. "What kind of information?"

"About a possible ransom." Mark knew the danger of this revelation. They had to persuade the Jesuits to offer the money. A leak could spoil their chances, appear to put too much pressure on the Society.

"OK," George said. "Let's talk. Can you get here at six-thirty? The gate'll be locked, so just buzz. We're not far from the Camino. Be prompt. Tell the guards you're a friend of mine from the States. You got that?"

"I got it."

"OK, David, your turn," Mark said, handing the receiver to David. "Call up La Merced and make an appointment with that Hungarian."

"Yes, sir," David said, suddenly chipper, saluting Mark as he took the receiver.

After the phone rang eight times, a deep voice answered, the words rapid as gunfire.

"*Comunidad jesuita de la Merced. Habla Joaquín Chiyá.*"

"Oh, God," David said, tense as he tried to parse the Iberian rattle.

"I speak English," said the voice at the other end, sounding more gracious, oddly languid in the northern foreigner's tongue.

"English. Great," David said, breathing out his relief. "My name is David Jepson. David Jepson. I'm from the United States. I wish to meet with Father Eg—Father Eger."

"Father Eger. Si, *señor* Jepson. He says his prayers now. Can I arrange a call for later today, maybe in an hour?"

"Yes, please, I'm at the hotel Camino Montserrat. I'll await his call."

"And, *señor*, is there a message for Father Eger? May I ask the topic of your conversation?"

David said the obvious. "It's about Father Burns. I come from the United States with a—proposal. I'm not a journalist. It's important I speak with him."

"Very good, *señor* Jepson. I will give your message to Father Eger as soon as possible. *Buenas tardes.*"

"Buenas tardes," David said to the already dead line.

"What did he say?" Mark asked.

"That wasn't Father Eger. I left a message for him to call." David fidgeted with the hotel key in his pocket.

Mark knit his eyebrows and seemed to stifle a protest. He looked at his heavy gold Rolex and said, "I've got to hurry." He started to button the top button of his shirt and headed for his room. "You may have to meet with Father General's emissary by yourself."

"I know," David said, alone in the main room with its heavy dark wood, feeling his usual sense of surety evaporate as fast as rain water on the high summer prairie.

"What should I say?" David asked in a loud voice, hurrying down the corridor to Mark's room. David had envisioned Mark being there to meet Father Eger. Mark was the unctuous one, the dazzler. David had known for years the caustic effect of his own tongue, the ease with which his lips slouched. He'd hired a coach once, a Guthrie actor, but she hadn't been able to help. He was cursed, as if he'd been born with one leg too short.

David stopped at Mark's bedroom doorway. Mark was pulling his blue twill pants up over his thick legs and contoured Calvin Kleins. He turned around toward David and zipped up with the correctness of an officer readying for parade. "Tell Father Eger the facts. We have money for the ransom. We care about Tom." Turning back toward the full-length leaded mirror imbedded into the closet door, Mark added, "Tell Father Eger we love Tom."

Mark stared into the mirror as the sentence disappeared, then mouthed some of the words again, this time slowly and carefully as he adjusted the buckle of his belt. "We love Tom."

Mark's cab dropped him off fifteen minutes early.

He was alone on the street. For a second Guatemala City seemed quiet. A little red-faced family walked by on the sidewalk, their heads to the ground. The father padded forward in sandals. A belt of rough sisal twine held a pair of dirty tan slacks loose at the man's waist. The mother wore a billowing skirt of many colors, which shone bright against her white cotton blouse. One child lay heavy in a black *rebozo* at her back. A square boy, dressed the same as his father and wiping at his nose, tagged behind them.

The boy looked up at Mark. His round eyes, impassive, sized Mark up the way a grazing antelope might some loping cat. Mark stared back and smiled. The boy looked down again, hurrying forward to pick up a rock.

Mark continued to watch them for several minutes. When crossing streets they formed into a tight line, mother behind, father in front, boy in between. They seemed so determined, apace with their fate. Mark felt an object gather inside him. It was positioned over his heart, black and squalid as a tumor.

Mark looked away from the family and toward the squat walls of the embassy compound, reassuring himself why he was there: an errand of mercy. It just might purify him.

A row of cypresses, fifteen feet tall with the space of two broad-shouldered men separating each tree, stood guard just between the outer wall and the embassy itself. They were a woody battalion, fixed as papal teachings.

He saw no lights in the upper story of the building. Mark looked at his watch. It was six-twenty-five. He decided visiting hours were over. He walked up and pressed the buzzer, which was wired into the concrete wall next to an iron gate. The gate led into a courtyard. A grill of starbursts topped it off. The intricate design looked Arabic to Mark, exotic, excessive. He thought of the chain-link fence at home. They'd put it up to keep Charley corralled when he'd turned three. He'd been energetic that spring and one morning disappeared into the neighbor's orchard. Ann was frantic, checking every bush, calling the neighbors, the police, calling Mark at the office and yelling for him to do something. The fence went up the next day. By summer's end, the fence was unnecessary, another suburban scar. That fall they operated on Charley's valves.

Mark adjusted the fall of his suitcoat. He looked down at the crisp navy blue. The color of power. Uniformed in it he was an admiral, persuasive, rival to Neptune. Its authority should've entered into his pores and down into his muscles. At the embassy gate, however, he felt none of that force, that confidence to harness the wind. He'd always carried the day in negotiations. Ann told him he made people love him. He'd scoffed at her. She'd turned away, at first, shaking her head, then turning back, pleading: "It's your smile and your eyes. People want you to like them, even people who should know better!"

A black marine, youthful and strong, in battle fatigues and helmet with an M-16 held across his chest, appeared on the other side of the gate. Mark noticed the shape of another marine over this marine's shoulder, just off to the side of the concrete guard house. That second marine held his rifle barrel out at mid torso.

"Yes, sir, how can I help you, sir?" The first marine belted out his reply, his two rows of irregular teeth barely showing.

Mark stepped back. "I'm a friend of George Saxon. He told me to meet him here."

"And your name, sir?"

"Mark Sappingstone."

His eyes trained on Mark, the young marine signaled the guardhouse with his right hand. The gate swung inward a few inches, opening a narrow strait through which Mark could walk.

"Yes, sir. Please step inside."

Mark crossed over the rusted lintel, moving so that his suit didn't touch the metal. He noted how the second marine, an older black man, kept one hand near the clip of his M-16. The first marine signaled again to the guardhouse, and the gate clanked back into place.

The young marine stepped in front of Mark and gestured with his shoulder for Mark to follow. They crossed over the paving stones of the courtyard to a massive double door. The marine held down the speaker's button and leaned forward slightly to announce a Mr. Mark Sappingstone who'd come to see Mr. George Saxon. The marine seemed comfortable with Mark's full name. Mark assumed George was a stickler for details.

Mark heard the sound of a bolt being forced out of its barrel. One side of the door opened and another young marine, this one a thin white boy with a severe crew cut and a holster topping one thigh, greeted Mark.

"Please come in, sir," spoke this new man, his delivery as clipped as the other marine's despite the lilt of the Georgian hill country singing in his voice. "Mr. Saxon is waiting for you in the green room."

All the rules were observed with the utmost care. Was it because of the kidnapping? Or was it George's way?

The green room was a long rectangle ringed with maps of Guatemala and matted charts showing production levels and import/export statistics for coffee, beef, and bananas. A banquet table surrounded by twelve chairs, whose backs and bottoms were stitched with American eagles, anchored the middle of the room.

"Welcome," George said, rising from a chair at the end of the table. A briefing document lay open in front of him. He'd pulled out several sheets of paper.

George came forward to grab Mark's hand, shaking it vigorously, giving the impression that the two were old acquaintances.

"Have a seat, Mark. Glad you could make it. Sorry about all the precautions. The kidnapping, you know."

George turned to the armed escort and dismissed him. "Mr. Sappingstone will be leaving within the hour."

With the young man gone, George, tall, with thin blonde hair and fat round cheeks, wandered back to his seat and sunk down into it. He gave Mark a head look, half annoyed, that implied Mark should do the same.

Mark walked over and sat next to George. George shifted his chair several inches away.

"So, the Jesuits are going to pay the ransom?" George asked, rubbing his eyes with the pulpy palm of his right hand. "I find that—amazing."

Mark assumed George knew all the scenarios floating through the embassy. Paying the ransom must not be one of them

"I guess it is amazing," Mark said, certain he should not divulge any other details of their plan, uncertain of George, increasingly uncertain that he and David could pull off this rescue, which made him angry so that he clenched his teeth too tightly and nearly yelped at a sharp pain.

George didn't notice. He was staring forward across the table, away from Mark.

"What do you want from me?" George asked, stretching out in the plush chair and turning his head to face Mark.

"I want to know what the embassy's learned about the UDA. Is the UDA serious about the ransom? Is Father Burns still alive?"

George hummed in response, a shallow decrescendo, and began to finger his stubbly chin with the thumb and index finger of his right hand. Finally, "About the UDA, we know a fair amount. We know the UDA is a real threat. They've been an operating force for about six years, forming in 1985, the year the army declared a self-amnesty."

"Of all the groups that started then," George said, "the UDA is the best run, the best funded, the best connected. Don Francisco Orozco is their head. Although, he denies it. He's an aristocratic man, grandson of an earlier parliamentarian who's notorious for having arranged the confiscation of German-owned coffee fields during World War II." George smiled and hummed again, as if he were thinking whether to say more, or what to say. "1944, also the year that foreign-born clergy were permitted to work in Guatemala after a ban of over a hundred years, a ban that many of the ruling families wish was still intact."

"All right," Mark said, itchy with this useless data. "Is Tom still alive?"

"We think so."

"Has the embassy contacted the UDA?"

"Essentially."

"And . . ."

"No response."

"You talked with this Orozco?"

George paused.

"He's the contact, right?"

"There were other instructions."

"Other instructions?"

"For purposes of local consumption, we're sure."

"What other instructions?"

George sat up. He rubbed his chin again with his thumb and index finger. Haven't I given him important news, Mark wondered? Don't I deserve something? I'm a friend of Coleman's.

"Don Francisco's role is not official, you see. The UDA designated a neutral contact person, as groups sometimes do here. This time it was Father Antonio Garza," George said, drawing out each word, "rector of the Jesuit church of La Merced, here in Guatemala City. This fact is not well known."

Mark was stunned.

"He has carried two messages to the UDA."

Mark was sweating. What did this mean? He knew Jesuits whose cloister was an inner-city intersection, the factory and courthouse of barrio gangs. He knew a priest in Boston who absolved mafiosi souls. He remembered the story of Father Hutchinson, the blind priest at Marquette High, about his giving the last rites to a chicano kid who lay dying in a crack house on the north side. The kid had just slaughtered the family of a rival gang in a drug-crazed blood orgy and was himself mortally wounded. Father Hutchinson said he'd felt no fear. He was a priest, and he was blind.

"But why did they choose Father Garza? Another Jesuit?" Mark asked. He looked at his watch. David could be going to the La Merced residence as they were speaking. Mark's heart began to pound. Were they sheep led to the slaughter?

"Father Garza is not noted for his love of liberalism, either governmental or ecclesiastical."

Mark knew George had that phrase from someone else. Was Father Garza a dupe of the UDA? A Coconspirator?

"Can he be trusted?"

George shrugged his shoulders, then reached down to work the oval callus under his right thumb.

"Do you think the UDA will release Tom if a ransom is paid?"

Another shrug. It was clear George was done giving information.

"Has the UDA ever asked for a ransom before?"

"Never," George said, rising and extending his hand.

"Just one thing more," Mark added, fearing his request was useless. "Please keep me informed. Will you do that?"

George hesitated. "Anything important. And say hello to Coleman," he said, suppressing a yawn.

"No one cares about truth. No one cares about Tom," Mark murmured, kicking at a stone as he waited inside the compound for the taxi to arrive. He turned to look back at the embassy. "And I'm a part of all this."

Father Eger was on the phone with David seconds after Mark left for the embassy. In a brief conversation Father Eger laid out the plan, instructing David to meet him in half an hour at the Parque Concordia, a plaza dominated by the headquarters of the national police in commanding Renaissance-style splendor.

"It is a busy spot," Father Eger said. "The crowd movement makes me feel safe."

"How will I know you?" asked David, still wondering why the Jesuit residence at La Merced wasn't safe enough.

"I have a goatee and am wearing a light blue Panama shirt. And I am an old white man. I will be sitting on a bench, God willing, chasing away shoeshine boys, reading a newspaper. You will notice me. When you have spied me, walk slowly past and head west on Fourteenth Street for two blocks. When you reach the bookstore Anticuarios, enter. Speak my name quietly to the young woman at the desk. Do what she says."

David mulled over these instructions as the cab sped down the exhaust-choked streets of the city, still itchy with their furtive sting. His whole body now knew that he was involved in an intrigue the depths of which he couldn't imagine. "What's this all about?" he muttered to himself. "What's this all about?" He wished Mark were with him, wished he weren't alone.

All too soon the cab arrived, and David stepped out onto the sidewalk. The shoeshine boys, tight as a bee swarm, buzzed around him, blocking his passage. He looked over their greasy dark heads as he shooed them away with long arms and an angry peal of "¡No, gracias! ¡No, gracias!"

David spotted a lone white man with gray hair and a goatee sitting on a black iron bench in the middle of the plaza. Evening was setting in. David stopped for a moment to take in again the details of the old man, who seemed unaware of his arrival.

He felt near a coronary. He put his hands in the pockets of his Hilfiger blues, securing his wallet in one hand, shaking a little, and walked forward into the plaza with slow steps whistling as quietly as he could "I'm a Yankee Doodle Dandy," even as he passed the wrinkled old man. David glanced out the corner of his right eye, hoping for some contact, some brief exchange. As David walked by, the old man continued to read, his crooked index finger moving down the inked column, his attention to the printed story unwavering.

A few feet beyond the bench, David nearly stopped. He shut his eyes and quashed the urge to return, to say his name. The trust-in-God David took over and moved his body to the edge of the plaza. Surely that old man on the park bench was Father Eger, he thought.

The European intriguer's on his way by now, he said to himself as he started down Fourteenth Street.

David stopped once again to look into a furniture store window, as if he were merely shopping the street. He decided he could play along, for a while.

Five minutes and he was in the bookstore. No one was at the front desk. He saw no bell to summon the staff.

David looked around. He turned down the first aisle. There might be a clerk working near a side wall. He coughed. The scent of ancient dust thickened the air. The aisle was a narrow passageway that ended at a booklined inner wall. Bookcases towered on both sides. The shop was windowless. Long fluorescent bulbs hung high above, half of them switched off. It reminded David of the Jesuit philosophy library at Fusz Hall, another deteriorating space whose millions of foreign phrases had fascinated his imagination.

David began to examine the titles. One title, gold on light brown leather, filled the entire spine of its book with a single sentence. It was a recounting of the glorious and divinely inspired foundation of a Carmelite cloister where a bush had sprung up bearing thorns in the shape of a cross. David edged the book out of the stack and started to look through it when he heard a movement, footsteps followed by the scratchy sound of someone sorting through papers. He stuffed the book back onto the shelf and hurried up to the front of the shop. At the desk, the face of a beautiful *ladina* greeted him with a broad smile.

"May I help you?"

"I'm here to see Father Eger." David returned her smile as best he could. His body had stiffened.

"I am Rosaria," said the woman, who was cool as a Bemidji spring dawn. She smiled and placed her silver fountain pen onto the open ledger. "Please, follow."

They exited the bookstore proper into a corridor cluttered with boxes and old shelving. They passed two closed rooms. Neither spoke. At the end of the corridor, Rosaria opened a metal fire door and gestured for David to enter. She remained at the door and leaned in to switch on a light.

"Please wait," Rosaria said and left, clanging the door shut.

This new room was a work space where old books were rebound. The scent of glue and leather pressed in its confinement. A single clear bulb hung in the middle of the room. There were two shuttered windows, two work tables, both with lamps.

David stood under the ceiling bulb and its circle of light. Alone, he felt limp. His mind was blank except for a sudden awareness of the fullness in his bladder. He wanted to get out of that rebinding space as soon as possible.

Five minutes later a sharp, three-tap rap on the door sent waves of blood pumping through the fibers of David's body. He said nothing. A moment passed. The door opened slowly. The figure of the old man from the plaza entered and stretched out a knotted hand in greeting.

"You are Mr. Jepson?" Father Eger asked.

"I am."

Father Eger noted the fear on David's tight face. The American was barely breathing.

"And you are Father Eger?" David asked. "Do I pronounce your name properly?"

"I am, and your pronunciation will do. Please, sit down," Father Eger said, pointing to the single workman's bench alongside the first table. He'd not been in the room before, but Joaquín had described it in meticulous detail. "We shall have to share this plank. Plank is a good word?"

"Plank is a good word, a plank with two legs. A bench."

"Ah, yes, bench. Like *banco*." They both sat. Father Eger smiled benignly at David and reached over to pat his hand. He, too, had hopes about this meeting. He must not scare the American away.

"Tell me, why are you here, my son?"

"I'm a friend of Tom Burns. We were Jesuits together, Wisconsin Province. We entered the same year, Tom and Mark and I. Mark is also here, with me, well, not right now." David's words were stumbling out. "He's an aide to a very important American senator."

"You are no longer a Jesuit?" Father Eger asked, even though his sources had already supplied this information.

"No, Mark and I left the Jesuits in 1979."

"I see. A long time ago, no? And you are concerned for your friend?"

"Yes. We're like combat buddies." David smiled, a smile over pain. "And now we have a plan, Mark and I. We want to pay the ransom. I have the money. Two million dollars is sitting in the Guatemala City branch of Chase Manhattan."

Father Eger kept his face as flat as his first German superior's, a Prussian with a saber scar down his right cheek, which he constantly rubbed when he meditated after communion.

"We need someone to make contact with the UDA to offer the ransom," David said.

"I have already made contact with the UDA." Father Eger was hoping to sound polite, a Japanese man at tea, but also official and determined. He feared he would seem a Kafka character to this TV-bred American, only half human, the other half roach.

"I have told the UDA there will be no ransom money," Father Eger said. "We cannot respond to threats in this manner." Inside Father Eger was mulling new possibilities, but he would not tell the American. "I have also demanded the return of our brother Thomas."

David rolled his eyes. "You *demanded* his return? Why would they return him? For what reason?"

Father Eger was shocked by David's tone. Combative already. Not totally unexpected. "To make their point," Father Eger answered.

"That we should be afraid of them?"

"That they are in control. They take and they give, just like God."

"Then even better to kill Tom. That's absolute control."

"Absolute control is not control of the body."

"Oh, please, Father, this is a kidnapping. They captured his body."

"And not his soul."

"But—can't . . . Can't you just offer the ransom?"

"Do they really want money? Or attention."

"Both. But I'm sure they want money. It *is* the root of evil. And evil favors its roots."

Father Eger waited to respond. He wanted to stand up and pace, but forced himself to remain seated next to the young American. He sighed and began to weigh within himself his impressions of this man, how trustworthy he was, how sincere, how committed. Father Eger had made mistakes in the past, mistakes in judging the human character.

So much biographical data on David and Mark had flooded in over the last hours. How cunning of Father General to provide Father Eger with a mobile phone, releasing him from the ordinary vicissitudes of *Guatel* and the ever attentive ears of those listening. He spoke Hungarian with his North American contacts, a mountain patois riddled with Romany words and phrases, residue of a novitiate training among the gypsies. In North America were two of Father Eger's oldest Jesuit brothers, Fathers Boedy and Nagy, both exiles of the '56 revolution.

Father Eger was not against paying the ransom. He had jousted with David about paying the ransom just as his early Jesuit training had taught, perhaps to discover the truth through logical combat but certainly to get a glimpse of his opponent's unguarded soul as it shimmered in the moment when the words blew apart.

Father Eger knew too much about prisons and torture to abandon any chance to release the captive. Release the captive. That phrase had become his mantra in Berlin. For a while it had saved him from the pit.

Father Eger was starting to think there might be a better exit from this Guatemala mess than the sacrifice of another martyr. He wasn't sure of its details yet. The secret messenger from Managua who'd disturbed his and Joaquín's sleep the night before had also provided a new thread of possibility to weave into this Guatemalan cloth. He had yet to mention to Rome that nocturnal conversation. Those words were far too revolutionary for Father General. His friend, Father von Ehre, had asked for the unexpected. Father Eger smiled inside: The unexpected was more and more possible.

"All right, we will talk of this ransom," Father Eger said, pulling on his goatee. "Tomorrow morning. You and Mark meet me in Antigua, the old capital. Wear shorts and gaudy shirts. And dark glasses, yes? You must have dark glasses." Father Eger almost grinned at the tinsel town silliness of his suggestion. "I will be at the Museo del Libro Antiguo at ten. In whatever way you can, try not to be obvious about your destination. Wander about in town. When we meet, follow your instincts. They will guide you."

David gulped. "I don't understand. Why are we meeting in Antigua? Is this—this subterfuge, is it really necessary?"

The American seemed stunned. Father Eger had expected resolution. Was it not obvious Father Eger was doing research?

"Necessary, yes," Father Eger said. "The rest I cannot tell you now. I must gather more facts." He paused a moment and leaned slightly forward. "Be brave."

Pushing back the bench, Father Eger rose, slowly, one of his bones cracking. "I am getting old," he laughed, patting David on the shoulder. "Give me five minutes before leaving. And buy a book."

At the door, Father Eger looked back over the stuffy work space with its shadows and its glaring light. He flashed back to a cell in Berlin, to his first interrogation. He shook his head and closed his eyes for a moment. Then he looked down on David, staring into the American's pale face. He almost told David to have hope, but stopped himself before offering that exhortation. He was not yet ready to light that candle. He had not yet detected, with sufficient certainty, the most likely course of the unknowable will.

CHAPTER TWENTY

How happy are the poor in spirit; theirs is the kingdom of heaven.
Happy the gentle: they shall have the earth for their heritage.

— Two of the Beatitudes from the Gospel of Mark, 5:1-4,
The Jerusalem Bible

The five granite-faced men gathered Friday at 9:00 in the back room of the Rio de la Plata restaurant on Avenida La Reforma. The night's air was cool, and the fashionable women of Guatemala City wore their cashmere cardigans loosely upon their soft shoulders. Inside the restaurant, however, the sizzle of Argentine steak, proof that not all good things in Guatemala came from above, had crisped the air.

Three of the men were in their forties, two in their sixties. They were representatives of that special class in Guatemala, that small town accumulation of prominent families who ruled the nation. All those who partook in this particular circle of warriors had served in the military. Two were still active colonels.

Two of them were Protestants now, converts during the recent explosion of Pentecostalism, that liberating force of the individual's spirit, that spiritual craft movement that spun out rows of single, wide-mouthed vessels to hold the miracle water. This reborn pair had found religion and political philosophy through their alliance with the colonels who had tormented El Salvador for so many years, latching onto a religion that was largely mute about what the liberationist priests called structural evil such as a distribution of wealth that left much of humanity blank-eyed with hunger. The other three were still Catholics, holding on to the ancient faith and its rituals despite their abhorrence of what to them was devil's-foam spewing from the left-leaning clerics and activists who occupied too many of the country's pulpits.

The gathering of this clique in such a public place as the Rio de la Plata was beyond special notice. The plazas and all the public spaces belonged to them and their clans. The names of the individuals who attended these *reuniones* changed, of course, although the same family names recurred, redundant as entries in a highland village baptismal registry. These men represented those families who owned Guatemala, who controlled its commerce, its government, its armed forces, its schools, all of its institutions—including a portion of the Roman Church. Friday, this group was discussing the event that had brought international focus to their small country.

"So, no one is dealing with us seriously?" asked Don Francisco, the eldest and leader, a man whose wealth was reflected in the exquisite blue of his hand-tailored silk shirt.

"No one, although, there is activity," said Don José.

"Activity?" asked Don Francisco.

"There is talk that some American senator will hold a special hearing next week, which has forced Ambassador Riordan to request daily briefings from President Kepler García, such an intrusion on the American ambassador's schedule."

The other men nodded their heads and grinned.

"The United Nations threatens to send a representative, if that can be construed as a threat," said Don Carlos, sneering. "Amnesty International has made their normal contacts, exciting their little troop of twitching mice. Rome has instructed our Most Reverend Archbishop on several occasions to keep the Vatican constantly informed."

At this fact they all laughed, knowing how enormously torpid was the existence of their current archbishop, a second cousin of Don Francisco.

"And the Jesuits?" asked Don Francisco raising his voice over the din.

The room hushed.

Don José cleared his throat. "As you know, the Jesuits have sent an emissary from their General. This man is an old Hungarian, an archivist, an unknown. He was years in Asia. He is quiet. He avoids publicity."

"Is there recent news from Father Garza? About this emissary? Or news from Rome?"

At that question, all five men looked contentedly at each other, acknowledging how deep the tendrils of their control dug into Guatemalan society.

"Father Garza informs me this foreign Jesuit is another liberal. That this Father Eger is an old man, which is obvious." Don Carlos leaned in. "This envoy from Rome has done nothing consequential. He has visited all the Jesuit communities within the city, asking for their prayers, inquiring about the UDA. Only once did the Hungarian go to the Palacio Nacional, twice to the American Embassy. He has sent us a single verbal message demanding that we release Father Burns in the name of charity, assuring us that the young priest would be returned to the United States. Aside from these activities, the old man has spent the rest of his time with the domestics at La Merced or wandering through the city. He is a harmless man. As Father Garza says, a good man to give a funeral eulogy."

Laughter again filled the windowless room. The two guards stationed at the door looked at each other and grinned at the sound of the *patrones'* laughter.

"So, what do we do, *compañeros*?" asked Don Francisco. "We asked for the ransom within two weeks. Do we need to emphasize our determination?"

"I don't understand," asked round-faced Don Walter, the cruelest among them and the slowest of wit. "Do you mean, should we chop off an ear or a hand and send it to them?"

"No, no," said Don Francisco, growling, waving one hand, its index finger bent and pointed in dismissal. "Nothing so dramatic. Maybe a drive-by shooting of a seminary, perhaps at Sololá. Or the bombing of a church. We don't want these brainless idiots who infest our Church to think that we are merely trying to get rid of Americans. We are sending them *all* a message."

At this the grave men surrounding the pentagonal table nodded in agreement. Soon Don Carlos, the youngest of the council, a man whose middle-aged skin remained unnaturally taut over his thin body, cleared his throat. "I have spoken with my contacts in El Salvador today. Their new archbishop there, Endres y Juarez, threatened to begin holding weekly news conferences after his Sunday Mass, just as that pig Romero did in the '70s. They had to slaughter that swine at his altar in order to quiet his grunting." He looked around the table, stopping briefly to affix his gaze on each set of eyes. "That bullet sent a clear message."

"This Endres is Opus Dei," Don Carlos continued, his green eyes trained on the man at the head of the table, "as are you, Don Francisco. If even a cleric such as he begins to take the side of the radicals, then can we spare your precious Church of Rome?"

Don Francisco didn't flinch at this threat. He knew well that Don Carlos was the chief proponent of the destruction of the Church of Rome in the New World. He saw the dreams of men like Don Carlos, their idyll of the future Guatemala, a country as blessed by the Creator as the great United States, especially the California they loved to visit. Under Don Carlos's guidance, Guatemala would be productive, prosperous, Protestant, liberated, finally, from superstitions, those inherited from their Iberian ancestors and those still vibrant among the *indígenas* who had not yet been assimilated into their *ladino* culture.

"I need an answer," insisted Don Carlos, puffing out as much as possible his gaunt chest, signaling to the other three, Don Francisco assumed, that he and not Don Francisco should be in charge of the UDA.

"I, too, understand that Archbishop Endres will hold news conferences," answered Don Francisco, focusing his response on the younger man alone, his right eye narrowing as if he were sighting an object in the cross hairs of a rifle. "I also know that Archbishop Endres has made it clear to the pack of journalists who roam the streets of San Salvador that responsibility for justice is in the hands of the government. He instructs those peddlers of rumor to bring their questions to the government, not trot to him every time some civil offense occurs. Of this, I can assure you."

Don Francisco twisted the end of his gray moustache with the long fingers of his left hand, backward and forward, as if he were tuning his guitar. "Archbishop Endres finds great fault in Liberation Theology. For him, the distinction between the religious realm and the secular realm is as clear as the natural border between land and water. It is the same with all of Opus Dei."

Don Francisco paused a moment to make sure the others were listening. "Jesus commanded us to render unto Caesar what is Caesar's, no? In this country, we and our allies are Caesar. In El Salvador, it is the same. The archbishop understands this political reality. I only wish that all the clergy in our country were as clear minded."

After that brief flash of contention, the gentlemen returned to the point at hand, whether they should give a sign to the church of its need to respond to their demands.

They decided to deface the walls of La Merced that night and told Pepe, one of the guards, to send out the command.

Once this piece of work was decided, the five *caballeros* ordered their dinner, *tournadoes de bouef*. Only one other bit of work crept into their conversation, another piece of information gathered by Don Carlos and his many acquaintances in the regimes of neighboring countries.

"I have received notice from Managua that the Escobar woman has taken a sudden, unexplained vacation."

"She is the woman Father Garza had mentioned?" asked Don Francisco.

"She is. The rebel. And the woman this Father Burns sullied."

"I see," nodded Don Francisco. "How good it is to have ears inside the confessional." For the first time that night there slithered onto Don Francisco's narrow face that serpentine smile which often came upon him before he would order the execution of his enemies.

Don Francisco had devised the threat to the Jesuits and later the kidnapping of Father Burns. He understood why such dramatic means were necessary.

The forces of peace and democracy were closing in on the UDA's corrective activities. A battle was nearing its end. Don Francisco needed to set the tone for years to come, the same task George Bush confronted at the end of the Gulf War. The American president had had to decide when enough was enough, when sufficient damage had been done to ensure the fall of the evil tyrant of Baghdad.

Don Francisco had the same choice, only he would choose better than President Bush. He would cripple the evil tyrant of liberation theology. The kidnapping had been a pretense—a way to buy prolonged exposure for their message. Too bad for the young man, the young Jesuit. How could they let him live?

CHAPTER TWENTY-ONE

Sursum Corda.

Lift up your hearts.

An invocation made by the priest to the congregation before beginning those sacred acts at the center of the Holy Sacrifice of the Mass where elements of wheat and wine are enunciated into divinity.

Tom's days all began the same. Awakened by Marcos's raspy voice, "Cover your eyes, pig!" Tom would fumble with his cold hands to secure the blindfold. Soon the door would scrape open, and he'd hear Marcos deposit a bowl of *mosh*, the thick *indígena* breakfast gruel, two feet inside the hut. Marcos never left a spoon, only the bowl and its sticky contents, which Tom dug into with increasingly dirty fingers.

The first three days of his captivity Tom had remembered to wash his hands before he finished his last drink of the day. Now he had stopped that hygienic ablution. Only a few acts preoccupied his thoughts.

After lapping up the last flattened breakfast grains from the sides of the bowl, Tom would get up to walk, circling the perimeter of his prison. He had an hour before Marcos would march him outside to the rickety latrine shed—his only time before dusk. Tom wanted to be ready. Pacing his twenty steps, he examined every internal sensation. If things weren't right, he'd jump up and down, knead his stomach with his fists. This was his best chance to keep the stench of his bowels from filling his cell.

On his way back from the latrine he'd walk slowly, careful as an old man, each step a danger. For a few moments he could rejoice in the fresh breezes that blew around him. One day it rained, and he held his head up to catch the drops. But every morning after about twenty paces, Marcos would come up from behind and slap him on the back of the head with the flat of his hand, ordering Tom to hurry on, spitting out the proud man's word: *cagón*—coward. This battery had become a ritual for the two of them, a collision of spirits.

Tom didn't flinch at the attack. He'd come to welcome its predictability. He could survive these slaps.

Tom had spoken with no one but Marcos, but he'd heard muttered conversations outside the hut. He hadn't understood the Spanish; the phrases popped up suddenly, without context. He'd picked out only a few accented words. *Matar*. Kill. *Disponer*. Dispose of.

Tom abandoned the daily examination of conscience. He swam in examination, a fluid of remembered words, smiles, the shape of furniture, kisses of greeting, the warmth of a woman's skin, the coolness of wine in the deep bowl of a golden chalice.

He abandoned the structure of the Exercises. His mind meandered, its course unpredictable, suborned as his spirit was by the war between fear and trust.

In the mornings, after his trip outside, Tom would kneel, his eyes still covered, and place his forehead onto the dirt floor, as if he were a Muslim in the prayer of submission, and sing snippets of chant from his youth, *tamtum ergo sacramentum veneremur cernui, dies irae dies illa solvet saeclum in favila,* heavy, arching words that had once formed a vault for an ancient faith and its reverences and fears.

Tom remembered standing under that vault as a child and ingesting its centuries-cured fervor, smelling Thomas à Becket at his execution in the great house of the Lamb at Canterbury, hearing the unmuffled drumbeat of that saint's defiant resistance. With those memories Tom's spirit would curve back into a sacred dome, soaring with the high arc of a baseball batted into the night sky, coming to rest somewhere beyond the playing field lights.

As the day warmed, he sang the sunnier songs written by his brother Jesuits while he was studying philosophy at St. Louis University in the 1970s.

He remembered the hope of those days, the resurgence of spirit. People were looking everywhere for renewal, renewal in the ways of worship, renewal in the ways they lived their lives, renewal in the types of songs they sang, renewal within the structures of the Church itself, some even whispering theories about radically different roles for women, perhaps roles of gesture and sacred utterance at the altar itself.

Tom had been an exemplar of that renewal.

His classes in languages and philosophy loaded his afternoons and late nights with Germanic enormity and mind-ripping exercises. And despite that burden, he spent several evening hours tutoring children from St. Louis's inexhaustible, glass-strewn, gun-popping ghetto. But on Thursday nights and Sunday mornings, he sang with the choir.

The Sunday Mass of the Jesuit community at Fusz Hall, where hundreds of scholastics studied to fulfill the Roman requirements for philosophical grounding, was immensely popular, drawing people from the university community and beyond.

Within the chapel, all blonde wood with narrow strips of colored windows, the pews had been angled, undoing the old compass of the space as Vatican II had undone the Tridentine compass of the Church, tilting its very axis several degrees.

The chapel was stark, clean, and warm. But the draw was the energy that suffused the long room. These young men wanted to lead the Church in new directions. The preachers were recently ordained, the best of the Society, those special ones chosen to guide the younger men. Their preaching unveiled a new set of sensibilities, a recasting of the interior existence to acknowledge psychology and all the modern analyses of what it meant to be human. And they loved the words of the prophets. They used those words to aim lightning bolts at the alienating and consumer-driven society of the modern Western world. And there was music, new music written by new musicians.

Tom sang with these men. His tenor vibrato was one of the chief attractions of that Sunday panoply. The instruments were simple, guitars and single bass, sometimes a piano or flute for a more glittering voice. All songs were written for soloist and choir.

When it came time for the solo, Tom would step up to the mike, radiant in bell-bottoms, dappled shirt, and wide, striped tie. When he lofted his first round note into the chapel, every head would turn, looking over to the choir, drawn by his exquisite voice and relishing a view of the seraphic young man who employed it.

"One bread, one body, one Lord of all, one cup of blessing . . ."

Tom had been kneeling on the rough dirt floor, singing along with his memory, the John Foley tune, ever so quietly, hearing in his mind the unison strumming of the guitars, listening again to the congregation's audible hunger for contact with divinity and feeling for a moment that sense of unity within the human family that had so often overwhelmed him when he sang.

But he could not continue with the song, try as he may. He began again to sob, still finding tears to raise up. Again he tried the song, *"One bread . . . one body . . ."*, but now his voice was cracking.

Tom felt himself being silenced. By his captors, his fear, his sinfulness, his despair. His breathing speeded up, deep, rapid, almost overwhelming his lungs. The bootblacked creature of terror choking him with oxygen, fuel of life. Deep, deep breaths. And then in a moment, everything nearly stopped.

He heard nothing.

Absolute silence, mysterious and kind, engulfed him, wrapped him. The ineffable, emptying *nada* of Juan de la Cruz. It was the sudden presence of air that was not air, more amniotic fluid. His ears heard what could not be heard, his eyes saw what could not be seen. For only an instant he was on the other side, on the side that had transformed Ignatius.

Others had been there. Francisco, Pedro, Edmund, Robert, Isaac, Noel, Paulus, Stanislaw, Jan, Alonso . . . *la compañia*.

They were still there.

On that side he was ravished with music. The purity of sound itself surrounded him, shaped as a wave. It turned him inside out.

Finally, exhausted, he slept. The day was not yet half over.

When Tom awoke, the sun was high in the sky, energizing the great masses of corn that fed on the volcanic nutrients of the valleys of the western highlands. His mouth was dry, but he managed to raise a thin foam of saliva, carefully layering it over his parched lips. He walked to the eastern side of the hut where the slats of the wall let in the most breeze. There he knelt down and strained to look outside, past the mud and dry stalks of the wall, to imbibe some quotient of that life-giving Guatemalan light he so loved.

He thought of his first experience within the dim dwellings of the poorest of the poor of Guatemala, huts dark as caves with earth floors, the structures pegged to steep hills until the next mudslide. Whether a hut's siding was wood or cardboard, or tin or tarp, the floors were dirt. The only opening would be a narrow doorway, in which half-naked children or the sick elderly would linger, watching the world pass by.

In one hut, however, Tom had found wood floors.

It was Tom's second Sunday in Guatemala. He'd offered Mass at the crumbling brick Chapel of San Pedro Claver in Colonia Samaria. The wood-floored hut was the house of Louis Richmand, a tall, slightly stooped American in his 60s, divorced, past-president of an early Silicon Valley success story.

Louis's divorce had changed his life, leaving him both childless and loveless. On a trip to Guatemala in 1976, traveling to visit the tree-covered pyramids of the northeastern jungles, he got sucked into Colonia Samaria. Louis's traveling companion, a photographer, had wanted to get pictures of the Missionaries of Charity at their orphanage and hostel for the dying in the flat center of the Colonia. These sari-draped nuns and their Mother Teresa were all the rage that year.

It was a fateful photo shoot. Louis looked too carefully at their need, asking the quantifying questions: "How many? How much?" The sisters, unhampered in their zeal, responded with their own question: "What can you do for us?"

First Louis sent money. He came down the next summer to help out. He was an able craftsman. He could help expand the orphanage.

Then two more summers. He picked up enough Spanish so he could speak about life, not buildings.

The fourth summer he never left, choosing to live in Colonia Samaria, to spend the rest of his time on Earth running his own version of an orphanage. His children were street boys who had no family or were better off with Louis, where at least they could hide when the death squads went child-hunting.

His only concession to Western luxury was the wood floor made up of six-inch-wide oak planks. Within several years his money was nearly gone, drained by other obligations, providing him only a trickle of income, which barely kept him and his refuge alive. He was on the verge of a poverty so profound, he explained to Tom, that his heart beat out its rhythm with an "inexplicable joy." After Louis spoke that phrase, Tom stepped back in amazement, unnerved, still adjusting to Guatemala and its extremes, wondering if starving Brother Lamb and mangy Sister Rabbit had taken up residence inside the aging American, expecting, in their animal innocence, the parousia any moment.

This Louis-in-transformation had waited for Tom after that first Mass in Colonia Samaria. Tom was speechless and couldn't escape. Coaxing and gentle, Louis brought Tom, who was hurried and hungry for lunch, to the compound of the Missionaries of Charity, pointing out that the floors of the sisters' buildings were cement and the walls stucco, telling Tom that "here miracles begin."

No fencing or stone walls separated the institution from the rest of the slum. The ground surrounding the compound was the flat, well-patted earth of Guatemalan hillsides on which children ran and dug and sketched.

Louis left Tom with Sister Martha, a Bombay Ph.D. in quantum mechanics. First she brought him into the kindergarten and their quarters for abandoned toddlers. In a pale-blue sick room, they stopped so Sister Martha could explain the patient population, the average stay, the goal for expanded facilities. Fifteen young children slept around them, their breathing a soothing hum, the smells of their young bodies warming in the gentle afternoon heat.

A girl, maybe eighteen months old with a black mop of hair and the round face of the *indígena*, scrambled up in her crib and moaned her presence. Unperturbed, as if a tea kettle were beginning to whistle, Sister Martha continued her explanations and walked across the room to the child. As she touched the girl's head, a one-legged man rushed in announcing that old Eduardo was having a seizure. Sister Martha ran out, leaving Tom alone in the room with the whimpering child.

Tom looked about. The girl was staring at him. Her cry was deepening. Tom had never dealt with children this young. He never had a younger sibling, and his nieces and nephews lived far away. But no one was coming, so he walked over to the little girl and smiled. He cleared his throat.

Her cry intensified. With the long fingers of his right hand Tom reached out and smoothed the hair of her head. She stopped crying, her coal-black eyes locked onto his. Then she began to cry again, a sharper sound this time. Tom inhaled, bit his lip. She's small as a puppy, he thought, and picked her up, awkwardly, by the armpits.

For a second he held her away from him. She continued to cry. Then he hefted her into a more calming embrace, just as he'd seen on TV, and cooed into her small ears in his still labored Spanish. *"No llores, niña. No llores."* Don't cry, little girl, don't cry.

The girl quieted down and nestled herself into his chest, her head on Tom's shoulder, the way a bear cub curls up in its den. He could feel the humidity of her breath on his neck. It was ticklish, gentle. The compact softness of her skin pressed against his arms. She breathed, and her chest molded into his.

Tom cuddled her, rocking his upper body back and forth, his body responding to her, uninstructed, a tall tree waving slowly in the wind.

Minutes passed. Finally Sister Martha returned to continue with the tour of the compound, a flicker of annoyance in her gait, as if her spirit were bloated with some hot, hard feeling beckoning from a carved stupa in a distant Punjabi field.

"What should I do with this little girl?" Tom asked quietly.

"Oh, set her down, Father. She has not been well. We are leaving Elena inside until she is better."

As soon as Tom placed Elena back into the crib, she began to cry, this time with greater and increasing fury, her latest abandonment too harsh to bear. Sister Martha had already headed toward the playground of the *jardín de niños*, a scrap of land enclosed by a low mud wall.

At the doorway Sister Martha gestured for Tom to follow. "Come, Father," she said, her voice narrow and authoritative.

Tom stood near the crib with his mouth open and still. He was paralyzed.

"She will stop when we leave," Sister Martha said, this time using her mothering voice. "God gives us suffering to bring us closer to Him. Surely you know this, Father."

Tom began to follow the nun, in a trance, repressing a desire to tell her that God sent suffering to shock others into action, turning back for a moment at the doorway as the cell-fabric of his flesh was being shredded by the child's plea.

With that experience Tom knew he could never leave Guatemala. He had entangled himself with its soul. It had breathed on him.

That evening he strode up and down the grounds of Landívar University. The words of Jesus rampaged through him, mystery words, the odd, enticing English: "Suffer the little children . . . Suffer the little children . . ." Jesus was loud inside him.

There was so much to sort out. There was so much to do. Even the smallest acts were sanctifying, he thought. He was frenzied with a feeling of opportunity, with the ability to make a difference, of the need to persist.

That second Sunday in Guatemala he fell asleep around two in the morning. He dreamed of the simple wonder of human touch, of how he had comforted the child by holding her—and how the child's fierce cries followed him the rest of the day, ringing in the hollow moments, accusatory, primal.

CHAPTER TWENTY-TWO

David and Mark rode in silence to Antigua. They commented only when a rough-carved valley demanded expression. These comments were brief and breathless: "What a view. What beauty."

Imbedded in both, as deep into their skin as steel rivets placed to seal the bones of a skyscraper's spine, were electrodes of fear. These implants forced the pair to concentrate completely, solely on the next meeting with the old man who had wired them up and now fingered the switch.

A few minutes after 10:00, Mark and David were walking up the steps of a cavernous stairwell inside the *Ayuntamiento*. Their footfalls bounced off the marble walls.

"See that sign," David said, pointing at the black lettering of a faded white poster. "It says there's an early printing press that way. I'll bet you the archivist is examining rare books."

The pair walked down a second floor corridor, finally turning into a high-ceilinged room whose ample, dignified space was warmed by sunlight from a bank of clerestory windows. A wood and iron printing press from the 1600s dominated the middle of the room. Yellowing texts were displayed along the stone walls of the room.

At the far end, past three young Dutch tourists, stood an old white man dressed in wrinkled black cotton pants, shiny black leather shoes and a white Panama shirt. The old man was examining one of the parchments that hung on the wall, one finger following along the line of the script. Standing next to him and back a ways was an *indígena*, another old man, dressed nearly the same except that his worn cotton shirt was tucked neatly into his pants and he wore *caites* on his bare feet and held a straw hat ready in his right hand.

Neither of the old men moved, despite the intense stare of the new arrivals.

A minute passed. Father Eger leaned down to speak to Joaquín, his voice more audible than necessary, "Now let us go up to the village of San Antonio Aguas Calientes. I wish to examine the volcano."

"Yes, Father."

The two old men walked out past the younger pair, the European clearly straining against the protest of aging muscles, the *indígena* relaxed in his gait. Neither of them looked at the brightly colored gringos who stood close together attempting to decipher a Latin phrase from an early translation of *The Annals of the Cakchiquels*.

Father Eger and Joaquín were the first to arrive at the *pueblo* of San Antonio Aguas Calientes. They had their own car, and Joaquín drove as fast as any *taxista*. The village was noted for its refreshing climate and its view of the valley. Aside from several dozen locals, only a crowd of sturdy Germans wandered through the stalls of the market to examine its prized textiles.

"Let us go to the church, Joaquín," Father Eger said. "They will find us there. The guidebook calls the church 'regal'. I wonder why. Is it plastered with crowns? Or shaky as a throne?"

They tried the main door of the church, but it was locked. A sign tacked to the door informed them with pale lettering that the church would open again at 15:00 *horas*. The two old men sat down on the southwestern side of the stairs, where a triangle of shade had settled in, and waited for the gringos.

Father Eger prayed his thanksgiving that Joaquín had been able to drive him. Things had looked uncertain in the morning. Sometime during the night *bárbaros*, as Father Garza termed them, had come to La Merced and defaced the holy facade of the church with slogans about alliances with the devil, once again drawing a crude stick figure with its head rolling off into the air.

Father Garza had sputtered with anger as he raced through the residence that morning, ordering the servants to erase those evil markings, condemning modern society and all its ills, wailing about corruption, and making a point of insisting that Joaquín could not go with Father Eger, that this was a time of crisis and that he, Father Garza, the rector of La Merced, needed Joaquín to run errands and carry messages.

Fortunately for Father Eger, Joaquín had smiled his enigmatic *indígena* smile, half Buddha, half *santo*, and gone off to prepare the car.

What Father Garza did not know was that the old Hungarian and the old Tzutuhil had been sharing secrets and making plans.

Thirty minutes passed before Father Eger spotted Mark and David leaving the village market stalls and walking toward them. He nodded to Joaquín. The two old men rose. They headed up a steep street that lead onto the mountain, where the gravel turned into a dirt path, which disappeared into the dense pine forest.

Joaquín turned back twice to eye the gringos. The first time he noticed the two young men taking pictures of each other in front of the church. The second time, just before he disappeared into the forest, he saw the young pair laboring up the sharp grade of the road.

Father Eger and Joaquín stopped about two hundred yards into the forest, at the predetermined spot, next to a granite outcropping. There they could rest in the pungent coolness of the pine forest and wait for the other conspirators to arrive. A dozen previous visitors at the rock had carved inscriptions and dates, one of which read: "Sergio Martorell, 1731." Father Eger, still breathing heavily, had no intention of leaving any permanent mark.

"This will do, nicely," he said, patting the flattest surface. "Please, Joaquín, can you check further ahead, to make sure there is no one there?"

Joaquín, responding without eye blink or utterance, continued up the path and soon disappeared. He was gone for no more than three minutes. As he returned, the gringos were stepping forward to greet the Roman priest.

"Father Eger, this is Mark Sappingstone," David was saying when he heard Joaquín's footsteps and startled.

"*Buenos días*, Mark," Father Eger said, rising to greet this new American. "Do not worry, David," he quickly added. "This is Joaquín Chiyá, my driver. He works for the Jesuit community at La Merced, and he speaks English very well. You can trust him."

Joaquín bowed his greeting, still ten feet distant. He moved closer to the trio of white men, but remained several steps removed. Even though his face revealed nothing but the simplicity of his grin, Father Eger knew Joaquín was concerned about bringing the gringos into their circle. Gringo interference, Joaquín had insisted six or seven times in the past twenty-four hours, was always for the worst. This kidnapping was of Guatemalan concern, of holy concern.

Joaquín's repeated assertion had shaken Father Eger. The thought crossed his mind as he'd sat on the steps of the small village church, watching the stilted teutonic bargaining at the market stalls, that he might actually be a pawn of the old Maya, who himself was becoming nervous that the game was playing out in the wrong way. How many chess masters were engaged in this match?

"Please, there is room for us all," Father Eger invited, gesturing at the many flat spaces of the rock. "Sit. Please. Yes, you, too, Joaquín."

"No, Father. I will stand and listen," Joaquín said, stepping a pace further back.

"What's he listening for?" David asked. He peered up the path.

"Other—hikers. That is the word, no?" Father Eger asked.

"Yes, hikers, if that's what you mean, " David said. "But we don't need to fear hikers."

Father Eger smiled and shook his head slowly up and down, wondering if David were naive—or could go through with the plan. Then he turned to look at Mark, admiring his build and evident power and the energy in his eyes, a mature man with youth's vigor. This gringo's jaw was set tight. The muscles of his arms stretched out his knit shirt as if he were ready to throw a combatant to the ground. He was ready to act, determined. More fueled by determination than fear. But there was some other struggle inside him. It darted in his eyes.

Nevertheless, this Mark seemed a good choice for their band, Father Eger mused, a good candidate for this one act of courage, anyway, for merely standing in the shadow of death. He only wanted the gringos for their money and their businesslike aura. They were cover, camouflage, distraction. Yes, he thought, this Mark could play the part.

But then again, looks could mislead. Father Eger recalled the Russian who had saved him at the end of the war. He remembered the hulk of that grizzled man who had knelt in a heap before the Soviet officer, softly pleading with his increasingly annoyed captain to spare the awkward and thin, suddenly stuttering Hungarian holy man. "I am a s-s-socialist. A s-s-socialist," scholastic Eger had repeated again and again, in German, Hungarian, Czech, even French. The young Joszef had thought the word might save him. He spoke his declaration over the Russian soldier's babbling. He could only guess what the soldier was saying. Something about stupidity, he thought, or mercy.

Father Eger clearly remembered the bearlike hump on the soldier's back and the long scar that ran from his left eye to below his ear, and the stench the man dragged along with him that made everyone stand away. But his heart had been soft. No, it had been brave. And kind.

"Well," Father Eger said, clapping his hands together as if he were about to start a lecture with little children. "Let us begin. There are three alternatives to consider. Alternative one, let us call it the Gautama plan after the name of the Buddha, is to do nothing. We wade only ankle-deep into the tide of history and let it flow around us. In this plan, we have gone far enough. As the official representative of the Father General of the Society of Jesus, I have told the UDA that we will pay no ransom. And I have demanded the release of Father Burns."

The two northerners kept quiet. Father Eger had expected protests from the gringos. He kept on.

"Alternative two, let us call it the Hollywood plan because money is its star and its ending is easy and happy." Father Eger smiled broadly. Again the Americans only stared back with blank faces. He sighed.

"In this plan we pay the ransom. I must make another contact with the UDA. I will offer them an exchange, two million dollars for Father Thomas Burns. We will then meet, undoubtedly in a place like this," he said, pointing up and down the shadowed path. "An empty, unseen place. I will be alone, although Joaquín will accompany me. After all, I am an old man and a foreigner. They will drive up in a jeep, guns everywhere. Father Burns will be in the jeep, although I do not know if he will be alive. Maybe not a happy ending."

A blanching concern wiped across the young Americans' faces. Good, thought Father Eger. They understand the type of men we deal with.

"Alternative three, let us call this the Ché plan. In this plan we must find where they hold Father Burns and capture him by force of arms. It would be up to me and Joaquín to discover where Thomas is being held, then . . ."

"And who is going to do the capturing?" David said, his question exploding in the silence.

"*Guerrilleros*," Father Eger said, blandly. "Counterinsurgents, you might say. Such a long word, so Germanic. *Contras*. No, not *contras*. Wrong side."

Father Eger stopped himself, realizing that he had become cheeky, a constant problem when he approached too closely to danger, as in his first interrogation after his incarceration in Berlin. The shortish police officer had been uncertain how to treat him. Something about his height and his hawkish face commanded respect. The first thing out of his mouth had been, "Shall I kneel s-sir, the better for you to s-strike me?" The guards had had to carry him out of that blood-spattered room.

"What do you two think of these alternatives? Gautama, Hollywood, or Ché?" asked Father Eger.

"For me, I want to free Tom," Mark said, anger in his voice, "I'm for the Ché plan." The muscles of his neck flared, and his shoulders tensed high.

David turned fully toward Mark. "I can't believe you said that." Even in the dappled light David's eyes flashed as if he stood on Arabian sand. "Where did that come from?" Then louder. "This is not a movie! This is not your Washington posturing! Your press conference pimping! People could get killed!"

"And why should death frighten *you*?" Mark asked, matching David's tone.

Father Eger saw a form swim up into Mark's eyes, all dorsal fin and sharp teeth. He stared in fascination. He watched Mark set his feet apart. Something wild was about to strike.

"You're the one who reminds me every time I see you that all your friends are dead or dying," Mark said. "You're the noble angel of the plague. So haven't you seen AIDS do more damage than a bullet could ever do and . . ."

"That doesn't mean I want to *die*, Mark. I have no death-lust. And I'm not constantly reminding you . . ."

"Do you want Tom to die?" Mark puffed his chest out. "Do we let him die? Die!?"

"No! I'm the one who agreed to pay the ransom." David looked over at Father Eger, jerking his head, as if the priest should intervene in this madness.

"And do you really think they'll let Tom go? Did you hear what Father Eger said? His fate may be . . ."

No one spoke or continued Mark's thought. His shoulders slumped back down. Father Eger saw the marauder descend from the shallows of Mark's eyes into a deeper blackness.

"I don't know if they'll let him go," David said, exasperated, looking up into the green and black canopy. He paused. "I just want to get this over with and get out of here. I'm ready to cooperate with their demands, but I'm not up for violence. That's not for me!"

"I'm not for violence," Mark said, pleading. "But maybe violence is our only choice."

Father Eger had made that statement himself once. More than once. He knew the feeling inside. This Mark wants to tear something apart.

"You don't know anything about fighting!" David yelled. "This is ridiculous!" David rose from the rock. "What's gone wrong with you!?!"

The four of them were silent, tense. Joaquín remained several paces away. On occasion he looked up and down the trail.

Father Eger was making his decision. Of course, he never imagined putting guns in the hands of the Americans. Still, depending on negotiations, he might have to bring them along to an exchange. Mark would not do, he decided. That fine-looking American may not be able to control the creature inside. David, however, he was sure, had been properly fired in an earth kiln and would not break. He was made of martyr's clay, and his glaze was himself.

Father Eger turned to Joaquín. "Make the sound."

Joaquín hesitated, then brought two fingers to his mouth and whistled the call of the quetzál, a bird that was long gone from the high pine forests.

The four men could hear footsteps on the far end of the trail, not the soft pat of *caites* but the sound of boots slapping the hardened soil of the path.

Two figures emerged, one *ladina* woman and one *indígena* man, both dressed in camouflage fatigues. The man had tied a red bandanna around his neck. He held a rifle in his hands and wore a holster strapped loose around his gut. The woman wore no bandanna. Her neck was long, and her dark hair had been curled onto the top of her head, extending her height. She walked a few paces behind the man, but had the more intense eyes, Father Eger thought. Her right hand was on a pistol that moved up and down in the holster on her hip.

"We must make this quick," Father Eger said as this new pair joined them. His spirit was rising. It was his first meeting with Guadalupe. This Nicaraguan woman moved with the surety of a warrior princess, an Athena in helmet and shield.

"We have not met," Father Eger said to the pair. He remained seated on the granite outcropping. "I am Father Eger. This is David," he said, pointing to the very nervous blonde who seemed transfixed by the woman. "And this is Mark. Of course, Joaquín and Luís know each other. Luís, your daughter María sends her greetings. She is so wise in her silence, which is so unusual in the very young."

Luís repressed a grin.

"Guadalupe, have you gathered sufficient forces?" asked Father Eger. He tried to sound the commander. He needed everyone to look to him.

"We have." Her voice was curt, more full of authority than his—and cautious. He noticed she had a hard time keeping her eyes off the gringos, as if she were a biologist suddenly feet from extinct primates, as if she wanted to pat them, measure them, take them back with her.

"Then I will make contact with the UDA today," Father Eger said. "I will offer to pay the ransom." Guadalupe and Luís knew the three options. Joaquín had carried Father Eger's message.

"They will take the ransom and kill Tom anyway, in front of your eyes," Guadalupe said, disdain searing her voice.

Father Eger paused. She is for rescue, he thought. He, too, feared the same messy outcome with the Hollywood plan. The UDA may now realize that asking for ransom was a mistake. It muddled their message. Father Eger was glad Guadalupe had the same insight. It explained the morning's attack on La Merced, didn't it?

"Yes, it may be that they will kill him anyway," Father Eger said. "My offer is meant to stall them, to give us time so we can find where they keep him." Father Eger still wasn't sure Guadalupe would follow his lead.

"How will you find that out?" Guadalupe asked.

"From Father Garza. I believe he knows."

"They will not have told him," she said. "Too dangerous for them. And if we capture Tom, they would have to kill Garza, the informant."

He was losing her trust. She was playing out new scenarios. He hadn't considered this possibility. Would he have to sacrifice one priest for another?

"Perhaps." Father Eger kept himself calm.

He had told Joaquín she might be difficult to control, that Luís would have to watch her closely. "She might act on impulse, go on a rampage. Like a gypsy woman in Szeged who nearly slit my gut because I resembled her cheating husband."

Still, the Guadalupe in front of him was in control: of her breathing, her posture, her ideas. Next to her, these Americans were children. She seemed less haunted than they. Absorbed by her spirit, not haunted by it.

Father Eger had known many people absorbed with spirits. Ignatius had, too. Ignatius had put such men on a long leash and let them roam, but on a leash nonetheless, a tether that, pulled at the right moment, would return them to sanity.

"If Father Garza says nothing—or knows nothing, then we go ahead with the exchange, money for Father Burns," Father Eger said, staring only at Guadalupe. "Agreed?"

She nodded yes.

"And at the first sign of a deal gone bad, we seize him," Father Eger said.

She nodded again. Father Eger noticed David look over at Mark. Mark, however, stood silent as the stone he sat upon.

"It will be hard to arrange a place where your force can be near," Father Eger said.

"We are better trained than they," Guadalupe countered. "They are thugs, men who surround the weak and kill at night." She spat on the path.

There was the rage. Father Eger wondered if it were a storm as predictable as the monsoon. Or something more frightening. Tsunami or hurricane.

"If it is to be an exchange, make it on September 15, next Friday, Guatemalan Independence Day," Guadalupe said. She seemed a general sure of her maps and data. "It will be easier to move around unnoticed."

"Yes, it should be on next Friday," Father Eger said. "But that is also the day appointed for execution, the ending of the two weeks."

Everyone stopped to consider this message, breathing once deeply.

"And if Father Garza *does* know where they keep Father Burns, we will have to silence the old man after I extract that information," Father Eger said.

Father Eger turned quickly to David and Mark, who had turned a plastic white. They had misunderstood. "Not kill him. Put him away somewhere."

He turned to Luís and Joaquín. "If that comes to pass, you and your people must deal with the old priest." The *indígenas* nodded silently. "Or," he said, entertaining a new thought, testing again, "the gringos could handle the old man until we have finished our mission."

Neither Mark nor David moved. The defiant Mark was now silent. So he didn't want to be a prison captain.

"Tomorrow is Sunday," Father Eger said, rising from his rocky perch. "I will rest and pray. On Monday I will speak with Father Garza about the whereabouts of Father Burns. Are there any questions?"

No one spoke.

"Good. Joaquín and I will contact you when we have determined which plan to take, capture or ransom/capture," Father Eger said to the two *guerrilleros*. "Do not contact us unless there is an emergency. Our enemies have some idea that we are meeting, or that some subsets of us are meeting. At this stage of the game, they have as many theories and outcomes as we have. Let us not make their lives easier."

Just as that hidden meeting was ending on the slopes of the *Volcán Agua*, Father Garza stormed into the ascetic study of Don Francisco Orozco, a building separate from the main house of Don Francisco's city villa, tucked away at the back of the great man's Guatemala City compound. It had no windows and only one steel door. It was really a bunker named The Eagle's Lair.

"What have you done?!" Father Garza demanded, stomping past the guard, his cassock's hem flying open as he sped in. "Why have you attacked La Merced, my church? I thought we were on the same side!"

"Calm down, Antonio, calm down," Don Francisco said, rising from his chair. "It was only a message for the old Hungarian, not for you. I'm so sorry we had to deface La Merced. But you understand the times we live in. And this messy situation . . ." Don Francisco paused, gesturing aimlessly into the air.

"So sad that your order could not send that gringo away. He does such damage here, spreads such lies." Don Francisco's voice was lush with the tone of a father dealing with a wronged child.

"Please, sit here." Don Francisco pointed to one of the two overstuffed chairs that offered the only comfort within his hideaway.

"You know, Padre Antonio, our Church is making things very difficult for me these days. Others in our group have already converted to the Protestant sect. They are urging us to eradicate our Roman Church from Guatemala. You know these radical, political priests make it difficult for loyal Catholics to defend our Church."

"Don Francisco," Father Garza said, shocked to hear these sentiments from his old acquaintance, "surely you know these liberal priests and nuns do not represent the Holy See. The Holy See is with us. Besides—besides, how could one abandon one's faith—you cannot be considering it, to join with that noisy rabble. Those stompers of feet whose services are as chaotic as market day. They are hawkers of truth, and only little shanks of truth! You could not be considering joining that group. . . ."

"No, Padre Antonio, no. You misunderstand me. I'm talking about political realities. The pressures I experience. My point: The inaction of your order has forced us to reemphasize our demands. That is why we sullied La Merced. It saddens me."

"But how am I to explain this defilement to my family? They will think I'm involved in these modern idolatries." Father Garza stared into the eyes of his old acquaintance, then continued his complaint. "I am a traditionalist. I submit to the authority of the Pope. And his Holiness has made it clear that priests are not to be rebels. Your action will make people think I'm in opposition to Rome."

"No, no, that will not be," Don Francisco said, displaying his bright teeth, most of them false. "After all, your nephew Marcos is playing an important role in this affair."

As soon as Don Francisco had uttered that phrase, Father Garza's face turned flat, revealing nothing of what had burst inside him.

Marcos was involved. His nephew had laid his hands on the gringo priest, performed the work of a henchman. Marcos, a precious flower of the family, a man who could accomplish much, perhaps return the family to political prominence—he was a thug.

Father Garza knew the times required many things of many people. Guatemala was at war. War with the communists who would take away people's lands and redistribute them to the lazy and ignorant *campesinos*, most of them superstitious *indígenas* who continued to practice their old rituals in hidden places.

Father Garza was no fool. He knew that much of the piety of the New World was devil worship. He had tried to remove it, even in his youth when he had worked on his family's *fincas* and *cafetales*. He had preached to the workers telling them about saints and how holy people should live, encouraging them to marry and to baptize their children.

Even before he had entered the Jesuits, Father Garza had tried to correct the practices of the *indígenas* who worked on the Garza plantations. His efforts had led to that awful event at *El Susurro*, his favorite plantation, way up near Lake Atitlán. He had prayed so often to have that memory taken from him.

Late one afternoon when he was seventeen, only months before he would cross the stone lintel of the Jesuit novitiate, during a particularly severe dry season, he had come upon a *zahorín* who was living in one of the huts of the plantation. The old man was making what Antonio had thought must be *cush*, the local moonshine, a substance the *zahorín* sold along with his other remedies. When Antonio had looked closer at the iron pot, he saw that the mixture contained blood.

"*¡Tu ofreces sacrificios a dióses falsos!*" Antonio had exclaimed as he began to rampage through the hut, beating the old *zahorín* and his wife and finally, fatally, knocking over a small iron bowl that contained several hot coals.

One thing led to another. The coals ignited a stack of dry corn husks, which sent a spark upward and set the thatch roof on fire. The wind had been against him. It took the blaze to other huts. The flames quickly reached a small field of corn stalks, which ignited. Then the nearby pine forest exploded, individual trees booming as they were consumed by flames.

Eventually an entire *caballería*, about 45 hectares, burned down, including that wonderful house made of volcanic stone and fresh, clean pine with windows that constantly tricked the birds with their invisible expanses.

Inside that house the youngest child of the Garza family, Isabella, a girl of nearly three, had been playing *escondite*, hide-and-seek. She had bundled herself into her mother's huge sewing basket. Her charred body, studded by melted needles and thimbles, was found afterwards.

The night of that fire had been unusually warm, and even the refreshing breezes of the place could not dry the tears of the family. His brother complained, even to this day, that the land of *El Susurro* was vexed by some curse. Nothing grew there. The plantation remained abandoned. Even the *indígenas* left it alone. He had no need to post guards.

Father Garza knew at that moment that Father Burns was being kept at *El Susurro*. He did not betray this knowledge to Don Francisco. His face was a block of stone, carved only by a meaningless fragment of time. After a few seconds, he began again to rant at the colonel, complaining about the defacing of La Merced, leaving the impression that he was a foolish old man who could not deal with the difficulties life sent him.

Within him, however, a new sadness was growing in a long-untilled soil.

CHAPTER TWENTY-THREE

Contemplatio in actionem.

Prayer in action, a distinctive characteristic of Jesuit spiritual life.

While David and Mark had spent their day edging down the narrow tunnels of conspiracy, bumping into the dark messes and unnamed creatures of that underworld, others were speaking on Main Street.

Ann had called and left a message, which the staff at the front desk of the Camino Montserrat wrote down on a small sheet of gold-embossed letterhead.

Mark stood motionless as a backroads fencepost while the clerk held out Ann's message, "*Señor*, for you." Mark didn't move. He was a pearl diver at work, breath held in, eyes wide open. David finally grabbed the note from the confused clerk, who kept repeating: "*Señor*, for you, take. Señor, for you, take."

David shoved the note at Mark, holding it flat against the firmness of his companion's chest until Mark, slow to react, reached up and took the paper.

While the head clerk watched this strange pantomime, his assistant opened the safe under the counter and pulled out a sealed envelope in whose upper left-hand corner sat a bald eagle, its talons bulging with arrows.

Mark was quick to grab this government envelope. He tore it open and read the single sheet of the ambassador's letter, then handed it to David.

Ambassador Riordan had stated, with the fewest possible words, that he wanted to know what the two uninvited Americans were doing.

"So George turned us in," Mark said, looking at David, who paid him no attention as he turned to start up the stairs.

David counted the curving steps, slowly moving his lips, hoping to dull his friend-anger and friend-despair with an exercise of enumeration. Halfway up the stairs he started to climb more quickly.

"Coleman said George would keep his mouth shut," Mark said, catching up to David at the landing. His voice pleaded for attention. "I guess the news about the ransom was too good to keep to himself. But we can't do anything now, can we? We can't talk to the ambassador, right?"

David continued his silence. As he walked and counted steps, his inmost brain was reviewing the new script, the dialogue Father Eger had scribbled on the volcano's skin, the jihad language of his friend. David was revising the odds of pulling off a peaceful exchange. These odds, once elegant and high-masted, had become a dinghy disappearing over the horizon, rudderless and caught in a rough current.

David despaired of saving Tom. He despaired of saving his friendship with Mark. A part of his life seemed to be ending, abruptly and without notice, as if he himself had heard a death squad's midnight knock, as if the condom had broken and his obit had acquired the fearful line.

Back at their suite, the two men went to their separate rooms. David never turned around to look at his troubling companion, despite Mark's call: "David . . .David . . ."

Mark went to his room. He had yet to read Ann's message. He walked to the end of his room, fifteen paces, and leaned against the outer wall. There he read the message, crumpled it back up, then opened it to read one last time. It was pure dictation. "Senator Brandon wants to know what you are doing. Have you gone nuts?"

He memorized the two sentences, speaking them quietly to himself. The words, so meager. Containing little of concern. Nothing of pure, clean anger. He read rebuke and disgust. Gritty, oily words. Words impossible to swallow.

Mark went out onto his balcony to stare up into the ancient Guatemalan sky. Last night he'd thought of calling her, but hadn't. He feared that hearing his voice, distant and attenuated, confused and hopeless, would be enough to send Ann, who'd inhabited his cluttered world for years, packing for the heartland. He'd pushed everything to the edge.

A great weight pressed in on him.

But he could not find tears.

He had ruined his family. He was his own disaster, a wolf sneaking up on a clouded winter night. He should've been sentry. Once he had wanted to be shepherd.

He'd thought fatherhood would save him. It hadn't.

Nor had marriage. He had betrayed them both, son and wife, and himself, father and husband. He had betrayed them in the slow loosening of their moorings, daily little unravelings that went unnoticed until the fleet had sailed out. He was so caught up in his success, in his Hill struggles. But so were all the other guys he knew.

But there was more, wasn't there? Was it the old story, once a vocation riddle?

Whatever it was, it had taken to writing itself with jism and the red rush of heart. For the last three years, every time Charley went into the hospital Mark spent afternoons and evenings with hookers, sometimes two a day. Always someone new. Black, blonde, Hispanic. It made no difference. There was no kissing. Little foreplay. Sometimes he kept his clothes on. He loved the feel of the cotton shorts riding up on him, catching the hair on his legs. He loved it better than the indifferent touch of his paid women.

He used funds from the office. He had ways.

His mind told him this sex was a sick thing ("You fucker, what have you done!" he would cry to himself as he left the apartments and their perfumed candles and stained carpets), but he felt no guilt, no remorse, no confessional turmoil. If he felt anything, he felt relief. But this relief ripped through his soul, unlike the soothing vesper-tides he had once floated in, and left him battered and exhausted on the shore.

After Charley returned home from his latest hospital crisis, Mark would resume chastity. He and Ann had stopped having sex. Stopped being intimate. Neither of them touched each other much any more, not the curves and folds of reproduction or the spirit-haunts of brain. They were Trappists, all concentrated on the son. Bowing when necessary. Gesturing for food and water. Firm in this one silent commitment.

But this past summer! Charley was having a good summer. He hadn't gone to the hospital, even for tests. So Mark had no excuse. What he did wasn't the same as those pumping moments with the nameless ones. It was a step further.

The night Mark made love to Gloria, he'd been at the gym. It was Gloria who'd convinced Mark he might feel better if he kept in finer shape, might deal better with the tension that was boiling inside him, that made him sit distant in important meetings, never taking a note.

That evening, after Gloria's aerobics class and Mark's two hundred free weight reps, they would eat Thai and plan a NAFTA commentary. Mark called home to tell Ann he'd be late. He told her he was still at the office, a lie he had never used before. No, he had not lied to Ann, because she had never asked the worst questions.

Gloria left the club in her workout clothes, telling Mark she was out of shampoo and conditioner, that she had to shower at home. Mark drove his silver Mercedes to her house and waited with public radio on, something funny from Minnesota. She turned around at the door and gestured for him to come in.

"I won't be long," she cried from the door, as if this invitation were a sudden idea. "Don't be shy," she said as he entered her home. "Mix yourself a drink," she said, pointing to the black Chinese cabinet and the two rows of thick tumblers lined up on its glistening top. "But don't drink too much, you're driving," she added as she walked down the hallway to the bedroom, lifting off the single layer of her top and revealing her sports bra with its gentle indenting of her unmarried skin.

Gloria had once studied for the Episcopal priesthood, and people had mistaken her for a nun.

Mark stood watching Gloria until the bathroom door shut. It had been years since he'd had sex with a woman who wanted just him.

He thought of that dark bar in Wisconsin, of the temptress on the Mississippi. He'd come to believe that if he'd never confessed that temptation, Father Gorman would never have been so opposed to letting him take vows. And if Father Gorman had supported him, maybe he would never have left the Jesuits, maybe he would have been able to work things out, or maybe he would have left a better man, maybe his life would have been . . . "I've screwed up everything," he muttered, as he poured his drink.

Mark's marriage was dying and he didn't know what to do or if he cared or if he should care. Right then he only wanted to lay Gloria down on her bed and sweat over her. "Diddle her." He loved that phrase. Women had always been amazed by him, his shape, his cunning, his stamina. He swallowed his first scotch and poured another. Maybe there was no such thing as a good life. Maybe there were only a few good moments. He looked down the corridor. A light shone underneath the bathroom door.

She and he were alike, he thought. They had sipped from the chalice and gone away parched. Was it them or was it the dryness of old blood?

Gloria opened the bathroom door, yelling down the hallway that she needed to defog the mirror in order to apply her lipstick "better than a kindergarten kid with a crayola."

Mark was sitting on her gold love seat, a cat poised at the mouse's hole. He could see the length of her body, the heart shape of hips. He caught a glimpse of her breasts. They were smaller than Ann's, just as he had surmised. He made no attempt to look away. He watched as Gloria dried herself. His heart started to pound. He checked his watch. Gloria turned around, barely displaying that bud at the tip of her torso. She was bold. It ratcheted him. He began to untie his shoestrings.

Two minutes after he came skin-on-skin inside her, Mark rolled out of Gloria's bed. He reached into his pile of clothes for his underpants. Her smell was still sharp in the air. She told him to stop, to stay. There was no desperation in her voice, he thought, perhaps nothing more than hospitality or a desire for more later.

"No," Mark said and pulled up his briefs. His heart was pounding again, a different rhythm. "I'm so sorry," he said. His voice was humid. He didn't feel the old emptiness. He felt something sharper.

"I'm sorry. I'm sorry."

He wasn't apologizing to her.

He cried the entire way home and slept the night in the foyer with his suit still on. Charley screamed when he discovered his father in the morning. Ann said nothing as she herded Charley into the kitchen and away from the doorway vagrant. Mark told her later he had drunk way too much that night with some visiting Japanese who had discovered him at work.

Mark avoided Gloria for the next month. When they were finally alone after a planning session for testimony at a Senate committee hearing on the School of the Americas, Mark told Gloria he couldn't sleep with her again. She put her hand on his lips, saying, "That's all right. We're both adults."

He had told no one else, not with words. Of course, Ann had noticed. He was sure. He read it in her eyes, especially the night he staggered in, unraveling as swiftly as a mummy floating up the Nile, after Gloria had informed him: "You're some fertile stud. I'm pregnant. One time and I'm pregnant! We were stupid."

Gloria hadn't decided to have the baby. "It's my decision, Mark. My decision alone."

Out on the Guatemalan balcony, Mark covered his eyes with his hands. He rubbed his wedding ring deep into his cheek. He thought of scratching his face, of wounding his eyes. They had betrayed him, hadn't they? What if he'd been born blind? Had never learned to throw a ball. Had grown up shy and physically unsteady.

He wanted to yell, but only a deep sound rumbled inside him. He couldn't picture his family. Her soft blonde hair. His big eyes. Mark ground his teeth. His head burned. His whole body ached as if he'd swallowed something, and it was coming up. The thing was stale and tarry as grief. He shuddered, and his body contracted hard. Again and again.

David sat at his desk and opened up his diary: Opus Fifty. Some years he'd written constantly, several times a day, words and tales flowing out of him, often soulful as Slavic drama from the pen of Dostoyevski. Some years his life was spare, and he only wrote the date of each day and the line: "I am alive." This had begun as one of those lean years.

> Mark's getting on my nerves. He's either a jabbering goon or he's moping around like a soul lost between Purgatory's steam bath and Hell's cauldron. That man needs help. Am I supposed to step in here? I told Ann I'd deliver her final message, her ultimatum: I won't be here when you return.
>
> I'm not speaking her words. She can hire Bill Bennett. I'm not getting involved with these two, not that way.
>
> Guadalupe is here. What does she want? What good does she want?
>
> This ransom plot is way out of control. I might fly home tomorrow. I'll write out a check, leave it with Mark. I'd be no good in a shootout.
>
> I feel sick writing that. They may kill Tom. Hack him to death. Can

I walk away? What if it weren't Tom? What if it were Randy? I'd be in fatigues, then. I'd hire mercenaries. Buy squadrons of helicopters, highways of tanks.

I wish Randy were alive.

I wish AIDS were a war.

"Can we talk?" Mark asked, appearing over David's shoulder.

David turned and looked up, shocked, covering his diary. "Talk? I don't know if we can *talk*. We could harass each other, the way we did out on the mountain, you asshole."

David shot up from his desk. They stood face to face.

Mark stepped back, his eyes wide as a child's. He hadn't been thinking of David. He could smell David's anger.

"What was that shit you gave me about AIDS out there!?! It's nothing but a dirty *word* to you! A *tired* word! Well, to me its been my *world* and the struggle of my *life*! Cleaning up the feces of the unchained Beast." David took a step forward and thumped Mark's chest with his right hand. "And what's this crap about strapping ourselves with guns and bandoleros and shooting at people! Have you ever shot anyone? Have you ever killed anyone?"

David thumped Mark's chest again.

Mark tensed his muscles. He stepped back further. His back was against the wall.

"I feel like punching you out, you asshole. YOU ASSHOLE!" Spittle from David's scream settled on Mark's eyelashes. Mark moved to wash it away, but froze. He wasn't angry. He was focused.

"Don't you have anything to say?" David slapped Mark on his right cheek, a pat.

"Hello. Are you there? Are you so far gone? Hello?" David slapped him again harder.

David stepped back. "Why am I doing this?" He turned to look out the window, both hands on his hips, and waited.

He turned back to face Mark.

Mark was still at the wall, his back straight, his breath regular.

"You were always somebody," David said. "You were king of the hill, the muscled boy who pushed all the others down. You were glory boy. The only rip in your wings was Father Gorman's rebuke—and you patched that up with hardly a scandal, didn't you? A year later you were on the Board of Directors of St. Louis University. Jesus H. Christ!"

Mark saw a darkness appear around David's eyes.

"I got caught loitering in Forest Park with my dull sorrow and my exhausting desires, and they almost threw me out of the Society! I was told I could stay if I went into therapy. And everyone knew my story the next day. The next day everyone knew. A decade before CNN! Who told?"

Mark remembered a locker room conversation with one of his new friends, a California province scholastic he played handball with, a witty, energetic mover who later left the Society and became CEO of an Internet startup. Mark had not anticipated the pain that his jock-wet revelation would cause. For a moment he closed his eyes in shame. He'd forgotten that incident. He'd been too caught up in his own resurrection.

"I never asked you—or Tom—how everyone came to know." David slumped into a smaller self. His voice lost its bite.

"My declaration of freedom that night in your room, my coming out, was revoked by dawn. Up comes the sun and I was back in the land of self-hatred. The snubbing, the stares, the little notes that showed up in my mailbox: 's.j.—sodomite jack-off; are you Greek or French?' I assumed I deserved them all. Even the other gay boys kept their distance. I was haz-ardous material. I was Hester with her Scarlet A. She and I, we both feared the forest and stayed within the holy village even though it scorned us!"

For a second David brought together the thumb and index finger of his right hand and examined them the way a jeweler holds a well-cut stone. He looked away, then right back at Mark.

"You know, all the while I was in St. Louis," David said, his finger and thumb still together, "some thread of me knew, just as Hester must've known, that freedom was out there . . ." David waved his right arm toward the courtyard, "out under the trees."

Mark said nothing. He thought of the great oaks that surrounded his boyhood home. He loved to climb them and stay hidden on a high limb all afternoon. He'd pluck off nuts and fling them at squirrels. He'd study the slouching movements of preying cats. He'd pretend he was a baby angel, fresh-born and wingless, defiant of gravity and its intense, watchful, fatherly pull.

Mark wanted David to keep on raving. Mark was a thirsty man smelling fresh water. David had water, the water of knowledge. He said things, and they were.

David's eyes narrowed. He leaned over to pick up his diary. He flipped back a couple of pages. Looking up, "OK, so you're going to be silent. Pretty boys can get away with silence. You know that. Pretty boys get the benefit of the doubt. They're not stupid, they're deep."

David paused and glared at Mark. Mark thought David's eyes lasers. Something was being burned away with those eyes. Mark was breathing regularly. He felt lighter, purer. Something was lifting. He could feel the muscles of his frame relax, the tendon-coils release.

"I wrote this last night:

> *Jesuit phrases keep popping up.* Nemo dat quod no habet— *nobody gives what he does not have. As scholastics we were taught to bless anyone who insisted we were priests. Instead of the real words of blessing, we said "*nemo dat quod no habet*" as we made the sign of the cross that should have layered grace on the recipient.*

> *The phrase haunts me. If you don't have it, you can't give it. I think that's Mark. He's trying to give, and he keeps coming up empty handed, or holding something hideous. But if he doesn't try to give something, anything, what will become of him? Maybe there's magic in trying to give what you do not have. Maybe giving, even giving from nothing, nudges the hidden creature. Maybe that warm animal trapped within Mark's clothes will escape, big-eared or dove-winged, wrinkling its nose or cooing. Maybe I'll applaud. Out of relief. Out of joy. Out of surprise.*

> *He wants so much to help Tom, but he really needs to help himself. So, are we here as rescuers or . . .? It's clear Mark wants to revive an old spirit, mouth to mouth, if only he could find the mouth. And*

me?

"Tell," David said, his gray eyes moist, his voice pleading, both hands firmly holding his diary as if it were a ritual text, sacred and directive, "why are we here?"

Mark flinched. He reached up to tug on his ear. An unformed idea was knocking about in his brain.

"I think you've got it right," Mark said, pointing to the diary. He was unsure of the words. They were too fresh. But his eyes were white again. "I'm in free fall. I either fly or crash. You—you're still trying—I don't know—trying to help a friend cheat death. That's what's yours to give."

CHAPTER TWENTY-FOUR

"I only see clearly at dawn or at the cold stroke of midnight. By see, I mean understand. It is only at those pivotal times of the day's cycle when I connect with the sacred forces most powerfully, with the sorrowing Sacred Heart of Jesus, with our holy father Ignatius and other saints, with the angels attendant on this world. At dawn and at midnight. Why? Why are the holy so active when most we need the luxury of sleep and a chance to nestle childlike at the open gate of infinity?"

Snippet of a conversation between Father Beltrán and the gangly Hungarian theology student who had gone to him to complain of his inability to concentrate on his studies, of his nights interrupted by horrid dreams, of the deep, sad, sorrow that seemed to chase after him with padded cunning, of a demon of hate and anger that had squeezed into him, of a soul adrift in a sea of questions, as recorded in the personal diary of Joszef Egcr, S.J., May 10, 1947, Rome.

On Sunday morning Father Eger struggled to unknot himself from the bleached threads of his bed linen as the rays of the blood-fed Mayan sun edged up the western wall of his bedroom. One leg and one arm had been immobilized for hours, restrained and encircled by the bedding cloth. He fought to bring those limbs back into life, into communion with his body, rubbing their loose, wrinkled skin and lifting them slowly into the air.

Father Eger sat up in his bed and watched the rays of dawn inch over the room's black crucifix. He watched the ivory corpus, hung in stately desolation with its deep-set eyes wide open to measure a new day, brighten in the light. The corpus's eyes, Father Eger thought, painted with cave-worn sorrow, stared with an intimacy only parents conjure as they examine wayward children sheepish at their doorstep.

With that thought Father Eger clamped shut his own eyelids and prayed his current mantra. "Sweet Jesus, have mercy. Sweet Jesus, have mercy. Sweet Jesus, have mercy."

All night Father Eger's body had danced the choreography of a troubled soul, tangling itself again and again in the worn cotton sheets of his bed. His rest was no nourishing dip into the saving waters of the unconscious. It was fitful, part anxious plotting, part blood-red disbelief. How could a man such as he, a vowed servant of the Prince of Peace, engage in the possible manufacture of death?

Father Eger rose shortly after dawn, time for his half hour of hatha yoga, the practice of which Father Beltrán had instilled in him so that the anguished theology student could quiet his soul before heading to his celibate bed. Now Father Eger both began and ended his days with those meditations of the body, those preliminary, sinewy steps toward enlightenment, what he called mystical union—entry into the land of wordless, plotless knowing.

This particular morning he was in desperate need of the graces of that renewing discipline. Questions plagued him. He cringed as his inner companion pounded these questions into the membranes of consciousness, as if it were a cook intent on the tenderest meat: Why do you plan this act of violence? You know it satisfies your need for vengeance, your need for bold revenge. When will you truly forgive your captors? When will you learn detachment?

Even his conscience, he moaned, did not understand his soul. It was ignorant of his soul's complexities. Had the conscience only been an organ of relaxing mischief in the Garden of Eden? Secondary and trifle? Connected to the rest of the body by a narrow isthmus of veins and ducts? Now it was the source of that animating human ooze, the green liquid of doubt.

Father Eger knew why he had not been executed in Berlin or sent to a camp. He was a Jesuit, and the municipal prison's commandant had heard that Hitler himself was much impressed by the way the Jesuits manipulated history. The commandant, a political scientist, thought he might learn something from the Hungarian. So certain details of Eger's crime were laid aside, allowing the commandant to keep the near-priest in his own protective custody, as the focus of an entertaining experiment.

Scholastic Eger had been a defiant prisoner to begin with. A few pistol beatings stopped his resistance, or the obvious expression of it. As the jail days proceeded, the commandant kept Eger under close watch. He instructed his staff to observe Eger's every move, to listen to his words, to ask other prisoners what the Hungarian had said. Later the commandant would inscribe these observations in a logbook titled: Jesuit Study. These treasures of human behavior would be data for the commandant's research into the methodologies of political influence.

This was the commandant's experiment: by sending in different types of prisoners as cell mates he would test the Jesuit's reactions, observe how the Jesuit interpreted and influenced the new cell mate's condition within the *polis*. The commandant sent in several faggots, a communist who stubbornly protested he was an ex-communist, a Bulgarian monarchist, a multitude of common criminals, a pair of intellectuals, a businessman who had demanded too much for his wares, even a fresh Jew recently uncovered in a small Brandenburg bank.

Although the commandant soon learned to despise Eger, so distasteful was the Jesuit's disdain for his captor, sometimes the commandant would bring Eger into his office so he himself could ask why the Hungarian had said this or that.

"You told that one-legged pickpocket Hans to examine his life, to remember the times when he was most happy, to think why those times had made him happy. Most cunning, young Jesuit. Emotion is such a powerful force." The commandant always smiled when sharing one of his insights and batted his eyelashes as if he were flirting with cameras. "But what if this Hans thinks the life of a pickpocket is the happiest of times. Would that not lead him to conclude, ever more clearly, that his calling is to steal? What would you say to him then?" There was glee in the commandant's voice.

Eger stood quietly with his hands clasped behind him, pulling back his shoulders until his clavicle was taut. He stood without quick answer before the dark-uniformed little man, who sat hunched over his logbook and waited to write the response. Eger felt the pressure of Ignatius within him, the pressure to speak just the right amount of truth to Inquisition jailers, to stare egoless into the false eyes of flatterers.

"I would have asked Hans again why that act made him happy? Was it the adventure? Was it the very moment when he placed his hand in someone's clothing, the moment when his skin evaded the cloth of the other's coat with the surety of a mouse that darts through a knothole in the floorboard. Was that the moment in his life when he felt most alive? Perhaps the skill of that act made him feel monumental." Eger would puff out his chest with that word: monumental. He didn't know why he loved it. "Or was it the danger? Or did he steal to feed his aging mother? If so, he stole for love, surely."

Before writing down Eger's response, the commandant looked up at his prize prisoner over his silver pince-nez glasses.

Eger imagined a hateful, bloating analysis pass through the commandant's ratlike mind. This captor of his could never have been good at philosophy. The man's talent, undoubtedly, had been in organizing, in fashioning discipline, in mapping the maze with the fattest of the rodents.

"So, what if Hans had said it was the skill of the crime that pleased him?" asked the commandant.

"I would say to Hans: Let me employ that skill to a different end."

"To what end?"

Eger hesitated, swallowing the word "resistance."

"To steal souls for Christ," he said, with the calmness of a man who speaks the obvious.

Hans had been released the next week. After he was arrested again for pickpocketing, he was shot. Eger was dragged out of his cell to witness Hans's execution. At first it had been unclear whether Eger, too, was to be shot that day.

With the sound of exploding shells still echoing in the courtyard, the commandant turned to Eger, throwing off two quick questions before marching off: "So, Jesuit, was Hans happy? Is he happy now?"

Eger had no answer.

As the commandant's laboratory studies continued, Eger became ever more depressed, fearful that his soul was being eaten away by his captor's experimentation.

There were no more moments of peace or acceptance. He spoke the words: *fiat voluntas tua*, but they were dead words, dead before his tongue had settled back into its new lethargy. No part of him, not his heart nor brain nor gut, resonated to them. He forced himself to pray, but prayer lost imagery. He ached for ripped organs and the latinate seduction of autotermination, noble Cicero's final friend. Only death seemed an escape, and suicide a sensible release.

With each new cell mate Eger withdrew deeper into himself, pulling his knees up to his chin. With each new cell mate, the commandant wrote more and more. The commandant sent Eger more pitiable companions, crippled men, kind men, old men. Eger tried to say nothing, but these men—they wanted to talk.

Eger noticed the commandant whistled constantly, a cheerful whistle. The commandant was whistling even as the Russians slugged their way through western Poland. He whistled as he packed up and disappeared two months before Berlin fell, one hellish block after another.

Eger's freedom from prison did not release him from his jailer's snare. The memories from his captivity still sullied him, spattering him freshly with the gore and anguish of the commandant's victims as if he, Eger, had chosen willingly to participate in the many experiments of the diminutive Prussian political scientist.

After Eger's aborted post-liberation execution, the Russian commander had provided Eger the Nazi's logbook, tossing it and other tidy files containing the details of his case at Eger's feet as he ordered Eger to pick them up and get out.

Eger had not read the logbook, not in its totality, not every word, every crimped thought. But he had kept it. The other files he had dropped in a muddy gutter outside the prison, crushing them with his own thin soles. Perhaps his accuser's name was in them. He did not want to know that name. He feared knowing it.

The logbook now lay on a shelf within the Vatican archives, neighbor to a set of documents from the Inquisition in southern France, a trial of Albigensians, one of those sects who declared matter and body innately evil, whose perfect ones starved themselves to death so their spirit-selves could return again to the holy realm.

After his initial meditation of the morning, more a trial of his spirit than a breathing in of peace, Father Eger said a private Mass in a side altar of La Merced, a dark niche crowded with statues and votive lights and dedicated to St. Peter Claver, a new world saint insistent on nourishing the bodies of slaves arrived in Cartagena before feeding their souls. Give the slaves time, Claver had decided. Time. Time to come back to the shores of life. *Primum est vivere.*

Father Eger hurried through the words and ritual gestures, still blocking out those nagging questions, praying to Jesus for quiet, for solace. It had not been this bad for years.

Father Eger had spent what seemed to be centuries tormented by those thoughts he named, never with pleasure, the children of his own curiosity, an incessant poking at actions and theories and motivations, an unstoppable riddling. His own life, the great events of the war, the discipline and insight of Ignatian spirituality, the thoughts of every generation of Western philosophers, the caravan of wisdom that trekked in from the East—all were seeds milled together in his mind. He had never been able to stop the grinding, although the past nine years of obscurity in the Vatican archives had been the best, and when he sat with his old friend. This event in Guatemala had sent a flood through the waterwheel, churning everything at a horrifying rate.

"*Lavabo me . . .,*" he prayed at Mass. "Cleanse me," he thought. "Cleanse me." He stopped and cried for a moment.

Later he ate a simple breakfast, fried eggs, toast and coffee, with the Jesuit community at La Merced. Afterward he went up to his room.

He read the Gospels for hours that day, especially Mark. The community had a good biblical concordance in the recreation room, which Father Eger carted up to his room. With that book he could do serious research, checking references and following up on other foundational passages.

Father Eger was reviewing the work of a young American Jesuit who did research into the similarities and differences between Jesus' instructions at the Sermon on the Mount and those moral and social principles of Confucius. It was a good text. Father Eger was happy to see the Church in dialogue with non-Christians, one of the great insights opportuned by the round, holy Pope. Father Eger thought of his mentor and friend, Father Beltrán, and of the Castilian's explorations into the other knowings, how Father Beltrán's curiosity had infected the student. Sometimes, he recalled, he had lost himself in that exploration.

As the day wore on, Father Eger's ability to concentrate lessened. The harsh voices of conspiracy took over.

Father Eger's concern was hard to nail down. He had never been a pacifist. During the war, he had prayed incessantly for Allied victory. Suffering quietly was no less a liberation of the soul than fighting valiantly. Both parts added to the sum of the human drama, both spoke a truth about a reality rooted in events long past. The world was harsh, spearing babies, extinguishing the hearts of lovers, yet it was also the buoyant home of music and art, a hopeful world of planting farmers and dancing harvesters.

Throughout his life, Father Eger had discussed these basic truths for hours, wrestling with their contradictions, savoring the ability of anyone who could, for a moment, make sense of them all. Yet at times, certainly now, they were only a dumb pack of thoughts and images, depressing in their immensity and mystery, bothersome in their dense meaning, a swarm of watermelon flies on a sticky June afternoon.

And now, in Guatemala, he was about to add to the conundrum. The responsibility frightened him. His actions would have consequences, on lives, on organizations, on the kingdom.

Whenever Father Eger's musings brought him to that center point of the Galilean sea storm, the only sure island of tranquillity was his belief in

Jesus' kingdom, in its presence, perhaps only single-celled and primitive, squirming with the essential element of life in every spin of every atom, in every beat of every heart.

For Father Eger, the most radical concept ever spoken by Jesus was his bold assertion that the kingdom is now. The time to live justly is now. Jesus-law rules *this* moment. Love *now*!

That teaching was magical for Father Eger, letting him imagine reality transformed, full of different dimensions, *gratia plena*. Building the kingdom, even if only within himself, with small personal chapels and scriptoria and portals for alms, gave meaning to his life. This he had told every spiritual father since Beltrán.

Finally that Sunday evening, Father Eger found himself pacing the courtyard after the community's light supper of vegetable soup and bread. He wore his black cassock, his acknowledgment of the special nature of the day.

Particles of conjecture and memory, surviving fragments of previous battles, continued to whirl through him. His thoughts raced. He tried to sit and meditate in the evening's enticing calm, but found himself fidgeting, theorizing about detachment rather than achieving it.

He turned toward the kitchen and saw Joaquín staring at him. He gestured for Joaquín to approach.

"Yes, Father, can I help you?"

"I am—full of energy, restless energy," Father Eger complained, wringing his hands. "I am ready to act."

"To speak with Father Garza?"

"Yes. Let us meet with him now. Can you lock him away somewhere, if we need to?"

"We are ready," Joaquín said.

The heaviness of the chore weighted down the words of the old *indígena*. Is this how servants feel toward masters? Father Eger wondered. Had he ever felt that burden? Perhaps. With Beltrán. And for Jesus?

"Father Garza is in a sanctuary where we keep the most precious statues and relics," Joaquín said. "It is often locked during the day. Someone must be in attendance when people are allowed in to pray. Many times Father Garza goes there at night. He has a special devotion to one of the images, to the statue of Jesus carrying his cross."

"Do you need Luís?"

Joaquín grinned, an odd meshing of flesh and muscles on his placid face. "Luís is hidden there, in that chapel, in the base of one of the statues. The base is as big a small room. He hides within the statue of the archangel Michael."

Father Eger's eyes sparkled for the first time that day. "The Archangel has gathered his hosts." Then dark again, "But you will wait outside. I must speak with Father Garza alone, Jesuit to Jesuit."

The two old men moved back into the residence and headed down the hallway that connected the residence to the sacristy of La Merced.

Along the length of the corridor hung portraits of the previous rectors of the church, seventeen of them, some fine paintings, others amateurish renderings with large eyes and single-dimensional faces. Each portrait hung on a thin metal wire from a strip of wood two-thirds up the high brown wall. Father Eger noticed there was room for only one more picture and that a narrow space.

As he passed through the corridor, Father Eger tried the hallway's three doors. All were locked, just as Father Garza would have left them, Father Eger reflected.

Inside the sacristy they stopped to pick up a tall candle and a book of matches from a sloping mahogany closet.

They walked past the annunciating bell and through a rounded doorway into the main sanctuary of the church. A trio of red lights glowed in the darkness.

Joaquín, whose white clothing shone bright in the murky light, was the first down the flight of steps that led through the marble altar railing into the nave.

Father Eger followed more slowly, stepping with great care. In front of the high altar Father Eger stopped to genuflect, a momentary supplication, part habit, part conscious supplication.

The atmosphere in the church had chilled, sending a shiver up Father Eger's spine. He sniffed the air, taking in its wax-scented smell, a smell he had come to associate with the sacred places of Catholicism. The smell reassured him. Surely a holy event would occur. Surely Father Garza would reveal where the UDA kept Father Burns.

When the two conspirators reached the rough wooden doors that sealed off the statuary chapel from the church, Father Eger whispered to Joaquín, asking whether those doors would also be locked. He squinted at an iron keyhole.

"No, Father, these doors are unlocked. I know his ways."

Joaquín reached over and put his hand on the door handle. "See, when you are ready, I will open it for you." Then Joaquín lit the rust-colored funeral candle. The sulfured fumes stung the lining of their noses.

Joaquín handed the candle to Father Eger and put his hands back on the door's handle.

With but a moment's pause, assuring himself that the flame had taken, Father Eger nodded his readiness, and Joaquín opened the door.

The hinges creaked. Their sound ricocheted off the sacred walls.

Father Eger hurried in and saw Father Garza rise from where he'd been kneeling in front of the cross-bearing statue of Jesus.

"*¿Qué pasa? ¿Quién hay aquí?*" yelled Father Garza.

The old Guatemalan nearly fell over as he scrambled to get up, but quickly regained his balance and began to rush toward the doorway.

"*Ego sum, pater,*" declared Father Eger in loud Latin, striding further into the dampness of the statuary chapel, a rectangle some fifty feet long and twenty feet across. The air was musty and stale. To Father Eger the forms of twenty statues seemed figures of menace in the brackish darkness as they stood along the sides of the chalk-white walls.

Ten long paces into the chapel, Father Eger stopped.

Father Garza halted his onrush only five feet from the European.

An image of Attila staring down the defenders of Rome clipped through Father Eger's brain. He knew he had to establish his authority to be successful.

His eyes adjusted to the dim light. He stared at the life-sized statue of Jesus in front of which Father Garza had been kneeling. The form of the failing Savior was flanked by two standing electric lamps with bulbs encased in milky glass. There was enough light for Father Eger to make out the color of Jesus' red cape and notice that the cross was rough-hewn, the ax marks still obvious. Dark ovals drooped under the cross-bearer's eyes. The Savior's carved head was tilted to one side, frozen in a questioning amazement, his statue-spirit forever resisting the blinding pain of convict humiliation as he took in the world.

"*Et quare me nocte visitas?*" Father Garza asked in Spanish-tinted Latin, breaking Father Eger's reverie. "You could have spoken with me at any time today, Father. This is my time to pray. Please." The Guatemalan was calm, careful. His arms hung at his side.

"I have needed to seek you out at night. You know why."

Father Eger moved forward, holding firmly onto the candle, thinking he must seem a frightening creature to the old Central American, tall and pale-faced as a vampire.

"No, I do not know why you choose this hour," Father Garza said, backing away as the figure of Father General's Magyar emissary stepped toward him. "I do not know why you must seek me out at night." His voice rose a register, achieving boyish excitement

"We speak at night because the things of which we speak are most unpleasant. They are best kept *inter muros*."

Father Eger took two more steps forward, deeper into the sanctuary, hoping his brother in Christ would stand still. Father Eger wanted to stare into the eyes of this other soldier of Christ. He needed to observe the Guatemalan's soul as best he could. Some of the soul would be in the eyes.

"Of what do *you* speak?" Father Garza said, taking two steps back. It was once again a rector's voice, stern and demanding.

"I speak of secret arrangements between you and the UDA."

"What can you mean?!" Father Garza bared his teeth.

Now he knows I've figured it out, his allegiance and its scope, thought Father Eger. The Guatemalan could become dangerous. Should he edge him back toward the statue of Michael? Would he need Luís?

"I have no secret arrangement with the UDA," Father Garza said with an angry, labored calmness. "I am merely a contact person. They could have chosen anyone. I am an old man, a man of little consequence. They demanded that *all* Jesuits leave the country or we would *all* be executed. Of course that threat included *me*." Father Garza pointed to his own chest.

"But they have only exercised their threat against a young American. You, surely you know, are inviolable." Father Eger stepped forward a foot. "But you are not without sin!"

Father Garza held his ground.

"What do you mean *sin*, Father? Are you crazy? Have you drunk too much wine? Is your food spoiling in your stomach?"

Father Garza inched slightly forward, his hands now formed into tight fists. Three feet separated them.

"I accuse you of collusion with the UDA. I know not all the details, but I know enough."

"What do you know?!"

"I know that you visit Don Francisco Orozco."

"So? He is an old friend of my family. Only rumors associate him with the UDA."

Father Eger laughed. This man is a child, evil and innocent, but not much innocent.

"I know you turned in the father of María. He escaped into the night, but others died in the attack. You are a collaborator!" Father Eger's anger deepened. Let the old man deny this evil act! "You told the UDA where he would meet her. She saw men killed!"

A swift pain crossed Father Garza's face. Perhaps he felt remorse, thought Father Eger. That would be a good sign.

"Do you deny it? Your silence is confirmation. Perhaps—perhaps even a sign of remorse."

Father Eger was steeling himself for the end. "But remorse is not sufficient. More will be asked of you."

The candle trembled in Father Eger's hands, as if it were coming alive and struggled against him. Hot waves surged around him.

"We are at war," said Father Garza. "Awful things happen in war."

The Guatemalan sounded stunned. The memory of Luís must sting.

Father Eger moved a foot closer. Two feet separated them. He began to circle the old Guatemalan. Their eyes locked. Father Eger knew the awful things that happen in war. He understood the loss of innocence.

They both turned in a circle, chess bishops come alive. Around and around three times. Hate everywhere, magnetic, pulling and pulling but keeping them separate.

"What do you want of me?" Father Garza asked.

There was a tremor in his voice. Fear? Exhaustion?

"I want to know where the UDA keep the American, Father Burns."

Father Garza's face was blank now. The candlelight flickered on it.

They continued to circle.

"I do not know where they keep him."

"Yes, you do. I see it in your eyes. Your deceit shines even in this obscurity."

"I do not know where he is kept! I deceive no one. Our eyes are different from European eyes."

"I have seen eyes like yours all over the globe. The eyes of deceivers. No, Father, your Guatemalan eyes are no different."

"This is insanity!" Father Garza cried, stopping a moment, then rushing past Father Eger.

Father Eger hurried backward to position himself between the Guatemalan and the door, gripping more tightly onto the thick candle. The flame jumped high. Globs of wax dropped onto the floor.

Father Garza scurried wide around Father Eger.

Father Eger lunged and caught the smaller man's shoulder, turning him around. "I order you to tell me where the UDA are keeping Father Burns! I order you with the full power of the General of the Society Jesus, which he has invested in me, Joszef Eger!"

"Ridiculous!" Father Garza spat on his holy floor. He stood his ground. His hands were fists again. The door was behind him, Father Eger in front.

"I will have you expelled, old man!" The force of Father Eger's threat nearly extinguished the candle. "I will have you expelled! Dare not transgress a command of your superiors!"

Father Eger trembled. His impulse was to strike Father Garza with the candle. The old men stood two feet apart.

Father Eger tried more Jesuit logic, but the words spun out like well-armed assassins into the night air. "Remember Igantius's letter to Coimbra? His insistence that you drop your pen in the middle of a word if your superior should call upon you! Did your novice master not instruct you in this practice of ours?"

Father Garza's face was one *hidalgo* smirk.

Father Eger remembered the noble face with which his confessor, Father Beltrán, had gone off into a final exile. He remembered the farewell tears at the Stazione Termini and the waving of moist handkerchiefs. He felt himself blistering with the heat of that Italian engine and ready to roll toward the sea.

"You dare not trample on our vow of obedience! Too many have suffered for you to trample upon it! Tell me where the American is kept! Tell me! Tell me *now*!"

Father Eger drove forward to grab the old cleric, thinking he would shake the truth out of him.

Father Garza jumped back, quick and agile as a sewer rat. He put his hands up to cover his ears and turned to speed out the chapel, running past the crouching figure of Joaquín, screaming out a resounding "¡NO! ¡Nunca!" which flapped through the baroque cavern of La Merced.

Joaquín rushed in. "Do we take him?"

Shocked, his adrenalin swiftly evaporating, Father Eger shook his head. He had been defeated. The kingdom was no closer.

"Let him go," Father Eger said. "He knows that someone here has betrayed him. This confrontation might have been a mistake! You and the girl and her grandmother must leave! Tell them to prepare. It is too dangerous."

Father Eger was thinking again of his own betrayal, of the day he had been hauled into the Reich's prison. He had never returned to the thoughtful quiet of his Jesuit residence that day. But he had survived. Now he feared for the members of the household of La Merced. He had put them at grave risk.

"Does Father Garza know where the young American is held?" asked Joaquín.

"I think so, but he has not said," Father Eger sighed.

"Then we will have to arrange an exchange, and capture the young priest?"

"Yes, Joaquín, our path is more difficult now. They will be prepared. At least they do not know we mean to use armed force rather than moral argument."

Late in the evening, as Father Eger was kneeling and making his final examination, he heard something at his door, a rustling of cloth and paper. He got up, afraid that Father Garza's friends had already come to clean out the house. Instead he saw a patch of brightness at the foot of the door. It was an envelope. He flipped on the overhead light and tore open the envelope. Inside was a handwritten message.

When I attended the Colegio Loyola, we had a scholastic teacher

from Spain, a grossly fat Castilian who spoke our language so soft-
ly and with that ridiculous lisp. To make things worse, he had
buckteeth. We were merciless in our jokes, referring to him as the
whispering pig.

Father Eger read it again, wondering what it meant, at first thinking it a threat, then realizing there must be a message there, something hidden, that his tirade of the evening might have loosened Father Garza's resolve, melted an inner hardness. He studied the words, but saw nothing, no clue.

Was it a cryptogram? Would he have to take it apart, digging around for a significance buried in the ordering of letters? He decided to show it to Joaquín.

Joaquín was busy in the first-floor quarters of the housekeeper and her granddaughter. He was gathering up the belongings of the old woman and young child. All three moved about with wild eyes, their fear filling the space like a sickbed stench.

Joaquín paid little attention to the puzzle Father Eger put before him. He was intent on removing his dependents from harm.

"I see nothing here, Father. I do not understand all the words," Joaquín said, shoving the paper back toward the insistent priest. "What is that word, *buckteeth*?"

"*Diente saliente.*"

"Ah. I see," Joaquín answered, taking the paper back at the same time he ordered the María to be sure to gather her two dolls. "And this word, *whispering*?"

"*Susurrón.*"

"Please?" Joaquín said, asking for the word to be repeated.

"Whispering. In my dictionary it translates: *susurrón*. The whisper. *El susurro.*"

Joaquín stepped back. Breaking out of a momentary vision, jubilation in his eyes, he smiled.

"What? What?" Father Eger cried.

"He has told us where they keep the young American," said Joaquín. "He has told us! The old man will not betray us. Thank you, Father. Thank you." Joaquín knelt down and kissed Father Eger's hands, again and again.

Father Eger protested, pulling his hands away from the newly emotional Joaquín. "Stop! Please, stop!"

"I do not understand," Father Eger said as Joaquín arose. "Where are they keeping Father Burns? How do you know? How could you trust Father Garza?! And why does he use riddles? To delay us?"

"He can be trusted, Father. Believe me." Joaquín dusted off the knees of his trousers. "The circle comes together. He will do no harm. This message is his way of telling us."

Calm had returned to Joaquín. He gestured for María to come closer. He picked her up and hugged her.

"I do not understand," Father Eger said, pressing his concern. "This . . . This . . ." he said, pointing to the sheet. "I do not understand."

"You do not need to understand," Joaquín said, sharply.

A different Joaquín was speaking. "They keep Father Burns at an abandoned Garza plantation. It was destroyed when Father Garza was a young man. He will not allow evil to occur there, Father. Not again. I assure you."

At that instance the church of La Merced, the Jesuit residence, and the entire central zones of Guatemala City shifted right, left, then right again, the result of a brief tremor, an event not uncommon in a city whose bedrock was volcanic. However, this time the loud sound of rock grinding on rock accompanied that evening tremor.

Joaquín looked to the old woman. The eyes of those descendants of the ancient ones locked briefly onto each other. The old woman uttered two phrases, then covered her mouth as if she had spoken a profanity. "*¡Gemió el temblor, desde tierra a dentro!*"

Yes, the land is groaning, Father Eger thought as he held his hands in the air, an unconscious attempt to steady himself. He looked around, checking the ceilings and walls, wondering if they could sustain this shaking, wondering whether the four of them should be fleeing, should be rousing the other inhabitants of the residence. He barely noticed the rapid communication that took place between the *indígenas*, that message conveyed through unhooded eyes. He marked is as nothing unusual, as any human's response to the destructive power of the earth's slowly shifting mantle. As nothing more.

CHAPTER TWENTY-FIVE

Contemplatio ad amorem.

The Contemplation to Attain the Love of God, one of the final formal meditations from the Spiritual Exercises of St. Ignatius.

The image of the slight woman would not abandon Tom, even in his highland captivity.

She had been his first failure as a priest. Still, sad figure as she was, she had taught him a good lesson: that he, himself, priest of God most high, had not within him the power to heal. He was vessel. He could break. He would flow out.

Her body was bent from age, her shoulders collapsing inward. Her hair had thinned, though not enough to detract from the beauty of its shape, a fierceness in the way the fibers still gathered in long waves. Her hands were mottled, signs of happy times in the sun and failing internal organs.

Her face had not wrinkled from smiles of kindness, yet it was a beautiful face. An interior struggle had etched it, a struggle that far outlived any other of her battles, her fight to control her lust and her anger and her quick tongue and her self-pride. Those combats were petty whims of human nature.

Many times he heard her confession. At St. Bridget's when he was a young priest, still studying for his doctorate. Saturday afternoons at 3:00. The bell of the church's tower would ring the hour. He knew she was either the next penitent or the following one.

Over the course of two years she had explained her Saturday habits to him. She had arisen from her nap at 2:00. She would wait fifteen minutes before getting out of bed. It took her twenty-five minutes to dress. It would take her fifteen minutes to walk the five blocks to church. Always fifteen minutes, whether the sidewalks were freshly swept or whether they were slick with snow and ice.

Everything in her life had time attached to it, Tom learned, sewn into the fabric of her days and thoughts. Tick, tick, tick. Constant as the tides. Time was everywhere about her. Shake her, and you would find yourself in its swell.

She lived not alone, her husband, her dear companion, still alive. Her children were nearby, often welcomed into her home. Her grandchildren nestled around her when they could. Yes, she could smile and laugh. But inside . . .

"Bless me, Father, for I have sinned. My last confession was one week ago." Her voice was already weak. He strained to hear her, leaning toward the grille, even though he knew the tale.

"Twice I was angry at my husband. Once I had a bad thought about our neighbor Dorothy. Twenty-three times I despaired of the Lord's forgiveness." She stifled her tears and placed a hand over her mouth, which filtered her words.

"I tried, Father, I tried to fight against the evil spirit, just as you have counseled me. I prayed to Mary and thought of my blessings, of my family, but I am stained for life, forsaken." That last, perfectly chosen word snapped out into the confessional with the fury of a coiled snake: forsaken.

"I committed the sin against the Spirit, the unforgivable sin."

The pause, inevitable, eternal though brief. Her voice now dim as a grave. "I aborted my baby."

The rest of the story, fruitless elaboration, flows out. "I wasn't married. I couldn't abide the shame of it. I hated myself, I hated that growth inside me. I killed it. I don't even know its sex, how to name it. I have no remains. Were they thrown into the trash? How do I know, the man never told me, it wasn't something we talked about. Was my child's flesh eaten by . . .? Oh, Father, please help me . . ."

As she devolved into tears, Tom could hear her arthritic hands fumbling with the black beads of her rosary. Her sobs broke the regularity of her breathing, sometimes nearly choking her.

This confession emptied him, hollowed him out. Her sin was a vacuum. One of its tentacles attached itself to his chest and sucked him into the nether world of Beelzebub, the demon whose eyes were embers and whose fingernails wrapped round into scimitars. It was the one sin he could not tolerate: her pounding, hammering despair. It was a bloodied chain she dragged across her spirit in defiance to the gift.

She could not accept what was offered: redemption, forgiveness.

What horror, personal, cultural, kept her caged in that foul pit? He wondered: maybe she needed drugs, psychotropic drugs. Or what? A funeral?

In any case, he could not stand to forgive her one more time. He could not bear to absolve her one more time. Her confession was a cross cutting into his own shoulders, the beam pressing directly onto his exposed heart.

"He died for your sins," Tom wanted to yell out through the confessional door, each word slamming into the vaulted silence of the church. "He . . . died . . . for . . . your . . . sins!"

Tom could feel the rage and the cleansing heartbeat and the hungry love of the Savior.

"He dies saying: 'Enough!'"

Tom saw a young man with angry, loving eyes struggling against the nails and the lashings.

"He cries from his cross: 'You are free!'"

The young man is joyous, somehow unbound, hovering in sanctifying air.

"He screams: 'You are desert! My blood moistens parched land!'"

The land quakes.

"Let green things grow! I shower you with life giving blood!"

The pain of this wounded mother's confessions was clarifying, especially in the hut. Because of her agony Tom glimpsed, for a moment, the passion of Jesus, its singularity and its depth, with a human truth harboring there, an ancient life form drifting in warm, oceanic stillness.

In the highland hut, Tom held tightly onto his vision of Jesus on the cross, of the near-naked redeemer man.

"I am loved," Tom began to murmur in the night, the words enchanting the air. "I swim in currents of love."

CHAPTER TWENTY-SIX

The conspirators at La Merced rose early, well before the wakening sun could tease even a blue-gray hue back into the city's dirty streets. They had miles to go. They wanted to perform their acts in the early morning while their wits were freshest and their enemies still rubbed sleep from clandestine eyes.

The grandmother and María would stay at the residence, living proof that Father Eger and Joaquín expected Father Garza to conduct himself in a manner proper to a rector of La Merced, showing concern for his staff, doing nothing that might lead them into evil hands.

Joaquín stopped Father Eger in a corner of the kitchen to ask whether he should contact the gringos.

"I think not," said Father Eger. "They would be of no value to us today; they do not understand this battle. They are from a different era, a different people—their battles are not like these."

Joaquín nodded, happy with the old European's decision.

Luís had gone with a message during the night to their forces in hiding. Guadalupe, Luís, and the platoon of Guatemalan rebels and ex-Sandinista guerrillas were to meet them at a peasant shrine on the mountain nearest *El Susurro*. A simple pinewood cross marked the shrine. Only *indígenas* came to pray, to leave offerings, a cup of *cush*, a flower. Joaquín had set aside a coin wrapped in strips of bright red and yellow cloth and placed it in his shirt pocket, patting it twice. He planned to leave it at the foot of the cross.

By car, the first leg of the trip took two hours. There was little traffic outside the city. The second leg was on foot. No road lead up the mountain to the shrine. From the shrine, the approach to the *finca* was a series of mountain paths.

Joaquín explained it all clearly to Father Eger before they left.

"There is a single-room mission school about five kilometers from the mountain shrine. We will park the car behind the classroom building. I will leave a note instructing the teacher, a cousin of mine, to distract anyone who might come around."

Joaquín tried to convince Father Eger that he, too, an old man, a cleric, a possible hostage, a potential burden, should not partake in this battle. Joaquín was troubled about the distance from the school to the shrine. It would be a challenging trek for the old priest. If things went poorly, it could be a hazardous run back. If things went wrong, what could the tall white archivist do then but be captured or killed?

"I must accompany you," Father Eger had insisted after each argument. Joaquín finally acquiesced to the inevitability in the old European's voice, the sound of submission. If the sharp-nosed Jesuit were ready to accept the consequences, so be it.

Guadalupe and the troops she commanded with Luís rose early. She had not slept all that night. Too many feelings squeezed through her veins, dilating them, then contracting.

As soon as the night finally stood still with Luís's unexpected information, she left her tent and ordered the march, calculating in her mind the necessary speed, thinking back to forced marches in Nicaraguan jungles. They only had nineteen kilometers to cover. With luck, they had positioned themselves near the rendezvous.

Luís looked on quietly as she uttered her commands: break down the tents, hide them in the cave, leave your last letters with old Jorge. It was dark in the highlands, but Guadalupe could feel the radiance within her and knew that the other warrior eyes were glued to it.

Guadalupe was pleased with this force they had gathered. The troop was silent and disciplined as they gathered their gear, lifting packs and rifles, checking ammunition, click and load. They headed out in two rows. So efficient. It was a good omen. Theirs would be an easy task if they could catch the kidnappers by surprise.

She knew the men she commanded cared little about Tom. They would fight to show the UDA who was the more powerful, to demonstrate the extent of guerrilla control. So many had died in Guatemala. Another death, especially of a gringo, even a priest, did not stir them.

For Guadalupe, there was only the desire to save this single man. It glowed within her. She hoped to release him and to release her. She was a clipped canary who'd discovered how to open her cage. She was on the verge of renewal. Feathers were regrowing on her wings. Soon she would fly. That's all she knew.

Guadalupe had begun her political struggles because a band of *contras* had killed her father. He had writhed in pain for an hour before dying from wounds that had burst his large intestines, stomach, kidneys, and liver—the organs of daily life. But that was years ago. She needed to fight again for someone with a name, with a face she knew. She could feel the energy move up and down her body, in her agility, the way she maneuvered through the forest, the tightness she felt in her stomach.

There was another desire, although she feared it, kept its name unformed. She remembered Tom's long, sinewy body. She remembered standing beside him on gringo street corners and thrilling. She wanted to walk again within a foot of his body, to feel the warmth flowing from it, to consider reaching out to touch it, perhaps to touch it, to linger, to kiss him, to embrace.

But she would not be undone.

Father Eger trudged behind Joaquín through the narrowing valley behind the school building. They moved along the edge of the forest, along that space where the cornfields stopped abruptly and battalions of red-trunked pine trees stood their ground. At the end of the valley, a path led up onto the mountain. From there the climb was steep.

The valley was quickly heating up, even with only an early blink of the sun. Father Eger had begun to feel his sweat, despite the wind that seemed to grow in intensity as the day aged. If they would only stop to notice, Father Eger was sure, they could see the vines of black beans stirring, beginning to crawl up along the stalks of corn, clinging to them for stability. This land was alive.

About three hundred paces up the mountain, the climate changed. The air cooled. He noticed the thinness of oxygen. They charged forward.

Father Eger concentrated on his feet as he pushed himself onward. Only once did he ask for a ten-minute rest. For the first time during his visit, he saw anger on Joaquín's face. Father Eger felt the burden of his age. He rested only five minutes, then hurried forward.

Father Eger and Joaquín arrived at the shrine before the others.

Someone had recently made vigil. The ground was covered with fresh pine needles, still green, soft, oozing their sanitary odor. Both men stood next to the cross and blessed themselves, uttering private prayers of supplication. Joaquín placed his offering of color-wrapped coins at the base of the rough cross and bowed deep. Then he knelt.

This offering unbalanced Father Eger. It was foreign, pagan, an offering to another face of the deity. He did not want that confusion on this day. Today must be filled with Ignatian sutras.

"Do you think we will be successful?" Father Eger asked the praying Joaquín. His question snapped with the brevity of a command.

The *indígena* said nothing. He mumbled words, Tzutuhil. He clapped his hands and bowed deeper.

Father Eger knelt also. He closed his eyes and began to pray: "*Pater noster qui es in caelis sanctificetur nomen tuum . . .*" He needed to remain focused on his goal. He wished to undo an injustice, to free at least one prisoner. He was archangel. There was precedence: Peter in chains. But how could he explain this to Rome? His heart beat fast. His fear was not of death. He feared making everything worse. Was he again the accomplice of evil?

Soon Father Eger heard the platoon of guerrillas forge its way up the mountain, their boots trampling the leaves and forest debris. He'd heard the same sound in the '30s and '40s, young men marching through parks in the fall. Nothing was different. They were herd animals announcing the strength of the band. Several gray squirrels hurried past the two praying men. Father Eger looked at his watch. It was nearly six-fifty. Joaquín rose and turned toward the noise.

There were no introductions as Guadalupe and Luís and twelve heavily armed rebels appeared among the trees. Their faces were striped with black and green. The four principals greeted each other with nods and a few polite phrases, "*Buenos días. ¿Qué tál?*"

Father Eger was nervous. The day was getting late. "How long until we reach the *finca*?" asked Father Eger of Joaquín.

"Another ten, fifteen minutes. But we must be very careful now, *hay que tener cuidado*," Joaquín said looking at the fifteen pairs of eyes watching him, stressing the fact that many people lived in the area, that none of them could assume the loyalty of anyone who might see the troops' movement.

After that cautionary remark, Joaquín, Luís, and Guadalupe knelt to the ground and built a relief map of the *finca*. Luís' mother had lived there as a child. He knew it best. Luís drew in what he thought were the remains of buildings and then placed an **X** at their destination, a point on a mountain ridge next to the flat land of the valley of *El Susurro.* From there Luís alone would go to scout out the *finca* and the men there, returning to devise the final positioning for the assault.

Marcos woke up late that morning. He stumbled from his hammock to the latrine. He was in a bad mood. He'd drunk too much the night before. He and the two guards with him were starting to get nervous. They'd been vigilant this past week after the news that the madwoman from Nicaragua might be headed their way. They began to do everything in pairs, someone always on the lookout, checking the forest for a glint of steel or the peering white of enemy eyes.

They knew an execution was set for Friday. Even if the ransom were paid, this priest had to die.

All three of the UDA men had killed before, butchering in their fury or slicing in their cold hatred after a long torture. This one they would merely kill, in the morning after emptying their hut of trash.

Tom was uncertain how much time he had left. He had not been tortured. He had not been interrogated. He had been treated as if he barely existed, as if he were of little value. It doubled his anxiety.

The guerrillas would take up three positions. Because it was a windy day, the sound of their movement would be disguised by the rustling of leaves and needles. Another good omen.

One group would take control of the roadway onto the *finca*.

Another group, including Father Eger and Joaquín, would settle in on the ridge at the base of the western slope of the valley, one hundred yards from the prison hut. Theirs was a clear view of the back of the hut and on toward the ruins of the old homestead.

The third group, with Luís and Guadalupe at its nucleus, would occupy a clump of shrubbery and squat trees that grew across a narrow, overgrown field fifty yards from the door of the hut.

Luís had counted only three guards, two *ladinos* and one *indígena*. "There are only three, but they are well armed and watchful."

He would use no words to command the final exchange. When the time was at hand, he would begin to shoot. The men guarding the road were to stay in place. The men on the ridge were to shoot only if they had a clear site on the enemy. Luís' team would rush in.

"Do not shoot into the hut. If the UDA men hide there, take cover. I will instruct you on the radio. Otherwise, stay off it."

Guadalupe was silent as Luís commanded the attack. She examined her rifle.

"Everyone has ten minutes to get in position," Luís said.

"Go."

By the time Marcos walked out of the guards' hut, only the guerrillas on the ridge were in position. Father Eger clasped his hands together and prayed to St. Jude, wondering where Luís's men were. He watched as Marcos and another *ladino*, who had followed Marcos, sauntered over to Tom's hut. The *indígena* on guard, who slouched against the door and slept standing up, jerked his head as Marcos arrived and yelled out his command: "Put on your blindfold!"

Father Eger began to shake. Their timing was off. The risk of failure curved upward. And failure meant death. Even success might be disaster. Guadalupe had taken him aside, a school marm with her favorite pupil, and explained to him the randomness of destruction wrought by a gunfight.

Bullets had no sense to them, she had said, instructing the old priest. "Many rifles fire differently each time. Many people fire with little aim, their fingers more guided by agitation than concentration. It might be that even one of the rescuers' bullets would hit Tom."

Father Eger thought she had been looking into his soul during this instruction, hoping to see in there the outcome of the day, as if his old priest eyes might mirror the future.

His eyes only saw the present. He saw Marcos open the door to Tom's hut and enter.

Then he saw Luís's band arrive at their position. They began to squat behind trees or stones. The two UDA guards had not noticed. They were grim-faced, but unaware.

Then Father Burns was in sight. He was taller than the three captors. Marcos shoved him along a newly trampled path toward another, smaller structure.

Luís rose slowly from his haunched position, hidden now behind a young *ceiba* tree. The sun caught some object on Luís's body and flashed. Father Eger held his breath.

Luís was aiming at the walking men, sighting with his right eye. A sharp, new thought flashed through Father Eger's mind: They are marching Father Burns off to execution. He had seen it many times. The slow, terrifying movement.

Just as a memory of crippled Hans at the courtyard's wall filled up Father Eger's brain, a voice rang out in the serpentine valley. Everyone turned toward the old homestead, now a pile of tumbled stone and rotted beams.

The voice cried out again. The two UDA guards raised their rifles. Marcos drew a pistol from his holster. Even Tom slipped his blindfold down, low enough to see.

An old man appeared from within the rubble of the homestead and stumbled toward the kidnappers over rough ground. He was dressed in a black cassock and wore the vow cape of a Jesuit priest professed to the fourth vow. That great black bolt of cloth billowed out behind him. A sudden gust of wind blew in his face, fighting his advance, forcing him to struggle forward. In his right hand he held aloft a Jesuit vow cross, a five-inch-tall piece of metal with a black inlay of wood and silver corpus.

Father Garza was yelling out, again and again, his biblical commands, *"Tén piedad. Tén piedad. ¡Suéltenlo al cautivo!"* Have pity. Have pity. Release the captive! His voice was strong for an old man and rang clearly across the terrain.

Of a sudden, another sound rang through the valley, a sound grating as a factory whistle that signals the end of a midnight shift. It bled an eerie, metallic energy. Loud, then soft. Louder again, then nothing. Then piercing through the valley again.

On the ridge Joaquín murmured in astonishment as he crossed himself multiple times, *"el susurrón de los dióses de la tierra. ¡Señor nos proteja!"* The words registered in Father Eger's mind, their meaning coming a second later. He paid the words almost no attention, unable to take his eyes off the scene before him. "The whispering of the gods of the earth. Lord protect us."

What appeared to be a cloud of smoke arose from behind Father Garza. The whistling increased in shrillness. It deafened. Joaquín would explain later that the *finca El Susurro* was named for the sounds that emanated from a fissure in the rocky ground at the head of the valley, sometimes releasing the unvented anger of the earth, sometimes only murmuring its pain. It had not spoken for over fifty years.

At the sight of this creature, dark as a denizen of the underworld, struggling toward him, the *ladino* guard raised his rifle and aimed at Father Garza.

Time was slowing for Father Eger. He saw each action as if it were stretched out for later recollection.

Marcos turned to the guard and yelled, "*¡No tires!*" Father Eger could see the young man's lips open wide as the words flowed out.

Marcos was too late. As his lips bounced back together, the shot rang out. The bullet's noise was soon swallowed by the rock-cries escaping from the fissure.

The guard's aim was good. Blood spurted from Father Garza's heart. One. Two. Three. The old priest stopped in his track, his right hand still held up in warning and petition. Four. Five. Six. He fell backward, blown over by a gust of wind, or weakened by the rapid loss of blood. His head bounced once upon hitting the ground.

Father Eger knew each moment was now precious. The guards had been distracted.

Luís shot. Two shots. He hit one guard and Marcos.

Guadalupe stood out from behind her tree and screamed over the horrid shrillness echoing through the valley, "Get down, Tom! Get down!"

Her scream was too late, or unheard. Before Marcos fell to the ground, a hole gaping in his chest, he spun around and aimed his pistol at Tom's head. The bullet burst into Tom's temple and shattered his brain.

Tom, too, had been caught up in that moment of apparition.

He barely had time to express his final thought, the resolution he'd been preparing in the hut hermitage, a sentiment as fragile and potent as spiritual conviction lettered onto goatskin and hidden deep in Dead Sea rock.

His last phrase, only the first word out: "Take . . ."

CHAPTER TWENTY-SEVEN

Everything is groundwork. When the change happens, it is swift. No one knows the shape of its swells. Some are lifted up; some are born under to begin again from below.

Nearly illegible phrases found on a crumpled sheet of paper stuck in the pajama shirt pocket Father Beltrán wore the night of his death, August 15, 1951.

When Joaquín and Father Eger returned to Guatemala City and to La Merced, their hearts added another ache as they examined the damage done by the morning's three-second, highly localized earthquake. As if struck by lightning, a large side of masonry had blasted away from one of the church's towers. The resulting pile of stones and rock and mortar, all of which had once united to crown the majesty of La Merced, remained in the road when the two men returned early in the afternoon. The large mound blocked traffic.

News of the morning's killing had swept through the city. People were afraid to go near the dusty rubble. A small crowd had gathered, mostly fervent old women, kneeling, praying their rosaries, sheltering their heads with *perrajes* or scarves, their eyes wide with expectation. There was a fear murmuring through the onlookers, that somehow this detritus still radiated with the anger of the Deity.

Inside the statuary chapel the news was even more disturbing. The statue of Jesus carrying his cross was weeping. Drops of water oozed out his eyes. And only his eyes. At first the flow was abundant, quickly filling two tumblers. Now the drops came less frequently, but each drop was tinged with red, each new drop becoming a bit more viscous. Still, no one seemed able to stanch the flow. Rags didn't work. Father Mendoza had tried a hair dryer. Father Rodriguez found a can of varnish and attempted to seal the statue's carved-out eyes with this carpenter's substance.

The air in the reliquary chapel was heavy with humidity, as if the chapel were transforming itself into a hothouse, generating its own atmosphere.

At least the Jesuit community of La Merced had managed to keep this news secret. At least there was no large crowd of believers gathering outside the doors of the statuary chapel. The adorers of the rubble were problem enough. In that mess of debris, the people had found no obvious message from God that would give life to the event they contemplated. There was no image to be found in that pile of dirt.

The whole Jesuit community feared the consequences of what had been found within the chapel, of what could easily be construed as an overt act of God, as a miracle—the weeping of the statue of Jesus, a statue that portrayed the Savior as he labored under his burden of the cross, recording a moment in that drama of the Savior's last day, a scene from the Gospels, and a story that never mentioned a Jesus who broke down into tears the day he bore the sins of the world to his end.

If they could not stop the statue's tears, then the community would have to figure out how to interpret them. And who had the authority to do that? Who had the wisdom to do that? Why now the Savior's tears?

Luckily, the statue stopped weeping when the body of Father Garza was transported from the morgue and placed within the chapel on that night of his death. By that hour there was only one drop every half hour. And the last drop was thick as blood.

Don Francisco resigned that Monday evening from the leadership of the UDA. He resigned not because the kidnapping had been botched or because three of his men had been killed. He didn't care about the death of underlings. He didn't care about the death of Father Burns. The death of Father Garza sickened him.

Don Francisco had grown to dislike the old man, to dislike his fussiness, his rationalizations, his need to feel important. But the old man was a respected cleric. He had officiated at the marriages of all of Don Francisco's children. He had confessed Don Francisco many times, freeing him from the torment of sin. Father Garza was known to be a pious priest, a devout priest, perhaps even a holy priest. And Don Francisco had been responsible for his death. He had committed sacrilege. Oddly, given the great slaughter perpetrated by Don Francisco, this one single human demise unsettled him, distressed him, formed a knot in his core.

Not only did Don Francisco resign from the leadership of the UDA, he resigned totally from the UDA. He abandoned his luxurious compound in Guatemala City and retreated to his *finca* near Chimaltenango where rumor had it he prayed often and lit candles to the Virgin and to St. Ignatius, sometimes placing rose petals at their feet, begging silently for forgiveness.

Don Carlos took advantage of Don Francisco's exit to grab control of the UDA. Within a week of his ascension, he published an edict declaring that the UDA would not tolerate religious interference in political matters. This edict clarified for all members the limits of religion in the organization of the UDA and in their lives. Religion was to purify the spirit, to gain discipline over evil tendencies, to set one on a righteous path. It was the warrior's discipline and nothing more.

Personally, Don Carlos was disgusted by the happenings at *El Susurro* and the events that transpired later in the capital. He hated the theatricality of it, the image of an old priest mowed down while waving his sacred symbol, the superstition of the people regarding just one more earthquake, and the rumors of the weeping Jesus that had made Guatemala a laughingstock among the nations, certainly in the opinion of Don Carlos and his Pentecostal *compadres*.

At least these latest events had clarified his own goals. Don Carlos now understood more clearly than ever the need to sanitize Guatemalan culture of all its leftover superstitions, Catholic and *indígena*, the need to plant cash crops in the *milpa*, to spend less money on saints and their expensive *lanchas*. He knew that a well-run, modern nation could not tolerate such aberrant thinking or behavior.

Two hours after Father Eger's flight landed at da Vinci Airport in Rome, he was in Father General's office, standing at attention. It was a cloudy, rainy fall day, a massive cold front having covered the boot of Italy and all the northern Christian half of the Mediterranean.

Father von Ehre was not happy. He was cold and tired and nearly bereft of hope. He did not rise to greet his old friend. He remained seated, studying the draft of a document, a proposed *bulla* that would rewrite the Constitution of the Society of Jesus and put it under greater control of the Papal Curia, meaning delivering his beloved Society into the hands of those entrenched conservatives.

The possibility of handing over control of his cherished *Gesellschaft Jesu* to these aging princes infuriated Karl von Ehre, boiling his blood so that he could barely concentrate, could barely think rationally. This was the one thing he had worked to avoid, his single goal over these past many years of authority.

Father von Ehre had sent his friend, the reserved archivist, to deal with this matter in Guatemala. He had expected the old man to talk, to persuade, to pray, to show the world the face of a long-suffering son of the Church. Father von Ehre had not expected armed rescue. None of Father Eger's communications had warned him of the horror that occurred.

Holding his head in both hands, still gazing at the words of the *bulla*, not yet looking his friend in the eyes, Father von Ehre moaned, "What did you do there? What did you think you were supposed to do? Didn't you know how delicate is the Society's position within the Church?" he asked, finally raising his bloodshot eyes to look at a very tired Father Eger as he waved the *bulla* in the air.

"The situation in Rome has been unsettled for years," Father Eger said, his voice calm, resolved. "I acted in what I thought to be the best interest of the Society and of Father Burns."

"And what was that? To expose him to so many rifles?" Father von Ehre's anger was unrestrained, rumbling on with the fury of a Bavarian avalanche. "What a stupid plan that was! How could anyone survive?!"

"All plans have their risks. When dealing with violent men, the risks are greater. Surely you know that, Karl."

"Yes, Joszef, I know all about risks," Father von Ehre said, his sarcasm heating each word. "And I know to avoid certain risks. And I wonder, why did you *take* this specific risk: attempting to free Father Burns with force of arms? So crude. So unlike us. Please, sit. Explain!"

Father Eger sat as requested, a reluctance in his movement. Father von Ehre watched his old friend fold his hands in his lap.

"Explain!" Father von Ehre commanded again.

Father Eger shifted in his chair. "An old Maya laid out the plan for me. I remember it clearly. It was late at night, my second night. That day I had spoken with the rectors of the Jesuit communities in Guatemala City and with the provincial of the Central American province. They said what I had expected, that we should pray and beg for our brother's release, that we should work the media, that we should talk face-to-face with our enemy."

Father Eger looked over to a copy of the death mask of St. Ignatius, which hung between two tall windows with their view onto the brick and marble Roman fall.

Father General von Ehre had thought the life of the founder still reflected through the impressions of his metal eyes, so he kept the mask near him. He told his intimates that he needed to feel the visionary passion of the founder. Staring half at the mask and half at Father Eger, Father von Ehre saw his old friend mouth the word, "*Iñigo.*" Then his comrade's lips moved again, as if adding, "*mi dispiàce.*" As the English slur, "I'm sorry."

Father von Ehre almost ordered Father Eger to speak to his living General, but kept his mouth shut.

"This Maya," Father Eger said, still facing the death mask, "he sat holding a young girl in his lap, letting her play with his gray hair—he felt sure we could rescue the young priest, if only we could discover where they were keeping him. He was certain it could be done. That there were powerful forces willing to help us."

"Communist forces!" Father von Ehre cried out from across the desk. "Look at me!"

"Forces opposed to the UDA," Father Eger said, turning slowly away from Ignatius's sockets.

In that stump of a sentence Father von Ehre heard Father Eger's desire to avoid the political words: communist, liberal, fascist. On many occasions, when they were theologians or in the last nine years in Rome, Father Eger had proclaimed that political systems were of little interest to him. In both epochs, Father von Ehre had doubted his friend's assertions. The Hungarian was political to his roots. That was his struggle. He was a politician without the guts for it.

"You should have dealt with the Guatemalan government," Father von Ehre said. "That was the right thing to do. I had instructed you to deal with the government."

Father von Ehre disliked impractical people, but he loved this old man before him. That love had often pained him. He felt a sadness sink again into his thick cheeks.

Father Eger looked back out through the window. "I allied myself with the trees."

"What?! What nonsense is that?" A hot rush of blood flushed out Father von Ehre's sentiments of love.

Looking surprised—or eager, Father Eger turned back from the window view to stare at his friend. "You recall the old Castilian, Beltrán y Lanzarote, don't you?"

"Oh, no," Father von Ehre said, waving both arms in the air as if to force away a foul smell. "Why do you bring him up?"

"I mention him because he used that phrase. 'I ally myself with the trees.' I think it means . . ."

"I don't care what it means! I don't care about that old man! I don't care about any explanations you have to offer."

Father von Ehre rose to pace through his office, his hands clasped tightly behind his back.

"You clearly lost your head. You got caught up in this adventure and didn't stop to realize what was going on. You didn't weigh your choices. You didn't weigh the consequences of your actions. You failed!" Turning to face Father Eger, centering his gaze, Father von Ehre ended, stating with a heavy certainty, "And you let me down."

His old Hungarian friend seemed to shrink into his chair. For a moment Father Eger's lips moved, but nothing came out, only the motions of a baby's mouth.

"I'm sorry I disappointed you, Karl. I acted as I did during the war. I relied on my instincts."

The skin of Father Eger's face turned as gray as the day's coverlet of clouds. Father von Ehre wondered if his Hungarian comrade were diseased, with that depression so many others complained of, especially the Americans and Europeans.

"I thought I was doing what you had expected of me," Father Eger said. "I only know two things thoroughly, as you are aware." He sighed. "Philosophy, mainly Buddha's logic-truths. And quiet subversion."

Both men paused.

"I thought you had better sense," Father von Ehre said, moving a foot closer to his friend, leaning to touch Father Eger's shoulder with his right hand, then stepping back.

"I witnessed a beatific event."

Father von Ehre blinked and his mouth dropped open, empty of words.

"Murder is not beatific," Father von Ehre finally answered, quickly shaking away images of the Savior and of martyrdom. He had never, himself, wanted to be a martyr. He was suspicious of those who sought out that blistering honor.

Father von Ehre returned to his desk and sat.

He picked up an envelope and reached it across to Father Eger. Inside were the orders he had prepared. He was transferring the archivist to the Jesuit community in Varanasi, India.

Father Eger unfolded the letter and read its contents, his eyes only looking up after he'd read its two paragraphs twice. "You return me to my spirit's best home," he said, his voice lined with amazement. "To the land of old-soul mystics. Why?"

Father von Ehre looked back at Father Eger, perhaps for the last time, he thought, taking him all in.

"Because you are not welcome in Rome, Joszef. There are those who would have you expelled from the Society." The General's brown eyes glistened. He looked down at the papers on his desk and tugged at the end of one sleeve. "I could not bear that."

Guadalupe and her men returned immediately to Nicaragua, easily traversing several countries where the national governments had long ago lost control of vast tracts of land, not just the hearts of the people.

Back in Managua she learned that Jim Meeker had received notice from his Jesuit superiors in the Central American province to abandon his work in the Nicaraguan government. He was being sent to become the pastor of a parish of three hundred Caribs deep in the jungles of northern Belize.

"I don't understand," Guadalupe said, stunned by his news. She had needed to speak with someone about Tom. She needed another Jesuit. She had not looked on Tom's shattered face in that highland valley. Instead she had slumped into the forest's undergrowth and waited for the troop's withdrawal. When she had seen the old white priest weeping over the sprawl of Tom's corpse, she had considered approaching, but hastened away instead.

"Ever since the events in Guatemala," Jim said, "the Society is tightening down—throughout the world. I know fifty Jesuits involved in government-sponsored justice ministries who've been reassigned," Jim said.

"But, are you going?"

He paused.

"I'm a Jesuit. It's who I am. I . . ." He rose from his chair to hide his face, turning himself to the wall, bending half over, already crying the tears of the exile.

Guadalupe got up and left. These priests were an enigma to her. And when she got close to them, she felt their pain. It wounded her in the center of her body.

She bled there for a while now; but the menopause, she feared, would be worse. So she resolved to head off on pilgrimage to Mexico, barefoot and with her hair in peasant braids.

And if the Virgin of the *cerrito* offered her no message, she would head further north until she found her spot.

Ann heard the news on a television broadcast. Stations all over the world were reporting the event. Some characterized it as nothing but another atrocity committed by another death squad. Others, beginning to mine the facts, were raising more complex issues, questioning the involvement of the clergy of the Catholic Church in direct political, especially revolutionary, activity. Certain right-wing American organizations were again stabbing with the question whether Catholics could really be both loyal citizens of a democracy and faithful adherents of their arcane and shadowy religion.

Jesuit communities throughout the nation were deluged with phone calls. Bomb threats mingled with prayers. Vigils had been organized. Thousands of candles were lit throughout the great Jesuit churches and shrines of the world and within the many small chapels the order tended.

Ann had called Guatemala City the night she found out, debating within herself the wisdom of being drawn too deeply into this Jesuit event. She had life choices to make. Her marriage was anesthetized and in need of surgery. She'd already cut the first incision.

But maybe her willingness to leave, to pack up and drive away in her Land Rover, she thought, coupled with Tom's death, maybe Mark would focus on their problem now. She'd rented a small apartment near downtown Alexandria. Their house was empty of life. She wouldn't move back. She hadn't even figured out how to tell him where they were. A note in the kitchen? A phone message?

She didn't feel any malice in her hesitancy before making the call, only a studying of options. She would not become her mother. She might resemble her, hips and hair, one stubby toe. But she would not be her inside. She would not suffer her way into the future.

"Ann, oh Ann, it's you," Mark said, the words gushing out as soon as the hotel clerk connected them. "I miss you so much. Really. Believe me. Please don't be angry with me. Not now. Have you heard? Have you heard about Tom?"

"I've heard," Ann said, moving past his request for forgiveness and onto the tragedy. It was easier to talk about that. She realized how much she had feared his indifference, how much it had hurt. "I'm sorry. I'm stunned, I guess. I've never known anyone who was . . ."

"Assassinated," Mark said.

"Not martyred?"

Mark sighed. She heard the sudden presence of tears. She hadn't heard them in years.

"I can't say that word. I think it, but I can't *say* it."

"You weren't there, were you?" Ann asked.

"No. We found out just like everyone else—later in the morning. But we knew the . . ."

David reached over to touch Mark's arm, holding his finger to his mouth, signaling to his friend to keep their involvement a secret.

"You knew what?" Ann asked.

"Nothing. We can talk later," Mark said. "We can talk, can't we?" he asked.

He was focusing on their rift, begging, she thought. She bit her lip.

"Yes, we can talk. But what's going on between us is serious. You've got to understand that!"

"I do. I understand a lot."

After hanging up, Mark turned to David, saying, "I'm more sad than I've ever been in my entire life. Lonely sad."

"About Tom? You and Ann? Charley?"

"Right. All that." Mark was slumped on the couch. He rested his elbows on his knees. "You know that phrase about having a hole in you. That's it—as if there's a hole in me, as if I'm not all there anymore. I'm still alive, but I shouldn't be. Do you understand?"

David nodded. "I understand. I've had those feelings, and hard."

David was thinking of Randy and the day of his funeral. He alone had remained at the grave, despite the family's uncomprehending stares: "I'll just stay awhile." He had stayed long into night, until the cicada sang their earth song, until the moon turned the grave markers into stone ghosts. He'd thought he'd never move again.

As if in a mystic union, quietly and unannounced, David walked over to their balcony and out onto its concrete width. He looked up into the evening sky and spoke loudly enough for Mark, who was still sitting next to the phone, to hear him. "It's over. We'll never be together again."

David leaned on the railing and looked down, staring unfocused on a brace of orange trees in the middle of the courtyard.

He didn't hear Mark get up, didn't hear him walk onto the balcony.

He shuddered when he felt Mark's hand on his shoulder and stood up straight.

He almost cried out when Mark embraced him from behind, both arms surrounding him, Mark's hands locking together on David's chest, Mark's head on David's shoulder. It was a lover's embrace, manly and unrestrained.

Slowly, abandoning anxiety, David settled into it.

Five minutes later the friends parted in silence and headed off to their rooms. Everything for tomorrow's departure had been arranged. The transportation of Tom's body was in the hands of the embassy, which had assured them they would do everything possible to get the body back to Minnesota with no undue delay.

That night Mark jolted awake, as if lightning had struck next to his bed. He came running into David's room, naked except for his underpants, his hair electrified, his hands rubbing his shoulders as if he were trying to scrub off rot, his eyes shooting amazement.

"He touched me. I saw him coming toward me. All dressed in white. In a cassock, dressed in white. Smiling. He said nothing. He seemed busy, with lots to do. He walked up to me. He touched me. He touched me!"

Mark's eyes were fevered. The muscles of his chest rippled, exercising his elation. "I felt it. Soft. Unreal. A feather brushing against my skin. Right here. On my right shoulder. God, David," Mark said, settling onto David's bed. "Did he touch you, too?"

"Who is *he*?" David asked, barely out of the fog of sleep.

"Tom!" Mark said.

"You dreamt about Tom. OK. That's OK. That's why we've been here."

David slumped back into his warm bed.

"I confessed to him," Mark said, speaking louder and shaking David's shoulder. "I told him everything. In an instant. He placed his hand on me. Maybe it left an impression."

Mark turned his back to David, flexing his deltoids. "See?"

David, lifting himself up a foot, saw nothing unexpected, only flecked skin, no aura. "I don't see anything."

"Tom was here. I know it."

Mark got up off David's bed and headed back to his room.

"Are you all right?" David, starting to wake, called out to his friend.

Mark stopped at David's door and turned around, his perfect form uncovered but for a thin layer of cotton hugging his groin. The perfect man, David thought. The figure at the center of Galileo's circle. Perhaps Lazarus arising.

"Yeah," Mark said, "I think I'm all right." Then he left.

The day of Tom's funeral began cold. The night before an arctic front had laid down the season's first juvenile frost. Soon, however, the sun warmed up by ten degrees the lowest layer of the atmosphere, where humans live.

It would have required a centurion to organize the stunned, angry cadre of priests who gathered to concelebrate that funeral. Each cleric had draped himself with a red stole, a symbolic link to their martyred brother, the stoles' dye vibrant as the blood that had dripped from Tom's skull onto his torso seconds after his politicized oblation. The priests talked, gestured, and barely formed into two shifting lines for the processional through the doors of the Jesuit Church of Saints Peter and Paul in Mankato.

The Jesuit American General assistant had arrived two days earlier from Rome. A man of few words, he would co-preside with the Papal Nuncio to the United States, another Italian, both of them from families of the Roman black nobility. Father Provincial Bob Fitzgibbons, round as a Midwestern prized pumpkin, would give the funeral homily. The General had appointed him provincial two years earlier because of his administrative capabilities, not his ability to stir the heart with oratory.

Under the close scrutiny of his Roman observers, Father Fitzgibbons spoke a careful three-minute commentary about the pivotal importance of obedience in religious life. The priests shifted their robed torsos as the homily ended abruptly, with no reference to the evil that stalked Central American roadways, or the land-link between right-wing death squads and American savvy. Looks of disbelief and despair shot about the sanctuary, rapid as guerrilla crossfire.

As the long train of clerics wound out the red-brick church, the entire congregation salved themselves and their pains by singing an old hymn, *Holy God We Praise Thy Name*, accompanied in post-Vatican II America by the strum of guitars and the whirring of two censers dispensing incense in every direction.

Mark, Ann, Charley, and David sat with the family, and followed the family as it joined the sacramental troop and Tom's body on the long walk out the nave. The only time they wept in that confusing liturgy was when Tom's mother, Finola, paused at the casket before turning to leave the church, dragging her gnarled hand fondly along a portion of its bronze top.

David had not seen Mark since returning to the States. They had separated in Washington at Dulles, where David saw Mark take out his cell phone and punch in what he supposed was Mark's home number and hang on waiting for an answer, ring after ring. Watching the scene, David was sure that Mark's family wouldn't continue to exist beyond the next weeks of mourning. Surely Ann had cleared out and even taken the answering machine.

After Tom's interment in the Jesuit plot on the cedar-wrapped hillside cemetery, Mark took David aside.

"I'm quitting my job."

"What? You're . . ." David had expected to hear about a divorce, or trial separation, at least as the first headline.

"Quitting my job. We're moving back here. Actually, further on." Mark nodded his head to the west. He was all factual, a first-year staffer reporting on the floor vote. "I'm volunteering at Red Cloud, on Pine Ridge. Temporary administrator. Subsistence wages."

"The reservation?"

"Yup."

"Without Ann and Charley?"

"They're coming."

"But there aren't any hospitals."

"I'm renewing my pilot's license. Ann's OK with it this time. We're using her inheritance for the plane. My first cross-country should be in a month, from Raleigh to Gettysburg."

"But you hated the reservation!"

"I'm defiant again. Or maybe for the first time."

"But the reservation?" David asked again, quietly.

"At least for awhile. I think He's still waiting for me out there." Mark paused, pawing the ground with his feet. "Or his answer." His face softening, "And Ann will give it a year, give us a year—but not in Washington—and not unless I do something . . ."

Mark moved closer to whisper into David's ear, hunching over. "Did you get a letter?"

"You mean . . .? The Hungarian? What'd he write?"

"About vocation. He said a vocation . . ." Mark was squeezing David's arm, " . . . is—now don't get offended—is like a viral infection. It toys with your DNA. Modifies the strand. Produces the unexpected long after entry." Mark was breathless.

The chill and the bright sun made David's eyes water. He blinked.

Two days back in Minneapolis from his Guatemala crusade, David had called up Daniel George Murphy, an ex-priest he'd once dated. He needed to talk about his loss, not as death-of-a-loved-one loss but as God-act.

Daniel George worked for Catholic Charities running a soup kitchen in an old tire warehouse near Elliot Park. David had liked him while they dated. Sex had been good, vigorous, but David couldn't envision himself married to a true believer, even if his chin were cleft and his arms the size of tree limbs. After two months, David had broken it off.

Now they were planning a getaway to Key West. David smiled at how the story of their renewed bond, accompanied by the standard "kneeling before priests" jokes, had swept through the Minneapolis Aquavit-sipping cocktail party scene in two days.

"Father Eger invited me to India," David said. "He wouldn't say why, precisely."

David could see several of their Jesuit friends staring at them. He knew their part in the saga of Tom's death was leaking out, becoming part of the legend. He wondered if they would be remembered as dupes or villains. He, too, began to whisper.

"Father Eger wrote about a collection of writings: notes, correspondence, sermons, all written by a teacher of his, a man who died in India. The stuff's still there, preserved in a teak box under the bed of some semiliterate Jesuit brother who was born an untouchable."

On Mark's fourteenth evening in South Dakota, the sun set under a storm wall of clouds. It was a fire sun, stoked with the day's sharpest passions. His next child would be born in six months. He'd convinced Gloria to let him and Ann adopt the baby. It was Ann's idea, even the stipulation that if they broke up, the baby was hers to raise.

Mark had sobbed for an hour that night of Ann's unexpected *fiat,* of her *magnificat,* so much the mother's act. He'd finally fallen asleep in their bed that night with his head resting on Ann's stomach, no longer as the other body laid out as the other corpse in unwrinkled linen, but messy and angled and seeing her, smelling her, from a lover's vantage, all fleshy risings and wiry hair.

Mark stepped from the prairie into their narrow, two-bedroom trailer home and picked up Charley, who'd been drawing pictures of painted horses at their kitchen table. Mark hugged Charley in silence.

Ann stopped peeling a fat Idaho spud and watched them from the sink. Mark could feel her pause, feel it envelop him with a wave of emotion, a wave charged with two equal currents, hope and fear. He'd been aware of her watchfulness ever since they arrived at Pine Ridge. He was using it to woo her. He knew that in reservation silence he was learning to speak a corporal language of love, communicated not by sound or symbol, learning to speak it with an increasingly native accent. He took that kitchen moment to enact a couplet.

Charley clung hard and wrapped his legs around Mark's waist. Mark ruffled his son's hair.

Mark wondered why Charley was less mysterious, less cat-eyed around him. Was it because they were together every day? Because their life had become a vacation? Because every night Charley's father would go out to a prairie knoll for half an hour and, among his other acts of examination and contrition, pray for forgiveness and send those prayers his son's way?

Don't worry about it, Mark instructed himself, holding onto Charley, embracing Charley as if his son had just kicked the winning field goal.

Mark's heart beat slower. Draped by his son's body in the thin-walled prairie home, he was feeling the way he had always wanted to feel, rugged and sure, and with a grip on his soul.

David's diary entry two months after Tom's funeral and a week before heading to India, the day he told Daniel George, as they both went about their early morning rituals, that he enjoyed watching him pray:

> *I'm liking things I never liked before. I like punks with safety pins in their eyebrows. I like farm kids who are too shy to breathe in front of me. I even like people in traffic.*

> *Some words have scent again. Love. Soul. They smell of Daniel, who comes home reeking of unfiltered cigarettes and unwashed clothing. They smell of Randy and Tom, whose smell is thinner and subtler and makes me breathe deep to bring it in. And soon the must of a forgotten man's scribblings?*

Author's Note

This is a work of fiction. All acting characters are imagined, and their experiences are fabricated. Although certain institutions, buildings and locations actually exist, I have modified them for use in this invention. Furthermore, this is not a rigorous theological or historical tract, nor a memoir. Any theological disputes are laid out in a slim way for narrative impact. All opinions expressed are those of the characters. Details of Jesuit life, the language of formation, and descriptions of conflict in Europe, Guatemala and the Catholic Church are not the product of a journalist's desire for objectivity, although all have a corresponding reality.

The slum of Colonia Samaria does not exist, although similar slums do. Some information about Guatemala has been pulled from guide books and from those who have worked more recently in the country and from the ever-growing Internet.

I was too strapped for cash to travel to Landívar to refresh my memory of its landscape, but their website shows a green campus. Tom's meditation spot and place of kidnapping is drawn from several locations. The Jesuit residence at La Merced is an accumulation of details from many religious houses. The American embassy in Guatemala city is entirely imagined, as is the topography of San Antonio Aguas Calientes.

There are numerous books about the Society of Jesus and the turmoil in Central America. Of great use in creating this fiction were: *The Jesuits, History and Legend of the Society of Jesus* by Manfred Barthel, William Morrow and Company, Inc.; *Stubborn Hope, Religion, Politics and Revolution in Central America* by Phillip Berryman, Orbis Books.

The assassination of the Jesuits in El Salvador, their cook and her daughter, is an undisputed fact, as is the execution of Archbishop Romero and the slaughter of hundreds of thousands. *Requiescant in pace.* The papal rebuke of Ernesto Cardenal is equally well documented. It bears remembering that Ignatius Loyola, founder of the Jesuits, was imprisoned and questioned by the Spanish Inquisition because of his spiritual teaching. Much of the Inquisition's concern was his lack of formal theological training, that he was solely informed by an inner light.

A peace accord was signed in Guatemala in 1996. As of 2000, the issue of the redress of human rights violations is still disputed. Slayings continue.

Even though Father Beltrán y Lanzarote never existed, in the conventional sense of that term, his spirit sat nearby on many Minnesota winter nights. *Gracias, compañero.*

If this book raises questions for you, here are a few websites where you can begin to find answers:

> on the Jesuits:
> www.jesuit.org
> www.redcloudschool.com
> www.muhs.edu
> www.url.edu.gt
> www.wjst.edu
> on the Guatemalan human rights situation:
> www.wola.org
> www.c-r.org

A Prayer of St. Ignatius

The following is a version of one of the most famous prayers of St. Ignatius. The *Suscipe* is a prayer kept close to heart and top of mind for many a Jesuit.

> Take, Lord, receive
> all my liberty, my memory, my understanding, my entire will,
> all that I have and possess.
> You have given all to me.
> To you, O Lord, I return it.
> All is yours.
> Dispose of it wholly according to your will.
> Give me only your love and your grace, for they are enough for me.

ABOUT THE AUTHOR

John F. Shekleton attended Georgetown University before entering the Wisconsin Province of the Society of Jesus. He received his BA in Philosophy and History from St. Louis University. He has taught school, led a student missionary group in Guatemala and interned at the Washington Office on Latin America, a human rights advocacy organization. After leaving the Jesuits, he began his career as a systems analyst and freelance writer. His articles on religion, computer software and gay issues have appeared in numerous publications. *A Jesuit Tale* is his first novel.